Dangerous Strategy

A Formula 1 Romance

Shut Up and Drive
Book 1

B. Randall

For my Formula 1 family
Thanks for being wild and passionate

Author's Note

For all readers:

In 2022, I watched a movie called *Rush*. If you haven't seen it, it's an incredible movie about Formula 1 legend Niki Lauda and Formula 1 World Driver's Champion James Hunt. At the time, I didn't know anything about motorsport. I didn't even know Formula 1 existed. My only exposure to motorsport was my father's casual NASCAR viewing and a friend of mine who's really into IndyCar. I watched *Rush* because I thought Daniel Bruhl and Chris Hemsworth are hot.

About halfway through the movie, I thought, *This Formula 1 stuff is cool. I should write a romance about a driver!* Of course, I didn't know at the time about the disparity between male and female Formula 1 drivers, but that's a story for another time. In the summer of 2023, I was ready to start researching Formula 1 so I could write a romance about an F1 driver. I started watching Formula 1... and it devoured my soul.

That's only sort of an exaggeration. Formula 1 very quickly became home for me. It became my comfort when I was anxious, my something to look forward to every week. I think people in my life found this startling because I'm not exactly a sporty gal myself and haven't been terribly into sports in any non-casual way in my life.

But here we are. When I wrote *Give Your Heart Away* (Lola's book) in 2023, it was as a casual fan. But by the time I wrote the last chapter, I had introduced a slew of other characters and was quite literally only interested in writing more F1 books.

And so, I give you *Dangerous Strategy*, my love letter to Formula 1.

For Formula 1 Fans:

When I discovered how much I love Formula 1, I was completely alone. No one in my life is particularly interested in Formula 1, even though they all smile politely while I blather on about my favorite drivers and what happened during the race this week. I sort of figured it would always be that way.

And then I discovered the Formula 1 community on social media. I can't properly put into words the way the F1 community took me in. Yes, we all know F1 fans who immediately try to give a pop quiz when a woman says she's a fan of the sport and the ones who don't want women in the sport at all. But when I found the inclusive, welcoming, gentle side of the community, I found true friends.

In a lot of ways, this book is just as much for you as it is for me. For the people on chat with me during the 2 AM races, for the ones who sent me friendship bracelets, for the ones who spent weekends watching old races with me to get through off-season, for the ones that share the memes and the hot takes and the hilarious videos. You're half the reason I adore this sport so much.

If you don't read anything else, please read this: I did my best to write a book that felt authentic. But at the end of the day, I don't work for a Formula 1 team, I don't know anyone who works for a Formula 1 team, and even though I watch all the races and all the media and all the socials, there's still stuff I'm going to get wrong. Please forgive me for anything I messed up.

There was also stuff I just had to change because it made more sense for the narrative. I'm sorry for that stuff too, but a girl gotta do what she gotta do to let the lovers kiss, you know?

Thank you to all of you,

B.

Content Notes

Although it is inevitable that I would be inspired by the people, places, and happenings in Formula 1 while writing this series, no characters are explicitly based on any drivers on the current (or past) grid. Everyone in this story is 100% fictional.

This book contains sexual content that is graphic and explicit and only intended for adult readers.

Possible triggers include light bondage, a significant age gap (17 years) between the main characters, physical violence, and discussions of multiple high-speed car crashes.

Please only continue if you feel comfortable enough to.

Playlist

🏁

Sports car - Tate McRae
older - Isabel LaRosa
Bad Reviews - Sabrina Carpenter
Mercy - Lewis Capaldi
magic - Kelly Clarkson
Shelter - Echosmith
Dangerously - Charlie Puth
BIRDS OF A FEATHER - Billie Eilish
Tú - maye
Do I Wanna Know? - Arctic Monkeys
LA FAMA - ROSALÍA, The Weeknd
Dangerous - Big Data, Joywave
Hymn to Virgil - Hozier
What If I Love You - Gatlin
But Daddy I Love Him - Taylor Swift
TOO GOOD - Troye Sivan
Anything - Griff

Curtains - Ed Sheeran
Fall On Me - A Great Big World, Christina Aguilera
Infinitely Falling - Fly By Midnight
Roadtripsong - Abby Cates

Dangerous Strategy

Dear Ms. Cedillo,

Welcome to Albatross Racing! We are so pleased to have you on our team. Attached is your intake paperwork, your employee handbook, and your racing season itinerary and flight information. Please take a moment to review the documents and return the signature pages. Once again, we are happy to have you here. We look forward to seeing you for the start of the 2025 racing season.

Felix Hoffman,
    Director of Albatross Racing

Chapter One
Pre-Season - Montreal, Canada

Arabella

A scream of excitement bubbles up in my throat, but I slam a hand over my mouth to stifle it. My neighbors are big fans of reporting me to management with noise complaints, and if they hear me screaming over here, I'm pretty sure I'm going to get fined or something.

I take a deep breath and open the text message that just came in from my mom.

> Papa got us a table at Casa Madera.
> Meet us there at 7. We're so excited!

I glance at the clock. Casa Madera is on the other side of Montreal from my apartment, much closer to where my parents live. If I'm going to make it by seven, I need to get a move on. I pull one of the dresses from the back of my closet, one of the ones I never wear. I don't generally have occasion for dresses, but tonight is a celebration. It calls for one of my best outfits.

I consider doing something with my hair, but it's pretty

much as set as it's going to be unless I shower. I toss some anti-frizz into my curls and call it a day. Snatching up my bag, I check the status of my Uber and go downstairs to wait.

Arabella

Casa Madera is packed, seeing as it's a Saturday night in the city, and I'm glad my dad had the foresight to make a reservation. My brain has been so clouded by the prospect of my new job that I haven't even thought about something like celebrating with my parents, even though I know, deep down where I don't want to examine too closely, that it's my father's influence that got me the job in the first place. Of course he's excited. Isn't it every parent's dream to watch their child follow in their footsteps?

When it's my turn at the host's station, I smile big. I can't help it. I'm so excited I feel like my skin is going to shake right off my bones. I can't even feel the tips of my fingers.

"Cedillo, party of three?" I ask, looking past the stand to see if I can spot my parents.

The hostess's eyes scan down the screen of her tablet and back up. Her brow furrows. "I have a party of four for Pedro Cedillo. That sound like you?" Her perfectly made-up smoky eyes meet mine, and she sends me a gentle smile.

Four?

"Sure, I guess." Papa must have invited someone else. He has a lot of professional contacts in the city, so it's probably just somebody he wants to show me off to. He's one of those dads.

"Okay, great. Just this way." She turns and moves quickly into the dining area, and I rush to keep up. I've been to Casa Madera a few times but never at night. The lighting is low over the tables and the bar lit from underneath. It's a casual atmosphere, with plants and globe lights on the walls, but it just has that smell of a place that's more expensive than it needs to be. It's something my parents love, going to top-tier restaurants when they have an excuse to.

Our table is half bench and half wood chairs, my parents rising from the booth side situated against the wall as I approach.

"There she is!" my mom says with a grin, leaning across the table to kiss me on the cheek.

Papa squeezes my cheeks between his big, solid hand and smiles. "A true miracle, you are, *cariño*."

I take a seat, already reaching for the margarita they've ordered for me, sitting at my elbow. "The host said four people. Are we expecting someone else?" I ask as I open the menu and peruse. The scent of the food on the air is starting to make my stomach rumble.

My father does a little pitter-patter on the tabletop with his fingers. "Mateo called me this morning. Said he was in town, so I invited him."

I choke on my margarita, coughing until I'm pretty sure an entire iceberg comes up out of my lungs. "Mateo is coming tonight? Here? To dinner?"

My father raises an eyebrow at me. "He wanted to congratulate you." His eyes move to something in the distance, and he smiles. "Ah, there he is!"

I'm not prepared for this. Sure, I knew I was going to have to face Mateo, and sooner rather than later, seeing as how I'm supposed to be in England soon for pre-season work, but I thought I still had time. Before I turn around, I take a deep breath to steady myself.

Mateo crosses the restaurant, sliding cooly by the bar, where everyone turns to look at him—either because they recognize Mateo Silva, one of the greatest Formula 1 drivers of all time, or because they're just drawn to him the way everyone seems to be, his magnetic field somehow stronger than a normal human's. No amount of deep breathing keeps me from feeling like I've been slammed into by a locomotive.

When his eyes meet mine, he smiles, bright and shining, and I think my heart goes into AFib. Holy hell, has anyone ever looked so delicious? He reaches up to fix the collar on his button up, black against the chinos he's wearing. I laugh when I see his trainers. You can take the guy out of sport...

"Arabella!" he says, his smile stretching all the way to his golden eyes. It's too dark to see them in this light, but I know the color of them the way I know the color of my own. When he finally reaches us, he pulls me up out of my chair and hugs me. I fear he can feel the chaotic thundering of my heart in my chest.

A hug doesn't mean anything to Mateo. Mateo hugs everybody, especially his best friend's daughter when he hasn't seen her in a while.

He hasn't seen me, but I sure as hell have seen him. Mateo Silva, Albatross's social media golden boy, who last year had his best season in Formula 1 since his last championship win over ten years ago. All the F1 media and fan sites never shut about him, either because they're tired of him and are leaving comments like, *was that Mateo I saw doing his track walk with a cane?* or because he's still their hero, and they're perfectly content to watch him race until his body collapses under the pressure.

I'm sure you can imagine which camp I fall into.

"You didn't have to come," I tell him when he lets me go.

"What, you don't want me here?" He smiles, clearly not actually offended by my comment. I'm sure it would never even occur to him that he might not be welcome, the guy who everyone wants at their table.

I clamp my lips together so I don't accidentally tell him

that I want him to be in every single room I walk into for the rest of my life.

"Mateo!" My mother's voice breaks through the haze that has surrounded me, reminding me that the rest of the world does, in fact, exist.

Mateo steps around me to hug my mother first and then my father. They have an entire conversation in Spanish that I try not to listen to. While they speak a million words a minute, my mother and I take a seat across from each other, and I try to settle my now swirling stomach. Mateo is here. He came here for me. When I try to plug that into the processor in my mind, the machine pops and smokes.

Mateo takes the chair next to mine, sitting so close that when he adjusts, his elbow brushes mine. I've forgotten how I felt five minutes ago. Now that Mateo is here, he's taking up all the space in the room, the heavy, confident curl of his Spanish accent the only sound I can hear.

He turns toward me slightly, a smug smile on his face. "I came because I had to congratulate you on your new position. I can't believe you're really going to join the team."

At his words, I feel some of my excitement fade, all the color in the room going gray. "Did you put in a good word for me?" It's not exactly rocket science to figure out that I probably got slight preferential treatment in the hiring process for Albatross's new art designer. My father was once a very famous Formula 1 driver and Mateo, his best friend and former rival, is a living legend. But if Mateo went straight to Felix Hoffman and asked him to hire me, that's something else entirely.

Mateo's eyes watch me carefully, that slight tilt to his mouth that's always there. Resting Kind Face. "Of course not. I didn't have to. From what I hear, your work spoke for itself. You don't need my influence to be successful in Formula 1. You'll do it all on your own."

He settles his hand on the back of my chair as he reaches

for the glass of ice water that's sitting in front of him. He doesn't even notice that his thumb is gently brushing the bare skin of my back. Doesn't notice that I'm watching him with wonder because what he just said to me is something no one else has ever said. Doesn't notice that I'm so in love with him that it's become a second skin that I couldn't shed even if I wanted to.

"Is Elena on a job?" my mother asks while I'm still trying to scoop my melted form off the floor.

Mateo takes a deep breath in that way he does when he's formulating a response in the processing center of his brain. I learned long ago that Mateo is like a computer, grounded in facts and statistics. He never says anything he doesn't mean to say, and he always says what he means.

"Elena and I ended things."

My stomach dips, like I just went over the crest of a roller coaster and am plummeting toward the ground. He and Elena ended things. Elena, the gorgeous Spanish model that Mateo was with for two years. And now it's just...over.

"Oh," Mom says, her face falling. "I'm so sorry to hear that. How are you?"

He shrugs. The end of a two-year relationship and the man is shrugging it off like it's a flat tire he had three weeks ago. "These things happen. They end. Women always think they want to date an athlete, but over time, all the travel, the long hours apart, it starts to wear on them." He leans back in his chair, taking in all of us. "Relationships are a hard thing, molding yourself around another person. It's hard to deal with every single move you make being that important to someone else."

He has no idea that I've molded myself around him so completely that I can't seem to get free.

※

Arabella

Somewhere around midnight, the four of us stumble out onto the sidewalk in the bitter February air, the alcohol in my blood just barely enough to keep me warm. My parents' car comes pretty quickly at the valet, and they wave goodbye to us as they climb inside.

And then Mateo's bright red Maserati—a rental while he's in town, I'm sure—pulls up to the curb, flashy enough that people walking by the restaurant stop to look. Some of them spot Mateo and take out their phones to snap pictures while others eventually just keep moving.

"Please, let me give you a ride," Mateo says as I shiver and pull my coat tighter around my body.

I look at the Uber app that tells me my car is still a few minutes away. A few minutes out in the cold won't kill me, even if I am wearing open-toed shoes. "It's okay. I don't want to inconvenience you."

He steps closer to me, until I'm forced to tear my eyes away from my phone and look up at him. Sometimes, I'm so certain that Mateo understands what his presence does to people. Not just women, but everyone in his orbit. When he walks into a room, everything changes, like a change in the chemical make-up of the atmosphere.

And other times, like now, when he's looking down at me with this look on his face like he's an alien from another planet trying to decipher what humans are made of, I think he has no idea that he's the most extraordinary person I've ever known.

"You aren't inconveniencing me, Arabella. I don't mind doing a little extra driving." At that, he smiles and steps away from me, a foregone conclusion. He takes his keys from the valet and shakes the man's hand, most likely passing him a very generous tip.

I stand by the passenger seat of Mateo's car and steady my

breathing. I can't help the small glance-around I do. Can anyone else feel the way the entire planet is shifting on its axis, or is that just me?

I get in the car. And holy shit, there is no way that the olfactory sensors in my body will ever forget the way the inside of Mateo Silva's car smells. Like cologne and leather and...I don't know, pheromones? Is that what that smell is?

I'm not sure what to do with my hands as Mateo expertly pulls away from the curb, merging into downtown Montreal traffic. I can't help but wonder what it's like for him to drive fifty kilometers per hour when he's used to driving two hundred. It must feel like listening to music in slow motion.

"You can put your address in here," he says, reaching out and tapping on the screen between the dashboard and the glove box.

There's a fancy GPS system, and I put in the address to my apartment with shaky fingers. Please, God, don't let him notice the shaky fingers.

"Have you thought of relocating?" he asks as we head toward my place. It's on the other side of town, but it's late now, so it'll take half the time it took me to get to dinner.

"No," I say, sitting back against the seat and watching the city lights go by. I'm definitely drunk, but not so drunk that I'm not going to remember every second of this drive for the rest of my life. "I like Canada."

When we stop at a light, he smiles over at me. "I like Canada, too, but there are so many beautiful cities in the world. And now that you're working for Albatross, you have the funds to pick somewhere new. Paris, Madrid, Tokyo, London."

"I like Canada," I repeat, rolling my head on the head rest to look over at him. "Not everyone wants to be a person of the world."

He makes a thoughtful shape with his mouth and then the

light turns green. "I understand," he says, pulling into my neighborhood. "I just wanted to make sure you weren't just staying put because of your parents. They must expect you to want to leave sometime."

I shrug. "Not everyone does. And besides, I did leave."

"Your destination is on the left."

He rolls up to the curb and nods. "Believe me, I didn't forget. All Pedro did while you were in New York was talk about how much he wanted you to come back home."

"Really?"

He shuts off the engine, which startles me more than if he had electrocuted me. Is he planning on staying? Is he coming inside? Oh, God. My apartment is a mess. There's no way I can let him see it.

"What it must be like," he says to himself, almost as if he's forgotten I'm even here, "to have people who always want to be around you. People who long for your company."

I open my mouth to answer, but before I can, he's already pushing his door open. I stare at his empty seat, my stomach roiling. If he only knew how I long for his company. How I would spend every day near him if I could. He honestly thinks that the people in his life are just...what, putting up with him? What about his sister? What about his parents? What about Arturo, the engineer at Albatross that has become Mateo's best friend over the last decade that he's been with the team?

What about the fans?

Mateo whips my door open, and I just stare up at him. This night is not going at all like I thought it would.

"Did you know that last season, during an interview, Thane called me boring?"

I can't seem to move, can't seem to unbuckle my seatbelt. My head is craned back, looking up at him. At this angle, he's all I can see. Him and the stars.

"He didn't say that," I tell him, the world starting to tip a little. "He said you wouldn't have anything in common with someone outside of Formula 1."

He bends, and next thing I know, he's in my space, taking up all the air, filling every crevice in the car. He reaches down and unbuckles my seatbelt for me. But before he straightens, he turns to look at me. We're eye-to-eye, so close I can smell his clothes, the smell of clean laundry. "And what exactly do you think that a comment like that means?"

He asks the question so quietly, so sincerely, like he's actually waiting for my answer, like he genuinely doesn't understand what the comment means unless I tell him what it means.

I can imagine him watching media coverage, watching that interview, wondering what Thane meant, reading into every word because people like Thane, they think that people like Mateo don't have feelings. They think that he's so focused on what he does that he doesn't stop to listen to the comments, that he doesn't have time to be bothered by whether or not his fellow drivers have a negative opinion of him or not.

But I've watched Mateo for the majority of my life, and I know that he's the best at putting on a mask and convincing everyone that he's far too busy and famous and legendary to be listening to driver interviews, when in reality, that's all he does, paying attention to what's happening on the track all the time.

"It means that Thane doesn't know anything about you. I mean, come on. The guy is going to fizzle out. He's not a serious driver. He thinks that always being the popular guy and always being the one in front of the camera is going to make everyone love him and it's going to help him win championships, but how many has he won and how many have you won?"

His eyes scan over my face, and I try to breathe normally, try to remember our very specific places in the world. Him, my father's best friend and possibly the most famous F1 driver there's been in a really long time. And me, a little nobody, the person who's just been obsessed with an F1 driver for six years and will never get close to him in any real way.

Mateo straightens, moving away from the car to let me out. In my head, I imagine him holding his hand out like some kind of Prince Charming, letting me slip my hand into his so that he can steady me, as if he isn't always doing that anyway, steadying me. In reality, he puts his hands in his pockets and waits for me to get out of the car before shutting the door behind me. He walks me up to the door of my apartment building.

"I got you something," he says.

"How did you...?" I start to ask but he ignores me and unfolds the cap, the familiar navy blue and silver of Albatross Racing, putting it on my head sloppily. He smiles down at me while I fix my hair which is awkwardly smushed beneath the cap.

I look up at him, feeling joy burst through my stomach, like all of the pieces of my life fitting perfectly together. "How do I look?" I ask him.

His eyes pop up to the cap on my head and then back down to my face, tracing over it quickly. "You look like you're right where you belong," he says.

Something hard forms in my throat and while I'm still trying to figure out what to say to him, he reaches out and adjusts the cap, fixing a strand of my hair that's caught in front of my eye. He tucks it behind my ear. "See you in England," he says and makes his way back down the steps toward his car, leaving me with my chest cut open and my heart beating just for him.

Chapter Two

Mateo

Pedro offers to drive me to the airport when I leave for Spain the next morning.

"So, what happened with the girlfriend?" he asks, almost as soon as we pull onto the highway.

The same thing that always happens. The slow fate of a seemingly successful relationship: I think things are going smoothly, and next thing I know, the person I'm with has met someone else, or she's telling me that the long distance is too much, that I work too many hours, that it's just too hard. And the whole time, I thought everything was fine. Because for me, everything is always fine. Just fine. If I had to sum up every relationship I've ever had in two words, they would be "just fine."

That's not to say that I didn't love any of those women. I did. I was in love with Elena. But I guess I was more in love with Formula 1.

Sometimes, I think I just need to find myself a woman who can handle coming second. But that's such a shitty thing to even think. I don't want a woman who's going to settle for being second. But I don't deserve a woman who needs to come first.

"I think I'm just done with relationships," I tell Pedro.

He sends me a look. This, *okay, sure* kind of look. Pedro's always been the wiser of the two of us. He's the one who retired to spend more time with his family.

Meanwhile, I'm still here fighting for another championship. And sometimes I can convince myself that if I just win one more championship, I'll be satisfied, even though I know it's not true.

I'll never be satisfied. It'll never be enough. It wasn't enough after the first three. It's not enough now.

"How are you feeling?" Pedro asks. "You know...about everything?"

Sometimes, when I look at Pedro, I think he looks so much older than me, even though he's only older by six years. He has wrinkles around his eyes and on his hands and one of those soft smiles men get when they have children.

"I don't know," I tell him truthfully. "Numb, maybe?"

He sighs, gripping the steering wheel. In a lot of ways, Pedro was a better driver than I was back when we drove together. Pedro was fast, but he wasn't ruthless, not the way I was.

"I think numb is pretty normal," he says, his tongue not rolling around the R's the way they once did. He's been in Canada too long.

I snort. "How would you even know, old man?" I say with a laugh in my voice. "You haven't been through a break up in thirty years."

He smirks over at me. "Sure, it's been a very long time, but from what I remember, it was very painful. And besides, you know that Melanie left me for a little while."

"It's not like that, Pedro," I tell him, because it isn't. I've never handled emotion the way that other people do. When I start to feel things too much, I just go to work. Focus on winning, focus on better cars, better times, studying footage and booking time in the sim.

I can't better myself as a man, but I can always better myself as a driver.

"Look, let's just talk about something else, okay?"

He shrugs, keeps his eyes on the road. Ever-responsible Pedro. "Okay. I was thinking about coming out to the factory next week."

That's a surprise. Although I guess it shouldn't be. Pedro has been known to show his face here and there, and it's going to be Arabella's first day with the team. Why wouldn't Pedro want to be there? But at the same time, I can only imagine this whole thing from her perspective. Her first day of work with a serious Formula 1 team, and her dad is there?

Everyone is going to want to talk to him. Everyone's going to question his involvement. Arabella is exceptionally bright. I know she's already considered what it means for her to take a position with the team when her father is who he is.

"Have you talked to Arabella about it?" I ask.

He looks over at me like he's surprised I would ask such a thing. Pedro isn't particularly used to asking permission, especially from Arabella, which makes sense because Arabella isn't really the type to be bothered by things. But he should still ask her.

"It's her first day, Pedro. Maybe she doesn't want her father there like it's the first day of primary school."

He makes a noise with his mouth, like a laugh or a cough. "Arabella is not going to be bothered like that. You know she's not like that."

"I know she isn't, but you can't just buy a plane ticket without consulting her first. Besides, pre-season is so delicate.

Everyone's coming back after a long break. People are working with their whole team for the first time. Cars are being perfected. The pressure is high. And since it's her first time working in Formula 1, it's going to be doubly stressful for her."

He seems to consider this, drumming his fingers on the steering wheel. "So you think I shouldn't come?"

"I'm not saying you shouldn't come. I'm just saying that you should consult her first."

He's quiet for a long time. Long enough for us to get in line for the airport behind people pulling suitcases from trunks and hugging loved ones goodbye.

"Okay, I won't come."

I sigh. "Pedro, I'm not saying you shouldn't come."

"You obviously don't want me there."

"Would you stop it?"

"I'm just worried," he finally blurts out. And I can tell that this is something that's been on his mind because his voice is serious. He's not joking anymore.

"What are you worried about?"

He chews on his lip, glances in the rearview mirror. "She's my daughter. In my head, she's still a little girl. And I know how brutal it can be out there. I'm worried that I'm sending her into the lion's den."

"Oh, come on. Formula 1 is nothing to be scared of."

"I know."

"And besides, you're not sending her anywhere. She chose this for herself. She decided to do this. She interviewed. She got the job. She's not afraid."

At this, his eyes go glassy and he smiles. "My Arabella is not afraid of anything."

I wish I knew if that was true or not. I've never known Arabella to back down from anything or anyone, but I don't know her the way Pedro does. What if she *is* afraid, and just isn't showing it? I can only imagine she wouldn't want Pedro to see her weaknesses.

"I know," I say, whether it's true or not. "That's why you've just got to take a deep breath and unclench." I slap him on the shoulder as he pulls into the drop-off lane.

He glances sideways at me, worry in his eye.

"Pedro," I say, gripping him a little tighter. "I would never let anything happen to her."

He shakes his head. "I know you wouldn't. But you can't be with her every second of the day."

"She's a photographer. She's not going to be part of all the drama. She's not going to be getting in fights. She's not going to be on the track. She's going to be okay. You've got to trust her, and you've got to trust me."

"I do," he says, without hesitating. "I know she'll be all right. She's just my baby."

"I know. I'm going to keep her safe."

He nods and I feel a sense of pride at the confidence in his expression. He knows he can trust me. I would die before I let anybody hurt Arabella.

Chapter Three

Arabella

For the first twenty years of my life, my father, the famous Formula 1 driver, Pedro Cedillo, and his racing rival Mateo Silva absolutely hated each other.

Okay, maybe that's not the entire truth. They were friends at first, back when I was just a baby, too young to be jetting all over the world to go to the races. Mateo was new to Formula 1 and not really a threat to my father. But as I got older, during my father's glory days, when he won four consecutive world championships, things between him and Mateo became more and more strained, until everyone on the paddock, even little ol' me, who had never met Mateo face-to-face, knew that he was persona non grata.

And then my father lost his fifth championship at the hands of Mateo, and as far as I know, they never spoke again. I remember that day clearly, the anger and defeat in my father's eyes as we all left the paddock together, my mother trying to cheer up both of us.

My father retired, and Mateo disappeared from our lives

after that, but not from Formula 1. He went on to win two more championships. And then, somewhere around my freshman year of college, he and my father started speaking again. It started in the paddock, and then they were meeting up to play padel and go skiing.

Then one night, my mother called to tell me Mateo was coming for dinner and to ask if I wanted to come home for the weekend to meet him. I was twenty by then, and by the end of that dinner, I was struck. I'd spent my whole life watching Mateo from afar, never cheering for him out loud but following his career nonetheless.

And just like that, he was in my life. Over the next six years, he visited Canada often, he followed me on social media, he slowly but surely became my father's best friend.

And I slowly but surely fell in love with him.

Arabella

I spent all night after Casa Madera thinking about how Mateo and I were in the same city, in the same time zone. It almost never happens. A couple of times a year, if I'm lucky. I laid in bed and thought about how the sky looked the same in whatever hotel room he was in. How we were seeing the same clouds, feeling the same air. I've spent so many nights, so many days, trying to imagine what the weather was like where he was, where the sun was in the sky. And today, when I woke up, only mildly hungover, I knew that the sun was in the same place for both of us.

And it made my skin ache because I don't want to be this close to him without being closer. I want to be in the same room he's in. I want him to look me in the eyes, smile that way he does, so generous with it. I want to feel the heat of his skin the way I did last night when his fingers brushed my face.

Is it crazy to be in love with someone's hands? They're just perfect. Big and calloused, tan, rough. I want them on me all the time.

And that's something I have to bury deep, six feet under, because it's all make-believe. If he ever found out, or my dad ever found out... I would feel so embarrassed for either of them to know how many hours of my life I've lost to just wanting Mateo so severely that it eats me alive.

Even though I know it can only end badly, as it has so many times in the past, I reach for my phone and open Instagram. I search Mateo's name.

Well, what I actually do is type in an M and the search results auto-fill Mateo's name. Because I do this all the time, regularly, on top of getting notifications every time Mateo posts to any social media site, which he does sparingly, unless it's race weekend.

As soon as the results come up, there it is. Something that I somehow missed over the last few weeks of turmoil. Between interviewing for the job at Albatross, interviewing for it again two more times, and then getting the job and signing all the paperwork, somehow I missed Elena announcing on her social media that she and Mateo broke up after their relatively long relationship.

I don't know why Mateo didn't post about it. Part of me thinks maybe he just doesn't care that much. But a bigger part of me, the part of me that knows Mateo better than that, knows he didn't know what to say.

Elena, on the other hand, knew exactly what to say. There it is, the long Instagram caption about how much they loved each other, how they were partners, how they'll still remain friends now that they've gone their separate ways.

I go straight for the comment section, even though I know

exactly what's going to happen, what I'm going to find. The same thing I find in every comment section anytime there's a post about Mateo that isn't on his own profile.

> Mateo really is a walking red flag, isn't he?
>
> Mateo Silva is looking to be alone for the rest of his life. Terminal bachelor.
>
> Is he really so stupid to break up with one of the hottest women on the planet? What an idiot.

I close the app and resist the urge to go through her photos.

That's something I do on a regular basis too, even though I turned off notifications for her profile a long time ago. I learned pretty quickly that while it was nice to have a little extra update on Mateo every once in a while, it was painful for those updates to always be him and his girlfriend on vacation, or him and his girlfriend at a beautiful restaurant by the beach, or just photos of Mateo that she'd taken, leaving sappy captions about how much she loves him.

Not that I can blame her. If I was with Mateo, I'd be doing the exact same thing: reveling. Or was she masking? Was it all just a show?

Either way, I reopen the app, unfollow her, and put my phone down on the bed beside me and open my laptop.

I also resist the urge to go through my saved posts, the ones that I go through at least once a week. All the videos I've saved, pictures, carousels on social media, so that I can remind myself on a regular basis just how beautiful Mateo is.

Like she knows that I'm about to go down that rabbit hole again, Lana calls.

"Hey," I answer.

"When do you leave town?" she asks without greeting.

A part of me feels bad for leaving Lana, my best friend, behind to join Albatross. Lana and I went to the University of Toronto together and then decided to get our MFAs at NYU together, too. And then she went back to Quebec City, where her family lives, and I came back to Montreal, where I've lived my entire life.

I know she's used to having me within arm's reach, and I love being close to her. The idea of leaving her and my family, and leaving home in general, is scary, but I also feel like I need it in a big way. Maybe I just need to be a little selfish while I figure out where my life is going.

"I leave next week."

"How long do you think you're going to be gone?" I can hear her pacing her apartment, the slow stick of her shoes back and forth across the floor.

"I'll only be there for a few days. It's just media stuff. A quick photo shoot and I'll be right back home."

She's quiet for a long time, and I can practically hear the question she wants to ask.

"Lana, what is it?"

"Are you thinking that you might move? Because I know it would probably be easier if England was home base or whatever."

I smile fondly to myself. On the one hand, it's nice to have someone in my life who cares this much. But on the other hand, I've lived in Canada my whole life, and the idea of moving to England actually doesn't sound that bad, even though I was adamant with Mateo about staying put.

"As of right this moment, no plans."

She lets out a sigh. "Good. Pencil me in for dinner when you get back."

"Done."

I mindlessly scroll down the page on my laptop while we

sit in silence. Lana and I do this a lot, call each other and just kind of exist while on the call.

So when she speaks again after a few minutes, it startles me.

"Hey, Ari? Are you sure you want to do this?"

My fingers pause on my keyboard, and I look up at the white board I have on the wall above my desk beside my bed. It currently has a to-do list for the final steps of my Albatross onboarding written in green marker.

"Am I sure I want to do what?"

I hear a rustle of clothing and I wonder if she's lying in bed too, like we used to when we shared a dorm room and we would work on assignments late into the night. "You know, join this Formula 1 team. I know it's a cool opportunity, but you've never really been super excited about following in your dad's footsteps."

"I'm a photographer, not a driver."

"Sure, but like, does it matter? You're going to be in that world. And I know you're excited about working with your dad's friend…"

At her words, my stomach clenches hard. I've never told Lana how I feel about Mateo. When we were roommates, I would watch the races, but I kept almost all other aspects of my obsession with Mateo to myself. I know how it looks— another silly girl obsessed with a celebrity. And it's not like I thought she would judge me for that, but it's also not the entire truth.

Hearing her mention him now makes me feel like someone just told me to take my clothes off and stand in front of a room full of people.

"…but this is such a big deal, traveling all over the world and stepping right into an industry that I thought you were trying to get away from."

She's right, of course, about the fact that I've spent my

whole life trying not to get roped into my father's world in any way that really mattered.

But this is different.

This is a chance to spend my weekends with Mateo. And I can't turn that down.

"I'm sure," I say, making sure my voice is light. "It's going to be great, and it's going to look excellent on my resume when and if I decide to move on to something else."

"When," she says. "When you move on, not if."

"Yes," I say, laughing. "When. Anyway, I'll see you next week, I promise."

Chapter Four
Pre-Season - Frome, England

Mateo

Shit. My phone falls out of my hand, clattering to the floorboard even as it rings and vibrates.

Shit, shit, shit.

I just got off the phone with Arturo to let him know I'm going to be late getting to the factory, and now I'm about to get into a car accident because I'm trying to fish my phone out of the floorboard.

I answer as soon as I've got it in my hand, expecting Felix to launch into one of his lengthy pronouncements, some decision he's made without consulting me.

Instead, a familiar, feminine voice comes out of the speaker

"Mateo?"

I'm focused on the road, but I'm not really seeing it.

"Elena?" I say, thoroughly confused. I can already feel that something bad is coming. Elena and I have barely spoken since we split up. Mostly because I've been avoiding any possible scenario in which I might be forced to speak to her.

She's done a very good job spinning the story in her favor, informing the whole world how happy she is. And I've done a good job of keeping my mouth shut, not telling a soul that she found someone better, someone who could give her the attention and future she wanted.

"Hi," she says, her voice small. "Listen, I wanted to tell you this before you saw it anywhere else."

"Okay..."

That sense of ominous foreboding rises up in me again. That feeling of defeat when you know you're not going to win a race. When you're on the last lap and there's too much space between you and the car ahead. I know this feeling well. I'm about to lose whatever this is.

"I'm getting married." I should have been expecting this. By the time Elena ended our relationship, she was fully immersed in her new boyfriend.

In the two years we were together, we never once talked about marriage. It never even crossed my mind. Marriage feels like something to do when you're excited. When you're young and in love and full of passion.

I don't know if Elena and I were ever full of passion. We were always steady. No ups and downs. No excitement or grand gestures. Just existing together. She must have been desperate to fulfill all the things she wanted with me but was never going to get as soon as she was with someone else.

"Why are you telling me this?" I ask her.

"I told you," she says, "I just didn't want you to find out on social media or in the middle of a driver's meeting or something like that."

"You think that we talk about you during driver's meetings?"

She groans. "That's not what I mean. I just mean that I don't want you to hear it from anyone other than me. I thought I was being nice but you're kind of being a dick."

"I'm not being a dick," I tell her. "I would have been fine, however I heard it."

She's quiet for a long time.

I start to feel like I've said something wrong but I can't figure out what I could have possibly said to hurt her feelings. This is how it always was with the two of us. She would get upset over things and I wouldn't even understand what I did wrong. She always read into every tiny, innocuous comment, and I never thought about anything before it came out of my mouth, always wrongly assuming I was safe to be myself.

"Yeah, I guess I should have figured," she says, "that you wouldn't be bothered to find out that I'm marrying someone else."

"Elena, that's not true."

"You were bothered about losing a race. You were bothered about coming in the back half of the grid. You were bothered by your career. Did you even care when I broke up with you?"

I'm not going to give her a response to that. She's trying to wind me up. One of the other things that she always did when we were together. She always hated that my emotions were level, controlled. She would say sometimes that she wanted me to be loud, to feel something big.

Maybe I never did, I don't know.

"Thank you for calling me." I hang up because I'm not interested in rehashing our unsuccessful relationship. I did enough of that when she left, and I have a very busy day ahead of me.

Chapter Five

Arabella

My first official day with Albatross is promo day at the factory. We've got a lot of photos to take of the car, of Mateo, of Jayce, of everyone at the team who's physically present. I'll be here for at least twelve hours today to shoot and edit, starting with arrivals.

I set up by the door of the factory, a big gray building that probably looks sleek and professional to everyone else but just looks boring to me. I adjust my tripod, snap photos of team members as they come in for the day. Mostly everyone is already inside but people not putting hands on the car today are popping in later.

When I spot a car coming into the parking lot that makes team members around the door crane their necks, my stomach jumps. But when the door opens and someone far taller than Mateo steps out of the car, I deflate.

It's Jayce, Albatross's second driver. I haven't even met him yet, but I ready my camera. I'm not the only one. There's a sea of team members and sponsors in professional dress lifting their phones to snap photos.

Jayce starts to walk by, so conditioned to ignore cameras, but then his eyes catch on mine and he skitters to a stop by the door. "Hey," is all he says, a genuine smile crossing his face. He looks freshly showered, hair styled and skin smelling like cologne, one of the tallest drivers on the grid.

I switch to video and pray I'm not going to miss a chance at catching Mateo's entrance while I'm distracted. "Hi! I'm Arabella."

"Right," he says, like he's remembering something. "Pedro's kid, yeah?"

"That's me," I say, and I'm appalled with myself when a nervous laugh slips out after. Even though I've spent the majority of my life around race car drivers, it's still a bit of a trip every time I get the chance to meet one of them. Growing up, I knew my dad's teammates well, but there wasn't a lot of cross-communication with the other teams, so the other drivers were a bit of an enigma, especially Mateo.

So now, even though I've never even really been a fan of Jayce's, the nerves still start to come alive.

He reaches out for a fist bump, and I can't help but smile as I return it. "Excited to see the car?" I ask.

His mouth twists in a weird way, and I can't decide if it's an affirmative or not. "Ready to get back out there," he says, and I still can't decide if that's a positive response, but either way, I have to get back in position.

"I'll see you in there!" I say, feeling a little silly at how desperate I sound. I just want everyone to like me.

He smiles over his shoulder. "Sure thing, Arabella."

As the door falls closed behind him, another car pulls into the lot, a sleek SUV that I suspect was a gift from the team. When Mateo gets out of the vehicle, I forget for a moment where we are or what I'm doing here.

Mateo greets everyone waiting for him, a whole parade of people, like he's a movie star on a red carpet, and then I'm the only one left, standing by the door with my tripod, clicking away.

Mateo stops in front of me, his hands in his pockets and a big smile on his face. "It's so good to see you," he says. He steps around my camera and hugs me, something I genuinely wasn't expecting. I guess I thought since we work together now, he wouldn't do things that we've always done. I guess he's not worried about workplace sexual harassment claims. At least, not from me.

"Settling in okay?" he asks when he pulls back, his body already turned toward the door.

"I've been here for half an hour."

He laughs. "Then I'll ask you later today." With that, he shakes the hand of the man holding the door open for him and then disappears inside, and I'm still standing there, snapping pictures of nothing.

Arabella

"Can you twist it this way? Just a bit, maybe?" I ask the lightning coordinator, who shifts the set light about three centimeters and then looks at me with his eyebrows raised. I nod and point my camera up at where they're fixing Mateo's hair.

My hands are trembling with nerves. My first day on the job, and it's taking photos of Mateo that are going to be used in every single piece of promo material for the rest of the season. No pressure.

As soon as everyone moves out of the way, I start shooting, first with Mateo holding his helmet at his hip and then a few of him offering it out to the camera.

I can hear my heartbeat in my ears. It never even occurred to me to do something like turn on music. Music would have been a good idea. Instead, there's nothing but the sound of my breathing as I lift my camera to my face and the soft footfalls and murmured conversations of the other people in the room. I can hear Mateo's manager chartering a jet to get him home on Monday, someone else talking about something the director of Onyx said in an interview.

I lower the camera and take a deep breath. Everything is wrong. Someone thought they should zip Mateo all the way up in his driver's suit and carefully gel his hair, but he doesn't even look like himself. He looks like a high school economics teacher.

"Um," I say, the word like a gunshot in the quiet room. "Actually, would you mind if we just maybe...?" I motion for him to unzip the suit, and his shoulders seem to deflate a little in relief. He reaches up to unzip the racing suit, tugging the Velcro at his neck open just a little bit, so that I can see his white fireproofs underneath. The sight of his muscular neck disappearing into the Nomex collar forces me to grit my teeth so I don't shiver.

I realize that whatever conversation was happening in the room has now stopped. Everyone is watching us.

"I actually think you could just let the suit hang."

Mateo hesitates, his eyes on me. One corner of his mouth creeps upward. He sets his helmet on the mat under him, tugs the zipper down until it's dangling around his navel and then he does that thing I love, the thing that makes my mouth go dry and my pulse speed up. He hooks his fingers into either side of his suit and yanks it off his shoulders. He carefully pulls his arms out of each sleeve and then lets the fabric hang around his waist.

And now I'm not sure this was such a good idea because

I'm thinking about what it would be like to lick him in a room full of my colleagues.

Mateo picks his helmet back up and plants it against his hip. "You think so?" is all he says.

I nod. "I do. You're going to look great, no matter what, but you look more...disheveled this way. More human."

One of his dark eyebrows hitches up. "Do I not look human otherwise?"

I bite back a smile. "No. You look like Spanish Formula 1 legend, Mateo Silva."

When he smiles, it's wide and dazzling. I snap a photo.

"One more thing," I say, taking a deep breath. "Could you just run your hands through your hair?"

Somewhere in a corner of the room, someone, Mateo's stylist most likely, says, "Wait, are you sure you should–"

But Mateo doesn't hesitate this time. He reaches up and presses his hands into his hair the way I've seen him do a million times. When he's done, he looks up at me, his hair a mess. He looks good enough to swallow whole. But it still isn't quite right.

I set my camera down and cross the room to him. As I move, my eyes meet his stylist's, who I'm sure spent a lot of time making him look their idea of perfect. But I see perfect Mateo every Sunday after he comes off the track, and this isn't him. Not yet.

"Trust me," I tell the stylist. If there's anything I know, it's Mateo through the eye of a lens. I know what it's like to lay in bed on a lazy morning and scroll his tag on social media, searching for any new content or fan edits that I can find. I know what looks good and what looks fake.

Stepping up to Mateo, I raise my hands and then pause. "Is it okay if I...?"

He nods. He's not smiling anymore, just watching me with curious eyes. My breath stutters out. I've never stood this close to him, seen his golden hazel eyes in person, seen the sharp contrast between his near-black scruff and his bronze skin.

I reach up and brush his hair back, fixing it so it looks less like he just rolled out of bed and more like he's been out on a run or playing a game of padel, the way he likes to. I step back, attempting to examine him in a clinical way and not as someone who's been in love with him for six years.

"Perfect," I say, feeling the word all the way down to my bones.

And like he knows, like he's been watching the comments too, seeing all the things that make women like me feral for him, he tugs at the collar of his fireproofs and turns to look at something at the side of the room. I snap the picture.

Chapter Six

Mateo

It's a relief to get out of the racing suit and back into my normal clothes. It's not like my race suit is uncomfortable, but there's something far different about wearing it for a photo shoot than wearing it during a race. Something starched and buttoned-up about knowing that I'm not even going to get a chance to sweat in it.

I head out to the cafeteria. There's still a lot to do, but I could use a break. I've talked to every single member of our team of over a thousand about every single component of the car, and now I need a sit-down.

Someone bumps my hip with theirs as soon as I step into the cafeteria, and I don't have to look to know that it's Arturo. He hands me a tea and sips at his own as we grab a table. "I don't know how you do it," he says.

"Do what?"

He gestures at me. "You come in here looking fresh as a daisy. You're forty-two, man. Don't you get tired? You got off a plane at like two in the morning."

I make a noncommittal noise. "I think that's the trick," I tell him. "I'm always tired. So this is just what I look like all the time."

He chuckles. "How's the car looking?"

I sigh. That's a complicated question. Do I think the car looks good and has everything we need in order to score some serious points? Yes. Do I think that it's going to be enough to beat Lola Castle? That, I'm not so sure of.

"You think I have a chance against her?" I ask Arturo.

He smiles into his cup. "You're asking a lot, man. I know you're still young and healthy, probably in better shape than you ever have been, but she's fierce. And she's got stamina and speed. God, she's fucking fast."

"Yes, I'm aware."

He chuckles again.

My eyes catch movement over in the corner of the room. It's Arabella. She's taking pictures of a plant. Arturo must catch that my attention has been diverted.

"What is she doing?" Arturo asks.

She's got her back to us, her hair pulled back in a ponytail and her Albatross jacket firmly in place. From behind, she looks like every other team member.

"I'm not sure," I say. "Arabella," I call out to her. A few people turn our way. People wandering through, stopping for lunch. And Arabella spins around, her hair whipping into her face. When she realizes it's me, she smiles, and I see her finger move on the camera button.

She's good at this. She knows that if there's anything of any kind of interest in front of her, she should be shooting.

She seems to hesitate, like she isn't sure if I actually want her to come over or if I'm just greeting her. I use two figures to beckon her and Arturo laughs again. I elbow him in the side, but I can't really blame him. I'm so used to dealing with people a certain way, and I'm having a hard time reconciling the way I generally am with my team with this person who I know from an entirely different world.

"Hi," she says when she steps over to the table.

"Have you had anything to eat?" I ask.

"I had a granola bar earlier," she says, smiling at me and then over at Arturo.

"This is Arturo," I tell her. "He's an assistant here. He's generally my shadow on race weekends."

"I know," she says, smiling at Arturo. "I've been following the Albatross social media accounts for a while, so I feel like I know everyone on the team."

Arturo leans back in his seat and says, "I don't need be introduced either. I knew what you looked like. I don't know if there's anywhere you can go that you're not going to be recognized."

At this, her smile fades, and I want to kick Arturo. I've been trying to do my best to keep Pedro out of all this. That night in Montreal she asked me if I had anything to do with her getting the job. I didn't lie to her. I really didn't have anything to do with it.

But I can't say her being Pedro's daughter didn't have anything to do with it. I wasn't the one making the decisions. I don't know how much weight that had on things. All I know is that I've seen her work. I follow her on social media. And while she was at art school in New York, I saw the work she was doing and posting online. She's good. Probably better than any of the other art designers that we've had here.

So when they asked me what I thought about hiring her, I told them the truth. That I thought she was talented and that she would do well in the position. But they didn't ask me about any of the other candidates and I didn't know any of the other candidates.

"Are you adjusting well here?" Arturo asks.

She makes an affirmative noise and nods. "Still just kind of warming up," she says. She gives Arturo an interesting smile. A co-conspirator kind of smile. Like he would understand better than I would what she's going through.

I guess it didn't really occur to me that even though Arabella and I are closer to each other than we are with anyone else, we're on opposite ends of the hierarchy where the team is concerned. And maybe knowing me doesn't really help her at all.

"If you need anything," Arturo says, crossing his arms and smiling up at her, his eyes bright, "you just let me know. I know it's kind of weird getting the hang of things, especially the schedule. Running around all day. You'll adjust quickly."

"Yeah, I think so," she says.

It's like I'm not here anymore.

"I think our schedules are going to be similar," he tells her, settling into shop talk. "I really do follow Mateo around for most of the day. And I think you're going to be following him around, too. So if you need help figuring out where anything is—"

"She'll figure it out," I cut in.

Both of them look over at me. There's a little pink to Arabella's cheeks, and I think maybe I've embarrassed her.

"I know that," Arturo says, a line forming between his eyebrows. "I wasn't implying she couldn't figure it out on her own. It's just that the paddock can get confusing. There's a lot of ground to cover sometimes."

I just nod, keeping my mouth shut. I think I've done enough here.

"I've got to go get set up for Jayce," Arabella says. "But I'll see you both later."

Arturo is quiet after Arabella wanders off.

"What was that?" he asks after a few bites of his oatmeal.

"What was what?"

His mouth is full, but he motions to the air in front of us as if Arabella is still standing there.

"Nothing." When he just continues to stare at me, I sigh. "I guess I'm just feeling a little protective."

He swallows his food, takes a drink of his tea. "She's going to be fine."

"You know how the guys can be."

He nods. "Yeah, I do know how the guys can be. But I also know that a woman doesn't apply to be in a male-dominated field without knowing what they're getting into. She'll be fine. She's a big girl. She can take care of herself."

He's right. I know he's right.

"Meetings?" Arturo asks.

"Yep," I say, pushing back from the table. I didn't exactly consult my itinerary, but it doesn't matter because Arturo will keep me in line.

"Engineering first, media second."

"Right.

"Sponsor stuff this afternoon."

"Yep."

Time to get started.

TurboDr1v3X: please tell me you gave Mateo a good car

PitStopPanic@: Why is Jayce still here????

SlipStream_88: Jayce DGAF

GridlockGiggles: MATEEEEEEEEO!

Chapter Seven
Round 1 - Sakhir, Bahrain

Mateo

"Mateo, there've been some rumors that Pedro Cedillo's daughter has joined the team. Do you have anything to say about that?"

I knew it was just a matter of time before someone asked. Felix knew, too. He told me that the decision not to announce that Arabella had joined the team was made strategically so as not to pull focus from testing and the start of the season. But people have seen her at the track. They know she's here, even if they don't exactly know in what capacity.

So now it's my job to break the news in the middle of our first pre-race interview, right before the first race of the season. On the seat beside me, Archer, casually holding his microphone in the vicinity of his mouth, smiles over at me, eyes glittering under the brim of his Onyx Racing cap.

I look out at the media crowd, stuffed into the room, far from where our couch sits, me, Thane, and Archer pressed close to each other on it.

"Yes, she did join the team," I say into my microphone.

"It's not something that's necessarily been discussed a lot. Not that anyone was trying to hide it. She's coming on as our art designer." I smile, thinking about her trying to explain exactly what an art designer is over dinner with her parents. "And I think that she's going to do a really good job. She's very talented and I think she will be an excellent addition to the team."

A different reporter stands now. "And did you have any say in whether or not she was hired?" he asks in a thick accent I can't identify. "Did you wish to bring her onto the team? How did that conversation go?"

"No, I didn't have any say in whether or not she was hired. She made it known to the right people that she was interested in the job. The only say that I had was after they had already decided they were interested. They came to me and just said, 'Are you good with this?' But she was already at the top of the pile. I was just an afterthought. And I told them we'd love to have her on the team, and I would love to get to work with her. Obviously, I've known her for a while, and I know what good she can do in a job like this."

I'm rambling. I can see it on the other drivers' faces as they peer over at me, but I can't seem to stop. It's like some kind of knee-jerk reaction, my need to defend her. I hate that they're asking me these questions. I know it will just sink into Arabella's mind if she catches wind of it.

"But she's not interested in racing like her father?"

A laugh goes through the room. I just watch their faces, all of them making Arabella the butt of the joke. I don't think it's funny, the way they're implying she couldn't be a driver if she wanted to, the way they're laughing at the idea that the legacy of Formula 1 can't be passed down from father to daughter the way it's been passed down from father to son for so many decades.

"We need people in every job," I say, raising my voice over

their amusement. I see their faces change, their attention catch. "We need an entire team to keep everything running and the whole team is important; every job is important. Having her in a non-driving position is excellent as well and she's still a very vital part of the team. She has never wanted to be a driver. She found the right place for her instead."

At that, I drop my microphone beside me on the leather couch and cross my arms. Out of the corner of my eye, I see Archer smile.

"Are we done?" he asks into his mic when no one else asks a question. We get an affirmative from an employee over by the wall, and I'm up off the seat before anyone can dare ask me another question.

Arabella

I take a deep breath, taking a seat for the first time all weekend, it feels like, and stretching my neck. I wouldn't say I'm a sedentary person. I like to jog and hike.

But that was nothing like this, always walking up and down the paddock, through the motorhome, down to the garage, around the track, a constant loop to always make sure I'm getting what's good.

And now I have almost an hour to rest and edit photos before prep will start for the race. I went for the first seat I could find in the motorhome, but now that I'm seeing all of the people coming through, I'm not sure this is the best place.

"Is it okay if I sit here?" someone with a heavy Swedish accent asks me.

The person doesn't wait for an answer before plopping a bowl overflowing with salad down beside my laptop and pulling out the chair next to mine. The Swedish woman, blond hair pulled into a tight bun on top of her head and wearing a navy-blue team kit that matches mine, smiles wide at me and holds out a hand. "I'm Brigit, it's nice to meet you."

"Hi." Is all I can say as I watch her make herself comfortable. It is obviously not her first day with the team. She shoves a huge forkful of salad into her mouth and her eyes scan all of my equipment.

"So, you are the new camera girl." Before I can answer, she puts up a hand to stop me. "I'm sorry, that sounded really condescending. I don't mean to be. I'm just a dummy who doesn't know what it's called."

I smile. "The official job title is art designer, but that makes me nervous, to be honest."

She makes a little humph noise. "Absolutely not. You wear that title with pride. That sounds so cool. I'll be honest, I don't really understand all that TikTok stuff, but I watched the last guy work on all of it, and he was always doing so much intricate editing work, so it's pretty impressive."

I pick up the smoothie that I chose from the catering bar and take a small sip. Strawberry banana. I can't fathom having a salad at eight in the morning. "Thanks. I don't feel terribly impressive."

Brigit's dark eyebrows wrinkle. "The team has not been very welcoming?"

"No, it's not that. It's just—"

"Look," she says cutting me off, but not in an unkind way, "I totally get it, okay? I was a big fan of your father's back in the day. Him and Mateo, they are the reason that I wanted to work for a Formula 1 team. And the only reason that I chose to apply to Albatross is because of Mateo, so I understand. It's got to be weird being here like this."

I immediately try to put Brigit on a timeline in my mind. I

was a kid when my dad was driving in F1, and Brigit looks like she might be my age, maybe even younger. She must have grown up on this stuff.

While I'm still processing everything she's said, she continues. "I always kind of wondered what it would be like to win a grand prix and then go home to your kid afterwards, you know? When you're younger, you go out and you celebrate and you drink and all of that, but you know, do you go home at the end of the day after winning a title and sing 'The Itsy Bitsy Spider' to your daughter?"

I love the way she says this, taking me all the way back to the days when my dad would disappear for races and then come back home to us.

"That's pretty much exactly what it's like."

She leans close to me, her eyes sweeping the room. "There are not a lot of women on the team, but that's okay. We'll stick together. You know enough about Formula 1 to know that men are always saying how women don't belong in motorsport. It's all bullshit. Boys just don't like it when they get outshined by a woman, but if one of these little rats says something to you, you just speak the name of our lord and savior, Lola Castle."

I laugh. Lola Castle, two-time world champion and Mateo's biggest rival.

"What's your job here, Brigit?"

"I am a mechanic. And I have the fastest tire gun time in the history of Albatross."

"That's really impressive." I take a deep breath, hope that I'm confiding in the right person. Brigit seems like the right person. "I guess I'm just afraid that everyone's going to think that I'm just here because of my dad."

She nods, munching away. "And they will. They'll all think it, but it doesn't matter what they think. You know the truth.

So you just ignore them. I know that I have the fastest tire gun time. I know that I put all of them to shame. They don't want to admit it, but that's fine because I know the truth." And she winks. "There's an empty office upstairs if you don't want to be bothered."

Chapter Eight

Arabella

I stand in the hallway outside Mateo's room as he prepares for the race. I feel like I'm in a dream. The energy at the track is completely different on race day. It's not like I didn't know this. I've been to so many races in the past, but when I was younger and my dad would take me to races—when he was still a driver and after he had retired—it was always just for race day. Very rarely for qualifying and never on practice days.

Over the weekend, I've seen the track get busier and louder from media day to qualifying and now it's like the place is alive, buzzing with noise and energy. I can feel my own excitement in my blood. Even though I've never had the passion for motorsport that my dad or Mateo have, I've always really enjoyed watching the races. The adrenaline is addictive.

But as I watch everything happen around me, I suddenly feel like I'm having an out of body experience.

I'm in a foreign country with a group of people I barely know working a job that scares me, and I did it all for a guy who's the center of everyone's attention.

I can't explain the tremor in my hands, the numbness in the tips of my fingers as I stand between Jayce and Mateo's rooms and wait to be called in to take pictures.

I lean against the wall, listening to Mateo and Arturo's voices on the other side of it, camera prepped, lighting perfect, ready, even as the anxiety pulls my chest tight.

Jayce comes out of his room first, his driving suit dangling around his hips and his white fireproofs tight against his skin. He's well built, tall, and a little gangly. Most of the drivers are under six feet, but Jayce well over. Mateo is well under.

Jayce runs a hand through his hair, smiles lopsided at me when he sees the camera. "Hey," he says as he makes his way over to me. I snap pictures of him, catch the change in his expression when the camera goes from my chest to my face, catch the way he laughs and then shakes his head, get pictures of his broad back as he moves past, his wide shoulders.

I want to follow him to give myself something to do, something to keep my mind off everything else, but if I've learned one thing in my short time with the team, it's that Mateo takes priority.

He's the face everyone knows. He's the one with the brand deals and giant fan base and the long history with the sport. Pictures of Jayce are important, but pictures of Mateo are my job security.

So I turn back to Mateo's room. When Arturo steps out, I get myself ready, poised to get Mateo as he follows.

But Mateo doesn't come.

Arturo turns to me as he closes the door shut behind him. He crosses his arms and sets his shoulder against the door-frame. He has a slouchiness to him that feels like it's trying to tell me something.

"Everything okay?"

He smiles. "Yeah. Just first race nerves."

"What? Mateo doesn't get nervous."

Arturo's gaze slides over to me. "I thought you knew him," he says with a smirk on his lips, a humorous tilt to his words, but the comment slices through me. Because I do know Mateo, but I'm also very aware of all the parts of him that I don't know, that I couldn't know before now. "Maybe you should go in and talk to him."

I press a hand to my chest. "Who? Me?"

He snorts. "No, the goblin hiding behind you. Yes, you. Might be nice for him to see a friendly face."

"Um, okay." I didn't think my anxiety about this day could get any higher, but here we are, my pulse pounding in my ears as I stare at the silver plaque on the door bearing Mateo's name. I knock.

"Come in."

His voice sends a shiver through me, and I crack the door open. Mateo is sitting on his small bed, already dressed in his racing suit. When he sees me, he sits back against the wall, knocking his team cap askew on his head.

I step into the room and shut the door behind me, not sure what else to do. He's trusted me with his privacy and I don't want to let anyone else into it. "All set?" I ask.

He nods. "Yeah, I, uh..." His eyes meet mine, and I can see the stress in them. It's a big day for him, and I can only imagine what he's feeling.

I walk over to the slender bed attached to the wall, not daring to sit beside him on it. He cranes his neck back to look up at me, and something about him now seems so small, when he's always seemed larger than life to me.

"I'm ready. I just—" He looks away, his cap obscuring his face so that I can't see it any longer. "I just need a second to get my head on straight."

"What can I do to help?"

He tips his head back so I can just barely see his eyes in the shadow of the bill of his cap. "You're here, aren't you? Did Arturo tell you to come talk to me?"

I can feel my face flush. I'm not sure if this is something he would find annoying or not. "Sort of. He's just worried about you." *I'm worried about you*, I want to say, but I don't.

He laughs. "Come on. I'm going to be fine. I always am."

Right before my eyes, Mateo transforms. He looks like Mateo, but at the same time, he looks like someone else, like a wax version of himself. He's pushing it all down, hiding so that no one will see whatever is behind his mask. Fear? Doubt? I've never seen him like this. I've always known Mateo as the most confident man in F1. Doing what he wants despite the opinions. But here he is, delicate, like he could crack from a single touch.

"You're still here, Mateo. You just go out there and fight."

His smile falls, and he stares up at me, his face unreadable. "Yeah, I'm still here." He leans away from the wall, fixing his cap.

"I'm going to get back to the garage. Don't hang around too long, or they'll start the whole thing without you."

Arabella

I hear Mateo's voice at the top of the steps and take a deep breath, surprised by the heavy relief in my blood. Like there was ever some chance he was going to back out.

Arturo comes down with him. They're laughing about something as they walk. Mateo adjusts his cap as he practically skips down the steps, his mouth pulled wide into that smile that I know so well. Is it real? Or is he just putting it on for everyone else?

His suit is zipped to his throat and fits him in a way that it definitely doesn't fit Jayce. I've had an obsession with the way Mateo's hip bones look in a racing suit for quite a while now. I want to feel them up against mine.

Mateo seems to find the camera then. Just a little glance at it and then up at me. As he walks into the garage, he fist bumps everybody as he goes. Then he passes me. He doesn't offer me his fist. Instead, he grips my shoulder in a quick squeeze and his hand falls away, sliding down my arm. It immediately sends goosebumps along my skin, the hair on my arms rising, but he doesn't notice because he's already moved on. He's got a big race to get to, after all.

I follow him into the garage. We still have a ways to go before the race starts. But I can already tell it's going to be a good one.

Chapter Nine

Arabella

I stand still, camera steady, lens focused. Every single mechanic stands perched, perfectly ready to go. Each one with their job, each one a cog in the wheel. I'm snapping photos, dozens and dozens of them as they remove everything from the car, take the covers off the wheels, and then Mateo peels out.

I can hear the crowd cheering. They're so excited, and I can feel the echo of that excitement in my chest. I turn to go, knowing that I'll need to be in Jayce's garage when he pulls back in for his pit stop.

I'm taking pictures of the pit wall from inside the garage when the team starts to scramble. It's far too early for a pit stop, but everyone is on their feet.

And then the nose of the car comes into view, slamming into the pit. I'm watching the whole thing through the lens of my camera, my stomach in knots. What's going on? I don't think anyone could bear a Mateo DNF on his first race, especially Mateo.

But it's not Mateo. It's Jayce. Jayce is fairly experienced, though a solid fifteen years younger than Mateo.

I watch the crew scoop his car up and back it into the garage, where they get to work.

I stay out of the way as Jayce climbs out of the car, not saying a word to anyone as he stalks out of the garage. I guess he's done for the weekend. My eyes rake over the car, but I can't see anything obviously wrong with it. Something must be wrong for them to have called Jayce's race like that.

As everyone shuffles around, taking the car apart, I slip out the back of the garage and move back to Mateo's side. I won't be needed on Jayce's side anymore, it would seem.

As soon as I step in, I spot Brigit. She grins at me from under the visor of her helmet. All the mechanics have to wear them when they do pit stops. "Hey!" She pats the spot beside where she's leaned against a shelf. I have to step around a tower of tires to get to her.

"Did you get a load of the action?" she asks, her eyes going back to the screen above our heads, where we can watch the race footage. I watch too as the camera holds steady to Mateo and Lola, already battling it out for first place.

"I didn't see what happened," I tell her.

"Issue with the cooling system. So terrible. Not what anyone wants for the first race of the season, especially not twelve laps in. No one's fault, really,"

I snort. "I think the engineers back at the factory would beg to differ. I'm sure they're busy pointing fingers as we speak."

She makes an expression that tells me she agrees. "I'm just glad that one's not on me."

I can't even imagine the pressure of having someone else's race be on your shoulders. I've seen drivers go from first place to middle of the pack with a bad pit stop. I wonder if you get demoted if your tire gun doesn't work.

"You should get in there," she says, nodding her pointed chin at the mouth of the garage. "Get the money shot and all that."

"I'll wait until I absolutely have to. I'm afraid that I'm going to get in the wrong place at the wrong time and get flattened by a car."

She laughs. "These men manage to not run into each other going 200 kilometers an hour. They get within centimeters of each other. And you think that one of them isn't going to see a whole ass human being standing in front of their car?" She claps me on the back. "I've got to get back to work. Take some good pictures of me and put them on social media, eh?"

"Will do." She steps over to a group of mechanics and they all immediately pull her into their conversation. I focus on the race, realizing that at some point while I was talking to Brigit, Mateo lost first place to Lola Castle.

In my peripheral vision, I see a figure standing to the side of the garage. Everyone else is watching the race on the TVs, but I can tell that this person's face is pointed at me instead.

I glance over, only mildly surprised to find Jayce's eyes on me. He stands tall, his hands crossed across his chest, and he's not giving any sign that he has any intention of looking away now that he's been caught.

I look back to Brigit, fully immersed in the race. She and the mechanic beside her watch the TV screen, their arms slung over each other's shoulders. Comrades.

The peace is shattered when a tall, red-headed man who I recognize as the head mechanic stomps into the garage, his hand in the air. The rest of the mechanics seem to know what that means because they batten down their helmets and rush out of the garage, onto the bright strip of concrete where Mateo will take his pit stop.

I follow them out, switching my camera to video. I think a video of the season's first pit stop will be well received.

Mateo's car slows in front of the garage, and my stomach does that thing it always does when I see him. There are so many different sides to Mateo, but this is the one I know best from my years of watching him drive.

I hold my camera steady and watch him. It all happens so fast. 2.4 seconds, to be exact. And in that time, I watch Mateo's bright helmet in the cockpit, eyes focused forward, waiting for his green light. The mechanics pull away, and he's gone.

I feel like I was just pushed through a whirlwind. I don't know if I belong here, but what I do know is that I don't know if I can belong anywhere that Mateo isn't.

Chapter Ten

Mateo

"Well done, Mateo, well done," Jerry says in my ear.

A loud shout erupts from my mouth. First fucking place. I haven't finished P1 in a Grand Prix in four years.

"Holy shit, thank you guys," I say into the radio. "Thank you, team. Thank you for your hard work." I wave at the stands as I pass on a victory lap. I pull up behind the first place sign and hop out of the car. I stand on the nose and wave to the crowd. Even with my helmet on, I can hear them. The sheer volume of their excitement matches the volume of my own inside.

I can't believe I just did that. As I'm getting down off the car, I see Lola pulling into the second place spot beside me but I don't wait to see her get out. I rush to my team, waiting behind the rope, and throw myself into them, like a swimmer into a wave.

They hug me and pat me on the back, and it feels like coming home.

Mateo

We file out onto the podium, and everyone below us starts to cheer. The noise settles just beneath my skin in the best way, a lightning bolt to the stomach.

Earlier today, sitting in my room in the motorhome and feeling it all hit me, I didn't think there was any way I was ever going to be here again, standing in first place. It's been a long road getting here.

I glance over at Lola. She's one of the best drivers I've ever met. She's focused, she's serious, she's hungry, and somehow, I beat her. She smiles at me, and I let out a sigh of relief, feeling some of the pressure ease off my shoulders.

Last season, when I ran into her after her brakes failed, she went into that wall and her car caught fire. I wasn't sure we were ever going to come back from that. It's a horrific thing, pulling someone you really care about, someone you really respect, out of a burning car, helping paramedics put the fire out that's raging over your friend's body, visiting them in the hospital. I've known people in this sport who've died. I've known people who have had permanent injuries. I don't know what it was about that wreck; it changed me.

But there's Lola beside me right now, smiling up at me, forgiving and grateful and kind.

They call my name last, and I move up onto the middle step. My eyes scan over the faces down below. Teams and fans and family, just a blur, a cloud of humans.

But right there at the front, amidst the Albatross wave of blue and silver, I see a black camera lens pointing right at me. And when the camera shifts, pulled away from the face that it was just pressed against, I see Arabella, and I smile.

She makes a face, a silly little scrunch of her nose, and then smiles back at me. And the world feels right again, like it's okay that I'm here, that it's *good* that I'm here, and good that she's here, too.

I'm used to just seeing my team or the fans that wave the Spanish flags above their heads or have their faces painted with my number. But it's been a long time since I've seen a face that felt so welcoming, and I can't seem to look away as they play the national anthem of Spain and then the national anthem of England. And all the while, I'm just glad I'm not alone.

Chapter Eleven

Arabella

My heart races as I scroll through pictures from Bahrain. There's got to be 10,000 of them. Practice, then qualifying, and then the race. But so many of the photos are from the podium afterwards. Which is ironic because I wasn't really focusing on the camera. I was just focusing on him.

Looking at the photos now, I see the progression. That man who walked into the paddock on Thursday in his designer clothes. Who changed into a racing suit. Who wore stress and doubt like a second skin. And then, on the other side of it, after the race. The sweat that curled the edges of his hair and gathered in patches on his suit. It's something I'm so familiar with, but it never gets old.

I'm deleting photos as I go. Ones that are blurry or just unflattering angles. But it's going to take me hours because I keep stopping on the good ones. The ones where Mateo is smiling. The ones where he's got his face turned up to the sun. The ones where he's tugging at the collar of his suit. Pulling on his gloves. Climbing over the side of the car to get out in that perfectly-formed arc that he always makes. Muscle memory. The exactness. He knows how to move his body. Something about that is downright intoxicating.

A knock sounds at the door of my apartment. I blink up, realizing that the sun set at some point while I was working. I straighten, my back aching. I've got to figure out a better system for this or I'm going to be a hunchback by the end of the season.

I'm not expecting anybody, but it's not unusual for the building manager to stop by to check on things.

But when I find my best friend, Lana, on the other side of the door, I'm surprised. "What are you—"

She pushes past me into the apartment, taking off her jacket as she does. When I got off the plane a few days ago, the shock of the cold startled me after spending the weekend in the warmth of Bahrain.

"I wasn't sure if you were coming back," she says, standing in the middle of my living room and staring out my window down at the city lights.

"I needed some time at home," I say, closing the door.

She makes a face, her nose crinkling and her lips puckering, and sticks her hands in her pockets. "An exciting couple of weeks, right?"

"Yeah. Sorry I didn't call. I was distracted and exhausted. What are you doing here?" I finally mange to ask her as she picks up one of the apples from the bowl in the middle of my table and takes a bite.

"A friend of mine is having a birthday party downtown so I thought I would drop by to see you." She smiles at me with her cheeks full of apple. "Aren't you happy to see me?"

"Of course," I say, shuffling into the kitchen. "Do you want something else to eat?" I just realized I haven't eaten all day. I've been really focused on getting those pictures out. The upside is that I can save a lot of them to divvy out over the week. There's no hurry on anything now that I've posted post-race content. But I'm putting a portfolio together anyway.

"I was thinking you should come," Lana says from the other side of my kitchen bar.

I shut the refrigerator door and look over at her. "Come where?"

"The party," she says, looking everywhere but at me, taking in all the bits and pieces of my apartment. Lana and I are mostly long-distance friends, meeting halfway between Montreal and Quebec City for day trips of brunch and shopping, so she's only seen the inside of my apartment once or twice. "The birthday party. It's supposed to be pretty classy. It'll be fun."

This is what Lana has always been good at, making sure I'm not hiding myself away, which I have a tendency to do if left to my own devices. I don't know that I really consider myself an introvert, but I'm fairly content to be on my own, to be where it's quiet, to be at home. But in college, when we were roommates, she always liked to go out at every opportunity and she liked me to go with her. She thinks I should be like her, wanting the noise and the crowds all the time. I'm sure it's very confusing for her now that I'm working a job where I have to be constantly in the presence of other humans.

But I still like the quiet, especially after a weekend of noise.

"I don't know. I have a lot to do." I motion toward my laptop and cross my arms. I'm not trying to be selfish, not wanting to go out with her when she came all this way, but it's not like she's in town specifically to see me and she dropped in without warning.

Over at my dining table, she's looking at the work that's still up on my computer. It doesn't occur to me until she's bent over, peering at my screen, exactly what I was doing before she barged in. But there he is, big on the screen. Mateo Silva in all of his sweaty podium glory.

She stares at the screen for a moment and then smiles over

at me, an oddly manufactured expression. "I just don't want you to drown in it," she says.

I get a plate out of the cabinet, go to the pantry for some bread and a jar of peanut butter. "I'm not drowning in anything. It's only been three weeks."

"I know," she says. "I just know how fast these things can happen. I'm just afraid you're going to become a workaholic."

I make a face at her. "Are you serious? All you do is work."

She rolls her eyes. "You know that's not true. Look at me right now, here, going out. I'm always out."

"Yeah, and if you're not out, you're working," I say, pulling a couple of pieces of bread out and slapping them onto the plate. "Look, I think it's okay if I'm a little buried in my work right now. I just started this job. I'm still trying to figure out how to work it all into a reasonable schedule. It's going to take time. Can I adjust, please?"

She leans on the bar between us and watches me. "Of course, you can. I'm not trying to make you feel stressed or anything. I'm just saying you have to make time for yourself so that you don't get obsessed."

I stop spreading peanut butter onto my sandwich and turn to look at her. She holds my gaze. We both know exactly what she's talking about.

We've known each other for almost a decade, lived together for six years, until I moved back to Montreal. She knows how many hours I spend watching Formula 1 and how many hours I spend looking up Mateo on the internet and how many times a day I zone out thinking about him. She knows all of it. And I guess she's never been very approving of it, though I've never known why and am too afraid to ask.

"Okay," I say, tossing the knife in the sink. "I'll go to the party with you."

She grins. "Great. What are you going to wear?"

Arabella

I don't dislike parties. In fact, I'm a big fan. While I like the quiet, I like the energy of a room full of people, too.

But it's hard to go to a party where you don't know anybody. That's the kind of thing that someone like Lana doesn't understand. She goes to a party full of people she doesn't know and fifteen minutes in, she's already best friends with somebody. She introduces herself and tells funny jokes and overshares and then suddenly everyone wants to be around her. They want to drink with her and they want to dance with her and people who are inclined to be interested in women want to go home with her.

But I have a harder time at parties. I'm not always sure how to start a conversation. So while Lana's having an excellent time, even though she seems to only know the birthday girl, I'm mostly observing from a spot on the couch.

It's a nice party on the fancier side of Montreal. There are twinkle lights all around the patio, expensive outdoor furniture, a DJ. It's that kind of party. At least the champagne is expensive and delicious. I've already had a glass of it and I'm starting to feel the warmth in my cheeks and my fingers, even though it's cold enough outside to be able to see my breath.

The person who owns the place has set up big lantern heaters to keep the outdoor warm. I'm sitting right underneath one, feeling toasty and watching everyone have a good time.

"Can I get you a drink?"

I have no idea where the guy comes from. He's sitting beside me on the couch like he's been there all night, but I'm really positive he hasn't been. Dark skin, jade eyes, cheeks that are a bit red and give away just how cold he's pretending not to be.

"I've had enough, I think." I don't mind getting tipsy in a room full of my friends, but tipsy in a room full of strangers when I'm not entirely positive how I'm getting home is maybe not for me.

The guy reaches out for my empty champagne glass. He shakes it between his fingers to indicate that he's surprised that one glass would be enough. "You're sure you don't want another?" He doesn't sound creepy or smarmy, more just curious.

"I'm pretty sure," I say.

Everyone here has definitely had more than one glass and there are still tables and tables of champagne. I don't actually know who the birthday girl is here, but I'm getting the feeling she comes from money. And that's coming from somebody who also comes from money, for the most part, but not this level of wealth.

"What's your name?" the guy asks me.

"Arabella." Now that I'm looking right at him, I think maybe he's cute. He's young. If he's my age, I would be surprised. He's probably just a little younger than me, maybe even still in university. Maybe he goes to school here. I think the University of Quebec is nearby. He has a very pink mouth and this haircut that tells me that he has an expensive barber.

"I'm Chuck," he says, putting his hand out toward me. I shake it, not surprised to find that his skin is very cold. We're like six stories up and it's early April in Canada. "How do you know the birthday girl?" he asks.

"Oh, I don't. My friend brought me. Well, she convinced me to come because, according to her, she's afraid that I'm going to turn into a workaholic."

There's a curl to the corner of his mouth. "Really? Aren't

you a bit young to be a workaholic? I thought only like Olympians are workaholics in their 20s. What is it you do?"

"I'm a photographer."

"Oh," he says, the sound coming out a few octaves higher than I was prepared for. He lifts my empty glass to his lips and then seems to realize what he's done and laughs at himself. "I guess I should get myself another drink, too." He lifts his other hand and I realize that he's got two empty glasses now. He sets them both on the table in front of him. "I'll be right back."

"Okay."

"Don't move," he says, and while he doesn't seem like a creep, the words are slightly demanding. I can't decide if they bother me or not. Since I didn't really want to move anyway, I decide on not.

My eyes find Lana in the crowd as I'm waiting for Chuck to return. She gives me a thumbs up and a smile, and I give her one back. She looks like she's having a great time. I'm not having a bad time. It's actually a really beautiful night. The sky is as clear as it can be in the middle of the city. In a few days, I'll be gone again. On a plane to another race, a triple header, which means three whole weeks away.

I turn on my phone and glance at social media, even though I didn't get any notifications and I know there will be nothing about Mateo. He's never posted much between races.

And then I get this pit in my stomach when I realize I miss him. I've always missed him between races, but this is something else. This isn't patiently waiting to see him on my TV again. It's patiently waiting to be near him, to be close enough to count his eyelashes, to hear his laugh and talk to him.

I shake away the thought and keep scrolling. Mateo is the only one that I have notifications turned on for, but I follow all the drivers and teams, and every once in a while, the F1 account or someone else will post about Mateo.

Chuck returns, sitting much closer to me on the couch

than he was a moment ago and handing me a glass of champagne. I choose not to be offended that he got me a drink even though I said I didn't want one. I just won't drink it.

"Listen," he says, leaning toward me, "I was thinking about it while I was away, and honestly, I think life is too short to beat around the bush. I think you're very pretty. And I'm worried that at any moment, someone else at this party is also going to realize you're very pretty and that you don't seem to be here with anybody. So before anyone else can jump at it, I would like to ask you out on a date."

I just blink at him. He just said a lot of words really fast, and I wasn't expecting any of them.

"Oh, okay."

One corner of his mouth tips up. "Okay?" he asks.

Oh. He thinks I'm agreeing to the date. *Am I* agreeing to the date? I can't really think of any reason not to. "Sure."

He smiles big, showing me all of his teeth. "Great. It's a date then."

A date. What could one date hurt? Who knows...maybe this guy is my soulmate...

"I'd like to take you to dinner," he says. "I can't afford anything as fancy as all this," he says, gesturing around. "I'm just a vet in training."

I narrow my eyes at him. "Do you mean, like, you're in boot camp?"

He laughs. "No, I'm not a veteran, a veterinarian. Or I will be, soon."

"Oh." I can feel the blush moving up my neck. That was really stupid. I blame the alcohol.

"What are you doing next Saturday?" he asks.

Next Saturday.

"Next Saturday isn't really going to work." I look down into my champagne glass, watch the bubbles rise to the surface and pop. "Yeah, next week isn't great for me."

"Oh," he says. He's clearly disappointed. But is it really reasonable to expect someone to have a wide-open calendar a week in advance? I guess I probably would have been wide open if I hadn't taken this job.

I put a hand on his knee, feel the surprising warmth of him through his chinos. "I'm just going to be out of town for work." I don't want him to think that I agreed to a date just to dodge him.

"Oh," he says. This seems to cheer him up a bit. "Where will you be?"

"Saudi Arabia."

His mouth drops into an O shape. "Saudi Arabia. Well, that's...fun. Are you...taking pictures of stuff there?"

"Yep." I lean back and, without thinking, take a sip of my champagne, the one I didn't want.

"Okay," he says. "Well, maybe the weekend after." He's definitely going to think I'm trying to blow him off.

"Actually, I'm going to be out of town the weekend after, too. I'll be in Monaco."

At this, he really looks confused. Like he's trying to solve a calculus problem in his head. His mouth becomes even more ovular and he glances to the side, his eyes narrowing. "You're going to be in Monaco? What are you photographing there?" He could have just asked me this the first time, or even when I first mentioned I was a photographer. But some people just hear photographer and think I work at a portrait studio at a mall somewhere.

"I'm a sports photographer," I say. I don't really like the way it sounds. Mostly because that's not how I would categorize myself. It's not like I'm hopping from place to place, photographing soccer players over here and hockey players over there. I'm not working for *Sports Illustrated*. "I work for a Formula 1 team."

He blows out a heavy breath, bowing his head and looking

at me from under his eyelashes. "Listen, I don't want to sound like a incomplete idiot, and from what you just told me, I'm going to assume that you hang out with a lot of macho guys on a regular basis, but I have no idea what Formula 1 is."

For some reason, I find this refreshing. I laugh. "Formula 1 is a motorsport. I take pictures of race cars all weekend." This is obviously a bit of an understatement. I'm taking far more photographs of race car drivers than I am of just race cars. But for now, I'll leave that bit of information out.

"So you're gone a lot," he says.

"Here and there," I tell him, severely downplaying the amount of traveling I have to do. "It's a triple header this weekend, so three races in a row in three weekends. But then I'll have two weeks off before the next race. So maybe I could see you then."

I fully expect him to pull out of this. How weird is it to meet a girl at a party and ask her out only find out that she has to pencil you in three weeks down the road like a dentist appointment?

"That sounds great," he says.

And while I'm still trying to get over the shock of that, he pulls out his phone and hands it to me. "Can I get your number?"

Arabella

I don't stay at the party much longer. Chuck and I talk a little bit more. He tells me about vet school and then he asks me more about my job, and I keep it pretty surface level. It's not something I want to get into. It's hard to explain why I want to be a Formula 1 photographer to a complete stranger without giving away more than I want to.

Nevertheless, we're going on a date in three weeks. I end up taking an Uber home by myself. Lana stays at the party because by the time I'm ready to go home, she's just getting her night started. She doesn't seem to mind when I tell her I'm leaving. It's not really that she wants my company, it's that she doesn't want me to be alone at home.

I go up to my apartment, lock the door behind me, and lean against it. It's been a long day, all things considered.

But I go straight for my computer, wiggling my finger on the track pad so the screen turns on. And there he is, Mateo, staring back at me from the screen.

CircuitPhantom52: Everybody say thank you admin.

PaddockNoah33: These edits are fire. More Mateo content please.

MickAerolyn: What is Jayce even doing? Someone send him home.

Ferr4ri_FL500: MATEO, GO BACK TO FERRARI. YOU'RE TANKING YOUR CAREER.

Chapter Twelve
Round 2 - Jeddah, Saudi Arabia

Driver Standings:
Mateo Silva - 25 points
Lola Castle - 18 points
Archer Hayes - 15 points

Arabella

The whole crowd gasps as Mateo goes into the wall, and I feel my heart sink. It's beating faster and faster, even as it falls straight into my stomach. On all of the televisions in the garage, I see his helmet move from one side to the other, even as race control is trying to speak to him.

"Mateo, are you okay?" Jerry's voice calls over the radio. Everyone can hear it.

There's no answer from Mateo, but we can see him moving around in there. The car isn't even that damaged.

"Are you okay?" Jerry asks again.

"I'm okay." Mateo's voice comes through, and I take a deep breath. I know how safe those cars are. I know that the chances that anything truly horrendous is going to happen are very slim. But I still absolutely hate watching any of the drivers crash, especially Mateo. Lola's crash last season, Mateo pulling her out of a car while half of her suit was on fire, is still fresh in my mind.

As soon as Mateo's out of the car, I start dismantling my camera, sticking it back into my bag. I'm not going to take photos of this. I'm not going to post things on social media about his DNF. I always post a final result on social media, and I can do that, especially since Jayce is still out on the track, but I'm not taking any pictures of Mateo.

The team goes to retrieve his car, and he gets into a golf cart and is driven back. As he walks down the pit lane toward the garage, the cameras are on him. Taking off his helmet, then his gloves, and then his suit, unzipping it, pulling it off of his shoulders. He's still being broadcast on the networks because everyone knows he could be in the title fight and that a DNF not only hurts his chances but could be an indicator that the season won't be going smoothly for him.

The camera pushes in on his face, twisted and upset. It wasn't even his fault. These things just happen sometimes. He wasn't the first to lose it at Turn 10.

I'm pressed against a wall when Mateo walks into the garage. The cameras have finally left him alone. He walks through with his head low. I know there will have to be strategy meetings and engineering meetings. I know there will be debriefs, discussions about what went wrong and how the team can fix it.

I feel like a ghost, everyone moving around me. The crew will have the biggest job, fixing up the car in time for the next race. I watch Mateo move through. I can see everything happening behind his eyes. I know he's upset. The moments after the race for any driver are always the most emotional. It's when the drivers are the most angry or excited or disappointed. It's like a sunburn, happening so quickly and then fading by the time the press is over at the end of the day. Tomorrow, anything they say in post-race interviews will be apologized for, all the anger will have burned off, and they'll all just be normal people again, ready for the next race.

So I know Mateo is upset now, upset about all the potential points he just lost, everything he just handed to Lola on a silver platter, but I also know by this time tomorrow, he'll be okay. He'll have his eyes on the next race.

Technically, I'm supposed to interview both of the guys after the races. It makes for really good social media content. People want to hear from the drivers themselves about how it felt to execute a strategy from behind the wheel. It's proven to be one of my favorite parts of the job, following Mateo through the paddock, watching him get that crinkle in his forehead that means he's really considering every single one of his words before he says them.

But today, I'll let him be. I don't want to force him to talk about what just happened. He should have his moment to get all the bad energy out.

I walk around to Jayce's garage. He'll be the star of the show this week. I know it's only been a few weeks, but I never get requests in the comment sections for more Jayce content. I think his fans are always happy to see him, but the expectation that he'll be the focus of the social media account just isn't there. Mateo is clearly the number one driver. And Jayce is just the young guy who gets to work with one of the most famous drivers of all time.

Arabella

Jayce comes in eighth place, which, all things considered, isn't bad. It could be better, but no one expects Jayce to be making any moves above fifth place. No one expects Jayce to win a race, really. He's a good driver, but he's not that good.

Everyone in the garage pats him on the back as he moves through. I take photos, trying to be as precise as I am with Mateo's. But to be quite honest, it's kind of difficult. I don't know what it is about Jayce, but he's just not nearly as photogenic as Mateo. His hair always sticks up in this weird way, and he's uncomfortably tall in that way that makes him slouch all the time, like he's not really sure what to do with his limbs.

I adjust some settings, get some good shots. He has a great jawline.

And then, all the action is over.

In the motorhome, I take my time. I pack my things slowly. I scroll through photos. I make some notes on a pad of paper about some content ideas.

By the time I'm done, the motorhome's empty. Everyone's already gone back to the hotel or gotten on their flights home. I'm still here, lingering. My flight to Monaco isn't until tomorrow morning.

When the lights start turning off, I head back out into the paddock. I know I should leave. I know if anybody from the team saw me lingering, they'd tell me to go. But I can't. I just want to make sure that Mateo's okay. I just want to see his face. I just want to make sure that he's good.

So I linger.

I pretend to have things to do. Things to take pictures of. Watching people start to tear down. Watching last minute fans walk back out to their taxis or to the train.

And then, finally, the team emerges from the meeting room. They're all exhausted. They all look unsatisfied, like even though they just sat in a two-hour meeting, they're still contemplating the outcome.

I know that tonight, Mateo will go back to his hotel room and he'll go over the race again and again. He'll obsess. He'll beat himself up. That's what he does. So I wait for him to emerge. Because I have an idea.

Chapter Thirteen

Mateo

After a bad race, when I just don't end up where I thought I would—like in a wall instead of across the finish line—my brain is like a blizzard. And when I'm trying to focus on one thing, it's like trying to catch a single piece of snow in the middle of it all.

The sun has already gone down by the time we come out of the garage, the team and I. There was a lot of discussion. Most of it about me, my strategy, my car. But some of it about Jayce's, too. The fact that I got taken out, sixteen laps in, means that Jayce should have finished higher. One less car to compete with. But he didn't. At least I wasn't the only disappointment in the room.

I try to focus, clear my mind, wake myself up, even though I'm just going to go right back to my hotel and pretend to go to sleep. I have an early flight in the morning with a couple of the other drivers. I know I can just sleep on the plane.

"Hey," a voice says as I'm walking out of the garage, my arm around Jayce. If possible, he's taking the race even harder than I am. It wasn't that he didn't race well today; everyone else on the track just raced better.

I'm surprised when I turn and find Arabella. The paddock is mostly empty, just her left on the empty street. I always like the paddock at night after a race. It's like being in an amusement park after it's closed.

"Hey," I say to her, pulling my arm off of Jayce. "Why are you still here?"

She shrugs. "I just wanted to check on you."

She just wanted to check on me. She's still here because she was worried about me.

Jayce goes past her, bumping her with a friendly elbow before turning to look at me. There's something about the smile he sends me. I can't decipher it. But it's gone in an instant as he keeps going.

"I'm fine," I tell her, the truth for the most part. "It's not as if it's the first time that I've put my car into a wall."

She shrugs. "Sure, but it's the only time I've ever seen you put your car into a wall that early in a race."

I look over at her, curious. "What are you, my strategist now? Do you have all my stats in a system somewhere?" I'm in a bad mood, but she doesn't take offense. She must be used to dealing with drivers when they've lost races, dealing with her father through his career.

"I probably do know more about your stats than some of your strategists do," she says, her voice quiet, like she didn't mean for me to hear.

I'm surprised how much I like the idea of Arabella watching all the races, cheering me on from her living room at home. I guess because I never considered that she might have kept watching them after Pedro retired. Having this information now, knowing that she's chosen to keep watching, that counts for something.

"If you know about my stats," I tell her, "then you know how often my good seasons turn to bad seasons."

Her smile falls when I say that. Because she has to know; everybody knows. It's happened so many times—starting out a season strong and then slowly being overtaken—that they've started calling it the second-half curse. I can already see the edge of the roller coaster, the slow downward angle of the rest of the season.

"For someone who's so competitive and has won three championships, you certainly are quite the pessimist."

I slide my gaze sideways to see her as we go through the gate out of the paddock. "A pessimist? What kind of pessimist would stay with a sport for twenty years when they haven't won in almost fifteen?"

I shrug. She shrugs.

"A person who just wants to keep doing something they really love."

Of course she would think that. That's what she wants for me, I can tell. To be in a sport I love. It's kind of her to care so much. But even if I am a pessimist, I'm not a masochist. I wouldn't stay in the sport if I thought there was no chance that I would ever win a championship again. There's too much money, too much strain on my body, too much sacrifice.

"What did your team say in your meeting?" she asks.

We stand on the street corner under the deep blue sky that's as wide and dark as the ocean.

"The same thing they always say," I tell her. "Keep pushing; improvements are coming; this is our season."

She smiles. "I like it. And here I thought I was going to have to cheer you up."

I cross my arms. "And what exactly were you going to do to try and cheer me up?" I don't like the way it comes out of my mouth. It sounds... suggestive.

But she doesn't seem to hear it because she smiles and starts to walk backwards. "Well, there are a lot of really fancy hotels around with a lot of really fancy pools."

I raise an eyebrow at her. "A pool? That was your grand plan?" I know my voice successfully comes out playful because when she looks at me, the light from the street lamps sparks in her eyes.

"You said in an interview once that you thought swimming was the most relaxing thing in the world. I know it's no ice bath but…"

I'm struck by her comment. "Did I, now?"

She nods, still walking, unaware of how she's taken me off guard. "Yeah. In one of those mini-interviews that Albatross does for the website. Like, maybe two years ago?"

Two years ago. Two years ago, she read a mini-interview I did for the website, one of those things I didn't know anyone read. The media team is always asking me questions and then parceling out the answers during off times during the season. I guess that's her job now.

"You know, they never ask Jayce to do those things," she says over her shoulder. "Maybe because he's blander than a box of Saltines." I laugh, not even paying attention to where we're going until Arabella says, "This one over here?" I realize she's talking about the hotel on the corner. I glance behind us at the hotel where I'm staying. I don't know why I expected her to know which one was mine.

"No, it's that one," I say, skittering to a stop.

But she doesn't even pause. "No, that one is the one with the rooftop pool."

"What?" I ask, and when I realize she's going to take off without me, I rush to catch up to her. "Ari, there's a pool at my hotel. Probably one at yours, too."

"I don't care," she says, grinning over at me. "It's more fun to go to someone else's hotel."

"We can't just swim in some random hotel's pool," I say on a laugh.

We sidle up to the hotel and the valet standing outside doesn't hesitate to open the door for us, either because he recognizes us or because we look too confident to be questioned.

"You're Mateo Silva," Arabella whispers to me in the grand lobby, all bright lights and gold accents. "I'm pretty sure that, legally, you can do whatever you want."

At this point, I don't care if we get kicked out. And maybe I don't care that I didn't finish the race today and that I fucked up the car. Maybe I just care that Arabella looks like she's having the time of her life as we slip down an empty hallway toward the elevators.

The doors open and we slip inside with a trio of teenage girls, clearly tourists, their hair wet with the smell of chlorine and towels wrapped around themselves. I expect them to get off the elevator. They rode all the way to the lobby, after all. But one of the girls reaches forward to hit the button for the sixth floor, and Arabella does the same, her finger landing on the button for the roof.

But the button doesn't light up.

"Oh, you need a key card for the roof," one of the girls says, her eyes darting to us and away again.

"Oh," Arabella says, pretending to check the pockets of her kit and come up empty. "I think I forgot mine. Do you think one of you could...?" She gestures at the key card held firmly in the hand of one of the girls.

She looks back at Arabella skeptically, and then her eyes slide over to me. "Um. Aren't you that race car driver?"

My smile comes easily, pulling wide across my face in the way it does when I have cameras pointed at me, a perfected disguise. It's muscle memory after all these years. "Yes, I am."

"My dad is obsessed with you," the girl says, scratching at

her freckle-covered cheek with chipped purple nails. "I'll key you up to the pool if you give us an autograph."

I snort. "A bit young for bribes, aren't you?"

She raises her strawberry blond eyebrows at me. "A bit old to be sneaking into hotels that aren't yours, aren't you?"

Mateo

And that's how we end up at a pool in a hotel that isn't either of ours.

I look over to where Arabella's standing at the edge of the pool, her toes hanging over. She took off her polo, the one with the Albatross logo on it, and settled it over a chair a few minutes ago. She has a black tank top on underneath, and she takes out her ponytail so that her curly hair cascades around her shoulders.

And now she's just standing there, looking down into the water, her skin blue and the ripples showing in streaks of light across her face.

"As a kid," she says, "when I had a really bad day, my dad would always take me swimming."

"Why the pool?" I ask her.

She smiles over at me. That perfect smile that Pedro spent a lot of money on. "I used to check to make sure I didn't have superpowers."

I stand beside her, my hands in my pockets, and just laugh. "What?"

She must know how absurd she sounds because she shrugs, biting her lip. "I always thought that if I had a super-power, it would be the ability to breathe underwater. I used to watch a lot of superhero movies back then. Anyway, I would check periodically to make sure I hadn't developed the ability to live in the ocean. You know, go down to the very bottom with the really scary fish."

My cheeks are beginning to hurt from smiling. "The scary fish?"

She gawks at me, her mouth open comically. "There's stuff down there that we don't even know about, Mateo. And I would go down there in a heartbeat. So yeah, he took me swimming. It sort of reminds me that in the grand scheme of things, there's a whole planet out there. And my bad day, it was just one bad day in the whole, huge universe. Just one person living on the planet." She tilts her head to the side. "Although, you are kind of one of the more important people on the planet, compared to me."

"Don't say that," I tell her, feeling some of my amusement wear off. "You are a very important person."

All of her excitement seems to leach out of her then. "I'm not so sure," she says. "I'm not so sure that I *want* to be some important person." Her eyes glaze over, not focusing on anything anymore. "It's a lot of pressure, being important. Having everyone know your name. I don't think it's for me."

I don't know how to respond to that. I knew when I made my choices when I was young, when I begged my parents to let me follow this path, that I wanted to be the kind of person everyone knew, that everyone recognized. There are a lot of days where I don't like it. There are a lot of days where I wish I could just get everyone to forget who I am. During the race, sure, I want the attention. But when I'm just living my life, not so much. It's like I'm always looking for a way to hide.

"Are you sure that joining Formula 1 was the right move then?" I ask her.

Her eyes find mine again, focused. There's something there, some secret thing I can see going across her mind that I know she's not going to share with me.

"Yes," she finally says. "I know I made the right decision."

She smiles big, reaches down, wraps her hand around my wrist, and jumps into the pool, pulling me in behind her.

I should have seen it coming.

My clothes are wet and heavy when I resurface, pushing my hair out of my eyes. I should have gotten it cut. I usually do for the start of the season, but I didn't this time.

I take my wet shirt off, tossing it over the side onto the edge of the pool as Arabella comes up beside me, using one hand to sluice the water off of her face. Then she smiles at me, laughs a little. Her eyes go to my wet t-shirt in a lump on the edge of the pool and then back to me.

I reach out and push a chunk of wet hair off of her face, use the tips of my fingers to brush it back out of the way so that I can see her eyes. She swims back a little bit and then forward, like she's restless, like she has to be moving.

But I just stay where I am, my feet firmly on the bottom of the pool. It's not a terribly deep one. I sink down to warm my skin in the water and watch her swim, hair like a jellyfish around her.

She's so pretty. I've known Arabella for so long and when you spend that much time with someone, you start to look around them instead of right at them.

But I'm looking at her right now, bobbing in the water, the wetness shimmering across her tan skin, her dark brown eyes looking almost black in the low light of the moon. She is undeniably beautiful.

When she sees that I'm not swimming, more just enjoying the calm of the water, she comes over and presses her back to the wall beside me. She turns to face me but doesn't say anything. I know she's giving me an opportunity to start a conversation, and also giving me the opportunity to stay quiet.

"Lola will win the championship," I say. It's not something that bugs me on a fundamental level. It's just fact. The only reason she didn't win last year was because of the accident. She had to sit out the rest of the season to heal.

"What makes you so sure?" she asks, even though I know she knows. She's too smart not to.

"She was way too good last season. And since they fired the principal and sacked their engineer, they've leveled up in a big way. They're unbeatable."

"Unbeatable!" she says, moving closer, until her shoulder's pressed against mine, slick and cold. "She's not unbeatable. You just beat her in Bahrain." She rolls her eyes. "I know what you mean. Lola's incredible, but she's not superhuman." Her eyes flicker back and forth between mine. She turns her body to face me. She's so close that when she speaks, I can smell the chlorine on her skin. "Why are you putting yourself on the bottom shelf? Like you're not a legend? An icon of the sport. You're going to be in history books, Mateo. You have your portrait on every circuit in the world. Don't sell yourself short."

I tip my head toward her. "I don't need a pep talk from you. I've had pep talks from millions of people."

She laughs, not fazed even a bit by my grumpiness.

"I know there are better drivers. I'm not having my feelings hurt by seeing the next wave come in and sweep me off my feet. They're good. They deserve to win. Lola deserves to win. I don't feel bad about it. Neither should you."

She swims a little closer, and I'm surprised when my pulse picks up.

Should I back away from her? She's not processing that she's this close to me. If I moved either of my arms, I would brush against her body.

"Maybe my pep talk isn't for you," she says. "Maybe it's for me. Because there's no way you could convince me you aren't going to win." Her mouth stretches wide into a smile. "I always think you're going to win, every single season."

That makes me laugh. "You must be really used to disappointment."

She shakes her head and smiles. "I'm never disappointed. All I ever want is to see you do your best."

When I don't say anything, her eyes roam over my face. Maybe she's had the same thought that I have, that she hasn't really been looking directly at me for such a long time. Everything's different now. She's been an observer for so long and now she's part of it. She's seeing the whole world differently.

"I have an early flight," I tell her. I'm done talking about this day and this race. It's behind us now. It's time to move forward.

"Okay," she says. I can hear the way she's trying to hide her disappointment.

I start to swim away from her and stop. "But wait. One more thing."

She circles her arms out like propellers, waiting to hear what I have to say.

I swim back to her, until I can feel the movement of her legs beneath the water. "We have to test our superpowers."

A smile stretches across her face, her eyes lighting up. I hold out a hand beneath the water, and she takes it. Together, we drop below the surface. Her hair fans out around her, and I'm mesmerized by the color of her skin as the pool lights shine on her. She looks like a ghost in a dream. Or maybe an angel.

I don't actually know how to test whether or not you can breathe underwater without drowning for real, so I just let the air out of my mouth in an exaggerated huff, watching the bubbles rise up between us. Her mouth opens on a laugh, her bubbles twice the size of mine, and we spring back up to the surface.

She laughs as she pushes her wet hair out of her face.

"I don't think I did it right," I say, laughing as well.

She grabs onto my arms, trying to stay upright as she belly

laughs up at the sky. But the laughter has died in my chest at the heat of her hands on me, the slide of her wet skin.

I jerk back away from her, and she lets out a startled sound, covering her mouth with her hand.

"Sorry," I say, not even sure why I'm apologizing. I turn toward the wall and lift myself out of the pool. When I reach down to get my shirt, she looks away from me quickly, ducking into the water one last time.

LewaDrivxoxo: The guy finally gets a good car and he can't keep it on the track

StellarHawk_5: Someone explain to me why they're still giving Silva a seat?

CyberPanther: Replace Mateo

HeliosDrive66: Why is Mateo personality proof?

AliaIsAName: Second-half curse rearing its ugly head

Chapter Fourteen
Round 3 - Monte Carlo, Monaco

Lola Castle - 43 points
Archer Hayes - 33 points
Mateo Silva - 25 points

Mateo

"So what are you saying?" I ask, leaning over Felix's desk. I wish we weren't doing this today, not when we're supposed to be doing sponsor events. But that's the thing about working in an industry where everyone is scattered across the globe. If I want to speak face-to-face with the man who has my career dangling over an alligator pit, I have to do it here or do it on the phone. I'd rather do it here.

"I'm saying that a championship doesn't have to come this year, but we both know it's a big part of why the team offered you another contract. If we can't make it happen, I don't know that there's a future here."

"Yeah," I say, keeping my cool, the way I'm good at. Because it's not as if this comes as a surprise. I'm not stupid enough to think they're just going to let me drive forever.

"I'm still bringing you points," I tell Felix.

"Are you?" He pauses for a beat. He doesn't have to mention Jeddah, even though I know he wants to. "Look, I know we're only three rounds in. I'm just saying that the team is starting to look at this season and worry that it's mirroring our last few seasons: a strong start with a slow downhill progression. We need someone who's going up."

"I'm sitting third in the championship right now," I tell him. "You're going to tell me that's not going to get me a seat next year?"

"I'm saying not to take your foot off the gas. Celebrate your wins, but don't forget that one podium does not a championship make."

"You're going to replace a driver who's still fighting, who's still hungry?" I say.

"This is not personal," he responds, leaning back in his chair and running his hands through his dark hair the way he always does when there's something he doesn't want to say. "You, of all people, know that. We respect you. We want to work with you. But we have to keep our options open. We don't have a choice. We're a top team. You have to know that the younger guys would bring more money. Bodies that are more equipped for what you're doing."

"There is no one with a body more equipped than mine. All I have done my entire life is make myself a perfect vessel for this sport."

"You're forty-two," he finally says. It seems to burst out of him like he's been holding it in this whole time.

"Yes, I'm aware," I say.

He sighs so loud that I know he's done it just so I can hear it. "I just need you to be reasonable, mate. You have been in this sport longer than anyone. You know what it's like. You know what's at stake, and your name is not going to be enough forever. You haven't won a championship in over a decade, and at some point, you might have to swallow the fact that you're not going to win another one."

As if I don't know that. Everybody knows. I've had a bad stretch of years and this is our last push. If I don't win a championship this season, I'm done.

I think most people are expecting me to retire but I'm far too stubborn for all that. This is where I want to be, and if that means I have to go to a worse team and drive a worse car, is that something I can stomach? Is that a decision I want to make for myself?

"Look," Felix says, his voice soft, understanding. "No one respects you more than I do, Mateo. Nobody wants you here more than I do. I've got a lot of pressure on me from above and it will take a lot of money to keep you. You're expensive because you're a champion. Three times. Look, let's just table these discussions until the summer, okay? Focus on winning."

I nod, but I don't say anything. I just get up and turn for the door, shutting it behind me with more force than I intend to.

I understand how this sport works, and until now, I've been able to fight my way into my seat, to hang on to it when the younger guys were clawing at me. Because of my name, because of my reputation, because of my history with the team, and my championships.

I always knew that at some point they'd give up on me and I guess a part of me thought that it would be easier for them to give up on me than for me to give up on myself. If they want me gone, they're going to have to force me out.

I head down the hallway, stand at the top of the stairs, looking down into the lobby of the motorhome. It's quiet back here, if not dripping with tension. Once I step back out, it will be into the current, the waves of people and activity, things to do.

I press my back to the wall, put my hands in my

pockets. At the end of the long staircase, the building is full of people. I watch them all through the archway.

Hospitality workers, sponsors, mechanics, so many people that it would be impossible for me to learn all their names, all their jobs. Then I spot a familiar face. She's standing right in the middle of the lobby, everyone moving around her like a rock in a waterfall.

She's doing something on her phone, brow furrowed. Arabella. Her eyes flicker up and find mine.

I always think you're going to win, every single season.

She smiles, not some polite thing, not some fabricated thing. She smiles big, all teeth and freckles and sunshine.

I start to walk down the stairs. She meets me halfway, and by the time we're standing in the doorway, her smile is gone.

"Is something wrong?" she asks.

I thought I was hiding it. Thought I was doing well enough. But Arabella has a knack for seeing right through me. She doesn't buy anything that I put on.

"Yeah," I tell her, even though I know she'll know I'm lying.

I can't pile any more on her. She's already believing in me more than she should. She's already supporting so much of my weight every week.

"Everything's good," I tell her.

She watches me carefully and then reaches up to push away a curl that's fallen in front of her eyes so that I can see both of them. Dark, rich brown.

"Are you sure?" she asks, her voice quiet.

She knows I'm lying. But she also knows there are ears everywhere.

I shake my head. That stray curl falls back into her eye and I reach out to push it behind her ear, shove my hand back into my pocket. "I'm okay, I promise. Just busy. Lots to do."

"Mateo." There's something in her eyes. They're wide, but

full of concern. Her brows furrow in, a line drawn right between them.

"Don't worry about me, Ari," I say. I leave her there, floating in the middle of the ocean.

Chapter Fifteen

Arabella

I can't keep the smile off my face. It's been a long time since Mateo won at Monaco. Six years, to be exact. He's grinning so hard right now, talking with Jayce as I set up the shot for the team's celebration photo, that it looks like he's going to crack right in half.

I don't know what conversation he and Felix had earlier, but whatever it was, it seems to have made a positive impact. As they pose for their photo, Felix wraps one beefy arm around Mateo's shoulders, like a proud father.

I wave my arms. "Okay, everybody ready?"

Mateo turns to me, his eyes glittering in the sun. He holds onto the sign that's positioned between him and Jayce where they crouch in front of the whole team that says **Silva P1 Baros P9**. He's got his winner's trophy on the ground in front of him. He holds onto it with one hand like someone might try and snatch it away.

I take a few photos, twisting the camera just a little bit in between each one to get a different angle. And just before

I've clicked the last one, someone runs into the photo. Arturo, a bottle of champagne in his hand aimed right at Mateo.

The guys jump up out of their squats, shielding themselves as Arturo sprays champagne over the whole group. It covers Mateo's hat, his team kit. He tries to grab it out of Arturo's hand, laughing all the while. There's a bit of a struggle, then Arturo lets it go and Mateo turns it on him, splashing him with fizz.

I'm watching the whole thing with a smile, full of life and happiness.

And then Mateo rushes toward me.

"Not the camera," I shout, running in the other direction. Mateo soaks me in champagne, sticky and sweet when it splatters into my mouth.

Luckily, my camera is safe.

I'm rubbing champagne out of my eyes when Mateo comes over and fist bumps me, like we're old pals.

"Are you coming out tonight to celebrate?"

I shake my head. "No way. I'm not going to party with you animals." I know he's just asking to be kind. Crew members don't go out with the drivers after the races.

"Come on," he says, grabbing hold of my shoulder and giving me a friendly shake. He looks good all covered in champagne, and for a minute, I imagine what it would be like to lick it off his skin, the taste of him mixing with the sweetness of the bubbles. I sigh. I've got to stop thinking these things when he's right in front of me.

"We're going to a yacht party," he says. "I think Jayce said it was his cousin's yacht or something." He sounds like he's been drinking, the adrenaline and happiness clearly loosening him up. "Drinks. Cigars. Come on. It's been a long time since I've won Monaco. It's *Monaco*."

"I know," I say, biting back a smile. He's not giving up. His eyes stay steady on me. And that's when I start to realize he's serious.

"Why not?" he says. "A lot of the team is going to be there, some of the drivers too, probably. I want you there with me. You deserve to celebrate, too."

I'm starting to feel uneasy. I don't think I could stomach going to a party with Mateo, only for him to disappear with more interesting people. I'd rather sit in my hotel room alone. "I'm a photographer," I say, reaching for my camera like I need physical proof. "It's not like I helped you win a victory."

"You help me win the hearts of the fans," he says, his voice cheesy, and I roll my eyes.

"It's not my victory, Mateo."

He steps up to me and I'm surprised when his smile drops, his voice quiet and serious. "It's your victory because you're my friend. Celebrate my victory with me, please."

My stomach does a big *swoop*. He's being sincere. He actually wants me there. I don't know what to do with that information.

"Okay," I finally say. I can't fight him.

He asked me to go, so I'll go.

🏁

Arabella

I've been to more Formula 1 races than most people have ever seen in their lifetime. More than I could count. More than I could calculate. But because the majority of those races happened when I was underage, I've never been to any of the post-race parties.

I remember when I was younger, going back to the hotel with my mom while my dad went to parties. I don't think my mom minded very much. It was sort of like girl time. We'd go to the hotel and order room service and watch rom-coms. It never really bothered me, and I never really questioned it. My dad was off doing adult things, professional things. Formula 1 driver things. He always got to do things that we didn't. Going to meetings, driving in tons of different race cars, hanging out with people that we would never get to meet.

If I was any other person, I wouldn't think so much about what F1 drivers did after races. It wouldn't really matter. They go home. They have big meals. They watch TV. They sleep. Whatever.

But I'm not a normal person.

I'm a person who's been obsessed with one specific Formula 1 driver since I was old enough to understand I didn't want a guy my age. So instead, I would look for any kind of evidence I could find of what Mateo was doing before and after races. Social media, my dad's phone calls, footage online. I was always looking for something. I never really found a lot of evidence that Mateo was a big post-race partier. There were occasionally photos of him at a club or a bar or a fancy restaurant celebrating.

So tonight, I'm desperate to see a piece of Mateo I've been trying to see for years, like finally getting a glimpse of the wizard. And I want it so badly that my hands are trembling.

I look at myself in the mirror. I'm worried that it's going to be obvious that I tried too hard, that I spent time putting product in my hair and carefully working with it so it curled correctly, that I put on makeup, that I bought perfume from the gift store downstairs.

I don't look like myself and I can't figure out if that's a good thing or a bad thing. Would not looking like myself make it easier for Mateo to see me as an adult, as someone that he could like as more than a friend? Or would not looking like myself make it harder, like I was a stranger and he just wanted a familiar face?

I have no idea. Either way, it's too late to undo it now.

I opted not to wear a dress even though I considered it. I don't want it to be too obvious that I'm trying to get his attention. Mateo's undivided attention is like gold. It's like a winning lottery ticket when he looks at me and only me. When he's not distracted by a race, when he's just there with me.

What if I could actually do something about all of these feelings building up in me? Is it insane to think that maybe I could tell him about them? Maybe not the whole truth, but just a tiny piece of it? The way he makes me feel. The things I think about doing with him. How, in my mind, he's somehow already mine.

What if I tell him any of those things and he tells the team to get rid of me because I crossed a line that we can't come back from? The thought makes me sick to my stomach.

I get an alert on my phone. It's my Uber, waiting downstairs to take me to the yacht that Mateo sent me the location of almost thirty minutes ago.

I fix my top, a silky spaghetti-strapped thing, cream colored, and the long pants that went with it. I think I look nice, but do I look nice enough for someone like Mateo? Someone who dates supermodels and athletes?

I grab my purse and rush downstairs. The yacht isn't far, down by the pier, close to the track. When I get there, the guy at the end of the dock glances at me, scans me from the top of my head down to the points of my shoes, and says, "I think you're in the wrong place. No kids allowed."

My hands clench into fists. "I'm twenty-five," I tell him, trying to keep my voice friendly so that he doesn't toss me out on my ass just for getting an attitude.

"Nah. No way, sweetheart. This is a private party."

If this were any other party on any other night in any other city in the world, I would turn and leave. Go back to my hotel room and watch reruns of *Great British Bake-Off* and order room service.

But Mateo is on this boat. He invited me here. And I can't bring myself to walk away without trying.

But I know that trying means I have to give him my name. My name is currency, especially in Monaco, and especially at a party full of F1 drivers. "Look, I'm—"

A hand finds my hip and I turn to look who's touching me just as a voice speaks into my opposite ear. "She's with me."

I spin around the other way and find myself eye-to-eye with Jayce. And if we're eye-to-eye, that means that he's bent quite a bit. He smiles at the man, who quickly waves us up the ramp to the boat. I want to move away from the hand that's still holding on to my waist as we go, but I don't. I don't really have an issue with Jayce. I don't even have an issue with him thinking it's okay to touch me. It's a hard thing to say no to attention from anyone, especially an objectively cute boy.

Especially when another cute boy whose attention you want much more doesn't see you as anything more than a friend.

So when a six-foot-three, brown-eyed dreamboat starts paying attention to you, you go with it because what else is there to do?

Inside, it's loud. I scan faces, but I don't see anybody I know before Jayce leads me over to the bar, a gaudy square number in the middle of the room, surrounded by windows showing off the water.

"What do you want?" Jayce asks, signaling for the bartender.

"Surprise me."

I don't miss the way his eyes scan my face and land on my mouth before ordering our drinks. I'm fairly certain he doesn't have any actual interest in me. He mostly ignores me on the track, but when you're together every week and you're spending all your time together, you just kind of hang out with whoever's around, flirt with whoever's around, an occupational hazard of working away from a normal life that you can just go home to at the end of the day.

"I didn't think I'd see you out tonight," Jayce says, leaning against the bar.

"I wasn't sure I was going to come out. I didn't think I was allowed." I don't mention that he wasn't the one to invite me. If he wanted me here, he would have, right?

Jayce makes a face, a scrunching with his mouth, as if it's a given that I would be allowed to be here. Which, of course, is preposterous. I don't believe for one second that he thinks I belong here.

He puts my drink in front of me and takes his own. "We've got a spot in the corner," he says, lifting his chin towards a dark section of the room, up against a window. "The team is over there. I just stepped out to make a call."

I nod and turn in that direction. And when Jayce reaches down to take my hand, I don't stop him. Because there are a lot of people here, and it's very dark, and I don't want to be separated from him. He's the only thing that's keeping me tethered to reality.

Chapter Sixteen

Mateo

There's something comforting about noise, about crowds. The way it can make all the noise in your brain go quiet by replacing it with something louder.

The music, the voices, the pop of champagne corks. It seems to shut the rest of it down. It seems to whisper in my ear, *this is not the time to worry. This is not the time for thinking about race strategy or engineering or contracts.*

Sometimes it feels like race weekends are on fast forward. They're going too fast. Two times normal speed. And then when the weekend is over and I go back home for a little while, it's like everything is going in slow motion.

Speed up, slow down.

200 kilometers an hour. A slow meander through the rest of it.

And right here on this yacht, it feels like a combination of both things. It's fast. It's loud. And maybe it's a little bit two times normal speed. But sitting in the middle of it feels like a quiet walk on a winter day.

"Mateo," someone calls and I look over.

It's a miracle I heard him. Jayce is kind of a soft-spoken guy. Doesn't always seem to have much to say.

He waves at me now. He's wearing a pair of khakis. They're cargo shorts. And he looks like a university student, his hair sticking up in a way that people seem to think is fashionable and attractive. I think it's lazy.

I nod at him, and it takes me a second to process the context of him. He's got his arm tucked behind him in a way that tells me he's holding on to someone. And like it's happening in the slow part of the universe, the rest of his arm appears, fingers wrapped around someone else's.

And then another arm appears, lighter than Jayce's olive-toned skin. Elbow, shoulder, face. It's Arabella. But for a second, she doesn't look like Arabella. Her hair is wild. She's wearing a cream-colored number I feel like I would have seen in some kind of perfume ad, makeup, and some kind of shimmer on her skin that makes her look like she's already begun to sweat, but in a pleasant way.

"Look who I found," Jayce says.

I watch as she tries to extract her hand from Jayce's, but he doesn't seem to want to let the grip go. I resist the urge to reach up and separate their hands myself only because she manages to wiggle free right at that moment.

Without hesitating, I'm halfway out of my seat, extending a hand toward her. Arabella's palm slides against mine. Everything is in fast forward again.

"You made it," I shout over the noise.

"I did," she shouts back, standing in front of me, gripping my hand like it'll keep her from drifting away. She glances at the room around us, full of bodies. I'm not sure the yacht won't just sink into the Ligurian Sea. "But now I'm not so sure about this."

"Come sit," I tell her, scooting over on the couch to make

room for her. There's a second—slow motion again—where everybody processes what's going on.

Jayce's eyes fall to the couch first, and I watch him realize that I did not make enough space for him as well. I see Arabella's eyes drop to the space next, her face careful as she sees that she'll have to squish in close to me.

And then I try to process it myself and can't.

Everything's happening in a language I don't understand. It feels like nothing more than instinct to let her come and be close to me, to send Jayce away from her, only to find myself behaving just as badly.

But before I can figure out how to somehow backtrack, change my mind, make it so she doesn't have to make some kind of uncomfortable decision, she's moving toward the couch and Jayce is wandering off. I watch, amused, as she turns on the flashlight on her phone and scans it over the couch.

"The pants are white," she says when she sits beside me, as if I couldn't tell. She *is* wearing white pants, but she's also holding a drink that's very fuchsia-colored.

"Here," I tell her, taking the drink and setting it on the table in front of us. It's low and oblong and kind of looks like a glob of mucus with no actual pattern to it.

"Thanks," she says. "It's disgusting. Way too sweet. But I told Jayce to surprise me so…"

I smile. "Did he order one for himself?"

She laughs. "No. But maybe he wanted to. Should I offer it to him?" She settles back into the couch and it really hits me how very little space there is for us. She's pressed all along my side, from shoulder to hip.

She starts to move away, but when she does, she bumps the man on her other side, and he looks at her over his shoulder, not a nasty look, but not a kind one either.

I raise my arm and drape it along the back of the couch,

turn my body in so that she can move in closer. Now we're facing each other with less than a foot of space between us.

"Are you enjoying yourself?" I ask her. I'm not good at starting conversations. I can finish them. I can carry them. But the articles, the reporters, they've called me words like abrupt, stern, distanced. And I get it. I just don't know how to fix it.

Talking to Arabella has never been difficult before, but in the midst of all this, she feels like someone else. It doesn't quite feel like she's the Arabella I know.

"I guess," she finally says, her eyes taking in everything, like she can't settle on one thing. "It's kind of hard to think straight in here."

"Do you want to go out to the deck?" I ask her. It's a warm spring. There might be a little bit of a cold breeze, but I was out on the deck earlier drinking and it was pretty nice, all things considered.

"Sure," she says.

I stand and turn for the door that will take us out to the deck. There are two levels to this boat and we're on the upper level. Down on the first level, there's another bar, another DJ, people partying half-naked. I start to gently push through the crowd when I feel Arabella grab onto my hand.

I turn to look at her over my shoulder. Her eyes meet mine. And there she is again, the Arabella I know, and we're just at a party together in Monaco. I grip her hand, knowing that she's doing what she can not to be separated from me.

We step out onto the deck and the wind off of the water immediately hits both of us. It's cold, even though the air is warm. There are others out against the railing, drinking and talking quietly away from the music. I can just hear the thumping of the bass down at the front of the boat.

Arabella immediately moves to the edge, putting her elbows on the railing, dangling her small, delicate hands over the side. She takes in everything. The stretch of black water in front of us. There are so many yachts, some of them out on the water and some of them still at the dock like we are. I don't suspect we'll be going out onto the water anytime soon.

"I've never been on a yacht before," she says, turning her face just slightly toward me. I've never seen her in this kind of light. It's dark, but the moon is full. And there are lights, strings of them along the boat so that her skin is lit. She looks like something out of a fantasy movie. She sets her chin on her fist and looks over.

"You've been to Monaco before though," I say, finally stepping up beside her, finally remembering that I have feet and that I'm the one who asked her out here.

"Sure," she says, "but you know that Monaco F1 isn't exactly family friendly."

Right. She definitely has a point. Yacht parties, alcohol everywhere, money, glam, sex.

"I came a few times when I was older," she says, and I see her eyes roll up like she's trying to remember all of the years. I know how she feels. They all start to run together after a while.

I can remember the races. My brain is like a textbook, filing them all away, time margins, podiums, pit stops. But I can't always remember everything else. The parties, the dinners, the interviews, who was there, who wasn't. It was something Elena always hated, when she would bring up something I had said while we were out at a race and I couldn't remember having said it. She said it was selective memory, that I was shutting her out, that I wasn't listening unless it was about F1, and maybe, to an extent, that was true, but it was never intentional. It's just the way your brain is wired when you've taught yourself to focus on one very important thing your whole life, putting everything else second.

I look over at Arabella and I wonder if I'll remember this years from now. When everything has slowed down and I've retired from F1, will I remember this moment, standing with her? Who knows?

"What is it like, being away from all of it?" I ask her.

She hums at the question. "Away from what? F1?"

"Yeah."

She has a crease between her brows, so I backtrack.

"When you were at school and weren't coming to the races. You were so disconnected. What was that like?"

Her features seem to soften, but not entirely. Her face has shifted from confusion to something else that I can't read. "What makes you think I was disconnected?"

I don't know what made me think that. I guess maybe the way it always felt like Arabella was on the outside of everything. I've seen the way people cling to their parents' interests when they've been raised to orbit those things. But then the shackles come free and you find your own interests or choose those things for yourself. Arabella, she found photography. I know she found it before she left home, but it's different when you're gone. You realize that your life can revolve around anything you want it to.

"I don't know. I guess I just wasn't really sure how interested you were in the whole thing."

She laughs, her face pointed down at the water below us where it's splashing against the side of the boat in a gentle, rocking rhythm. "I'm here, aren't I?" she says. But there's something about the way she says it. It's not straightforward, not simple. There's more to it, but she's clearly not going to tell me.

I grab on to the metal railing and lean back to look up at the stars. "I guess a part of me thinks that once I'm not doing this anymore, I'll forget about it. I'll be able to move on. I could focus on cycling, play padel, watch movies like normal people. It's sort of like a black hole, but not in a bad way. Anyone who escapes it, who gets free of the suck of it, there's so many things to experience in the world. So many things out there I've never done."

She tips her head to one side. "What do you mean? You've done so many things."

I shrug. "I've played sports. I've been to a lot of countries. And yes, I've done so many things, but there are also so many things out there that I haven't had the time to do. Like, I've never been to a ballet or climbed a mountain or been on safari."

She smiles at me softly. "And do you think that once you retire, you'll do those things?"

I sigh. "That's not really what I mean."

I'm frustrated that I can't express myself as easily as she seems to be able to. I say too many words, not ever really sure I'm getting my English just right, and then she responds calmly, easily.

"I just mean, what is it like to live in a world where everyone you know isn't tied to the same thing all the time?"

Something I've said makes the smile fall from her face. I'm not even sure what it was. But her mouth turns down at the corners. Her hair blows in the wind, long and curly and brown.

"I was still tied to it," she says. "I was still watching every Sunday." But she doesn't say it like it's something she's happy about. She says it like it's something she regrets. A curl flies into her mouth, sticking to her lipstick. I reach up and pull it away, tuck it behind her ear. I'm frozen for a moment at how soft her skin is.

Her eyes meet mine in the dark.

"You're here!" someone says behind us, and I turn to find Brigit walking up to us.

"*You're* here!" Arabella says back, turning and taking the hands that Brigit holds out to her.

I'm just as surprised to see her as Arabella is. It's not that the crew is not allowed at these parties, but most of the time, they want to party with each other instead of partying with the drivers. It's a different scene. We're in the same orbit, us and the crew, but we're on different planets once we leave the garage.

Brigit shrugs. She has her hair down now. I've never seen it like that. I've only ever seen it up in her familiar bun. Her very Swedish bun.

"I was invited," she says, planting her hands on her hips. "I met a guy in the paddock who happens to know a guy who knows the guy that owns this yacht."

"Jayce's cousin or something..." Arabella says, glancing at me for confirmation, even though I know about as much as she does on the subject.

But Brigit bounds ahead. "I didn't know you were going to be here."

"Here I am," Arabella says. There she is.

Brigit wraps her fingers around Arabella's and tugs her toward the door back inside. "Come on, let's go dance. This is not a night for quiet. This is Monaco. We party. Let's go."

Arabella laughs, but turns toward me. "Sorry," she says.

I have this strange urge to reach out and pull her back. To tell Brigit no, she can't have her. Then that urge turns sour in my stomach, and I take a step back.

"You go," I tell her. "Have a good time. It's Monaco, after all."

She doesn't hesitate. She sends me a closed-lipped smile. Then she's gone, and I feel a little stuck, not quite existing inside with the excitement but not quite existing out here with the cold wind either.

I stay out anyway, with the full moon and the wind and the stars and my thoughts. I watch through the windows as Brigit and Arabella make it to the dance floor, a stretch of floor between the bar and the DJ. Immediately, they start to dance to a familiar song from the early 2000s that I can hear through the glass. It's a song I couldn't get away from when it was popular. But on the dance floor, it doesn't matter how old a song is, as long as it gets people moving.

Brigit takes Arabella's hands and they sway their hips. Brigit twirls Arabella, and Arabella laughs so loud that the sound of it carries out all the way to me through the open door. And when Brigit pulls her back in, they light up against each other. I watch as their hips move, their arms wrapped around each other. Something inside me stirs. They bend their knees, push their hips together. Brigit's hand goes to Arabella's lower back.

And then a tall, dark figure comes up behind Arabella, breaking the spell between the two women. Arabella tips her head over her shoulder and looks up at Jayce. She smiles and lets go of Brigit, who puts space between them to let Jayce move in. I watch Brigit for some kind of sign that this is intrusive or that she's jealous, but she easily lets Arabella go and continues to sway on her own, her arms in the air, long and pale.

That's when Arabella turns toward Jayce. His hands find her hips. And while they're not as entangled as she and Brigit were, they're still right up against each other. At first, they just speak. She says something to him and he bends to put his mouth closer to her ear. He nods. And I think maybe they'll leave the dance floor, go and get a drink.

But instead, he spins her around so that her back is to his front and grinds her up against his pelvis.

Something hot and angry shoots through my veins. I'm not even thinking. I'm just moving. I stomp back inside, heading towards the dance floor just as Jayce's hand moves up onto Arabella's rib.

As soon as I'm close enough to reach them, I yank his hand away.

Just like that, everything is on fast forward again. Me shoving Jayce away, grabbing onto Arabella's arm, pulling her out of the room, right off the damn boat, where it's quiet enough for me to hear her yelling.

"What the hell are you doing?" She yanks her arm away from me as we stand on the dock, ignoring the people milling about, watching us.

"What the hell are you doing?" I growl back. "Is this why you wanted to come tonight? So you could sleep with Jayce? Or were you satisfied, no matter which driver it was?" I regret saying it as soon as it leaves my mouth.

Anger flashes across her face. "How dare you speak to me that way? You invited me to the damn party, Mateo."

"Exactly, and I'm supposed to be looking out for you."

Her mouth falls open. "I'm a capable adult! I don't need anyone looking out for me."

"Clearly, you do. You think guys like Jayce are looking for someone sweet like you? They want someone they can use and throw away like a tissue."

"You would know all about that, wouldn't you?"

Her words sting, but I'm not going to argue with her on that point. Maybe I don't use women at the rate that Jayce does, but I've had my fair share of one-night-stands with women I picked up in the paddock on race day or in a club afterward. "You're better than that."

She grimaces. "Better than what? Being in the same room with men who might want to have sex with me? Wanting to have sex with them too?"

"Don't say that!" I say between my teeth. "You're not having sex with any of them!"

"You're not my father, Mateo! Not that he has any more say in who I sleep with than you do. And I'm not a child." She points her finger at me, her long hair falling around her shoulders in waves.

I can feel myself starting to calm, like waking up from a dream. "I know that, Arabella." I don't even know what I'm saying, don't understand how I'm acting. Running on pure instinct.

She shakes her head, and her disappointment stings most of all. "You need to get a grip."

With that, she stomps into the night, and I want to follow her, want to make sure she gets back to her hotel safely, but I know that would just make her even angrier. So I stand on the pier, watching her walk away in the glow of the moonlight.

I feel Jayce step up beside me before he speaks. "What the hell is up with you, man?"

I look over at him, stick my hands in my pockets so I don't hit him. "Stay away from her."

He chuckles. "You don't get to make that call, grandpa." He gives me a sarcastic salute and turns back for the yacht, and I know he'll just find someone else to warm his bed tonight.

Chapter Seventeen

Arabella

I'm at the airport, getting ready to fly to Miami, when I get a text message. I'm expecting it to be my mom, who always makes sure I text her before I fly so she'll know if she needs to look out for news reports of fallen planes, but it's a text from Mateo.

I stare at the notification for a long time before I actually click on it. The plane is boarding, the line ahead of me moving even as I stare down at my phone.

Mateo
I'm sorry for how I acted last night. It was unacceptable.

The man behind me in line, bogged down in duffel bags draped over his body, clears his throat, nodding forward to let me know to go.

But I can't go. It'll be eleven hours before I get another

chance to talk to him. I step out of line, pulling my suitcase over to an empty seat in the terminal.

> **Arabella**
> Why DID you act like that?

Last night was a fever dream. I thought the party was going well. I thought we were having a good time. And yeah, I danced with Jayce. It was fun, and he was being flirty, and I was just feeling good and wanting something. I certainly didn't have any plans to sleep with him, but why in the world should that matter to Mateo?

Because he sees me as just his friend's kid. Because he's trying to protect from the advances of an adult man when I am very much an adult woman and can sleep with whoever I want.

Just thinking about it is making the anger start up again. I can't believe he pulled me off that yacht like a crying child being dragged out of a toy store.

Mateo
Because I want to protect you.

I sigh, look up at the line that's boarding while I think of how to respond.

> **Arabella**
> Do you really hate Jayce so much?

Mateo
No. Jayce is a good guy.

> But he's still a guy. I don't want to see
> you get hurt.

He's acting like I was ready to propose to Jayce. It was one dance.

> **Arabella**
> You don't have to worry about me,
> Mateo. I can take care of myself.

His dots appear and then disappear. They appear again and while I wait for his message, one of the women at the gate says, "Ma'am? Are you boarding this flight?"

Shit. I have to go.

His dots are still there.

I stand and get my passport and boarding pass ready, trying to kill time. And then his message appears.

> **Mateo**
> Your happiness is extremely important
> to me. You don't know how much you
> mean to me, Ari.

All I can do is stare down at my phone, my heart pounding in my ears. He has no idea.

"Ma'am?"

I put my phone in my pocket. It's not like I would be able to formulate a response after that anyway. But I think about his text for the entire eleven-hour flight.

FormulasFormula: Wait, who is that dancing with Jayce? Is that Arabella Cedillo?

racedaydrew: Jayce and Mateo fighting on a yacht? WHAT IS GOING ON? *gif*

Formula1er: Proof that F1 drivers never grow up.

Lolaslovelies: Whatever. Lola wouldn't be caught dead doing this shit.

Chapter Eighteen
Round 4 - Miami, USA

Lola Castle - 61 points
Mateo Silva - 50 points
Archer Hayes - 48 points

Arabella

"Arabella, where is Arabella?" I hear Julie, the team's media director, say as I'm loading up my lenses for the day. I have two cameras slung around my neck when she comes into the back room and spots me. "Arabella," she says, out of breath. Why is she out of breath? When she gets closer, I realize she's sweating, too.

"Is everything okay?" I ask. "Is it Mateo?" Panic lances through me.

She has her hands up, like she's about to delve into a long explanation, but then stops. "Why would you think something is wrong with Mateo?" She waves me off before I can give an answer, which is a relief because I have no idea what I would have said. Something along the lines of, *Mateo and I got in a fight and he apologized a week ago, but I never really accepted and now enough time has passed that I don't know if things are weird between us or not.*

"Cassie Reese is coming to the race today."

"Okay..." I say. *What does that have to do with me?*

"We need pictures, and I'm getting you fifteen minutes of time alone with her."

My brain finally catches up. "Wait. She's coming here? To Albatross?"

"Yes." She's already tapping away at her phone, moving on to the next thing that needs her attention.

"Alone?" I say, still trying to catch up, but she's already gone. She's rushed out of the room as if she's the town crier, who has to go spread the word to the next person.

I'm not positive what to do with this information. Fifteen minutes alone with Cassie Reese. Cassie Reese is a very famous pop star. Cassie Reese has won something like a dozen Grammys. Cassie Reese is that kind of pretty that makes you think maybe she's not even from the same planet you are, because how could the two of you exist on the same planet and be the same species, and she looks like that and you look like this? What am I supposed to do with Cassie Reese for fifteen minutes?

I don't even have an opportunity to really digest it because I have to get down to the garage. The guys are going to start moving in soon to prep. I've got to make sure my camera is in the right place because now I have a pop star to take into account.

"Did you hear?" Brigit says, ambushing me as soon as I get into the garage. She's got her hands wrapped around my upper arm so tight I'm worried she's going to unhinge her jaw like an anaconda and swallow me.

"I heard," I say. "And Julie says I have to be alone with Cassie for fifteen minutes to get content."

Brigit scoffs. "Of course. This is a huge publicity thing."

She pulls me off to the side and lowers her voice. "All the teams wanted her, and she chose Albatross's garage to watch the race from."

"Why?" I ask.

Brigit raises an eyebrow at me. I feel like I missed something, like maybe I've walked into this story in the middle of it. "She's coming to meet Mateo."

"Oh." Once again, I have no idea what to do with any of the information being thrown at me. I feel stuck in time, like I'm frozen and everyone around me is moving too fast.

"Aren't you excited?" Brigit asks. Her eyes are shooting over to where the mechanics are starting to stretch for the race.

"Sure, I'm a big fan," I tell her. Cassie Reese's music is great. It's the kind of music that I find myself singing in the shower or that I listen to in the morning to wake myself up. It's not that I'm not excited. I just wasn't really prepared for this today.

"I have to get to it," Brigit says.

As soon as she's gone, my brain starts to untangle what everyone has told me.

Cassie wants to meet Mateo. Brigit didn't say anything about Jayce. Cassie Reese, one of the most beautiful and desirable women on the planet, wants to meet Mateo. She's coming here specifically to meet him. Is she a fan? Is she looking to get to know him better?

I feel like someone has wrapped their hands around my throat. I feel so stupid. What did I think was going to happen? Did it really not even occur to me that in the whole year that I'm contracted to work with Albatross that Mateo might want to date someone, or even multiple someones? Did I think he was going to be a monk for a whole year just because he has me hanging around?

What if he's...already seeing someone that I don't know about?

He and his ex, they would post about each other some-times on socials, her more than him. He didn't want their private life in the open, that much is obvious. But just because he hasn't been with women out where everyone could see or because he hasn't posted about anybody on social media, doesn't mean he doesn't have a girlfriend. Doesn't mean he's not meeting women, sleeping with them.

He and ex-girlfriend have been broken up for months. Maybe he's ready to jump into a new relationship.

And suddenly this whole thing feels like the biggest fucking mistake I've ever made. Because if he does decide that he wants to date the prettiest pop star on the planet, I'll have to sit back and watch him do it. It's literally my job.

Mateo

"You just have to say hi," Arturo tells me as we walk down to the garage. I've just been informed that I am expected to say hello to Cassie Reese. And while I'm happy to meet Cassie, a woman whose music I hear everywhere I go, whether it's in the car or at the shops or at a cafe or even in the motorhome, meeting people right before a race is not my favorite.

It's not as if we get to sit around and get to know each other. I usually have five minutes to say hello, shake some-one's hand, give them a pat on the back, and then I'm off. Race day makes me feel like a piece of putty that's being pulled in twenty different directions at the same time. I'm never going to snap. I'm never going to break. But I'm going to be stretched so thin that you can see the sky right through me.

"Is she here for something specific?"

"What do you mean?" Arturo asks, running both of his

hands through his curly hair, clearly trying to make sure he's pop star ready.

"I mean, is she here to talk about investing? Is she here to promote an album? What is she here for?"

Arturo shakes his head. "You're something else, you know that?"

"What?" I ask, stopping for someone who has politely called my name so we can take a quick selfie together.

As soon as we start walking again, Arturo says, "She's here because she wants to date you."

My brain turns to static. "What?"

He makes a sound in the back of his throat. Arturo definitely has his information mixed up. That isn't why she's here. We head down the stairs into the garage.

"Isn't she dating some hockey player? She didn't come all the way here to see me."

Arturo stops, turning towards me. "Why do you say it like that?"

"Say it like what?"

"Like you can't understand why a desirable woman would want anything from you."

I don't have an answer for that. So I just keep walking. He's probably right. If this was ten years ago, if this was before Elena, would I have questioned this? God, when I was in my 20s and had just won my third championship, women threw themselves at me. I'd find them waiting outside of my hotel room half naked. They'd pull at my clothing at bars. They'd ask me to sign their breasts. They'd leave their room keys in my pockets. I won't pretend I didn't have my fun.

But now...

It's not that I'm not interested in women. I am very interested in women. But more often than not, I'm too busy. I know that finding a woman for a one-night stand is easy enough. Strangely, I think it might be easier for me than it is for some of the younger guys. People know my name. They know my face. Especially when I'm in Spain or England. But I don't think high-profile pop stars go searching for one-night stands. I don't think they'd cross an ocean for one.

"We were thinking you could give her one of your helmets." As soon as we pass through the doors into the garage, there's Arabella, her camera pointed at us. The sight of her interrupts my brain function. We haven't spoken to each other since Monaco, apart from the texts, a conversation that doesn't feel like it was ever finished.

I gave her space, and she took it, not making contact until right now, when she pulls her camera away from her face and looks at me.

The corners of her mouth lift just slightly into a smile, and I feel something that was wound tight inside me loosen.

"Do you think she wants one of my helmets?" I ask Arturo, reaching out towards Arabella the way I always do, take her elbow in my hand and give it a squeeze, pray that everything is okay between us. I want her to know that I see her. That I know she's there. On race day, my brain is always so cluttered, and I don't want anybody to think I'm looking right through them, especially not Arabella. I could never look through her.

She trails behind us as we walk.

"Sure, why not?" Arturo says.

I send him a skeptical look. "I think you're reading the situation all wrong."

"And I think," he says, "that if you're not careful, you're going to end up in a relationship with Cassie Reese."

Something clatters behind me, metal on metal. I turn to Arabella. She still has her camera in her hands but she's knocked over a bunch of stuff on one of the mechanics' benches.

"I'll get it," I say, stepping forward.

"No," she hisses at me, pushing me away. "You're supposed to be meeting Cassie right now."

So she's here to photograph me with Cassie. Excellent. She waves someone over, and Brigit appears, gently moving Arabella out of the way and scrambling to fix everything that she's knocked over. Everything has to be perfect so that the mechanics can function without hesitation.

"Is that her?" Arabella says, her eyes flying over my shoulder.

I turn to find Cassie Reese striding up to me. I recognize that confidence. It's the confidence of somebody at the top of their field, someone who can't be touched. I know because I've worn the same confidence many times.

She's wearing a sensible dress, dark green, wearing a denim jacket, except her arms aren't actually in it. It's just draped over her slight shoulders. It's there for fashion, not because she's cold in Miami in May.

"Hi," she says, coming up to me with her hand already out. Pink lipstick, long brown hair so dark it's almost black, sunglasses that match her outfit. "I'm Cassie." She has two very large men flanking her. Bodyguards. "It's so nice to meet you," she says in her English accent. "You're such a legend."

I never know how to respond to a comment like that. "It's nice to meet you, too."

Someone prods me with something, and I turn in time to see Arturo holding out a helmet towards me. It's one I've already signed.

"You like Formula 1?" I ask her, taking the helmet. It feels good in my hands.

"I'm kind of new to the sport," she says.

"Because of that guy," Arturo says. And when we both look over at him, I can tell he regrets saying it. And by the look on Cassie's face, I can tell she also regrets him saying it.

Yes, *that guy*, the ex-boyfriend. He was a hockey player and apparently a big Formula 1 fan. He spent a lot of time in the Mercedes garage while the two of them were dating. And now I can't help but wonder if she's here as some attempt to get back at him. If he's a big fan of Formula 1 and she dates a Formula 1 driver, does that mean that she won the breakup? That would make more sense to me than Arturo's assumption that she wants to date me just because she wants to.

"It's really an honor to have you here," I tell her, my typical, scripted speech. "We wanted you to have this, to remember your time here."

She takes the helmet, and I can see in her eyes that she's not really sure what to do with it, but she turns and passes it to one of her bodyguards.

"Thank you. That's very cool. How many helmets do you think you go through in a season?"

I shrug. "Maybe twenty or so. Depends on the races. We have special ones made for certain races and they can sometimes get damaged easily. Not the helmet itself. They're extremely sturdy. But the paint and whatnot. They want them to look perfect for the pictures."

I can feel myself descending into that place people don't like, that place where I start talking about Formula 1 and can't seem to stop.

"We usually do one or two special lids every season for special races. For example, they always have a special lid for Silverstone because Albatross is an English company. I often have a special lid for Spain as well because it's my home race."

Her eyes are glazed over, but I don't know what else to talk about.

"I was just listening this morning to one of your songs," I say.

"Oh!" she says, her mouth pulling into a diplomatic smile. "Really? You don't really seem like the type."

"What type?" I ask.

She shrugs. "You know, to listen to pop music."

Beside me, Arturo laughs. "This guy listens to nothing but pop music. He doesn't know anything else exists."

A little snicker sounds to my left, and I glance over to watch Arabella clamp her mouth shut. My brain buzzes at the sight, offering some kind of biological reminder of how much easier it is to talk to her than anyone else, how I rarely feel lost for what to say in a conversation with her.

"I think it's really cool that you listen to pop music," Cassie says, and I realize that I'm still staring at Arabella, that she's staring back.

I turn to Cassie. "I like upbeat music. It keeps me in a good mood."

"Very cool," she says. "Anyway, I'll see you after the race. I know you have to get going."

"I do, yes," I say, relieved that this conversation is going to be over and that I wasn't the one to end it. "Maybe I'll see you again later."

"Once you're done on the podium," she says, giving me a wink.

Right.

***

Arabella

"Thank you for coming. I really appreciate it. It was nice to meet you," Mateo says, shaking Cassie's hand one more time before turning around and heading to the back of the garage to finish getting ready.

As soon as his back is turned, Cassie makes this goofy smiling face and clasps her hands together. When she realizes I'm watching her and that I still have my camera turned in her direction, even though I wouldn't use it at a time like this, her smile drops.

"That's embarrassing," she says, her face flushing.

I wish I could tell her that that thing she just did on the outside is what I've been doing on the inside every time Mateo has walked into a room for the last six years.

"Not at all," I tell her instead. "The team was hoping that I could spend a few minutes with you. I think they were just hoping to get some pictures of you in the garage."

"Oh, of course," she says, stepping toward me and lacing her hands together behind her back. "Yeah, just tell me where you want me."

I'm trying really hard not to be sour toward her. It isn't her fault, this situation I've found myself in. I've always been a fan of Cassie's. It's hard not to be. The whole world loves her. She has more top hits than years she's been alive.

But any question I might have had before about her intentions are gone. Her intentions are pretty clear. She wants to make a move on Mateo. And it's not her fault I'm in love with him. And it's also not her fault that she is who she is and I am who I am and that only one of us actually has a shot with him.

I take her over to the garage entrance. There are huge Albatross signs everywhere and I ask her to pose with them. When Jayce walks by, I rush over to him, grab onto his arm and ask him to join us.

We haven't really spoken since that night in Monaco. I don't think he's upset about what happened, but I think that whatever interest he had in me that night has definitely vanished, if it was ever real at all.

I snap photos of them as they engage in much less awkward small talk than what she had with Mateo and then while Jayce video calls his sister, who freaks out at getting to speak to her idol. It makes for good content. Maybe I can get the internet to like Jayce, after all.

And then our time is up.

"I really appreciate it," I tell Cassie, settling my camera against my chest. "I'm a big fan."

"That's really nice," she says, pushing her jacket off her shoulders and handing it to one of the men escorting her. "Do you like working for the team?"

"Yeah, I love it." It's an automatic response. Do I love it? Or do I just like being around Mateo all day?

She steps closer to me, crossing her arms and lowering her voice. Right up against me like this, I can smell her perfume. Sweet and floral. "How long have you been working with Mateo?" she asks.

"This is my first year with the team."

She nods. "Okay."

I can tell this is not the answer she was looking for, so I amend it. "But I've known Mateo for several years. He's friends with my father. They go way back."

Chances are good she has no idea who my father is, which means that she doesn't know who I am.

"Oh," she says, her eyes lighting up. "That's really cool. So you know him very well."

"Yeah," I say. Sometimes I think the only person who can really know Mateo well is Mateo. He's so particular about what parts of himself he shares with people. Trying to decipher what's real and what's for show can sometimes be a bit tricky.

I think about that night in the pool. The water clinging to his eyelashes. Him telling me how confident he is that he'll lose the championship. That was the real him. I'm sure of it.

"Do you think there's any chance he's interested?" Cassie asks, pulling my attention back to this bizarre scenario that I find myself in. The world's biggest pop star is asking if I think a boy has a crush on her. In that moment, I relate to her so much. Not because I'm anywhere near her in terms of looks or status, but because I know what it's like to be desperate for someone to look at you. To want you. Especially since we're both desperate for the same guy.

"It's hard to say," I tell her. "He just gets really focused on race day. He can be hard to read."

She nods, suddenly looking very serious. I can't help but wonder why she's set her sights on Mateo. I know all the reasons I want him, all the little things about him that have made him the only person to ever make me feel this way.

But what is it about him specifically that appeals to her?

"You think he'll be in a better mood after the race?"

I laugh. "I guess that kind of depends on how the race goes."

She laughs, too. "Right. God. Of course. I'm so not used to this. Sports are just a whole different animal, you know?"

"Yeah, I do. When I was in art school, I used to take pictures of abandoned churches and small animals in the morning before everyone else was awake. And now I take pictures of race cars. I understand how this world is different from seemingly everywhere else."

She smiles. "Thanks for your help," she says, reaching out to grip my elbow with a squeeze before walking away. And I'm caught for a moment on how that's exactly what Mateo does every time he sees me.

Chapter Nineteen

Mateo

I can't explain how I ended up on a date with Cassie Reese.

One minute, I'm getting out of my car behind the plaque for third place, everyone's slapping me on the helmet, patting me on the back, congratulating me, spraying me with champagne.

And next thing I know, I'm at a dinner table ordering oysters, sitting across from Great Britain's sweetheart. The whole experience is sort of like trying to explain a dream hours after you've woken up.

I've been on dates with dozens of women. All of them beautiful. Bottle service, five course meal, private restaurants, the whole shebang. And I always have a good time. They make me laugh or they make me horny or they seem genuinely interested in my life and what I do.

I made the podium today. Not quite the interval I wanted. Not first place. Not as many points as I need. But Lola DNF'd, and with my biggest competitor out, it didn't really matter what place I finished in. No matter what I did, I was closing the gap between us.

So, I should be in a good mood. But I'm sitting across from Cassie and I'm not feeling anything. She's telling me a story about tripping during a show. And it's an interesting story. She's a good storyteller. She doesn't linger on unnecessary details or go back way too far, long before the story has really begun. She hits her punchline and looks at me expectantly. And I laugh because it's funny. She's funny.

"What's your karaoke song?" she asks me.

"My karaoke song?" I've been asked a lot of questions, but I don't think I've ever been asked that one.

She nods. "Yeah, you know, if you went to karaoke with your friends, what's your go-to song?"

I don't have a karaoke song because I would never sing karaoke. But I know exactly what she's expecting from me. I've gotten so good at answering questions the way I know people want me to answer them. So, I say, "'Oops!...I Did It Again.'"

This makes her laugh hard. "That would be hilarious. I would love to see you sing Britney."

She is decidedly pleasant. And so, so pretty. I can't find a single flaw. Everything is exactly where it should be. Every hair in place, not even a lipstick smudge. Nothing.

"Do you think you're going to win this season?"

I tap my fingers on the table. "Do you think you're going to win another Grammy?"

A slow smile stretches across her mouth. "Yeah, I think I probably will."

"I think I probably will, too," I lie.

Because that's what she wants to hear, right? That's the connection between someone like her and someone like me. Confidence, success, never-ending drive to be better. She already has a million Grammys, or so I've been told by Arturo.

And I know why people would like to see the two of us

together. Because it makes sense. The same reason she was with that hockey player she was with. The same reason she dated another Grammy winner. And a movie star.

Because this is what you do to make the stars align correctly.

So why does it feel so uninteresting to me?

We split a slice of cheesecake. She drinks three glasses of wine.

And then we go outside, where the valet pulls my car up to the curb. We met at my hotel earlier and I drove us here. And now, as I help her into the passenger seat, I look up and discover cell phones pointed at us. At her bodyguards that are following us. Cameras everywhere. And more than anything else that has happened tonight, that makes me feel something.

Exhaustion. Pity. Not for myself, but for her. She'll have more to answer for than I will when this night is over. People are far more interested in her love life than they are mine. Although they *are* also interested in my love life, for some indecipherable reason; I just give them less of it than she does.

"Where to?" she asks when I get in the car. I imagine a karaoke bar. Any kind of bar, or a club. Someplace quiet, where we can sit close together. I can put my hand on her leg. She can put her chin in her hand and tell me secrets.

I'm not interested in any of it, not today. Because I'm trying to stay focused. The only thing I care about right now is this championship.

"You're going to think I'm an old man," I say. I'm already trying to turn it into a joke, the way I'll reject her. "But I'm actually very tired."

"I bet," she says pleasantly, wearing a smile. "It must be exhausting. It's totally fine."

"I have to fly back to Spain tomorrow."

"Of course you do."

"An early flight."

"Right."

And so, I drive her to her hotel, where I pass her over to her bodyguards. And as I drive back to my own hotel, I feel nothing.

Up in my room, I sit on the edge of my bed, staring out over the city. I have this odd feeling in the pit of my stomach, like...emptiness. I've felt it before but this time, it's different. Like something is missing.

I go over some data that the team sent over after the race, scrolling through emails and text messages, but my eyes glaze over quickly. No one is going to mind if I just ignore it all for the night.

I pick up my phone and see a text from Arabella that I must have missed while I was at dinner with Cassie.

Arabella
Back in Montreal! See you in two
weeks!

I stare at it for a long time. Arabella didn't get to stay in Miami an extra day like I did. She had to go all the way home immediately after the race.

The distance between me and Montreal isn't something I ever really considered before. When you take private planes and travel to a different country every week, things like distance between countries becomes irrelevant. Everything is a quick flight away.

But now, sitting in the middle of Miami by myself, my mind starts to calculate miles. Flight times. I've visited the Cedillos' home in Montreal more times than I can count. It's never really seemed far away before, but for some reason, it seems unbearably far now.

F1WORLDWIDE: Whoa. Cassie Reese much?

RacingChili: I wasn't ready for adorable Cassie videos!!!

Rallypop: Why does Jayce kind of remind me of a department store mannequin?

asktaylor4: These pictures of Casssssssie! She's so gorgeous!!

Chapter Twenty

Arabella

I'm three days into my two-week stay in Montreal when my phone rings. I'm busy scrolling through social media, trying to get a handle on things that are trending at the moment, and I glance quickly at the screen on my phone, half expecting it to be my parents or Lana.

But it isn't. I look at the number, a 212 number. New York. I get a feeling it's the same one that's been calling me for the last couple of weeks.

The last time this particular number tried to get a hold of me was in Monaco. I don't normally answer numbers I don't know, but this one's been particularly insistent.

"Hello?"

"Oh, thank goodness."

I halfway recognize the voice on the other end of the line, but in that weird way you recognize someone at the grocery store but can't quite place where you know them from.

"Sorry, who is this?" I ask.

The man chuckles. "Arabella, it's Mark."

As soon as he says it, my brain catches up at full speed. Mark Whitaker, my professor at NYU. For some unexplainable reason, I pull the phone away from my ear and look at the screen, as if I've somehow answered someone else's phone.

"Professor Whitaker," I say when I put the phone back to my ear. "It's nice to hear from you."

"None of that. It's Mark. I hope you don't mind," he says. "I got your number from one of the emails you sent me last summer. I'm contacting you about a job opportunity."

"A job opportunity," I say slowly, things already running through my mind. Answers, excuses. I'm not looking for a job, after all.

"Look, before you say anything, I already know you have a job. That's actually why I'm calling. As you know, I was extremely impressed with the work you did in my class. And a colleague of mine found out you were working for that race car team."

I hold in a laugh.

"Anyway, I looked into your work. The stuff on the website, the social media, it's really good. I really think you would be an excellent fit for this project."

I interrupt him. "Whatever it is, I really appreciate it. But if you know I'm working for Albatross, then you know I'm contracted until the end of the season."

"I know," he says. I can picture him in his office, the one I sat in many times. Professor Whitaker is one of the kindest men I've ever met, an extremely understanding professor. Someone who really wanted to see his students succeed. To teach them something, make them feel something. Not just lord over them.

"This job doesn't start until next summer, so you would have plenty of time to prep for it. And, you know, to consider."

Okay. I wasn't prepared for that. And now my excuses are no good. I'm only contracted for one year with Albatross. So, whatever he's offering me, I would potentially be available for.

"What's the job?"

"I'm taking a documentary crew out to Everest next August."

I blink, feeling outside of my body when he says it, even though I'm firmly planted at my desk. I stare down into the city. There's a gray haze over Montreal today. A light mist.

"I'm sorry, did you say Everest?"

He chuckles in my ear. "I know that probably sounds very intimidating, and I understand. But the documentary is actually about base camp and a lot of the Nepali religious practices around people going up the mountain. And I need a crew. I've got a lot of spots filled, but I'd really like a great photographer to follow us out. You are certainly not expected to climb Everest."

He chuckles again. "I'm not going to say it's going to be easy. Base camp in and of itself is quite the trek, and not exactly a five-star luxury hotel. But I really think you could do some great work based on what I've seen from you in the past. I'm going to be honest with you, I've talked to a lot of people about this position. There's some interest, but I really have my sights set on you."

"Professor Whitaker, that's very kind."

This is the kind of thing I've dreamt of. A creative position falling into my lap. An opportunity to make something important with someone who's passionate about it.

Except I would have to leave the team. I'd have to tell them I'm not coming back for another year.

Not that anyone has offered me any contracts, but... I can only assume that unless something goes terribly wrong in the next nine months that they are, in fact, going to offer me another contract. And I worked hard to get here. Do I want to walk away to go be part of some job on Mount Everest?

"I know it's a lot to digest," Professor Whitaker says, voice warm in my ear. "And I'm not expecting an answer right now. I just want to put it in your head. I want you to think about it. I really want to have my crew put together by the end of the year. That gives us the first half of next year to get everything ready. It's going to require a lot of preparation and planning. So, I want you to think on it. Will you think on it?"

I take a deep breath. Let it out. "Of course."

"Excellent. I've still got your personal email address. So, if you don't mind, I'll just send you some forms so that if you decide this might be something you want to do, everything is there at your fingertips. Okay?"

"Okay."

"Excellent. Hope to hear from you soon, Arabella. Really. I would be delighted to have you on this job. I'll talk to you later."

"Professor Whitaker?"

"Yeah."

"Thank you for thinking of me."

I spend a solid half hour processing, staring off into the distance, trying to figure out how in the world that just happened to me. This number has been trying to get through to me for almost a month. That means Professor Whitaker wants me on this job enough that he pursued me for a month, even when I've been ignoring the calls.

And even though I don't think there's any way I could do this, that knowledge alone, it does something to me. Feeling wanted. Feeling respected. Especially by someone with the kind of educational and professional background that Professor Whitaker has. What an honor.

My computer dings.

A message from Professor Whitaker. It's an application form.

And just one line of text.

Please don't write me off yet.

Arabella

As Chuck is telling me about a golden retriever he worked with today who could dance a waltz with its owner, my cell phone rings.

I know how dreadfully rude it is to have my phone sitting on the table, but the Thai restaurant Chuck brought me to is fairly casual and Chuck's phone is on the table by him, too. Except his isn't ringing and his doesn't have Mateo's name flashing on the screen.

My eyes wander down to it and when I look back up at Chuck, I can tell he's seen it, too. The vibration is loud enough that I'm sure the people at the next table can hear.

I stare at Mateo's name, at his smiling face. I know I shouldn't answer it. I should be here with my date, the one I waited three weeks for.

But Mateo is calling. Mateo has never called me. Only texts here and there over the years. The idea that he might need something from me now...

"Do you need to take that?" Chuck says when I don't immediately reach out to silence it. I almost feel guilty. He doesn't know who Mateo is. All he sees is that some other guy is calling me, a very familiar photo of him—taken in the motorhome in Monaco—on the screen.

"I'm so sorry," I say, grabbing the phone, "But yes, I do. It's my boss. I'm really sorry. It's probably important."

"Oh." Chuck's whole face seems to fall. He clearly thought I was going to say I could ignore the call. "Okay, that's cool. I'll order dessert."

"Okay." I'm halfway out of my seat.

I also know it's dreadfully rude to answer my phone in the middle of a restaurant, but I can't wait until I get outside. It's already been too long and I'm afraid he might hang up. So as I'm rushing for the door, I answer and press the phone to my ear.

"Hello?"

"Ari," he says, and I want to melt. I've never heard his voice in my ear like this before. It sends a shiver down my spine, just those two deep syllable in his Spanish accent.

I step out onto the sidewalk, the air cold. I forgot my jacket inside but that's okay. It doesn't matter.

"Is everything okay?" I ask him.

"I watched that movie," he says.

I'm perplexed for a moment. Not even sure I remember English.

"A movie?" I ask. Did we talk about a movie? Was he supposed to watch a movie? Was I supposed to watch a movie? Is this a work thing?

"The one about the boat."

Okay, now I'm even more confused. A movie about a boat?

"Mateo, I have no idea what you're talking about." I can't stop the smile that crosses my face. I may be very confused, but I'm having a conversation with Mateo, standing on a sidewalk in the middle of Montreal, and there's an unfamiliar excitement fizzing in my blood.

"You told Pedro once that it was your favorite movie. I overheard."

There's a beat of silence as my mind starts to make sense of things. "Are you talking about *Titanic*?" My eyes catch on a group of people across the street heading into a restaurant, laughing and talking loudly. I'm smiling so big my cheeks hurt.

"Yes," Mateo says "Yes. That's the one. *Titanic*. I watched it."

"You watched *Titanic*."

"It was sad but good."

I shake my head, even though he can't see me. "Are you trying to tell me you watched *Titanic* for the very first time?"

"Yes," he says, so matter-of-factly. "I work a lot. I don't watch a lot of movies. Anyway, I thought it was good so I called you to see if you had any other movie recommendations."

This might be the strangest conversation I've ever had. With anyone else, it might seem mundane. Borderline small talk. *Seen any good movies lately?* But this is Mateo. Mateo, who talks about race strategy and wind speeds and tire erosion.

"You want movie recommendations?" I ask him.

He groans a little, and I can't decipher what the groan means. "I'm not feeling very well. I've been laying on the couch for two days. And I got bored. I got tired of watching old races. And I got tired of scrolling social media. And I got tired of reading this book. So I turned on the TV. Tell me what to watch."

My smile falls. The thought that Mateo is somewhere in the world sick and alone makes my skin ache, makes me want to get on a plane and go to wherever he is, feed him chicken noodle soup and take his temperature.

Everything in me is starting to speed up. My heart, my breath, my brain. Because Mateo called *me*. He could have called anyone. He could have called my dad. He could have called Arturo. He could have called Jayce.

But he called me.

"Are you okay?" I ask him when I can find the right words. "Do you need anything?"

At this, he chuckles. "Arabella, if I did need something, what would you do about it? Aren't you in Canada?"

"Yes," I say, a bit dejected.

"I don't think you could help me. But I appreciate the offer. I'm alright. It's just a cold or something. I'm going to be okay. You can help me by telling me what to watch next."

"Okay." I glance back inside. I can see through the big glass windows straight down the brightly lit room of the restaurant to where my date is patiently waiting. There's a slice of cake on the center of the table, with two forks.

"Right. Well, what about *When Harry Met Sally*? It's a classic."

"*When Harry Met Sally*," he says, and I can hear him clicking around like he's searching for it on his TV.

"Yeah, it's a different caliber of film than *Titanic*. Still a great movie, but funny, cheerful. It'll make you feel better."

"Talking to you makes me feel better."

My breath stops. I know he doesn't intend for me to read into that comment. He's clearly said it without even thinking. He's busy trying to find the movie on his TV. He's distracted.

But he said it nevertheless.

There's almost a full minute of silence while he searches, and I try to clear the frog out of my throat so I can speak. "I wish I could stay on the phone," I tell him, "but I'm sort of busy."

"Oh," he says, and the clicking noise of the search engine on his TV stops. "I'm so sorry. I didn't even ask if you were busy. It's a Friday night."

"No, it's okay. It's fine. I'm just out with a friend. So I've got to get back in there. I left him sitting at a table by himself." I don't know why I said that, not quite telling the whole truth. But what does Mateo care if I'm on a date or not?

"Out with a friend," he says. I don't know why he says it like that, repeating the words slowly.

"I'll see you on the circuit."

"Yeah. Have a good night, Arabella."

"Feel better, Mateo."

I don't think I've ever been this sad to end a phone call. I could stand on this freezing sidewalk well into the night talking to him. Instead, I have a perfectly nice veterinarian waiting for me back inside. So I go back in to him and the cake.

Arabella

Chuck walks me from our Uber to my door. He escorts me up the steps, and then we stand there on the stoop, shivering, neither one of us saying anything. I look up at him and he smiles down at me. He's really tall, at least 6'3", his hair perfectly slicked back and his eyes looking like twin oceans in the shadows of my stoop.

"I had a really nice time," he says, "I know you're really busy with work and stuff. You're like some crazy adventurer. But I'd really like to see you again."

I look away from him. Even if my crazy schedule wasn't an issue, I don't think I want to go on another date with him.

All I can think about is how that five-minute phone call with Mateo made me feel more excited than this date with this cute, polite guy. This feeling in my chest and my stomach and in every inch of me is insanity.

There has to be another guy on this planet who can be as interesting to me. There has to be another guy on this planet who will make me feel something like what I feel for Mateo. Because if there isn't, I don't know what becomes of me then.

"I had a nice time too, Chuck," I tell him. "But—"

"Oh. But..." he says, sticking his hands in his pockets and dropping his head like he just lost a competition.

"I'm really sorry. I promise it's not you. You're so great. I just, I don't know, my life is kind of crazy right now. I mean, obviously. I'm about to be gone for two weeks and I just... I'm traveling a lot and it's kind of a new job. And I just think maybe this is bad timing."

He nods, his cheeks pink from the cold. "Bad timing," he says.

"I'm really sorry."

He nods again. "Okay. It's just really nice getting to know you and, you know, maybe don't delete my number, just in case."

This makes me smile because even though I know I'll never use his number again, it's still a really nice thing to say.

He turns and heads back down to the Uber that's waiting at the curb. He gives me a small wave before he gets in, and I wonder if I just made a huge mistake.

A Match Made in Miami

Pop star Cassie Reese, currently in the middle of the North American leg of her Stars Aligning World Tour, was seen out on the town with Formula 1 World Champion Mateo Silva. An interesting match...

Chapter Twenty-One
Round 5 - Melbourne, Australia

Archer Hayes - 73 points
Mateo Silva - 62 points
Lola Castle - 61 points

Arabella

It starts with the photos online. They crop up on social media in clusters.

Pictures of Mateo and Cassie at her hotel.

Pictures of Mateo and Cassie at a restaurant.

Pictures of Mateo and Cassie talking to each other over the console of his car.

I can't escape them. And I know it's my own damn fault. I've trained my algorithm to throw Mateo in my face the second I open social media. And so it does exactly that. But this time, she's in all the photos. You'd think I'd be used to it by now.

But things are different now. I can't even really explain why. They just are.

I can only assume Albatross is the reason it took two weeks

for the pictures to come out. They were taken in Miami, but they don't start to sprinkle out into the media until Miami is a distant memory, until we're a day away from the race and people still have time to tune in to see what all the fuss is about.

It's not as if any of it comes as a surprise. I knew there was a good chance that Mateo would go out with Cassie. That their lives would become intertwined in a way that would make the press go crazy.

All day, Mateo is distracted by the attention, weighing on him more heavily than normal. As we walk through the paddock, people stop to ask him about the pictures and he just smiles and keeps walking. Julie asks me to film videos of him with Cassie's music on top and then leaves me standing in the middle of the motorhome, watching people pat Mateo on the back and wink at him as they go by.

In the media tent, someone shouts out, "Mateo, is Cassie coming out to the race today?"

To which, Mateo replies, "No comment."

By the time race day rolls around, all that's left of me is a shattered version of myself.

I prep for the day in a back room in the motorhome, pretending everything is normal, everything just as it should be, even as I feel hollowed out by it all.

A voice carries over to me through the open door. Jayce. He's kind of a quiet guy, but he can be loud when he wants to be. He has an inhumanly big mouth. "There's no way it's true," he says from somewhere out in the dining hall. "It's just some fucking story they picked up on to make things juicy."

"So how do you explain the photos?" someone asks. And I know it's Dan. He follows Jayce everywhere he goes, does everything for him, the way Arturo does for Mateo.

"The photos don't prove anything. Everybody knows Cassie was in the garage as a publicity stunt. The team wanted her there to get exposure. Why wouldn't going out and having drinks or whatever they did be part of it?"

"Yeah, she *has* been known to pull this kind of stuff in the past for attention. Probably has a new album to promote or something."

Could it just be for publicity? I bristle at Dan's implication that Cassie does things just for attention. It's the kind of thing people say when they're judging a woman's life choices just because they don't approve of them. There's no actual evidence of it.

Mateo looks his age. He has lines on his face. He doesn't have a six pack anymore. So, of course, someone like Jayce can't understand why someone like Cassie, the most desirable person on Earth, would choose him over one of the younger guys on the grid.

For me, what he has is far more attractive than those drivers, the ones who are my age. Those caramel-colored eyes. Those hands. That boyish smile.

It wouldn't really be that much of a surprise if Albatross were trying to get him in front of the cameras so that he could get as much attention as the young guys get on social media.

Except...I know Cassie wants Mateo. And doesn't that change everything? How could anyone say no to a beautiful pop star who's actively pursuing them?

But somewhere in all the mess, my heart finds hope.

Hope for what, I'm not sure. Even if he isn't dating Cassie, he's certainly not dating me.

"What would someone like her want with someone like him anyway?" Jayce's comment brings me out of my thoughts, turning my blood sour. I cross my arms, lean back in my seat, trying to get closer to the open doorway so I can hear his voice on the other side.

"You mean besides money?" Dan asks.

"Yeah, besides money," Jayce says. "She's a huge pop star.

She doesn't need his money. And if she did actually want a guy with money, there are nineteen other drivers on the grid who would probably happily hit that."

"Don't forget about the married ones."

"Even the married ones," he says, and I blanch. There are six married drivers on the grid and I'm confident none of them would cheat on their wives. Jayce is just projecting because he would cheat on his wife with Cassie if he had one. "Nah, there's no way," he goes on. "If she was going to date any of the guys on the grid, it wouldn't be Mateo."

"Why not? The guy's nice, and he's successful."

"Mateo is ancient. What would they talk about? All he knows is racing. The guy's got nothing to offer."

My head swirls with all the things I want to say: that Mateo isn't ancient, that he has so much to offer, that he's mature and experienced and gorgeous and has a status in this sport that someone like Jayce could only hope to achieve someday.

But of course, I can't say any of it because I'll get my ass sacked. So instead, I quietly gather my camera and sling the strap over my neck before stepping out into the hallway. I step up to Jayce's table, make a show of snapping photos of him and Dan as they relax, Jayce smiling straight at the lens a few times.

And then, because I can't hold it in anymore, I say, "You know, if you can't figure out what someone like Cassie would see in Mateo, maybe you don't know him as well as you think you do."

Dan stops chewing with a mouth full of granola bar, his eyes sliding over to Jayce. Jayce, however, smiles at me. He crosses his arms and leans back in his seat. "Is that so?"

I shrug, trying to seem casual when my blood is boiling with rage over how Jayce spoke about Mateo. I know I shouldn't get so defensive, but isn't it bad enough that Mateo has to listen to what they say about him online without facing this bullshit in the workplace, too?

"Well, maybe I just can't see Mateo through the eyes of someone who's hopelessly in love with him, yeah?"

At that, I stop breathing. When I meet his eye, he grins even wider.

"Maybe you can educate us on that perspective."

I should have kept my mouth shut. But then I think about Mateo on his first day back this season, the way he seemed like he might shatter at any moment. I lean on the table, my palm flat on the surface, and say as quietly as I can, so no one but Jayce can hear, "Jealousy is a natural part of life, Jayce. You'll get there."

His jaw clenches, and I straighten away from the table in time to catch Mateo's eyes across the motorhome. He's watching us with a furrowed brow, and before I can stop myself, I turn my camera on him and take a picture of the expression.

Then I take one of Jayce's, for good measure.

Arabella

When we're in the media pen after a race, I always feel, ironically, less like media and more like a little girl watching her crush from afar.

And after this particular race—Mateo coming in third and Jayce in fifth—I feel even smaller and less significant than usual. Because I know what the questions will be about. And they won't just be about the race.

My job is to keep my eyes open, make sure I know where the drivers are. With everyone all mixed together like this—media, crew members, drivers—it can be really easy to miss someone. But I see Jayce first. He steps up to the microphone.

The interviewer asks him, "It seems like you were really struggling out there with the car. What happened?"

Jayce takes off his cap, runs his fingers through his hair. It sticks up in all directions, and not in a cute way. "That was just a really complicated race. I wasn't being able to get any real downforce. So I just didn't have a ton of grip. I was sliding all over the place. Bad tires. Just not a good week."

"Mateo didn't seem to be having an issue with the car," the interviewer says, and I flinch. It's obvious to anybody with eyes that Jayce has a real problem being the number two on this team. The interviewer knows that and is just playing right into it to cause trouble and get a rise out of Jayce.

Jayce pauses. "Then maybe I shouldn't stick around, if you really want to talk to Mateo about his race. I can just move out of the way," he says, and I bite my lip, walking around the interviewer to the other side to get pictures, even though I know they'll probably have to be scrapped. Jayce wouldn't want anybody seeing him as angry as he currently is, even though this interview is just going to be all over the internet anyway.

"I think you've done a really good job holding your own." The interviewer sidesteps Jayce's comment. "I think you have a real chance to compete with Mateo. What do you think is holding you back?"

"I think I've made it pretty clear it's the car," Jayce says, and I hide behind my camera again. Jayce only made it up to fifth today because an incident managed to take out three cars right on Mateo's ass, letting Jayce squeeze right in.

"Thank you, Jayce," the interviewer says.

And then Mateo is stepping up behind Jayce, clapping him on the shoulder.

Jayce shrugs him off and walks away, and my mind goes

back to what he said to Dan earlier. Jayce might play nice with Mateo most days, but he clearly resents him.

"All right. No love lost between teammates."

I roll my eyes at that. This guy is really going for a good pot-stirring today.

Mateo steps up to the microphone, gives the camera a little half smirk. "Emotions are always high after a race," he says. "It was a tough one in the car for Jayce. That's just how it is sometimes."

"You don't seem to be struggling at all," the interviewer reiterates, and Mateo smiles. The interviewer launches into a long question about strategy and tire performance, and while he listens, Mateo unzips his driver suit, pulling open the neck.

A shiver runs through me, even as I keep my camera steady on him. I'm taking video now, making sure I don't miss out on anything.

"There's been a lot of discussion about whether or not this is going to be a tough season, if it's going to be a real race for the finish, with you, Lola, and Archer being so close in the points and none of you slowing down. Or maybe the second-half curse is still going to make an appearance. What do you think?" the interviewer finally completes his diatribe to ask Mateo. The question burrows under my skin, and I watch Mateo closely for his reaction.

He hesitates as he pulls his driver suit off his shoulders, giving a polite chuckle, letting the question roll off him. I feel like I should look away, like I'm looking at something I shouldn't be seeing, glancing in someone's bedroom window, but I can't tear my eyes away.

"I think it's hard to say," Mateo finally answers, adjusting the collar of his fireproofs. "We're still really early in the season. I really hope I'll be able to give Onyx a run for their money. But I also know how quickly the season can turn around, so all I can do is keep pushing, keep doing my best, keep hoping for the best."

I smile down at my camera, watching Mateo effortlessly handle the media on the screen. He sets both hands on the podium, leans on it in a way that tells me his lower back is aching, but yet, he makes it look so cool. That's when he spots me over the interviewer's shoulder.

His eyes hold mine for a second, some odd expression in them, and then focus back on the person in front of him, the ghost of a smile playing on his lips.

"Mateo, let's talk about Cassie Reese..."

76sheeanpie: Wait is this for real? Cassie Reese???

BronzeAvocado: What is it with Cassie and athletes?

xxHeartEyesCassiexx: Who is this guy? Never heard of him! Totally fake!

youandmebythelake: This is kinda hot button —>

Chapter Twenty-Two

Mateo

I shut off the screen on my phone and toss it onto the table.

"Oh good, you're back with us."

I look up, finding my sister's eyes across the table. She wasn't there a moment ago. At least, not that I can remember.

"Sorry," I say, leaning back and crossing my arms. "I'm distracted."

"You're always distracted," Jimena says. "It's kind of what you're known for." She shrugs, quirking a small smile at me. If I'm known for always being distracted, she's known for being kind to everyone. It's why I love my little sister so much. You can trust her to take care of the unlovable parts of yourself.

She reaches towards the other side of the table, where bottles of liquor are haphazardly piled up next to Crock-Pots and plates of finger foods. This is what always happens when my family gets together, when we all squeeze into the confines of my parents' house. We drink, and we eat, and we laugh.

I try to come into town when I get the chance but Madrid

is far from Barcelona, where I live to be close to the track, so I don't get to join the family get-togethers as often as Jimena, who's only an hour from our parents.

And then, when I am here, it's hard for me to turn it off. It doesn't matter where we are. It doesn't matter who I'm with. I can distract myself for small stretches of time, forget about racing, but my mind always comes back to it when there's even a moment of downtime. If I let myself wander, I'm back there again on the racetrack.

I watch Jimena pour a glass of sangria and push it across the table to me.

"Thank you," I say.

I've had enough to drink, but if she's feeling particularly festive, I'll have another one.

She leans forward on the table, her elbows digging into the tablecloth that my mother always covers all the tables with, like the card tables underneath need to be protected like ancient family heirlooms.

Jimena's eyes slide from one side to the other. "Listen," she says, "I'm not ready to tell everyone else yet, but I know I might not get a chance to see you again for a little while, so I wanted to tell you, and I didn't want to do it over the phone."

"Okay…" I say, glancing down at the liquid in my glass, swirling lightly against the side of the cup, the color of blood.

"You're going to be an uncle."

In moments like this, it's amazing how much the brain can fit into a single second. How fast you can process something, feel one thing, and then force yourself to feel something else.

When she says this, I'm ashamed that the first thing I feel is disappointment. Disappointment that I'll lose a little bit of my sister when she becomes a mother. That she won't be able to travel as much, come see me at the races. Disappointment for the way the world is going to shift just a little bit, altered irrevocably for the rest of our lives.

And then something even more selfish, disappointment that my little sister will no longer be someone I can compare myself to. I've told myself for years that it's okay that I'm not married yet because Jimena wasn't. It was okay that I didn't have a family yet, because Jimena didn't.

But now all of that will change.

She'll have a family and a life, and I'll still be driving.

Our family will start to pick at me. Wonder when I'll quit Formula 1 to have a family. When I'll grow up, as the commentators are so fond of saying.

Back when I was driving for Onyx, I heard one of the engineers say that it was pathetic for a forty-year-old to still be driving in Formula 1.

That forty-year-old wasn't even me back then. But I filed that comment away forever.

I've always had everything I've wanted in life.

Success. Happiness. The world at my fingertips.

I live a fulfilling life. I have a fulfilling career.

I've been told I'm an inspiration. I've been told I've changed lives. I've had people dissolve into tears at meeting me.

The one thing I've never had is a family of my own. And now, Jimena will.

Everything has slowed down. Slow motion in the split second it takes me to run through these things in my mind.

And then, it speeds back up all at once.

"That's amazing," I say, and the feeling is sincere. It's there inside me the same way all the other emotions are. Jimena deserves happiness. She deserves the life she wants.

"You look dumbstruck," she says, smiling.

I feel a real, authentic smile spread across my mouth. "I'm

just a little blindsided. When did this happen? Who's the father?"

"Well..." she says, with a downward curve to all of her features like she's about to deliver bad news. "That's why I haven't told Mama and Papa yet. It was sort of a one-night stand."

"Jimena," I chide. Not because I care whether or not she's having one-night stands. But because maybe if she's going to have one-night stands, she should be more careful about using protection. "So he doesn't know?"

"No," she says in a contemplative tone, pursing her lips. "Do you think I should tell him?"

"I think it's not any of my business." I finally lift the sangria to my lips. I down half the glass and set it back on the table. "Either way, I'm happy for you. Whether there's a dad in the picture or not."

She shrugs. "What do I need him for? He's going to have all the family he needs. He'll have Mama and Papa. And he's going to have you. The best uncle around. He's going to adore you."

"He?"

She makes a face, her red-lipstick mouth twisting. "I've just sort of gotten in the habit of it. Of course, it's way too early to know anything."

"But you're certain?" I ask.

She nods. "I'm certain. I saw a doctor. Six weeks along. Of course, anything could go wrong. But there's no reason to think it would. I'm in perfect health."

She's in perfect health. My beautiful, healthy sister.

"Congratulations, Jimena."

She smiles and settles her chin into her palm. "Thanks, big brother. Maybe we'll raise a little race car driver together."

Her words sock me right in the stomach. I would love that. To raise a little race car driver.

I just wish it was my own.

"Mateo! Jimena!" Our mother is waving us over from where she's lounging beside the pool, surrounded by my aunts.

"Come on, Uncle Mateo," Jimena says, grinning down at me as she gets up to join our family.

Chapter Twenty-Three
Round 6 - Baku, Azerbijan

Lola Castle - 86 points
Archer Hayes - 81 points
Mateo Silva - 77 points

Mateo

"Where is Lola?"

"Don't worry about it, Mateo. Focus ahead."

I hold in a growl. I know it's not Jerry's fault, but I want to know what happened to Lola. She was right behind me and then Thane somehow got ahead of her, and I lost her. And maybe it doesn't matter as long as she stays far enough behind, but if she's fallen out of the points, I want to know, for my own peace of mind.

We've got five laps left, and I'm sitting firmly in fourth place. There's a twelve second gap between me and the guy ahead of me, so I know I've just missed the podium. But it doesn't matter because Lola is far behind me. I know Archer is at the front of the pack, and that he's probably just as much of a threat to me as Lola is at this point, but all I can think about is Lola.

Archer's a great driver, but this isn't going to be his year, and we all know it.

But it might not be mine either.

The last part of the race is fairly uneventful, and then I'm hopping out of my car, my eyes sweeping over the cars behind mine to find Lola's teal car. Like she knows exactly what I'm doing, Lola, standing beside her car, her helmet still on, raises her hand to wave me down.

We meet somewhere in the middle and walk up toward the front of the pit to get weighed. "If we're not careful," she says, "Arch is going to knock us both out."

I smile over at her, though I know she can't really see it behind my helmet. "Had enough of the championship race, Castle?"

She shoots a look at me. "Better watch out, old man."

I throw my head back and laugh, reaching out to put an arm around her shoulders. "Listen to me, Lola. We've got too much at stake here. Archer will get his day."

We stop, and I let her go so we can turn toward each other. We're surrounded by cameras, crew, marshals, everything slowly unraveling from the machine it once was just moments ago.

"I think some would disagree with you," she says, and I'm surprised at how dejected she sounds. She's playing my part, and I'm playing hers, and I don't even know why. Something in the air.

Lola has two championships, one more than me, but the gap between her last win and where we are right now is significantly smaller than my own. She was heading for a championship last year before her accident ripped it away from her. I certainly wasn't.

"Maybe it's time for us to go, Mateo," she says, her voice

small. This is not the Lola I know, but the Lola I know hasn't come eighth in a long time. Her DNF in Miami wasn't her fault. Today's was due to seven people driving faster than her. It's a different kind of loss.

I set a hand on her shoulder, give her a little shake. "Let's make it through this season, yeah? One race at a time." I let her go with a pat. "Get your head out of your ass because I don't want to be fighting Archer alone, okay?"

She smiles. "I'm not missing the action."

"There she is."

We keep walking and it's only then that I realize we're walking right past the Albatross garage. I turn and watch the team already packing up. Right outside the door, camera pointed right at Lola and me, is Arabella. When she sees me looking, she lowers her camera and sends me a thumbs up. Then she cups her hands around her mouth and shouts across the pit lane, "Great race, Mateo and Lola! Let's go! World champions!"

Beside me, Lola laughs and says, "Jesus, she's sweet, isn't she?"

I tear my eyes from Arabella. "Yeah, she is."

Arabella

"Drinks tonight?" I hear a voice say out in the hall. I'm packing up my stuff, watching the sun drop in the distance. It's still early enough that I have a little bit of energy.

It wasn't the kind of draining race I'm used to. Not an emotional rollercoaster. This was an easier one. Even if we didn't get the result we wanted, Mateo coasted in fifth place. It certainly could have been better, but it wasn't bad, by any means. He settled in early, with a big gap in front and a big gap behind, and he just kind of stayed there. Worse track positions have been harder won.

"I heard about this great French place in town."

"Yeah," a couple of voices chime in.

I don't realize I've started rushing until I almost drop my laptop trying to get it into my bag. I don't hang out a lot with the team. Part of it is that I spend so much time with Mateo. And part of it is that I don't have the same kind of technical job as most of the people on the team, so we don't necessarily have anything in common.

So when I get an opportunity, I have to take it. If I want to make friends on the team, and if I want to figure out how and where I fit in, I've got to spend time with people.

I just want to be a part of something. So even as the voices are getting softer, moving away from where I'm at, I zip up my bag and sling it onto my shoulder. I rush into the main lobby of the motorhome and stop.

It's empty. There's no one left.

My shoulders slump so far that my backpack almost slips right off. I sigh.

I've never really felt lonely before. I've always had friends. I've always had my family. I've always had people around me, even if it was a small group.

But it's different being so far from home, having so many responsibilities.

"I thought you would have been long gone by now."

I jump, startled, and turn to find Mateo coming down the stairs from his room. The tips of his hair where they stick out from the bottom of his cap are wet. My eyes flicker over his shoulder. I knew he had a shower in his room. But there's something about knowing he was in the shower...completely naked...while I wasn't that far away from him that makes my skin go hot when I look back at him.

Please don't read my mind.

"I just had some stuff to finish." I gesture vaguely at the door, where I can still see the rest of the team through the glass heading out of the paddock. There's a whole group of them, six, maybe more, laughing, talking so loudly that I can still hear them.

"Did you need to..." he says, nodding in their direction.

"No, it's fine. They, uh, they didn't invite me or anything."

His eyes scan over my face. His is unreadable. "I was just going to go grab some food. Have dinner with me."

My heart starts to race inside my chest. *Have dinner with me.* Such an innocent statement. It would be so easy for me to dig deep, to read into the meaning of an invitation like that.

But I don't.

"Okay," I say, calming my heartbeat. "Sure, let's have dinner."

Chapter Twenty-Four

Arabella

Mateo takes me to the kind of restaurant that doesn't have the prices on the menu, a surefire way to broadcast that if you have to ask for the price, you're not their intended clientele.

They also have caviar on the menu, which I will not be ordering.

Ivy dangles from the ceiling and a sparkling light fixture the size of a swimming pool glows in the middle of the room.

"Why do you have that look on your face?" Mateo asks.

My eyes shoot up. "What?" For a second, I wonder if I've somehow been gazing at him adoringly, but I'm pretty sure I wasn't.

"You look like you've forgotten how to read," he says with a smirk.

I roll my eyes and put my menu down. "I haven't forgotten how to read. I just—" I glance around. "I know you like all of this luxurious stuff," I say to him. "I'm not really used to it is all."

His eyebrows raise. "Is that so?"

"You know that. My dad didn't want to be one of those celebrities who made a bunch of money and then blew it on, like, an island or a private jet or something, just to leave him broke and destitute in his later years."

Mateo laughs, showing me all his perfectly straight teeth. "Are you saying I'm going to be destitute in my old age?"

"You're already in your old age."

At that, he laughs even harder. "You're feisty tonight."

I shrug. "I just think maybe you overestimate how much Albatross is paying me compared to how much they're paying you," I say, with a very pointed look.

I expect him to laugh, but he just scowls. "Are you having trouble getting by?"

I wave off his concern. "Of course not. Albatross is very generous, especially to somebody who has no work experience and is fresh out of college."

"I don't think a year can be considered fresh out of college."

"That's exactly it. I had a year-long gap on my resume when I applied for the team," I tell him, putting my elbows on the table and leaning toward him.

The table is fairly small, and I don't miss the way he leans back away from me, his eyes scanning over me with a weird expression in them. "Is that a big deal?"

Of course he has to ask. Mateo's never had a normal job. Motorsport is what he's done since he was a kid. While other people his age were getting part-time jobs at service stations, he was driving race cars. He had a contract with a racing team before most people his age were graduating high school.

"Yeah, it's kind of a big deal. It doesn't look good. And it kind of makes me think—" I cut myself off. I don't want to bring this up right now.

"It makes you think what?"

I sigh and pick my menu back up, like I can hide behind it. "It makes me think that maybe I was just hired because of who I am. Would they have taken a chance like this on me if I wasn't Pedro Cedillo's daughter?"

He watches me for a long moment. I hold his eye, refusing to back down. "Maybe you were, and maybe you weren't. It doesn't matter. What matters is that you deserve to be here. You're good at what you do. And you enjoy it, right?"

"Of course."

"Then don't worry about it. Keep doing great and the team will keep bringing you back season after season." There's something about the way he says it. So sure, so confident.

Our waiter appears, setting down the drinks we ordered. "Are you ready to order your meals?" he asks.

"Oh," I say, glancing down again at my menu. I didn't even really process what I might want.

"Want me to order for both of us?" Mateo asks in Spanish.

I nod. He orders us both steak and hands our menus to the waiter.

"Thanks," I say. "My head's a little foggy."

He nods but doesn't say anything, and I immediately realize how idiotic I sound.

"God, you're probably a million times more exhausted than I have ever been in my life. I'm so sorry."

"Don't do that," he says, his voice soft. "Don't act like you don't struggle just because your struggle is different from mine. Tell me what's going on."

Mateo

There's something different about Arabella tonight. Something sad. I've known Arabella a few years. I know she always wears a smile, even if it's just to hide her own pain so that she doesn't ruin anyone else's time.

But she's not wearing it now.

"Tell me what's going on."

She shakes her head, bites her lip. "I don't want to sound ungrateful," she says. "I'm so happy to be here. I just don't know if I'm adjusting well, you know? You're so used to doing this. All the travel, all the being away from home. Being surrounded by people but only knowing them on a surface level. I don't know, I just... I wonder if maybe I don't fit in this job."

I watch her across the table, and my skin feels too tight. I'm overwhelmed by this sudden need to fix this for her. To fix everything for her. I don't want to see her l like this. I don't want to see her questioning herself, questioning her place on the team.

"What can I do?" I ask.

"Nothing," she says, running her hands through her hair. "This is why I didn't want to tell you. I don't want to worry you. I don't want to worry anybody. I'm just adjusting, you know?"

"It's a hard lifestyle. It takes a toll on you. And I've seen a lot of people burn out because it just wasn't what they wanted it to be. If you need to leave..."

Her eyes shoot up to mine, a deep, rich brown. "What do you mean?"

"I can get them to let you out of your contract. They can find someone to replace you so you can leave."

"You don't want me here?"

I sit up straight in my chair, surprised at the tightness in my chest. "Of course that's not it. Of course, I want you here. But I don't want you to stay if you're miserable. Having you on the team..." I hesitate, not sure if I should finish my sentence. I settle for looking down at the white tablecloth. "It makes me feel like I have a little bit of home everywhere I go."

Her eyes have gone wide, her cheeks a little pink, and I can't quite decipher why, but I know I shouldn't have said that to her.

I'm looking for the right words to say. Opening my mouth, closing it again, trying to articulate something, when my phone rings. I look down at it. There's no identifying photo. Just a black screen with a name in white letters.

Cassie.

Without hesitating, I reach out and silence the ring.

"Do you want to answer that?" Arabella asks, her eyes on the screen. She can see exactly who it is.

I shake my head.

"Are you—"

The buzz of a text message cuts her off. And then another. And then another.

Her eyes fall to my phone. But I keep my eyes steady on her.

"Let's just enjoy our dinner."

She sends me a closed-lip smile and nods. Just before the waiter brings our dessert, Arabella goes to the bathroom, and I check my phone. I pull up the texts from Cassie. There are three of them.

> **Cassie**
> Hey, I just tried to call.
> I was really hoping to see you soon.
> I'm thinking about coming out to your
> Canadian race. I'm going to be in
> town.

I swipe the notifications away and set my phone back down on the table. I'm not sure what to do about Cassie. In the past, I've been historically bad at saying no to women. And when you're always by yourself, it seems strange to pass up any opportunity for companionship that comes along.

Arabella comes back from the bathroom, and settles into her seat across the table from me. "Everything good?" she asks.

"Maybe it's selfish," I say, "but I don't want you to leave the team."

A slow smile spreads across her mouth. "Then I won't."

And I know it's selfish, but I don't care.

F1FanaticVibes: The second-half curse coming for Mateo

TracksideBanter: Lola too?

PodiumPulse: Anyone think they look like they were fighting after the race?

track_thrills_: Definitely. Their friendship is over. You can't stay friends when fighting for a championship.

Chapter Twenty-Five
Round 7 - Barcelona, Spain

Archer Hayes - 106 points
Lola Castle - 90 points
Mateo Silva - 89 points

Arabella

With the roar of the engines in my ear and the sound of Jerry in my headset, I shuffle through the pictures I took while the boys were getting in their cars. Following them from the motorhome to the garage and then recording them while they get into their gear and load up is probably my favorite part of shooting the races. Watching Mateo smile all the way to the garage and then put on a serious face for the race. It makes my heart gallop.

I shuffle through all the pictures, deleting the blurry ones as I go. I've been known to shoot thousands of photos on race day, a lot of them of the crew and the mechanics while they're getting the car ready, and there's so much movement in the garage that I often get more blurry photos than clear ones. Although, sometimes the blurry ones have the right vibe. The smudge of the blue and silver logos and jackets everywhere can sometimes have a nice look to it, like neon in a dark city landscape.

Flip. Flip. Flip.

I get to the bank of photos of Mateo putting on his gear. He stops to give fist bumps as he pulls on his balaclava and his gloves. He zips up his suit, fixes the collar of his fireproofs, puts on his helmet, and then turns right toward the camera.

When you're Mateo Silva, you're used to being followed around by a camera. The comments on absolutely every single media post I've ever made always say the same thing: "Give us more Mateo content." No one cares about Jayce, which I understand. The camera doesn't like the twist of his smile quite as much, his John Lennon sunglasses and the scrap of a mustache he sometimes lets grow out before shaving it off again.

But Mateo? The camera loves him. His chiseled jaw and effortless scruff. The way he runs his fingers through his hair like a goddamn fashion model. He's been doing this for almost twenty years, and he knows what to do to please the fans.

In the picture I'm looking at though, it's like he doesn't even see the camera. I had it down at my waist, the screen tilted up toward him, and I think I might have caught Mateo off guard, one of his hands still partially extended to fist bump a mechanic as he moved through the garage. All I can see of his face are his eyes, staring right at the camera through the open visor of his helmet. There's so much sincerity in those eyes, not putting on a show for anyone, just looking ahead at what's next.

It's like he's looking right through the camera and directly into the crack in my chest. How does he always do that?

"Box, box."

The words in my ear shake me out of my thoughts. I probably have less than a minute before Mateo slams into the pit lane, and my tripod isn't ready. I finish my adjustments, trying to be in the perfect position to catch a picture of the car without actually being in the way of anybody. Pit stops are chaotic and precise, and the last thing I want is to be the reason the mechanics took an extra second getting Mateo back on the track.

I settle in and wait for the stop. I always photograph the first pit stop for both drivers. Jayce has already come through. Once I'm done here, I'll walk the track and try to get some good snaps of the cars in motion.

The Albatross slides into the pit, comes to a hard stop. Less than three seconds. That's what I've got to get a good photo. But even as I'm thinking it, my eyes are caught on Mateo's gold helmet in the cockpit.

How many times have I been on the receiving end of these pictures, staring at that helmet on a screen and wondering what's going on in his head mid-race? I do it even now, imagining the thoughts moving through him in this split second.

I don't want you to leave the team.

Mateo sitting across the table, soft in the light of the chandelier, golden eyes shining, saying the words that have buried deep into the marrow of my bones.

I don't want you to leave.

I snap back to reality, realizing too late that I've missed the pit stop. When I snap a photo, all I get is the Albatross's rear wing.

Arabella

"Go, Mateo, go!" I scream, clasping Brigit's hand as hard as I can in mine. She's got her eyes on the screen, too, both of us watching as the drivers swing into the second to last lap of the race.

"There's no way," Brigit says in my ear. "There's no way. He's too far. He's not going to be able to get into DRS range."

"Yes, he is," I say, confident. The gap between him and Archer is closing. But I don't know if it's closing fast enough. I can't let myself think he's not going to win today. It's his home race, and he's so close.

I watch the space between him and Archer close on the readout. 0.6 seconds. Then 0.5. One more lap.

"Come on," I say. "Come on, you've got this, you've got this."

The whole crew is out of their seats, gazes fixed on the broadcast. 0.38 seconds.

"If he's going to do it, he's got to do it now," Brigit says.

They move around the last turn, and it's like Mateo's car turns into a rocket ship. There's barely enough room for him to even exist. He pulls beside Archer, the two of them neck and neck for just a moment.

And then Mateo pulls ahead.

Everyone in the garage screams. I can't make a single noise. I just watch, amazed. It's not over yet. But as they pull into the main straight, careening toward the finish line, Mateo is just far enough ahead of Archer, by just half a car length, the two of them beside each other again.

And that's how they cross the finish line. As the commentators shout out Mateo's name, I scream. And then me and Brigit are jumping up and down, hugging each other.

Because Mateo's back. He was down, but he's never out.

Chapter Twenty-Six

Mateo

"I'm kidnapping you."

I startle Arabella, and she jumps about a foot in the air before realizing it's me. When she does, she laughs, hiking her camera bag up on her shoulder. On instinct, I take it from her and sling it over my own.

"Where are we going?" she asks as we slip through the paddock toward the parking lot. People stop us every few feet to clap me on the back or tell me congratulations.

My insides feel light. Winning today was what I needed, like a salve to a burn. And now all I want is to celebrate.

"My sister is going to meet us at a salsa bar in Tarragona, but it's almost an hour drive, so we have to go." At that, I take her by the elbow and we laugh as we hurry to my car.

She doesn't even question me. She throws her stuff in the backseat and hops in, rolling down the window to let in the warm summer air as we drive along the coast.

"I forgot how beautiful it is here," she says, her hair flying in the wind.

"Jimena is so excited to meet you."

At this, she twists to face me. "I'm so nervous."

I wave her comment away. "Don't be nervous! It's just Jimena. She's going to love you!"

Even over the wind, I hear her snort. "Sure, I'll just stop being nervous. Thanks for your words of wisdom."

I laugh. "You're going to have a great time." I take her hand that's resting on the console between us and give it a squeeze, a short thing to let her know I'm here and that everything is okay.

After that, she goes silent, turning to look out the window as we drive out of Barcelona, and it's a long time before I realize I still have her hand in mine.

Mateo

We decide to go to El Ritmo, a salsa bar in the city. Jimena and I have spent hours in this place, filled with good food and even better drinks and live music. Two men are set up in the corner of the patio, one singing and playing the trumpet, the other on a keyboard.

Jimena is waiting for us outside, and when she sees us, her whole face lights up. She rushes over to meet us, immediately pulling Arabella into a hug and kissing her on both cheeks, leaving smears of red lipstick behind.

"It's so good to finally meet you!" Jimena says, pulling back but keeping her hands on Arabella's waist.

Arabella smiles. "I feel like I already know you from all of Mateo's stories."

As they continue talking, a few men at a table nearby look over at us. I see one of them recognize me. He smacks the guy next to him and then leans over and says something to him under the music.

I see it move through people like a wave, until, right there on the patio, the music still flowing over all of us, a chant begins. Quietly at first, slowly getting louder.

"Mateo! Mateo! Mateo!"

It's clear the moment Arabella realizes what's happening. She stops mid-sentence and looks around, her head perking up like a dog hearing a siren. A smile spreads across her face, and she spins toward me, immediately joining in with the chant. I don't look at anyone else, just watch her as she claps and shouts, like she's a cheerleader at an American football game.

"Oh, come on," Jimena says, rolling her eyes and then latching onto my elbow to pull me into the restaurant.

There are so many people pressed inside and I look over at Arabella to try and get a read on how she's feeling. She has a light sheen of sweat on her face that makes her glisten, and under the blue light of the bar, it's like we're underwater. It casts blue onto everything. The bar stools, the bar, the liquor bottles lined against the wall.

She looks back at me and laughs. "You look like one of those aliens from *Avatar*."

"From what?" I ask.

"You know," she says, "the big blue people from the movie."

"Do you mean like Smurfs?"

She seems to find this hilarious. She throws her head back and laughs, and I feel this strange joy fizzle in my stomach. I have this intense feeling of contentment, like nothing bad is ever going to happen again in the world, at least not to me.

"What do you want to drink?" I ask her.

She stands on her tiptoes to see the bar between the shoulders of the people crowded around it. "Let's just have some tequila," she says. "We can do shots."

I push up to the bar, leaving Arabella and Jimena to talk.

"Hey, man!" the bartender says in Spanish, pointing up to a flatscreen behind the bar, which I realize is still playing race coverage. My face is all over it. "Your drink's on the house tonight!"

"Thanks!" I shout over the music drifting in from the outside patio. I accept the shot of tequila and swirl my finger through the air. "A round of drinks for everyone, on me!"

Everyone nearby cheers, and I take two shots and a water back to Arabella and Jimena.

"*Salud*," I say, tapping my shot against Jimena's water glass and then Arabella's shot, and then we all throw our drinks back, Arabella hissing through her teeth when hers is gone.

"I ordered tapas," I tell them. "We just need to find a table."

"Let's go outside," Jimena suggests.

"But what about the vibes?" Arabella argues. Then, in the middle of the bar, with people pressing into her on both sides, Arabella throws her hands up and does this little shimmy with her hips.

"You can't possibly already be drunk after one shot," Jimena says, laughing.

"I'm not drunk," Arabella says. "I'm high on life. We're in Spain! Mateo won!"

This makes me laugh, too. "Of course you're in Spain," I yell back at her. "Two-thirds of us live here."

It's impossible for me to see the shade of her skin, but I'm almost certain she blushes. "Fine, let's go outside," she finally says.

"Did you order more drinks?" Arabella asks as we go outside.

"Margaritas," I tell her, not mentioning that Jimena's will be virgin.

We find a table not far from the band, but I can tell Arabella is sad to be sitting. She wiggles in her chair, like she can't sit still. Jimena watches her, a kind affection in her eyes.

Our tapas and margaritas arrive, and it's kind of nice, not talking. It would be exhausting to try and yell over the band. Instead, it's nice to just be here, to drink margaritas, eat Spanish food that I don't really get on the road, and listen to the man crooning into the microphone about his lost love.

My eyes tip over to Arabella. I know she says she's having a good time, but I can't help but wonder if she feels out of place here. Spain is her heritage, where her father came from, but she didn't grow up here. Pedro left Spain long before Arabella was born. He moved to Canada to be with Arabella's mother, but she seems to have it in her blood. She's scarfing down the tapas, watching the man behind the microphone sing as if he's singing right to her, as if she understands every word, even though I know her Spanish isn't strong.

By the time the food is gone and Jimena and Arabella have had two margaritas each, people have begun to dance on the slab of concrete in front of the restaurant. It's not a dance floor, but energy is high, and everyone's drunk and happy, so why not?

I'm laughing to myself at a couple that's pressed together a little indecently when a guy my father's age sidles over to our table. He looks sheepish, but apparently not sheepish enough to keep him from approaching. He puts out his hand, grabs my shoulder, shakes with a force that's almost shocking.

"I'm a big fan," he says, the way they always do. "You're gonna win this season. I don't think there's any question. There's no way you don't have it in the bag." His accent isn't Spanish. I can't quite identify what it is, something vaguely Eastern European.

"I don't have it in the bag," I tell him, feeling generous enough to joke with him. I'm full of good food and good feelings, sitting at a table with two people I care about very much. So even though I hate being approached in public, I smile at the man. "Lola will probably wipe the floor with me."

"Eh, come on," the guy says, crouching down beside my chair and waving my words off. "Don't you think Lola's had enough?"

I'm not entirely positive what he means by that.

"Enough what?" I ask with a laugh. "Trophies? I think she's still got room in her museum."

The guy laughs at that. "Nah," he responds when he's composed himself again. "How many championships does a woman need anyway?"

I grimace, all my good cheer fading quickly. "Well, the record is seven, so I'm guessing eight."

He shakes his head, rolls his eyes. He thinks we're still buddies, thinks I'm still in the mood to joke with him. "Women don't belong in the sport. She's just got a good car. Archer's proof of that."

By now, I can see out of the corner of my eye that Arabella and Jimena are listening. I glance over and see that Arabella's fists are balled in her lap.

I don't look back at the guy as I say, "Considering that Lola Castle will eat me alive if I so much as stumble on the track, I think that this sport is definitely a place for a woman. If you'll excuse me..."

I reach over and grab one of Arabella's clenched fists. I pull her up out of her chair. She doesn't question me, and I don't even really know what I'm doing. All I know is that I need to get away from this asshole who thinks he knows anything about Formula 1.

Arabella follows me into the dancing crowd. So many bodies, pressed in close to the band.

"That guy was a piece of shit," she tells me when we stop moving. "Lola could stomp him into dust."

"That's the point," I tell her, bending down to say it right into her ear. I take both of her hands in mine, warm and sweaty. "A man like that will never have any kind of true skill behind the wheel, and he's angry that a woman does. So he'll try to diminish her, turn her into nothing. But do you think Lola has ever spared a thought for a man like him?"

She grins up at me.

"No. Because Lola is going to continue to win championships while he sits at home and cries about it."

She giggles, her mouth pulling wide. She's sweating in the early summer air, the little curls around her face sticking to her skin. Her smile dims a little. "You still think she's going to win, don't you?"

I shrug. "I think she's been fifteen or more points ahead of me all season. She's in a position to dominate."

She shakes her head. "You won a race four hours ago! I think you still have it in you."

Instead of answering, I start to sway my hips, take a small step forward, take a small step back, hoping she'll join me.

"Let's dance," I tell her.

"What, here?" she asks, her eyes going wide. I never noticed how big her eyes are until this moment.

"We're at a salsa bar," I tell her. "Is there a better place?"

"I don't even know how to salsa," she says.

"You're fine," I tell her. "Just follow me."

She gets the basic step easily, her eyes taking in everyone around us, watching what they're doing. Some people are pressed close together, just moving their hips, and some of them are all-out dancing, swinging each other around with skill.

I may be one of the best Formula 1 drivers in the world, but I'm not one of the best salsa dancers in the world.

"Your parents never taught you how to salsa?"

"They tried," she says. "I'm just not very good at it."

"You just have to trust your body," I say. "Listen to the rhythm." I put a hand on her hip to guide her. She stumbles but I hold tight to her so she doesn't fall. When she's steady again, her eyes meet mine. In the rope lights, I can tell her cheeks have turned pink, and I watch the color get darker as it spreads across her skin.

"What is this song about?" she asks me, her voice just barely audible under the noise of the music.

This makes me finally rip my gaze from hers. I can't tell her what the song is about. I can't tell her the song is about sex. That it's about the shape of a woman's body and how it's perfect against the singer's.

"Love," I tell her instead.

She smiles, rolls her eyes. "Aren't they all?" She shifts, moving her hands up to my shoulders. I find myself straightening further, my skin suddenly feeling very sensitive under her hands. She twists her hips to the left and then to the right. My eyes drop. The sight of it is intoxicating.

"Like that?" she asks, rolling her entire body.

"Yes," I breathe. There's a layer of sweat on her bare shoulders and her chest, right above the neckline of her top. My eyes are caught there. I move them up her long neck to where she's looking at me with those eyes, like she's waiting to hear what I'll say next.

I take her hands, sliding my fingers all the way up her elbows, I see a shiver move through her, which seems impossible because it's so hot. Then she's against me. Our fingers intertwine on one side and I take her hip in my hand on the other. I'm shocked by how natural it feels. She fits perfectly against me.

As we move our hips and feet to the rhythm, I press my cheek to hers. I can smell the slight tang of her sweat and something else, some kind of floral perfume. I breathe it in.

The song ends. Before it can quickly shift into the next, I step back, letting her go.

What the fuck am I doing? This is Arabella. This is my best friend's daughter. She may be moving against me like it's completely natural. She may look good in those tight jeans she's wearing, the ones that show every single curve of her. But having my hands on her isn't innocent.

I leave her in the middle of the dance floor and go back to Jimena. Her eyes watch me closely as I gulp down what's left of my margarita, letting it cool my blood.

F1ReviewerX: MATEEEEEEEO!!

MFDiaz: A home race win from the GOAT!

Hulkster: Anyone checked on Archer Hayes lately?

HealthDrivenF177: Podium Mateo just hits different...

Chapter Twenty-Seven
Round 8 - Montreal, Canada

Archer Hayes - 116 points
Mateo Silva - 114 points
Lola Castle - 105 points

Arabella

I sigh and look out my bedroom window down at Montreal. I have to admit it's pretty exciting to not have to get on a plane this week. Sleeping in on a day when I would normally be fighting traffic to get to the airport was downright luxurious.

And tomorrow morning, I can casually make my way down to the circuit.

Even as I'm thinking it, there's a knock at my door. I scowl at it. Maybe it's my dad, coming to check with me before the race. Or maybe even Lana, who's coming into town for the after-party, even if she's not interested in coming to the race.

But when I open my door, it's to find Mateo on the other side.

My heart positively stops beating.

"Hi!" He grins. "I hope it's okay that I came by."

"Of course," I say, ushering him into my living room. But then I realize the mistake I've made. Because now Mateo is inside my home, and all the chill has left my body. All that's left is the knowledge that I will never be able to exist in this space again without seeing him in it.

I'm very aware that I have dirty dishes piling up and move into the kitchen to pretend that's exactly what I was taking care of when he knocked.

"So, what's up?" I ask him over my bar as I open my dishwasher.

"I thought you might want to grab some food," he says. This has become our thing, it would seem, eating dinner together after races. Only, it's a few days until the race and Mateo is choosing to spend his time with me.

Stay calm.

"Yeah, sure," I tell him, scrubbing some dishes from yesterday. "You don't want to go out with Felix, or one of the guys? Jayce?"

He shrugs, perching on the armrest of my couch, hands in pockets. "I'd rather go out with you."

The world tips over. "Okay, yeah, okay. Where to?"

"You decide." He jumps up. I scan him, taking in his baseball cap, his athletic shorts, his trainers. He doesn't look like someone who's about to go out for a nice dinner. He looks like someone who's about to go for a run. But that's just Mateo.

I put my shoes on and lock up.

"Are you enjoying being home on race weekend?" he asks on the way to the elevator. He presses the button, and I watch it light up red.

"Definitely beats yet another hotel."

The doors slide open and we step inside. I watch the numbers on the display count down and down and down. The doors open to the lobby and we both step out.

And then we both come to a stop. Because outside the

lobby doors is a tidal wave of people. They're lined up on the sidewalk, spanning the length of the front windows of the building. People with Spanish flags, signs, giant cutouts of Mateo's face. I know the drivers deal with this every race weekend outside their hotels, but... outside my apartment?

"You were here for thirty seconds," I say.

He groans and runs a hand down his face. "I don't even know how anyone knew I was here."

"Someone must have put it up on social media."

Luckily, I can afford an apartment in a building with a doorman, who is actively keeping people out of the building. But he can't protect us once we hit the sidewalk.

"There's a back exit," I say, grabbing on to the sleeve of Mateo's jacket and pulling him down the hallway. "If we hurry, we can get out before anyone has figured out what's happened."

We go down a long hallway and then take a right at the emergency exit that spits us out into the alley behind my building.

"What now?" he asks. "We can't get to my car."

And just as he says it, someone appears at the end of the alley, not much more than a silhouette in the setting sun. "Mateo!" they call.

We don't hesitate. We turn in the opposite direction and run. It's a short alley and we turn right onto a busy sidewalk, almost slamming into a group of fans, two of them wrapped in Spanish flags.

"Sorry," I say, even though they're the ones who are following us. And I think they're still trying to figure out exactly what's going on while we're already taking off again. We cross the street and take a side route between two buildings, then a right through another alley.

I keep pulling Mateo along, taking in where I am, trying to orient every time we turn on a street I'm not prepared for. There's a seafood restaurant down the next street that I know we'll be safe in.

But when I stick my head out of the alley and look both ways, I catch sight of the same group of fans, the ones with the flags, standing on the curb just outside the alley.

Before I have a chance to move, Mateo pulls me back into the alley, pushing me against the brick building behind me and putting a finger over his lips. I forget all about the fans, forget about where we are. Mateo is so close that his breath is puffing out onto my mouth. He glances to his right, his attention pulled, listening for footsteps. But all I can focus on is him.

If I wanted to, I could reach out and touch the scruff on his jaw. Trace the curve of his ear. Feel how soft his skin is.

"I think they're gone," he says, turning back to me. He seems to realize in an instant how close we are, that his hands are clutching my upper arms even though they don't need to, that our knees are touching, our shoes overlapping each other.

He opens his mouth to say something, just as his cell phone rings.

"Shit," he says, stepping back to pull it out of his pocket. He scowls at the screen and glances up at me. Those amber eyes, dark in the shadow of the alleyway.

"What is it?" I ask, imagining a call from my father, maybe even Felix.

Without answering me, he swipes the call, puts the phone to his ear. "Cassie," he says, his eyes never leaving mine.

I can hear her voice on the other end, though I can't make out what she's saying.

"Oh," he says, finally turning his back to me. He paces away from me down the alleyway, his head bowed as he listens. "I didn't know you were planning to do that," he says, rubbing the back of his neck while I watch.

I realize I'm still pressed against the building and push

away from it, hearing Mateo talk to Cassie as he gets further from me.

When he's almost to the other end of the alley, he turns and meets my eye. "Yeah, that'll be fine," he says, loud enough for me to hear. He comes back to me quickly and pulls the phone away from his ear. "Is it alright if Cassie has dinner with us?"

"Cassie Reese?" I ask, as if I don't already know. What a nonsensical thing to even ask.

He nods. "She's in town for the race."

"I can just go back to my apartment," I say, feeling the panic rise in me at the idea of having to sit at a dinner table with Cassie and Mateo, the two of them flirting and making eyes at each other. My stomach turns.

"No," he says, putting out a hand to stop me. "No, I promised you dinner. It's okay, it's not like it's..." He shakes his head.

"A date?" I ask.

His eyes meet mine. "No," he says, sounding far less sure now. "No, it's nothing like that. She said it's fine if you come. She just wants to know where we're eating."

Against my better judgment, I tell him the name of the seafood place that's just a block or two from here. He nods and relays the information to Cassie. I hear her answer in the affirmative before hanging up.

"Sorry," he says with a nervous chuckle. "I had no idea she was going to be in town this early. She didn't say anything."

"She probably just wanted to surprise you." The words taste bitter coming out of my mouth.

Mateo glances at me. "Maybe."

"There's no maybe about it, Mateo," I say, turning away from him and glancing out into the street.

When I don't see anyone suspicious-looking, I step out into the sun. I motion for him to follow me, and we start walking. There are no fans in sight, but every once in a while, someone does glance at Mateo. There are probably tons of people in town for the race, and we're only a few miles from the racetrack, so it's to be expected.

"She seems to really like you," I say, and I immediately want to clamp my mouth shut permanently. Why did I say that? Maybe because I desperately want to understand what's going on between the two of them. But I can't just outright ask, right?

Mateo makes a noncommittal noise. "I think she's just having a bit of fun. The team's been pushing it because they know it would be good for engagement."

My head snaps toward him. "What, so they want you to date her just so you look good on social media?"

He shrugs. "It's not like anyone's adding stipulations to my contract or anything. Everyone just agrees it couldn't hurt."

"But what do *you* want?" I ask.

He opens his mouth, face turned toward me, but again is cut off by the likes of Cassie Reese.

"Mateo!" Her voice floats toward us as a driver helps her out of the backseat of a town car. She bounces a little when she sees us, her long, dark hair swirling around her. The sight of her makes my steps stutter.

I wasn't expecting Mateo to show up at my door to whisk me off to dinner, so it's not as if I was dressed for this. I'm just in my casual clothes: jeans and a button-up blouse. But Cassie looks like she's getting ready to walk a runway in a corset top and a denim skirt.

She rips off her sunglasses and rushes over to throw her arms around Mateo. His eyes flash to me over her shoulder, then away again.

I don't know what that expression is about. If he feels guilty about inviting Cassie when he was supposed to be having dinner with me, then why did he insist I come to dinner with them?

"Arabella, right?" Cassie says, spinning toward me.

She smiles so big, like I'm her long-lost twin or something. And I'm surprised when she bends forward to hug me, too. She has to bend to hug both of us, me and Mateo. We're roughly the same height, and she's nearly six feet, even without the heels.

"Thank you so much," she says when she lets me go, squeezing my upper arms. "I didn't mean to barge in on your dinner."

"It's no problem," I say, even though it is. I can't imagine a bigger problem than this right now, than the fact that I'm about to sit in on a date with the man I love and the woman he might be seeing.

This is a worst-case scenario, if I've ever seen one.

"I've eaten at this place a million times, so I know it's really good. Great pasta." My voice doesn't sound normal, but seeing as Cassie has only met me once, I don't think she notices.

But from the way Mateo is watching me out of the corner of his eye, I think he might.

"Ooh!" Cassie says. "I love pasta. And seafood pasta is the absolute best. Shrimp." She does a little chef's kiss with her hand.

Mateo smiles at her. "Let's get a table," he says.

Chapter Twenty-Eight

Mateo

The problem is that I have a hard time saying no to people. Sure, I can say no to an F1 boss. I can say no to shitty contracts. But it's hard for me to say no when someone is asking me for something perfectly doable. Something like grabbing dinner.

And there was Cassie, on the phone, telling me she flew all the way to Montreal from LA just to see me race.

And there was Arabella, already with me because I dragged her away from whatever she was doing in the comfort of her own home. I couldn't say no to Cassie, just like I couldn't say no to Cassie the first time. But I also didn't just want to send Arabella back to her apartment. I wasn't ready for her to be gone.

So here we are, in the middle of a seafood restaurant, people glancing our way while we sit at a round table, me on one side and Arabella and Cassie on the other. Luckily this place is nice enough that no one takes out cell phones and snaps pictures of us.

"So how are things looking for the race on Sunday?" Cassie says, unwrapping her silverware. "Is this a track you feel really confident at?"

I make a face.

"It's not a good track for the car." Cassie and I both look over at Arabella. Her eyes flicker up to me, then Cassie. "Sorry, I just... I was talking to Brigit about it yesterday." She turns to Cassie. "She's one of the mechanics on the team. And she said you guys aren't really expecting a great result."

"Well, aren't you always expecting a great result? Or at least, hoping for one?" Cassie says.

I give her a so-so gesture. "We always hope for a great result, but we also understand that certain tracks do better for certain cars and certain drivers."

She leans forward, settling her jaw in her palm, like she's endlessly fascinated by the subject. "What tracks are you good at? Like, which ones do you expect the best results at?"

I find myself looking to Arabella again, surprised to realize that I expect her to know the answer just as well as I do.

"Baku," I say.

"Definitely Barcelona," Arabella adds. "Monaco, obviously."

"Why obviously?" Cassie looks back and forth between us.

"He won at Monaco earlier in the season," Arabella says.

"I don't really know a whole lot about the championship," Cassie says. "I'm kind of new to the whole sport. If you win one race, what does it mean?"

Arabella and I spend the next twenty minutes explaining the basics of Formula 1 to Cassie as our drinks are brought to us and then our food. I can't help but eye Arabella's shrimp pasta while Cassie talks about her upcoming tour.

"We're going to start in the U.S., of course, and early next year, we'll be going worldwide."

"Do you like all the travel?" I ask a little absently.

It's the kind of question it feels like you're supposed to ask, not because you actually care. While Cassie talks, Arabella raises her eyebrows at me, noticing the way I'm eyeballing her food.

She nudges her plate towards me, and I send her a questioning look, even as Cassie continues to talk about her favorite tour stops in Europe.

"You know all about traveling in Europe," Cassie says.

Arabella nods to me, and I extend my fork to spear one of her pieces of cooked shrimp and shove it in my mouth.

This catches Cassie's attention, and her words falter. She looks over at Arabella and then at me. I can't decipher the expression on her face. "Oh, did you want some?" she asks, offering me her plate.

I shake my head. "I just wanted a taste," I say around the buttery shrimp in my mouth.

I can't imagine taking food off of Cassie Reese's plate, a woman I've been in the same room with three times in my life. But it feels natural to reach over and grab one more piece of Arabella's shrimp.

She laughs. "You should have just ordered your own."

"I didn't want my own; I wanted some of yours."

This makes Arabella laugh again, and Cassie leans back in her seat, watching us.

Maybe we're being rude. I'm not sure. I'm not always very good at reading social situations.

Arabella's eyes catch on Cassie. She seems to notice the same discomfort I do because she smiles big and says, "I really love Italy, too. We're going there in a couple of weeks. What are your favorite sightseeing spots?"

That seems to rouse Cassie back to the conversation. We chat about our work through the rest of dinner, and then the three of us stand on the sidewalk, waiting for Cassie's car.

I know Cassie is hoping I'll get in her car with her. She's

made several comments about how the bar at her hotel is the best. I can tell by the way she stands with her car door open, moving toward it slowly, but there's no way I'm making Arabella walk back to her place alone.

"How about a nightcap?" Cassie finally asks under her breath, sucking her bottom lip into her mouth, eyes shooting over to where Arabella waits.

I'll be the first to admit I've slept with women I wasn't romantically interested in. I've slept with women I thought were boring or rude or just in it for a good story. But the thought of doing that now, of doing it in front of Arabella, makes me feel uneasy, like needles under my skin.

"Next time," I tell Cassie, leaning forward to peck her on the cheek before handing her into her car.

As soon as she drives away, I walk back to Arabella. Without a word, we turn toward her apartment, this time avoiding alleys.

Arabella shivers, and I slip off my jacket, quickly draping it over her shoulders without missing a step.

"Thank you," she whispers, like she's afraid she might speak too loudly and bother someone in one of the apartment buildings we pass.

When we get to Arabella's building, I walk her inside, heading for the elevator, but she stops.

"You don't need to walk me all the way up," she says, taking off my jacket and offering it to me.

I take it but still say, "I would prefer to walk you up. I would hate for something to happen in the corridor. And I don't mind. Nowhere to be." I put my jacket back on, and she doesn't protest as I walk to the elevator.

We get in, standing just as we did going down earlier this evening, but something has changed. I'm not sure what it is. It's like the light atmosphere from before, the way Arabella seemed to glow as we headed for the restaurant, it's all dimmed now.

The elevator doors close, and I watch Arabella in the golden reflection of the mirrored doors. She's standing far enough forward that she's almost in front of me. I can see her perfectly in the reflective metal.

"Are you with her?" she asks.

My calculating brain tries to make sense of what she's just asked me. "Am I with who?" I ask.

She crosses her arms, bites her lip, looks down at her feet. "Cassie," she finally spits out.

The question surprises me. Not just because I don't understand why Arabella would care, but because I don't know how she could still be unsure when she just sat through whatever that was with Cassie tonight. Then again, I don't even know what Cassie and me are. Maybe Cassie doesn't know either. And if we don't know, then how can I expect Arabella to know?

With her eyes on me, I come up with an answer. I look at her now, our eyes meeting in the reflection of the door. "No, I'm not with her."

She takes a breath, a long pause. "Do you want to be?"

I don't hesitate this time. "No."

Something seems to harden in her expression. Her chin comes up, her shoulders back. She drops her arms at her sides. I don't know what she's doing, what she's thinking, what's happening.

So I just wait. Wait for her to ask more questions. Wait for her to explain. Maybe she understands something now about me that I don't quite understand myself.

She spins in my direction. I expect her to say something scathing. She has an almost angry look on her face.

And then she takes hold of my face, her soft, warm hands cupping my jaw, leans forward and kisses me.

For a second, I'm so shocked that I just stand there. She holds her mouth to mine like she's never kissed anyone before, like she's afraid to move, and then pulls back just an inch.

Her eyes stay closed, while mine run over her face. The way her features have gone soft. The way she has just a light layer of eyeshadow on her lids. The way she's so warm.

I'm not sure who closes the inch the second time, me or her. But for just a moment, we kiss. A soft, gentle, barely-there thing.

I sigh against her mouth.

The elevator dings and the doors open. Arabella jerks away from me, her eyes springing open, her hands still up, now curled awkwardly.

"I don't know why I did that," she says.

I open my mouth to answer. But she's already gone.

Chapter Twenty-Nine

Arabella

Holy shit, holy shit. What did I just do?

I practically run down the hallway to my apartment, shove my key into the lock, and slam the door shut behind me. I scrub my hands over my face.

Why did I do that? I don't know why I did that. I temporarily lost my mind. Oh, fuck.

I just ruined everything. I've managed the last six years without anybody knowing I'm obsessed with Mateo. And now I have made it very clear to the very last person who should know.

And there's no taking it back. This isn't some drunk confession. This isn't some weird text message. It's not something I can pass off as something else.

I kissed him.

I set my head back against the door, wrap my arms around myself.

I know why I did it. I know deep in my bones. Because these last few weeks have been torture. Watching the media turn what was going on between him and Cassie into something it wasn't. Not being sure I wasn't reading it all wrong. Feeling this desperation under my skin because all I want in this world is for Mateo to be mine. And maybe there was a time in my life where that was a ridiculous, idiotic dream. But not anymore.

In my logical brain, I know this could never really happen. He's my father's best friend. Papa would kill us. Not to mention I'd probably get fired. I don't even know what the rule is about team fraternization or whatever it is.

And the cherry on top: Mateo doesn't see me that way.

Except... he kissed me back.

All I know is my heart belongs to him and will always belong to him. And all the other stuff doesn't really matter because if I thought for one second that he might want it too, that there was any way he could be mine, I'd throw all of it away in a heartbeat.

Mateo

When the elevator doors open in the lobby, I just stand there. Somewhere down the hallway, I can hear voices. I can't seem to make myself move.

The doors close again. The elevator doesn't move because I haven't hit any buttons. I'm still just standing here, trying to sort through what just happened.

Arabella kissed me. I kissed Arabella.

I loved kissing Arabella. It was sweet, and she smelled amazing. I could feel the gentle weight of her against me.

What am I doing? What am I doing?

Even as I'm asking myself, trying to talk some sense into

myself, I reach over and hit the button for her floor again. The elevator moves just as slowly up as it did before.

When the doors open, I step out into the hallway, stare down at the ugly pattern on the carpet, and then I realize this is a terrible idea. What am I going to do? If I go and knock on her door, and she opens it, then what?

What the hell am I going to do then? Kiss her again? Touch her? Do things with her I can't take back?

I press my back to the wall. Stand there.

I have no idea what's going on, but my skin aches. My blood is boiling.

Because I want to kiss her again. I want to taste her again. I want to taste much, much more of her. I don't even know when this happened. I don't even know what this is.

I just know it's not okay. I turn around, get back in the elevator, and take it down to the lobby.

As I'm stepping out into the night, I pull out my phone and text Cassie.

Mateo
Hey, it's been really great getting to know you, but I don't think you should come to the race tomorrow.

Chapter Thirty

Arabella

"This is so exciting." My father is practically bouncing in his seat like a child on his way to Disneyland.

"Dad, you have to calm down," I say, pulling my car into the team parking lot.

"It's okay, I'll be chill once we're inside," he says, "but let me be excited about it, yeah?"

I smile over at him, remembering that this is the reason I did all of this, the reason I know I can't leave. Because he's always wanted me to be part of his world. And now I am. And once I got a degree in photography and had the opportunity, it just made sense.

We get a parking space, and I grab my bags out of the back, my father taking one of them as we head for the turnstile.

"So what do you do all day?" he asks.

I shoot him a look and pull his paddock pass out of my pocket to hand it to him. "What do you mean, what do I do all day?"

He shrugs. "Is all you do is take pictures?"

"You make it sound like an easy job."

"Well, don't you have a degree so it will be easy for you?"

"That's not how it works," I say, rolling my eyes. "Yes, I take pictures all day and then I edit them and I post them, but it's not like taking a selfie on your phone."

"Well, I would hope not," he says, patting the camera bag that's slung over his shoulder. "I would hate to think you're carrying these things around when all you have to do is snap photos on your phone."

I just smile and keep walking. He doesn't mean anything by it and he doesn't think I have an easy job. He just doesn't understand the work that goes into getting one really good shot, especially when cars are flying past you at 200 kilometers per hour.

"What are you going to do all day?" I ask him. "You can't just sit around and bug Mateo. He's going to be extremely busy."

He rolls his eyes back at me. "You really think that I need someone to explain everyone's responsibilities on race day?"

"It's been a while since you've been a driver. I thought maybe you forgot what it's like to be a high-performance athlete."

He gives me a gentle shove that just barely knocks me off balance.

I see his eyes sweep back and forth as we move through the paddock. Yes, he gets to be in the paddock, but Albatross is the only team that invited him to spend the day at their motorhome, which means he's going to be a little limited. When my dad was driving twenty years ago, Albatross didn't exist. Back then, it was called Turner, and my dad drove for their biggest rival.

"I'm going to run down to the garage," I tell him. "Get an idea of when the mechanics will be ready for me. You'll be fine in the motorhome?"

He grimaces in my direction. "Would you stop? I'm not going to be bored."

"Right," I say, turning for the garage as he turns for the motorhome. "Don't bug Mateo."

"What are you, his babysitter?" He shoots at look at me and then smiles as one of the Albatross garage techs passes by. "If I want to go bug my best friend, I certainly can."

"Sure," I say, and hand him my other bag. "Drop these in one of the offices, will you?"

Mateo

The door to my room slides open, and Arturo sticks his head in. He's got a ghost of a smile on his face. "There's someone here to see you, and he won't take no for an answer."

I scowl. "What?"

Before Arturo has a chance to tell me who it is, Pedro sticks his head around the corner. "Hey, man."

I laugh. "Hey. Fuck, I thought I was going to have to kick someone's ass." I gesture for him to come in. He gives me a hug, squeezing me tight and patting me once on the back.

"I didn't want to have to share you with anybody," he says as Arturo closes the door. I have to keep myself focused on him so I don't ask him where Arabella is. I can only assume by the fact that Pedro is all smiles that he doesn't know what happened between us.

I put a foot up on my bench to tie one shoe and then the other. Sitting back down, I reach out and flip the badge hanging down onto Pedro's chest.

He picks it up, wiggles it back and forth.

"Nice to be back?" I ask.

"Yeah," he says. "Can't believe it's been so many years since I've been to a race." He shrugs. "It's what happens when you get old. You stop wanting to do the crowds and the noise."

"Forty-eight is hardly old."

Pedro smacks me on the arm and walks over to my desk, his eyes scanning over my itinerary, my meal plan. He knows all this stuff as well as I do. Pedro did it all for ten years before he retired. "When are you going to give all this stuff up?" he asks, turning around and perching on the edge of the minuscule desk, barely big enough for my laptop.

"I don't know," I tell him honestly. "I'll probably stay as long as they want me." I don't tell him that I don't think they'll want me much longer. "There are young drivers chomping at the bit to get into Formula 1, proving themselves in Formula 2. I know I can't hold this spot forever."

Pedro reaches for the one picture frame I have in my room. A framed photo of Jimena and me from the day I won my second championship sixteen years ago. She's got me in a chokehold, blue braces shimmering at the camera.

He doesn't say anything, just sets it back down. "Be honest with me," he says, "how's Arabella doing?"

I keep myself still, make sure I don't visibly react. How's Arabella doing? Well, last night Arabella was kissing me in an elevator.

"She's doing fine," I say, looking away as I pull my suit up over my shoulders and zip it up. "She took to the job really quickly." My mind races back to what she told me at the restaurant all those weeks ago. That she doesn't feel like she fits in. That the traveling is taking its toll on her. Maybe I should be honest with Pedro. But I know if I open the floodgates, all of the honesty will come out, and I can't even begin to guess how much she would want me to tell him.

"What about Jayce? What's the deal there? Word on the street is he's been sniffing around her."

He switches the conversation so quickly it takes me a moment to catch up. "Jayce? Nothing going on, as far as I know." I think about her mouth on mine in that elevator. If there ever was anything going on with her and Jayce after Monaco, it sure as hell better be done now.

He nods. "Okay."

"But, you know, she's a grown woman. She's going to see people." I should let the subject die before he realizes we're not talking about Jayce anymore, but the whole thing has me bothered.

His eyes shoot to me. "I know she's a grown woman, but I also know how these guys are." He doesn't elaborate. He doesn't have to. I've been in this world long enough to know what's going on behind closed doors.

"Maybe she needs to make her own decisions." I don't know why I'm fighting him on this. If Arabella's decisions include kissing me in elevators, maybe she should be making better ones.

Pedro scowls at me. "What, you think she wants to date one of these douchebags?"

I shake my head. "I don't know, but if she does, then it's her business."

For a second, I think he might punch me, his eyes hard and his fists clenched. "I don't care if it's her business," he hisses. "She's my daughter."

As far as I can tell, Arabella is not having flings with guys in every city we go to, although she's well within her rights to do just that. But seeing the fire in Pedro's eyes right now, even if it wasn't me she was kissing, if I knew she was hanging out with anyone else, I wouldn't tell him.

When he asked me to look out for her at the beginning of

the season, it didn't occur to me that this might be what he meant. Make sure she's fed, make sure she's safe. Make sure she's happy and comfortable. These are the things that came to my mind.

That is, until Monaco. Until I saw her dancing with Jayce. And even then, I don't know if that was really about Pedro at all.

Pedro waves a hand at me. "I don't want to talk about it anymore. What's your strategy? What are you doing when you go out there?"

We talk about the race for a little while, but honestly, trying to discuss it with Pedro, someone who is probably less aware of what's going on than anybody else in this motorhome, just gets my nerves up.

There's a knock on the door, like the back of one very small knuckle.

"Yeah?" I call out. The door slides open and Arabella stands in the hallway.

"Hey," she says, smiling at Pedro. "I got you a place in the garage, but we gotta get down there." Her eyes meet mine. I wish I could read her face, but she's very carefully not showing any expression. "Time to get to work," she says.

"He's always working," Pedro grumbles.

I zip up my race suit without doing up the Velcro at my neck. Arabella watches me, her face blank.

Pedro's already halfway down the hallway when I get to the door, squeezing out. Arabella doesn't move. They must have sent her to escort me. Arturo is nowhere in sight.

When I'm in front of her in the hallway, her eyes drop, frozen for some reason on my throat, where I haven't finished doing up my suit. Her eyes flicker back up to mine.

"You're going to do great today," she says.

I glance down the stairs toward Pedro. He's standing at the

bar, talking to one of the cooks, who nods and hands him a mixed drink. He must be planning to gulp it down right here because he can't take it into the garage.

My eyes fly back to Arabella. "We need to talk."

She glances over at her father, too. This is not the way I wanted to have this conversation, but it's a conversation that needs to be had right now.

"Now's not a good time," she says, as if I need a reminder of what our responsibilities are right now.

"I don't care," I hiss. "Why did you kiss me?"

I see the way the words affect her, a small gasp, barely audible. "Because I wanted to," she says, her eyes flying over my face.

Because she wanted to. I ball my hands into fists. Part of me wants to shake her, ask her what the hell she's thinking. But another part of me wants to grab her, slam my mouth down onto hers, and taste her all over again.

"Fuck," I grunt, running a hand through my hair. "Arabella."

Her eyes move up to mine slowly.

"Be honest with me. How long have you wanted to do that?" I don't know why I ask. Maybe because, in my mind, she's turned into a person I don't even recognize overnight. But you don't do something like that impulsively, not when you're in our situation. It doesn't just happen out of the blue.

She lifts one shoulder. "Six years or so."

All the breath rushes out of me. I can't say another word. I just turn away from her and start walking down the stairs. I shouldn't have asked her. Especially not before a race. I can't even process what she just told me. She's been thinking about kissing me for six years. It's insane. Can't she see how insane this is?

But after what I just said to Pedro, I have to put my money

where my mouth is. Let her make her own decisions. She wanted to kiss me, so she did. Simple as that, right?

I smack Pedro on the back as I walk through the motorhome. "Come on, mate."

He throws back the final dregs of his cocktail and follows me out.

Chapter Thirty-One

Arabella

"Woo!" Papa hollers as we walk through the paddock. I feel like a teenager whose parents are dropping her off in their pajamas.

"Dad, would you chill?" I ask.

"No!" he says. "I will not chill, okay? Mateo just won another race. He's a real contender for a championship."

"He always was," I tell him, the comment slipping out of me. This seems to finally calm him down.

"I know that," he says. "You know I believe in Mateo just as much as you do. But I guess I just didn't know if it was really going to happen."

Nothing has actually happened yet, but I don't say as much. There's certainly still plenty of time for Lola to pull way ahead. Or even Archer, seeing as how he's having a great season. There's still time for Mateo to come in third. A great spot, but not a championship.

"Where to now?" I ask my dad as we head back to the lot

where my car is parked. "Straight to your house? Is Mateo joining us? Did you invite him?"

"Oh, Mateo is joining us alright," he says, hopping into the passenger seat and shutting the door.

"Why did you say it like that?"

"Because we're having a party!" he cheers, his voice loud in the enclosed space of my SUV.

"Jeez," I say, plugging my ears. "Okay, I get it."

"My place," he says. "I invited everybody."

I pull out of our parking space. "What do you mean by everybody?"

"I invited a lot of people," he says. "Every driver that I came into contact with while you were busy after the race. But most of them already had plans."

I look over at him. I can feel my blood pressure rising. "Are you kidding? You don't even know these guys."

He shrugs. "They're drivers. We're family." He waves me off.

"Alright," I rumble. "Who else?"

"Your friend is going to be there."

I purse my lips. "Who, Brigit?"

"Who's Brigit? No, I'm talking about Lana."

"Oh, well, I knew she was coming."

"And Mateo," he goes on. "Of course. And the family, you know."

"The whole family?" I ask. There's a reason my parents chose to set up shop in Montreal when I came along. When they met, Papa was living in Madrid. Mom stayed there with him for a long time, but when she got pregnant, they decided to move to Montreal to be near her family. Even though my grandparents didn't really love the fact that my mom was married to someone who very dangerously drove 200 kilometers per hour in an aluminum can every weekend, they helped my parents out a lot when I was born.

My dad picked a place that was close to the track so he could come out to the race every year. Oddly enough, it's probably been four or five years since he's attended, even though I know he gets invited every single time.

As soon as we pull up, I realize people are positively spilling out of my parents' house.

It's going to be a very long night.

Arabella

"Oh, thank God," Lana says when she sees me. She pulls me into a hug and I laugh into her neck.

"What, you weren't having fun with my family?"

She grimaces. "Fun isn't exactly the way that I would put it. Your mom tried to get me to help cook."

I laugh. "Well, she probably just assumed you wouldn't mind."

"Yeah, well, you know what happens when people assume."

I laugh and scan her from head to toe. Lana is the kind of person that puts make-up on to go to the grocery store, but she's really outdone herself tonight in a cocktail dress and heels. "Are we going clubbing later?"

She grabs onto my arm. "Your parents said there would be drivers here. I know what those drivers look like. Don't judge me."

"Tell me what's going on with you," I say.

And just as she opens her mouth, the front door swings open and in walks Mateo. The whole room erupts in applause and shouts.

Mateo smiles, this shy little thing. "Gracias, gracias, gracias," he says. "Bueno, bueno." He kicks the door shut and comes into the room, immediately pulled into a conversation by my mom.

Lana starts telling me about this friend she has who just started a podcast, and I try to listen, but my eyes drift over to Mateo.

He looks delicious. His hair is damp from his post-race shower, brushing the collar of his white t-shirt under his black jacket. I can't believe I know what his mouth feels like against mine.

"So what do you think?" Lana asks.

"About you starting a podcast?" My eyes dart back to hers. Thank God I was listening.

"Yeah," she says, looping her arm through mine and walking us over to the table where my mother has laid out food. We start filling plates with snacks.

"Well, what would you talk about?"

"Art, I guess," she says. "Wouldn't that be so cool? I could, like, interview artists. And then maybe it would make me enough money that I could use that to fund my own work."

"Is that something you want to do, talk to people about art every week?"

"Sure, I love talking to people."

That much is true. She does love talking to people.

"Then you should go for it. You never know if you don't give it a shot, right?"

"Exactly," she says, chomping into a baby carrot. "That's what I'm thinking. If it's a total bust, then no big deal. But if it's a huge success, then maybe it will actually get me somewhere."

"Are you worried about not getting anywhere?" She studied art. I studied photography. And while those aren't exactly stable careers, I didn't think she was worried about that, especially with her parents still mostly supporting her.

Lana opens her mouth to respond but then stops, her wide eyes going over my shoulder. "Who the hell is *that*?"

I turn, watching two very tall men by the front door speak to each other and then look around like they're not sure how they've gotten here.

"Wow," I say, taking in their faces, their casual clothes. I'm so used to seeing them in their racing gear. My dad wasn't kidding. He really invited everyone.

"Wait, are those guys drivers? They're drivers, aren't they?"

Jayce and Thane. I can understand why they came. My dad is a legend in Formula 1. He and Mateo saw more action with each other in one season than most drivers see in their entire careers.

I can imagine they probably look up to my dad and it's likely that neither of them have met him before today. "This is a weird night," I say, turning back to Lana.

"Is that Mateo's teammate?" She hasn't taken her eyes from them.

"Yeah. He's kind of a troublemaker, to be honest."

"What do you mean?" she asks, stepping closer and lowering her voice. She wants to gossip.

I sigh, thinking back to Monaco, about the comments he made about my feelings for Mateo. "I just mean he's a little bit of a pot-stirrer, but it's whatever. He just likes to have fun."

"What about the other guy?" It's not surprising that Lana has no idea who Thane is. Not only is he not a particularly big name in the world of F1, but Lana doesn't even watch F1. She probably recognizes Jayce from following the Albatross social media account to support me. But anyone else is a no-go.

Back when we were roommates, she used to see snippets of races over my shoulder, but that was about it. She always said it was really boring watching boys drive around in circles for two hours.

"That's Thane," I tell her.

"Who does he drive for?"

"He drives for Lime."

Her eyebrow quirks. "Lime?"

"Yeah, it's an American team."

"Is he any good?" she asks.

"He's great," I tell her. "He just doesn't drive for a good team. Thane is the kind of driver that doesn't come across as being very serious, so the top teams don't want to take a chance on him. But I think if they did, he could win a championship."

Lana is practically salivating, which I get. Thane is very beautiful. He's Australian with this wild curly hair and goofy smile that is somehow extremely endearing and also kind of makes him look like a supermodel.

Thane is that guy in your high school who everybody wants to be friends with. The quarterback of the football team. And it doesn't really surprise me that he caught Lana's eye. Lana may be deep and artsy, but she's also a party girl. She likes all the cute boys.

"Do you want me to introduce you?"

Her eyes shoot back to me. "Would that be weird?"

"I guess not. They're nice enough, and you wanted to meet drivers, right?" I turn with a smile on my face. "Jayce!" I call across the room.

He's only just found Mateo, the two of them shaking hands, patting each other on the back the way boys do. But as soon as he sees me, he gives me a nod and heads my way, pulling Thane along behind him. I don't miss the way Mateo watches them join us, his brow furrowed.

"Hey there, beautiful," Jayce says, immediately reaching out to hug me.

Lana's mouth falls open. Over Jayce's shoulder, I lower my eyes and shake my head, letting her know there's nothing going on between me and Jayce. And that this, I have concluded, is just kind of how he is with everybody. It honestly might be a little inappropriate, considering we work together, but it's harmless enough. I have no doubt that if I had shown any interest back in Monaco, that Jayce would have slept with me. But it wouldn't have meant anything. And now, I guess he knows how I feel about Mateo. The thought makes me feel like I've broken out in hives.

"Guys, this is my best friend, Lana. She's lives in Quebec City. Lana, this is Thane and Jayce."

Both of their mouths immediately stretch into flirtatious smiles. Well, at least she'll have some options tonight. I wonder if they'll fight over her. Formula 1 boys are competitive, after all.

On reflex, my eyes find Mateo across the room. He's looking over at us, but as soon as he sees me, he looks away, smiling at one of my cousins, Sam, who just graduated high school and is obsessed with Formula 1.

It takes me a moment to realize Jayce is talking to me. "Sorry, what?" I say.

He smiles. "This house, it's really nice," he says.

"Oh, it's not mine," I tell him nervously.

"No, I know," he says. "It's your parents' place, right? Is there a room upstairs with your pink princess stuff in it?"

I snort. "No, but there might still be some Schumacher posters on the wall and like a shit-ton of Polaroids."

"I would have loved to have grown up in a house like this."

Thane makes a sound in the back of his throat, and we all turn to look at him. "Sorry," he says.

"What?" I ask.

He shrugs and then motions slowly around. "I don't know. I knew nepotism was quite the thing in Formula 1, but I've never really met anybody who was Formula 1 royalty."

I feel my face flush.

Before I have a chance to say anything, Lana has already

swung toward him. "Don't say that to her," she says. "Who the fuck even are you?"

"Lana," I say.

"Oh, I didn't mean it as an insult," Thane says in his bright Australian accent, with that smile on his face. He's the kind of guy who can say that kind of thing to someone's face and then laugh it off because he's just so charming that everyone will forgive him.

"Oh sure, calling someone a nepo baby isn't an insult," Lana barks.

"I didn't exactly call her a nepo baby," he says. "And hey, if I was the kid of someone famous in F1, I'd be doing the same thing she is. I'm not saying it's a problem. I'm just saying I've never met anybody like that."

"And what about you?" she demands. "What's your role in F1?"

"I'm a driver," he says, smile wide.

"I know you're a driver." She gestures towards me. "Arabella told me. She said you're a good driver, but that you drive for a shit team."

At that, Jayce throws his head back and laughs, clearly amused by the drama.

"I do drive for a shit team," Thane says, shrugging. "See, I'm not insulted, because it's just the truth."

Lana rolls her eyes. "You're a jerk."

He smiles big at her, like she just told him he's Prince Charming. "Do you like jerks?" he asks.

"Alright," I say, reaching down for her hand and turning toward the drink table. "Why don't you guys go mingle? Thane, I'm sure you want to meet my dad, seeing as how he's Formula 1 royalty and all."

We walk away to the sound of Thane's chuckle.

"What an asshole," Lana says, pouring herself a hefty

helping of Chardonnay. "If that's what F1 drivers are like, I don't know how you put up with them."

I snicker, glancing over my shoulder at Thane, who is now in a heated argument with Jayce. "Well, I really only have to deal with Mateo and Jayce, and they're not so bad."

She rolls her eyes and we take our stuff over to one of the round tables my parents set up in the dining room. We sit side-by-side, facing the room so that Lana can keep an eye on the goings-on while we chat.

"So I was talking to Professor Whittaker yesterday," Lana says, tapping her fingers on the tabletop. She's not looking at me, but in that way that makes it really obvious that she's not looking at me. Her eyes scan the room and then they stop. I don't have to look to know exactly what has caught her attention.

My eyes slide across the room and find Mateo talking to my father.

"Why were you talking to Professor Whittaker?" I try to keep my voice light, casual.

"He told me about the Everest job," she finally says, not answering my question. "You're not going to take it, are you?" Her tone is venomous, as if I've somehow betrayed her.

"I haven't decided," I lie. "I just don't think it's very good timing."

She's still not looking at me, even as she shakes her head, her long brown hair swaying gently. "I can't believe you're doing this," she says. She finally twists her face in my direction.

"Doing what?" I ask.

She motions around to everything in the room. "This. This life you said you didn't want. You didn't want to be a Formula 1 kid. You didn't want to go around being Pedro Cedillo's daughter. And here we are."

I shake my head. "You don't know what you're talking about." I suddenly wish I had more to drink. I wish my veins were hot with alcohol. Maybe then I would have the courage to say what I want to say to her, which is that she should handle her own fucking life and stop worrying about mine, that everyone should stop worrying about the choices I'm making for myself.

"Don't I?" she asks in an incredulous voice that's so high-pitched I'm pretty sure the dogs next door hear it.

"No, you don't understand. You keep acting like this job is working at a McDonald's or something. Like I've debased myself by taking a job with a multi-million dollar racing organization. This is huge."

"Yes, and as long as you're there, you will always be Pedro Cedillo's daughter."

"Who cares?" When a few faces turn toward us, I realize we're being far too loud. I glance over at my father and Mateo, but they don't seem to have noticed.

We stay silent for a while until everyone seems to have forgotten us again. And then much quieter, she says, "I care. You're going to throw everything away on some fucking fairy tale where this man who is twice your age falls in love with you. Is that really what you want? Do you really think that's what your family wants for you?"

My mouth falls open. "I don't know what you're talking about," I hiss.

"What other reason would you have joined this team?" Her eyes are steady on me while I try to find an answer. "I've known you for seven years, Arabella, and at some point, it's like something inside your brain snapped, and you've been focused on him ever since. You try to hide it, but it's obvious you're into him. Are you making a huge mistake in some attempt to be near him? Did you join the team to be near him? Be honest with me."

Of course I did. But she's acting like I flushed my entire life down the toilet for a man. I took a high-paying job for a successful team in a very desirable industry because it was the right thing for me at this point in my life.

"I signed a one-year contract. It's not like I just shackled myself to Formula 1 forever."

She analyzes me, her eyes sweeping over my face. "But what if he asked you to?"

"What?"

"If he asked you to shackle yourself to Formula 1 forever. If he asked you to stay with the team and to be in Formula 1 for the rest of your life, you would do it. I know you would. You would do it for him."

I feel like she punched me right in the middle of my chest.

My eyes slide over to Mateo, a drink in his hand and a smile on his face. He takes a sip from his cup, his eyes catching mine over the rim.

I look away quick.

I would do anything he asked me to. I would give up everything for him. That doesn't make me a bad person and it doesn't make me pathetic. It just makes me someone who wants someone, a specific someone, more than they want a dream job. More than they want whatever life they think that they've created for themselves. What do I have that's so spectacular that I wouldn't give it up if he asked me to?

"I just really think..." I finally say to her when I can find the words, "...that it's none of your business."

She bites her lips between her teeth and nods. "Sure, okay. But as your best friend, if this isn't my business, then I have no idea what is."

With that, she leaves her drink in the middle of the table and walks out. I can't sit still. I stay in my seat long enough to gather myself, to take deep breaths so I don't start crying, and then I stand.

I gently push through the crowd in the living room and

step out onto the back patio. The doors are open because it's such a nice night.

I still feel like I can't breathe. I move around to the side of the house, press my back to the brick wall there. I can still hear the party through the open door. I can see the light from the kitchen shining out onto the grass through the window above my head.

Maybe she's right. Maybe I have done all of this for a man who will never want me. Maybe Mateo will never see me as anything more than his best friend's daughter.

I just don't know if it matters anymore. It doesn't matter if he loves me back. I love him far too much to stop.

Chapter Thirty-Two

Mateo

I'm fairly certain I'm the only one who sees Arabella make a run for it. I saw her and her friend arguing earlier. Though what about, I'm not sure. They sat at that table, their faces angry. And then Arabella's friend got up first, disappearing down a hallway. Arabella sat there for a moment, her eyes down on the table before she got up, too. She walked right by all of us and into the backyard.

I don't think anyone else has noticed. They're getting themselves cake, pouring themselves drinks, having conversations, and playing cards.

I count to thirty. I scan every face in the room to make sure they're all truly preoccupied. And then I follow Arabella out.

At first, I don't see her. Just a stretch of grass and then the spot where the grass turns into tile before it hits the swimming pool. It's lit up in the dark, cerulean blue.

Arabella is nowhere that I can see, but I remember that

this yard is L-shaped and I walk slowly around the edge of the house.

Arabella must hear me coming because she's swiping at her face when I finally discover her. Swiping at what I can only assume are tears. "What happened?" I ask her, stepping forward and pushing her chin up.

The shadows are heavy in this corner of the yard. But in the light coming through the window above us, I can see her cheeks are red, her eyes swollen and wet.

"It's nothing," she says, pushing my hand away. "Don't worry about it. You're supposed to be inside having a good time."

I toss up my hands. "It's not exactly easy for me to have the time of my life when I know you're out here crying, *querida*."

I see her take one big breath, her chest rising and falling. And then another. Even with tears on her face, she's so beautiful. Her hair curly down to her shoulders, still in her team kit.

"You didn't talk to me all weekend."

The way she chokes the words out makes my stomach hurt. Is that why she's crying? Because I've been avoiding her?

"What am I supposed to do, Arabella? Can you really blame me?"

"What are you supposed to do?" she asks, her mouth curling around the words in a sad way. "You're supposed to talk to me. You're supposed to... You're my best friend." She must read the confusion on my face because she wipes again at her cheeks and says, "You're my best friend on the team. It's hard sometimes being so far away from home, being in the paddock with so many people and all the guys and I just need my friend."

I get what she means. I feel it, too. The way the two of us have begun to rely on each other's presence every week. I've found myself walking into the paddock and immediately looking for her behind her camera. Walking into the motorhome and scanning the faces. It's like it doesn't feel right anymore unless she's there.

"I'm sorry," I tell her. "I just thought I was doing what was best."

She looks away from me, her face hidden in the shadows. She wraps her arms around herself. "I just..." She trails off, but she doesn't need to say it. She made herself vulnerable to me. She kissed me even though she knew this wouldn't be easy, even though she didn't know how I would react. She put herself out there and I just left her dangling off the side of a cliff.

"You must know..." I say to her, stepping even closer. Close enough that when she huffs out a surprised sigh, I can smell the alcohol on her breath. "You must know that... Shit." I bite my lip.

What am I supposed to say? Am I supposed to tell her everything right now? Everything I've been thinking and feeling? If ever there was a can of worms that could not be shut, it's this one.

But she's looking up at me with her sad eyes. And I reach out, press my hand to her cheek.

"I'm trying to save us both," I say.

Her hands fall to my chest, grip the fabric of my shirt slightly. "I don't want to be saved," she says, the quietest of whispers. "Ruin me."

I kiss her.

Because everything in my body is pulling me toward her. And I know that I'm going to Hell for this, but I can't find it in myself to care. It isn't the sweet, tentative thing we shared in the elevator.

Her mouth opens on a moan, and I slip my tongue in, tasting her as I push her back against the side of the house.

Sometimes you can convince yourself you don't want

something. You can tell yourself it won't be as good as you imagine it will be. You can talk yourself out of craving it every moment you're alive.

But I knew—have known for weeks now—that when I touched her neck, her skin would be silk under my fingers. That when I forced her mouth open even wider for me that she wouldn't put up a fight. That when I pressed myself to her as close as I could that she would grip onto me like she doesn't want to let go.

She moans into my mouth and I pull away, breath heaving out of me, before going back in again. And this time, it's like the flames have been stoked even higher. My hands find the curve of her hip. I slide up her back until my fingers have found the softness of her skin at the back of her neck.

Even though she knows we have to be quiet, she still makes a sound in the back of her throat. I suck at her bottom lip and let my hands trail back down until they find her ass.

Something inside her changes then. In a split-second, she goes from willing and pliant against me to a hungry animal. She grips the collar of my shirt, pulling my face even closer to her so she can devour me. She hikes her leg up over my hip, and I have to stifle a groan when the movement presses us together at the hip. My pelvis grinds into hers. Hardness against so much soft heat.

She pulls her mouth away from mine to look at me with eyes that seem to almost be filled with panic. I understand it. This want, this need is almost panic-inducing. Her mouth falls open on a gasp when I rock once against her.

"Arabella?" Arabella's mother's voice floats at the edge of my awareness.

Without thinking, I clamp my hand over her mouth. She pants against my open palm.

We don't say anything. We stay frozen, locked at the hips

until Melanie seems to have gone back inside. Just before she shuts the door, I hear her tell someone she doesn't know where Arabella is. I feel like I've been doused with cold water.

This is why we can't do this. Because we could hurt people. Her parents, the team, each other.

I let her knee fall from my hip, then get close to whisper in her ear, "Go around the front. Pretend you were getting something from the car. I'll go back inside through the back."

She nods, but I can feel what she's not saying. Feel what she wants to ask.

What are we doing? What is this? What happens next?

And I wish I had an answer for any of it.

Arabella

As soon as Mateo is gone, I press myself to the side of the house and try to breathe. But I can't. My entire body is trembling.

I'm worried that any second now, I might wake up.

How many times have I fantasized about this happening? How many times have I touched myself and imagined Mateo's mouth against mine? Too many times to count.

I glance around the side of the house and watch him slip back in through the open door. I go the other way, popping open the gate and stepping around to the front of the house. I stop for a minute, let the cool air wash over my skin, and then turn for the front door.

But before I pull myself fully out of the shadows, I see two figures pushed up against one of the cars parked against the sidewalk.

For a second, I think nothing of it. We're in public, there are adults around, people are drinking, doing whatever.

But then my eyes begin to adjust to the shapes in the moonlight, and I realize it's Lana. It's Lana and she has Thane's tongue in her mouth. They're kissing like the apocalypse is right on their heels.

So much for her thinking he's a jerk. It took her all of thirty minutes to change her mind.

About the time that Thane grabs onto her knee and wrenches her leg up over his hip, I turn for the front door. I guess she's not upset about our argument, but her words are still ringing in my head.

If he asked you to stay with the team and to be in Formula 1 for the rest of your life, you would do it. I know you would. You would do it for him.

Those words cycle through my head, even as I can still taste Mateo in my mouth. I throw open the door to my parents' house, stomp inside.

"There she is," my mom says, immediately coming for me. She runs her hands up and down my arms. "You're cold. You shouldn't be outside without your jacket."

"I'm fine," I tell her, but her smile fades slowly. She puts her hands to my cheeks.

"You're all flushed," she says. "Let me get you some hot tea."

"No, it's okay," I tell her, pulling her hands away, feeling weird that she's touching me when my face is flushed because I'm turned on.

"It's all right. I think I'm actually just going to head home."

My mom's shoulders fall. "Did you get in a fight with Lana?" she asks. "I saw the two of you talking earlier."

She's giving me the perfect out.

My eyes scan the room, finding Mateo's. He's taking a seat with my father at a table, both of them laughing. Mateo claps my father on the shoulder, then his eyes drift over to mine.

I look away quick. He's recovered much more quickly than I have, considering he was just hard up against me a few minutes ago.

"Sort of," I tell my mom. "But I don't want you to worry about it, okay? I'm just really worn out."

"Of course you are," she says. "You've had a big day. So has Mateo. Why don't I ask him to drive you back to your place?"

"Nope," I say quickly. "No, it's okay. He's having a good time. I can drive myself."

"Okay," she says, putting her hands up.

But my thoughts have started to swirl over what she just said. My apartment is just on the other side of town. Mateo knows where it is. Just twenty-four hours ago, we were kissing in my elevator.

"I'll text you later, okay?" I tell my mom and turn back for the door.

I hesitate, glancing once more over my shoulder at Mateo. If I texted him right now, told him that he could come to my apartment, that we could finish what we started out there against the house, would he do it?

I don't say goodbye to anyone, but when I turn the corner back toward the front door, it's to find Jayce in the hallway, a whiskey glass near his mouth.

"Looking a bit frazzled there, Arabella," he says, eyes meeting mine over the rim of his glass. My feet skitter to a stop. All I can do is stare at him.

Whatever it is he's insinuating, he doesn't know what happened between Mateo and me. He can't know. But he still sends me a sly smile.

"Goodnight, Jayce." I'm not going to let him rile me up. I just keep walking until I'm out on the porch once more.

I close the front door behind me, relieved to find

that Lana and Thane are no longer playing tonsil hockey against a car. Said car is gone, so it must have been Thane's.

And I guess that's how Lana's going to spend her evening. After lecturing me like she just did, it's a little ironic that she just went home with F1's biggest playboy. I roll my eyes and get in my car.

I have far too many things to think about right now. The whole way back to my apartment, I think about Mateo, his mouth, his breath, his hands, everything that was pushed against me below his belt. And I know I won't be able to sleep tonight. As soon as I'm in my apartment, I pull out my phone, pace back and forth across my living room while I try to figure out what I want to send him.

Maybe the best thing to do right now is just be up front. I open up my text thread with Mateo.

Arabella
I'm home.

And then I take a deep breath, steadying myself.

Arabella
You have my address if you'd like to
come over later.

I send it before I can stop myself.

I'm so not this person. I don't know that I've ever made the first move in my entire life. Either way, my hands are trembling waiting for him to respond. My heart is pounding in my ears.

It takes him three minutes.

. . .

Mateo
I don't think that's a good idea. I'll see
you next week.

Cassie Reese seen dining out with suspected boyfriend Mateo Silva...and daughter of Formula 1 driver Pedro Cedillo?

Color me confused. For the last month and a half, we've had our eye on Cassie Reese's new romance with Formula 1 driver Mateo Silva, an interesting match, to say the least. It's not at all surprising that the couple was seen having dinner in Montreal this weekend, two days before the Canadian Grand Prix.

What is surprising is the fact that they seem to have invited Arabella Cedillo, Albatross Racing's photographer. Is Cedillo playing third wheel here? Or is there something we're not seeing?

Chapter Thirty-Three
Round 9 - Silverstone, Great Britain

Mateo Silva - 132 points
Lola Castle - 117 points
Archer Hayes - 116 points

Mateo

"This question is for Mateo," a voice in the room says. It takes a moment for my eyes to find the man sitting a few rows back.

"Yeah," I say into the microphone.

"You're having an excellent season."

Lola smiles over at me, and there's a small cheer from the back of the room, a little whoop.

"Thank you," I say into the mic.

"But we've seen you do well in the first half of the season before. This is not the first time that you've been hitting podiums, winning grand prix early on. Are you worried it's going to end soon?"

I try to focus on the guy's face, but the room has begun to blur a bit, including this guy's bald head and gray jumper.

What a stupid fucking question, I want to tell him. *Am I*

worried it's all going to end? Of course I'm fucking worried it's going to end.

I'm a human being, and I'm a person who has their mind set on exactly what they want. And it would be so easy for it to slip out of my grasp. One fuck-up with the car or Onyx getting Archer's shit into gear. All it would take is Lola making no mistakes between now and the end of the season, and that's it.

That's not what he's talking about though. Not just everyone driving at peak performance and knocking me out. No, he's talking about the second-half curse. Four years in a row now, I've started the season strong just to plummet halfway through.

"Of course he's not worried," I hear Lola say from beside me, her face bright, optimistic. We do this for each other, step in when people are crossing the line. I've done it for her, and she's done it for me. Countless times. "Mateo is a legend. And that's not going to change, even if he gets 20th place for the rest of the season."

I lift the mic to my mouth. "I don't think that was as encouraging as you thought it was," I tell her. A laugh goes through the room. "But in all honesty," I say, looking back out at the media, feeling steadier now, "the only thing I can control is myself. For the rest of the season, I'll be giving my all. I'll be fighting as hard as I can. The improvements on the car are fantastic. The team is working hard. That's all we can do."

The interview moves on. They ask Lola several more questions, and Archer, on my other side, a few as well.

I know this is what they want. What the media wants. The three of us in front of the cameras at all times. Because we're the three that could win it. I glance over at Archer. His arms crossed, shoulders back, eyes up at the ceiling. I don't think he really wants to win. He's a great driver, but... he just doesn't seem particularly interested in dethroning Lola.

"And one more for Mateo." This time, it's a woman. Long, blonde hair, sitting a few rows back. "What do your retirement plans look like?"

I hesitate, trying not to let in all those things swirling in my head. The comments from the interviewers. The commentators. The people online. The other drivers.

> When are you going to retire and get
> out of the way?
>
> When are you going to give up your
> seat to someone younger? Someone
> who might actually win?

"No retirement plans at the moment," I mutter and set my microphone down on the seat beside me, making it very clear I have no intention of saying anything else.

"All right, all done," someone says.

I'm up off the couch before the words are even all the way out of their mouth. I hit the back exit, shove out of the building, and close my eyes to turn my face up to the sun, sucking in fresh air. I'm relieved when the door stays shut behind me, everyone else going out the other way.

I press my back to the building and hunch over, grabbing my knees. The questions are just going to get worse. The comments are going to get worse. And I can't decide what's worse: people attacking me because I might be actual competition for Lola, or people attacking me because I don't do well in a race. I can't win.

"Here you are," a voice says.

I open my eyes, find Arabella standing in front of me. She has a slight sheen of sweat across her forehead, a worried crinkle to her brow. She's glowing in the sun. "What's wrong?"

I shake my head. "Nothing," I say, straightening away from the building. I need to be strong. For her. For that camera in her hand. "Nothing," I repeat. "I just need a little space."

She immediately takes a step back. "I'm sorry. I'll leave you to it."

Without thinking, I reach out and grab onto her wrist, halting her backward descent. "Not from you," I say. My thumb is pressed against her pulse, and I can feel it racing, feel her impossibly soft skin under my fingers.

She watches me for a moment, her curly hair blowing in the gentle breeze, and then steps back toward me. I should let go of her, but I don't. "Everything's going to be okay," she says. Neither one of us has brought up what happened behind her parents' house back in Montreal. We can't bring it up. We have to keep pretending these things aren't happening so both of us can survive whatever the fuck it is we're doing.

After the party, she invited me to her apartment. And I stood in her parents' living room and looked at that text message and knew that all it would take was saying yes and I'd be in her bed. It was what she wanted. It was obvious. It was what I wanted, too. But we've got to fight this thing. I don't even know what this thing *is*.

But whatever it is, it absolutely cannot happen. That's hard to remember when she leans against the building beside me, not speaking anymore, just offering silent comfort. Because she's the only one who can make me feel like this— calm even though everything is in danger of burning down. She quiets all the noise.

I look over at her. "They're all waiting for me to fail. Maybe it would be a better story if I did."

She looks back, pointed chin tilting to the side. "Better story for who?" She sighs. "You can't let them get to you. You can't let them worm their way in. They're trying to break you, and it infuriates them when they can't."

Something about the way she says it, chin lifted high,

makes me smile. "You've certainly identified their intentions, haven't you?"

She rolls her eyes. "It's not like it's hard to do. It's obvious. They're baiting you. They want to see you crack under the pressure. And they want to see you and Lola hate each other. They want drama. They want to watch you crumble." Her eyes narrow. She looks beautiful like this. Fierce and angry. Protective. "You're not going to give them what they want. You're going to go out there and you're going to hold your head high. You're going to fucking win this race."

Fuck, I want to kiss her. I want to take her face in my hands and taste that delicious mouth. A shiver goes through me at the thought, at the memory of her hot under my hands, moaning into my mouth. And I know I won't be able to stop thinking about it. This is going to make it much harder to concentrate on the race.

I clear my throat. "Thanks, Ari. I should probably get going."

She nods, clearly not offended by my cutting off the conversation.

"I'll be watching," she says.

🏁

Arabella

The whole crowd is screaming at the top of their lungs as Mateo hoists his trophy over his head. All I can do is watch him, my cheeks aching from how much I'm smiling, how much I've been smiling since the second he made pole yesterday.

I saw the interview from Thursday, the one that upset him.

Last night, sitting in my hotel room, I was scrolling

through social media, and it came across my feed. Those absolute dickface reporters asking him these baiting questions. What did they expect him to say? *Oh, yeah, it's definitely going to be a shitty rest of the season, and also I've decided to retire because I suck?*

He can't help but internalize all of it, which is insane. I know for a fact that Lola doesn't. She doesn't listen to it. She doesn't even hear it. She's so caught up in her own fucking magnificence, and I just want Mateo to see that. I want him to be wrapped up in himself, too. I want him to be so confident that all these comments just hit a brick wall, but instead he just marinates in them.

Not today. Today he fought off Lola hard, and he won, and he looks amazing up there on that podium.

I have chills watching him pop open his champagne and turn it on Lola. It drips down the bill of his cap as he smiles big, and then it's over, and the other two drivers file off the platform.

The whole world comes to a stop just for a split second as he turns to the crowd and looks down. He seems to find my face immediately, and his smile shines in the English sun.

And I am madly in love with him.

Chapter Thirty-Four

Mateo

> **Arabella**
> You did amazing today! See you in
> Italy!

I stare down at the text from Arabella, my brain unable to focus on what Felix is telling me as the team packs up their stuff so we can all leave for the night.

Felix is talking, his mouth moving, but everything is hazy and out of focus. The text message is still open on my phone. Arabella is in her hotel room right now, and just the thought of it...

My eyes meet Arturo's as we head for the door, and even as Felix is droning on, I press in close to him and say, "Tell me not to do something extremely stupid."

His eyes take me in, holding the door open for me so I can step out into the paddock. "You don't do enough stupid things in your life, Mateo Silva."

And maybe if he knew, he wouldn't have said that. But then, maybe he would have.

As soon as Felix has wandered off and Arturo and I head for the parking lot, I know exactly what I'm going to do. Nothing could possibly stop it. Not me, not an asteroid, not God himself. Not when I have all this heat and adrenaline fizzing through my veins.

Once I stood on that podium and looked down at her in the crowd, I knew this was where I was going to be tonight. I knew the second all the obligations were over, when everybody else was heading out to the clubs, that I would be taking out my phone and texting her.

It feels so simple in my mind, this thing that makes perfect sense. We're a super car driving right off the track, and no one can stop it.

Arabella is the only person I absolutely should not want. And somehow, she is the only person I can think about. I didn't even realize it was happening. Wanting to text her the moment I wake up. Feeling a nervousness in my blood every week as I head into the paddock on race week-end. Wanting to see her. Needing to see her.

It just happened. It just crept up on me. Like a shadow stretching in the setting sun.

And today, when I was up on that podium, something broke inside me. Whatever willpower I had to pretend this wasn't happening between us, to try and force it away into some back recess of my mind, vanished.

I want her. I want her and only her so bad I can taste it. So as I make my way out of the paddock with Arturo beside me, I pull out my phone and I send her a text.

Arabella

> **Mateo**
> Are you alone?

I stare down at the text, my fingers going numb the way they do when I've had too much alcohol, even though I'm almost offensively sober. Heat races over me.

He wants to come over. That's what this means, right? I have enough experience with the opposite sex to know that when someone you've been flirting with and kissing for the last few weeks asks if you're alone in your hotel room, it's because they don't want you to be alone in your hotel room anymore.

> **Arabella**
> Yes.

I wait a long time for a response, but I don't get one. There's never any indication that he's typing, and when five minutes pass, I realize he must not be responding because he must be on his way here. Right?

I rush to my bathroom, comb my fingers through my hair and swish some mouthwash. While I'm contemplating whether or not I should change out of my pajamas, there's a knock at the door.

I'm trembling so hard I can barely get my hand around the door handle, but when I finally do, I find myself looking into the caramel-colored eyes of Mateo Silva. I'm certain I stand there forever, the world rotating but everything frozen. I can hear my heart in my ears, my harsh breathing.

I don't know how long it is before his eyes dip down to my mouth.

And then he rushes forward. He plants his hands on my hips to push me back into the room and let the door fall closed.

He's so close, his hands on me, and I can feel the warmth of his body, the feverishness of his skin.

"This is a terrible idea," I tell him, even as my heart is telling me to shut up. What does anything matter compared to the desperate need I have to belong to Mateo? Everything I've ever wanted is right here; I've got my hands on it.

"I don't want to stay away," he says simply. He's not trying to justify it. He's not trying to give me reasons why it's okay. He's just telling me he's here because he wants to be.

"Then don't."

He bends forward, his lips brushing mine. But before I can get lost in him, I push him away and hold up my hand between us. Like I'm trying to stop a train from running me over.

"I can't do this if…"

He waits for me to finish, his eyes steady and focused on me the way they always are, that way that makes my blood pump faster, hotter with every passing second.

"If what?" he finally asks me, his voice gentle.

I don't want to say it because saying it might be the end of this. Saying it might mean him realizing what we're doing here and turning around and leaving, pretending none of it ever happened.

But it doesn't matter because it needs to be said.

"I can't be a one-night-stand to you, Mateo. I'm more than that. We're more than that. It's me, and the way I feel about you… I can't just be some girl you sleep with."

His eyes move over my face in the light coming in from the bathroom, contemplating, calculating. I wasn't expecting to see this version of Mateo tonight, the version that processes information like a computer that runs through odds and statistics before making a move. But here he is, right in front of me.

I wait. He takes a step towards me and I don't back away.

"That's not what this is," he says, his voice low, quiet.

"What is it then?" I ask, my voice trembling.

I don't think he has an answer for that. I don't think *I* have an answer for it either.

He reaches out and takes my hand, running his thumb across each of my fingers. "If this was just about one night, if this was just about wanting anyone, I can think of a hundred women who would be a lot less complicated."

His words make me smile. Maybe they shouldn't, but they do. Because if there's any way to describe the way I feel about Mateo, it's *complicated*.

He smiles, too, his eyes dropping to my mouth. "I don't want them. I want you. I want you wrapped around me. I want inside you."

A strangled moan leaves my mouth, and I throw myself at him and kiss him.

I was twenty-one when I realized I wanted to have sex with Mateo Silva. It wasn't something that happened all at once, but rather, a slow sneaking up on me, the monster that would plague me for the next four years. He's been there, in one way or another, in every kiss, every touch that I've shared with anyone else, something I always hated but couldn't escape.

And now it's him kissing me, walking me over to the bed, pressing me down gently. Every sensation in my body feels like it's been dialed up to eleven. The surface of my skin at all the points where he's resting against me, the smell and taste of his mouth, the vibration and timbre of his deep groan when I spread my legs to let him settle against me further.

His mouth travels down my neck, leaving goosebumps all over my skin as I clutch at him.

"Is this real?" I don't realize I've asked the question out loud until Mateo pulls back, his eyes meeting mine, not much more than shadow. "I never thought I'd be here," I tell him. And maybe I should be embarrassed that I'm saying all of this to him, but I can't seem to push away the thoughts.

Mateo presses his forehead to mine. "Me neither." He sighs, his warm breath puffing out against my mouth. "But this feels..." His eyes scan over my face. "...right."

My chest pulls tight, like a suitcase stuffed too tight to zip up. I take his face in my hands, mesmerized by the feel of his skin under my palms. "Can I see you?"

He hesitates and then seems to understand. He pushes off me, moving to stand beside the bed. He holds my eyes as he slips his shirt off over his head. I suddenly wish all the lights were on, so I could see every inch of him. In the light from the bathroom, I can just barely make out a tattoo where his right shoulder meets his chest. In the dark, I can't make out what it is.

I stand and move over to him, reaching out to touch the lines of dark ink. An image of Santiago, the patron saint of Spain. I know his face well. And on either side of him, the dates Mateo won his championships.

"I didn't know you had this." Mateo isn't often photographed with his shirt off, and all the photos I've seen of him bare-chested from his younger years, there was no tattoo in sight.

Mateo puts his hand over mine, flattening it against his chest. When my eyes meet his, he kisses me, hot, frenzied, his tongue mating with mine. I whimper into his mouth and wrap my arms around him, suddenly lamenting the fact that we're still wearing clothes. He could be inside me right now, but now the thought of parting long enough to get naked seems impossible.

I push back just enough to keep my mouth on his but to let my hands find their way between us. I run them down his warm chest, his flat stomach, and then to the button of his pants.

He doesn't stop me as I undo them, just licks into my mouth like he's trying to taste every inch of me. Finally pulling away, I shove his pants off his hips and watch his half-hard cock spring free.

For a moment, I forget about everything else. How can anything else in the world exist when Mateo is standing in front of me, completely naked? My eyes scan him from head to toe, and when my eyes linger on his penis, it gets harder under my gaze.

"You're beautiful," I say. I knew he would be, but I never could have prepared myself for this. Without hesitation, I drop to my knees in front of him.

"Hey," he says, hands taking my face. "You don't have to—"

"Please, let me." My hands itch to touch him, to feel him, to guide him into my mouth. "I want to so bad."

Burying his hands in my hair, he bends forward to kiss me, once, twice, and then he cradles my face and waits.

I reach for him, wrapping my hand around him. There's nothing soft about him now. He's hard in my hand, hard and thick, and my mouth is watering by the time I lean forward and swallow him down.

He groans, still holding my head gently as I slide down as far as I can and come back up. I don't even realize I'm making noise as I worship his cock, a sort of whine in the back of my throat, until he uses his hold on me to tug me back and says, "You've got to stop. You're killing me."

This time, when I make a noise, it's one of disappointment. I stick my tongue out, like I could reach him with it even as he pulls his hips away from me. "Please. Let me make you come."

He tugs at my hair, pulling my head back. "Absolutely not. I haven't even gotten you naked, Ari."

Something pulls tight inside me when he calls me that. Like a reminder of who we were before and who we are now. Everything will be different. There's no going back.

Grabbing onto my arms, he pulls me up to my feet. Without missing a beat, he reaches for my shirt, yanking it off over my head before moving to push down my shorts and underwear. Attaching his mouth to mine, he lowers us to the bed before pushing himself up off me to scan my naked body.

His hand comes up to cup my breast, and then he lowers his lips to my nipple, sucking on it gently. I gasp, watching his mouth, that mouth I know as well as my own, as it surrounds the peak. I can't stop myself from digging my hands into his hair, can't stop myself from indulging.

"I want you inside me."

He moans against my skin, and my hips buck with want. "Do you have protection?"

I laugh, cover my face with my hands. "No. I never thought this would..." I drop my hands and look at him. "If you're okay with it, I have an IUD."

He nods, what we just agreed on setting in as we look at each other. He's going to be inside me without anything between us. My fingers tremble at the idea. How did I go from loving Mateo from the other side of the planet to loving him with nothing between us but air?

He pushes up to his knees between my legs, and I can't help but smile as I watch him gently press my legs open wider and position himself against me. But then the smile is gone as he sinks into me, one inch at a time.

I grab onto his arms, feel the flex of his biceps under my

hands. When he pulls out and pushes back into me, my back arches, and I have to slam my eyes closed against the pleasure.

Mateo sets a rhythm, and I open my eyes, watch him watch where he sinks into me again and again. When he sees me watching, he smiles and lowers himself on top of me, and something snaps inside me.

It's like my brain turns on fully. I'm wrapped around him, gasping for air, but when I try to focus on the pump of him between my legs, it's like my mind is in overdrive.

All I can think is, *this is Mateo, Mateo, Mateo.* The man I've been in love with for six years is inside me. The reality of the situation is too much, and I have to turn my face away from him so he can't see that I'm on the verge of tears, that the emotion has become so big inside me that it's going to burst out of my chest.

"You feel so good," he says, his mouth sucking at my throat and then moving down to engulf one of my nipples again. His hands grip my hips, my thighs, my calves. It's like he's trying to touch every inch of my skin. He's so distracted by it that his hips slow, just enough that a whimper escapes my mouth because I need him to go at me hard. It's the only way I'll survive this, if we burn up quickly.

But Mateo doesn't seem concerned with finishing quickly, with making it short and sweet. He pulls one of my legs from around his hips and kisses the inside of my ankle, the act so tender I have to cover my mouth with my hand and bite my palm not to sob.

He reaches for my other leg and then he's hoisting them both up onto his shoulders, bending forward so that he's back where he was, the tip of his nose brushing mine. His fingers come up to my cheeks, and he wipes away the tears there without saying a word. He has to know. He has to understand what this means to me.

He slides slowly out of me and pushes back in. "What is

it?" he says, watching me with his pensive eyes, the way he does. "Where has your mind gone?"

God, does he think I'm thinking about something that's not him? Does he think I've disappeared into my mind instead of being present with him? Can't he understand that he's all my mind is ever focused on? That I'm trying not to look him in the eye and say, *I love you, I love you, I love you* with every thrust?

"I'm just a little nervous," I tell him. It's always been hard for me to focus during sex, to shut out the awareness I always have suddenly of every sound in the universe or the way I'm always unsure where to look, too embarrassed to stare into someone's eyes while they're inside me.

And it's a million times worse when it's Mateo. I can't even fathom the fact that this is real instead of some dream I'm having, and I'm worried if I stare into his eyes, he'll see the way I feel about him, but if I look away, he'll think I'm uninterested, not feeling every move he makes like being struck by lightning.

He stops thrusting, settling on top of me, his whole body against mine in a way that makes a sob rise up in my throat again. I want to spend every second of the rest of my life like this, with Mateo inside me and on top of me and looking at me like the rest of the world doesn't exist.

"Why are you nervous?" he asks, his voice quieter than I've ever heard it. "It's just me."

The comment is almost comical. *It's just me.* That's the problem. It's him. It's *him*. It's HIM. The only man I've ever truly wanted like this. The only person I think about when I'm alone at night with my hand between my legs. When someone puts everything you've ever wanted in the universe right in front of you, is it not normal to be a little nervous?

His mouth brushes mine, and I sigh against it.

"Sometimes I have trouble."

He kisses me, a deep, open-mouthed thing, like he can't quite help it, and then his golden eyes find mine in the near dark. "Trouble with what?"

His hips are moving against mine lazily, and my mind is caught once more on the knowledge that *Mateo's cock is inside me*. I want him so much I'm paralyzed by it.

"With...letting go, I guess."

He pushes up onto his elbows on either side of me, his fingers coming up to brush the hair out of my face. I shiver at the feel of his fingertips on my jaw and then my forehead. "Does it feel good?"

I nod enthusiastically. It does. So good. So, so good. But I'm terrified, already, before it's even over, that we'll never be back here again, that he's already regretting it.

"Good. Maybe I can help you relax."

"What do you—"

Before I've finished my sentence, he's already pulling out of me. He sits back on his heels, and if he wanted me to relax, the way he holds my knees open and looks down at where we were just connected definitely doesn't help. He's staring at my pussy like he's memorizing it, and it takes all my willpower not to cover myself.

"You're so beautiful," he breathes, running his fingers over me. "So wet and swollen." A chill runs up my body at the way he says it, spoken softly and gently, like he's commenting on a piece of art hanging in a museum. He stands, tugs me to the edge of the bed, and then gets on his knees on the floor.

"Mateo," I say, moaning out his name as if he's already licked me there, as if I can already feel him, because watching him get on his knees like that is just as hot as having him inside me.

"Arabella," he says back at me, his hands caressing the insides of my thighs. "There's no reason to be nervous. There are no expectations. You're not being graded. I just want you to feel good. That's all that matters."

He holds my eyes, like he's waiting for me to agree, and when I nod, he smiles. And then he leans forward, parts me with his fingers, and circles his tongue around my pulsing clit.

A sound bursts from my lips, and my hands move of their own accord, sliding into his hair. He groans when I tug and says, "That's it, baby."

And that's what finally rips me back into the room. Mateo's mouth is between my legs. He called me baby. He's *enjoying* himself. I am not some kind of convenience fuck. He's not doing this to be *nice* or as some kind of favor.

His teeth graze my clit and I gasp and moan at the same time, pleasantly surprised. His hands splay across my stomach, and I'm caught by how dark his skin is against mine, evidence of how much time he spends in the sun and how little I spend. I slide one hand back, running it up my stomach until I can twine my fingers with his.

His tongue swirls and swirls, his hand gripping mine, so warm and so big.

I start to feel the tug, that tug that tells me that with just a little more concentration, I'll come. "Wait!" I gasp. "Wait. Wait."

He pauses without moving his mouth away from me, his eyes flickering up to mine.

"I want to finish with you inside me." I'm not a multiple orgasm kind of girl, and I know that if I wait until he's inside me, the orgasm will be a million times better than what he can give me with his mouth.

He sends me a big, open smile, pressing a kiss to the inside of my thigh, and next thing I know, he's flipped us both, pulling me on top of him. Straddling him, my breath catches in my throat at how beautiful he is, his scruff dark in the shadows, his chest strong under my hands, his shoulders broad.

"What are you doing, Arabella?" he asks, not accusation but curiosity lacing his words.

I run my hands over his skin, feel the texture of it under my hands. "Enjoying you." And it's the truth. If this is my one chance, I want to memorize every inch of his skin. I do it with my hands first, down his arms and back up his stomach. And then I do it with my lips, tasting him on my tongue.

But when I start to move lower, wanting to taste every single part of him, he grabs onto my arms and hauls me back up. Pulling my mouth to his, he says against my lips, "Let me feel you, *cielito*."

He lowers me down onto him, and this time, it's like nothing but him exists. He pulls me close against his chest, wrapping himself around me as he pushes up into me. His hands find my hips, moving me in a rhythm so that my clit rubs against him as we rock.

And it doesn't take long at all before I get that desperate feeling again, like I might catch on fire from the inside. I rock harder, watching his eyes close and his lips part.

"Please," I tell him, for once not begging for my own release. "Please, I want to watch you come."

His eyes pop open, his brows furrowed, and he takes my face in his hands. "You first," he says, but I'm already shaking my head.

"No. You. Please. I need it." I know that if I get lost in my orgasm, I'll miss his. And if there is anything in this world I want to know, it's the look on Mateo's face when he reaches his peak.

Before he can argue, I squeeze my inner muscles tight, an act that sends a ripple through me that almost pushes me over the edge. But then Mateo groans loud, his head tilted back so I can see the long lines of his throat, the strain of his muscles, the bulge of his Adam's apple that dips with the sounds he makes.

"Yes," I whisper, straightening to watch, locking our hips together as he falls to pieces. "*Yes,*" I moan again, caught by the delicious sight of him coming and coming and *coming*. And then I follow him over the edge, the orgasm hitting me so hard that a sharp cry bursts out of me.

I pant against his skin moments later before disconnecting us so I can lay down beside him. He pulls the blanket up over us, and I watch him as he settles in, still staring up at the ceiling, his chest heaving a little.

"It's okay if you need to go," I say, even as the words are painful coming out.

He turns his head toward me on my pillow. "You want me to go?"

"Of course not." *I want you to stay forever.* "I would just hate to see your fancy motorhome go to waste."

He smiles and turns on his side, his eyes traveling over my face. "We'll have to use my room next time."

Next time...

He reaches out, wrapping a hand around my hip, and pulls me into him, until my face is buried in his neck. And with the scent of his skin in my senses, I fall asleep.

Arabella

When I wake up the next morning, Mateo is gone and there's a text from him on my phone.

Mateo
Had to catch my flight. Text me later.
You were incredible last night.

Last night.

I shift, pleased to find I'm a bit sore between my legs. Not to mention sticky. Covered in evidence of Mateo. He's all over my skin. I can still taste him.

I stare out the window at the bright sun. This is a whole new world. A world where Mateo is mine. And I don't know if I'll ever believe it's real.

Mateo
Last night was amazing.

Arabella
You have no idea.

Mateo
I think I do.
I think I'll be thinking about it every
second until I see you again.

Arabella
Me too.
Mateo?

Mateo
Yes, querida?

Arabella
Nothing.

Chapter Thirty-Five
Round 10 - Monza, Italy

Mateo Silva - 157 points
Lola Castle - 135 points
Archer Hayes - 128 points

Mateo

"I have a surprise for you," I tell Arabella, low in her ear, as we stand in the middle of the motorhome.

"Oh yeah?" she says, not looking up from the display on her camera. I love it when she's like this, focused, serious about what she's doing. She's not going to let me distract her, but I'm going to try.

"Yes," I say. Reaching out quickly to grab her hip, I give it a squeeze, and that's enough to get her to look up. A tiny little shock of intimacy to get her attention.

She immediately sees Jimena. Her face lights up, and something claws at my chest. I love seeing her like this, too. Pure happiness. Happiness that, in a small way, I put there, even if she's actually just happy to see my sister.

"Jimena!" she says, putting her camera down and stepping around me. "He didn't tell me you were coming."

"That was sort of the point," Jimena says, hugging Arabella.

"What are you even doing in Italy?"

"Work," she says.

I glance at my watch. I don't have much time. "Jimena has full access," I tell Arabella. "She's going to watch from the garage. Can you keep an eye on her?"

"Oh, no," Jimena says, scowling at me. "She's working. She doesn't need to babysit me."

Arabella grabs her wrist. "It's no bother," she says kindly, just like I knew she would. "It'll be nice to have some company."

I pat Arabella on the shoulder. I would never normally ask anyone on the team to be responsible for my family members, but I knew Arabella would enjoy having Jimena around.

"I'll see you both after the race," I tell them before heading for my room. It's been hell all day, not touching Arabella, not kissing her, not being able to pull her into a corner to tell her that she turned my entire world on its head when she kissed me in that elevator.

Before I round the corner into the back hallway, I turn and look back at them. Arabella is showing Jimena something on her camera. The two of them laugh, and I feel a rush in my veins. She looks so beautiful when she's happy, and everything about having her in my life just makes *sense*.

Everything but the fact that she's Pedro's daughter, of course. If he knew what I did to her in Silverstone, he'd cut off my balls and serve them at family dinner.

Mateo

Arabella has taught me how people—the media, the fans—analyze every tiny move the drivers make. The way they pass the videos around on social media, the same social media I try to pretend doesn't exist. So when I come in fifth, I can't slam my fist down on my steering wheel the way I want to. I can't toss my helmet the second I get out of the car and rage.

The fucking car. They've told me again and again this weekend that they can't tell what's wrong with it but the oversteer is insane.

Instead, I keep a straight face. I've still got my helmet on for now, a good way to hide. But eventually, the helmet comes off. Arturo takes it, and I very calmly walk to the media pen.

Mateo, how do you feel about the way the race went today?

This is their generic question. They ask it every time. They ask it almost in exactly the same way every time. I knew of course that they were going to ask it, but my brain is in a jumble. My thoughts are all written out on notebook paper and someone came and ripped them out of the spiral, crumpled them into little pieces, and scattered them into the wind.

I can't think. That voice in my head just keeps going. *This is it, this is it. It's over.*

"Yeah," I say into the mic, upbeat, voice steady. *Just get through the media shit and you can go home.* I can have dinner with Jimena and Arabella. "Obviously, not our best race," I say. I even add a little bit of a smile so they can't start rumors about how heartbroken I am. "Obviously, we wish for a better outcome, but we're still in the fight. Everyone out there on the grid is driving their best and I'll keep driving my best and we'll keep fighting."

Keep fighting. That's what the media team is always telling me to say. Keep fighting, keep fighting. The media wants a fight. They want proof I'm still in this, that I'm still willing to throw punches on the track.

"What is the environment like when you walk off the track and you and Lola are back there in the paddock?"

"If she's the best driver and she's the one who's had a better race, then she deserves to win. We both know that. We don't walk off the track and hate each other. We don't walk off the track and ignore each other. Lola deserves nothing but respect, and we understand that we both want to win, but that doesn't affect anything."

"Great, thank you, Mateo," the interviewer says. There are so many people over her shoulder, people hanging out after the race to talk to the drivers or get their pictures, get their videos, get their interviews.

I see Arabella standing to the side with Arturo and Jayce. Arturo waiting on me, Jayce waiting on the microphone. I expect her, like she always does, to lift the camera to her eye. She's so good at what she does, capturing the right moments, making me look good.

But she doesn't do that now. Her camera stays firmly in place on her chest and she just watches me.

I want to go to her. She's always been able to recognize all of it, all of the things I can't say to anyone. She seems to hear it, like everything I'm thinking echoes in her brain.

I steady myself like I'm good at doing, like I'm *known* for doing. Pat Jayce on the shoulder.

"Hey, man," he says to me, then walks away to do his own media duties.

Everything else feels like a blur around me, just moving too fast. But Arabella is standing still. She's the only thing that's in perfect clarity. As I pass by her, I reach out, let my fingers brush against hers. Just for a moment.

Chapter Thirty-Six

Mateo

"What happened today?" Felix says as soon as I sit down at the table for the team meeting. I don't want to do this right now. It was shit enough coming in fifth place. Now talking it over...

"You tell me. The car was impossible to steer today. It was miserable. It was fighting me on every corner."

"There was nothing wrong with the car." Felix leans forward on his elbows. "All the data was saying it was perfectly fine except for the wing damage."

"Are you kidding me? You saw it. The only reason I even managed P5 was because of pit strategy and because Archer had that miserable fucking pit stop. Every inch of my body is sore from trying to keep the car on the track."

Felix grinds his teeth. "We'll sort it out."

I settle back in my seat. I'm not feeling merciful today, not after they dragged me out of the paddock in a huff. "You'll sort it out. A second ago, you said there was nothing wrong with the car, and now you're saying you'll sort it out."

His eyes shoot to mine. "We'll figure out what was wrong, okay?" He adjusts his headset and directs our attention to the screens in front of us. The engineers start running through stats, data, feedback from the race. I don't want to be here right now. Not when I know Jimena and Arabella are waiting on me. We're all in Italy together, and I want to take my girls out and have a good time. Instead, I'm here.

An hour later, I rub my hands over my face. "Felix," I groan.

"Don't give me that," he says in a bored tone.

"It's one bad race," I say.

"One bad race." He laces his fingers under his chin and glares at me through the gap between our computer screens. "We all know that one bad race is not just one bad race, Mateo. One bad race turns into two bad races, and next thing you know, the gap between you and Lola is so big that you're not able to chase her down."

I hate it when he tells me shit I already know. Like I'm not seeing the information. Like I'm not running through the numbers in my head when I can't sleep in the middle of the night.

"Yeah, I know," I tell him.

The rest of the team is quiet, watching this interaction happen without interfering. They don't want to get in the middle of a fight, and I don't want to get into a fight at all.

"Look," I say, pulling off my headset. "I have to go, alright?"

"Excuse me?" Felix says.

"My sister is here, and she's waiting for me. I have to go," I snap back. I know I'm going to pay for this. But at the moment, I don't really care. I leave my headset on the table and walk out.

Across the paddock, in front of the motorhome, Arabella and Jimena are chatting. Arabella already has her stuff packed up, her camera case slung over her shoulder. I walk up to them and take the camera bag from her, unhitch her backpack from the other shoulder, and sling both of them over mine.

"Ready?" I ask them.

Jimena's gaze slides over to me then back to Arabella. "Yeah, I think we're good to go."

Mateo

Things are quiet at dinner and I feel bad because I know that Arabella and Jimena are feeding off of what I'm putting out: exhaustion, worry, fear. We order drinks, and Jimena refuses when Arabella asks her if she wants wine. Arabella still doesn't know Jimena's pregnant, but I can see little things about her changing, so it's just a matter of time before it's public knowledge.

We order food but then Arabella gets a phone call and steps outside. I smile across the table at my sister because she didn't come all the way here for this race to watch me despair over the fact that I came in fifth place. Is my smile wooden? Does it look real?

"Did you have fun at the race?" I ask her because from the footage I've seen and what they said in the debrief, it was an exciting one.

Even though I feel like someone's forcing me to swallow a bowling ball, everyone is very excited about the fact that I had wing damage and kept driving. We all agreed it would be better towards the end to just keep going than to risk a pit stop and put me even further down the grid.

An exciting race indeed, which will make for an even more exciting championship battle down the road. That's what everyone wants, right? Not someone who comes out clean and easy. They want us fighting until the very last race, and with the standings the way they are, unless one of us fucks up from here on out, that's exactly what they're going to get.

"Lola did really well," Jimena says, fiddling with her fork beside her on the table.

"Yeah," I agree, because that is an irrefutable fact. "Yeah, she's really having a good season. I think something about last season really put a hunger in her that—"

"What the hell do you think you're doing?" she cuts me off, and I see what wasn't there a moment ago. Anger. How long has it been brewing in her eyes?

"What are you—"

She cuts me off again. "Pedro is going to kill you."

I feel ice in my veins. Pedro. Why did she mention Pedro?

"What are you talking about?" I ask her.

"Please, just tell me that whatever this is that you're doing with Arabella, it isn't just sex."

I feel like I'm trying to run in a dream. Going as fast as I can, but not moving forward at all. "How did you—"

"I saw you grab her hand in the media tent," she says. "And for a second, I thought it was innocent. You know, you've been friends for so long and now you're colleagues, but I saw the way the two of you looked at each other all day. I've never seen two people look at each other like that and there not be something going on between them. So, be honest with me. What are you doing?"

I scrub my hands over my face. I really didn't think anyone would notice. In the media tent, the focus of every single camera is on someone, someone behind the microphone, someone who's giving interviews. They're not watching what's going on in the background.

But my sister is not the media. She'd have no reason to be watching anyone but me.

"It's really hard to explain," I tell her.

"Try," she says. I'm surprised at the way the anger in her has transformed into something else, something more desperate, something more confused. "Mateo, she's Pedro's kid. She's, what, seventeen years younger than you? Are you out of your mind? I mean, forget Pedro. What happens when the media gets wind of this? They already think you're crazy for going for another championship. And now you're dating a woman who's seventeen years younger than you? They're going to eat you alive."

"Are you done?" I ask her. I'm just as surprised as she is by my outburst.

We both sit quietly.

I glance out the front windows of the restaurant to see Arabella still on the phone, pacing back and forth in front of the door, like the phone call is not something good.

"I understand how this looks," I tell Jimena. "I understand your concern, but you have no idea what's going on here."

"Then tell me," she says.

But all I can do is shake my head. "I don't know how to tell you," I say. "I don't know how to explain this to you in a way that will make you not hate me right now."

I sort of expect her to tell me she doesn't hate me, but she doesn't. She just watches me, waiting.

"I don't know how to explain it," I say again. "We're just... together. She just makes me feel good."

She blanches, and I realize how that sounded.

"I don't mean like that," I snap. "It's not about that." I sigh. "It *is* about that, but it's not *only* about that. Arabella is so kind and strong and smart. She's understanding and compassionate. We just like spending time together."

"You can spend time with someone without fucking them, Mateo."

"That's enough," I say, crossing my arms. She made me feel guilty, but I'm done feeling guilty now. "You're my sister, and I love you, but I don't need you to understand what I'm choosing to do with my life. If you don't like it, go back to your own."

With that, her chin wobbles. I feel bad. I do. But she started this thing.

Arabella's shadow falls over Jimena, and Jimena turns her face away just in time to avoid being seen.

"Everything good?" I ask her as soon as she takes a seat beside me.

"Yeah," she says. "Just a weird thing. We'll talk about it later." She smiles, and I can see in the bright summer sun coming in through the front windows that it's fake. She turns the fake smile on Jimena. "What'd I miss?"

Chapter Thirty-Seven

Mateo

When I get off the elevator, my eyes slide back and forth, making sure I don't see anyone in the hallway before I head for Arabella's door. Using just my knuckle, I give it a tap, and it opens immediately. I like to imagine her standing there waiting for me, knowing I would come without us ever discussing it.

She smiles a soft smile that makes some of the pressure in my chest loosen and reaches her hand out for me. I let her pull me into the room, and as soon as the door slams shut, I wrap my arms around her, bury my face in the crook of her neck. The smell of her skin is comforting and familiar.

I wish I could shrink her down and stick her in my pocket, carry her around everywhere so that when I had to sit in driver's meetings or am being berated by my sister, I'd know she was there with me.

"Are you okay?" she asks, gently running her fingers through my hair. I sigh and pull back.

"Jimena knows about us."

Her eyes go wide, her arms dropping to her sides. "What? How?"

I raise my arms, let them drop, and walk around her to perch on the edge of the bed. The covers are already pulled back, and I realize she's in her pajamas, a t-shirt and a pair of athletic shorts. She was getting ready for bed.

"It seems we're not as inconspicuous as we thought we were."

She sits beside me on the bed, tips her face toward me. "Do you think anyone else knows?"

I shake my head. "I don't think anyone else is paying that much attention, but she is. Jimena has always been very in tune with her surroundings."

"Do you think she'll tell anyone?"

"No," I say. "She wouldn't want to cause drama with the family, and besides, she's got secrets of her own."

She narrows her eyes. She won't ask, but I know she wants to know.

"She's pregnant." I don't think it'll hurt for her to know. Just like Jimena, Arabella is not about spreading secrets and starting fights.

Her mouth pops into an O shape. "Is she happy about it?"

"Yes," I say, "but when my parents find out the dad isn't in the picture, they're not going to be very excited."

Her mouth pulls into a line, and she nods. "I can only imagine."

I reach over and take her hand, lace our fingers together. "I just wish it was easy."

"Wish what was easy?"

My eyes meet hers, almost black in the lamplight. "Anything. I just wish, for once, that anything could be easy." I move closer to her, until our hips are touching. "Being with you," I say, feeling like I'm exposing too much of my skin but not really able to hold it in anymore, "it's just so easy."

A line forms between her eyebrows. "Is that a good thing? Is it supposed to be easy?"

I reach up, stroke my fingers down her throat, watch her shiver. "I think, in a way, yes. It'll never be easy all the time. And this is, quite frankly, the most complicated relationship I've ever been in, but—"

"Relationship?" With my hand pressed to her throat, I feel the rumble of the word under my palm.

"I meant it when I said this isn't some casual thing. It can't be casual with us. We're risking too much."

A blush spreads across her cheeks. "I don't want casual."

I don't realize I'm leaning in until I can feel her warm breath on my mouth. "What do you want, Arabella?"

"I want you," she says, her voice quivering. "I've always wanted you, and only you."

I can't decipher what her words do to me, part panic, part excitement. I love to hear her say that, but it also terrifies me.

I press my mouth to her jaw. "Tell me about it," I say, my lips brushing her skin.

"What do you mean?"

"You've been holding on to this for a long time." I move my mouth up to her ear, speak directly into it. "I want to know, when did it start? How have you hidden it for so long?" I smile at her breathy laugh and lean back a little to see her eyes.

"I don't think I've hidden it at all."

"You hid it from me."

"That wasn't hard to do. You weren't really around. Everything I was feeling, I was feeling from afar. It was when I was in college, when you and Papa stopped hating each other. It was like a veil lifting."

Something happens in her body then, her shoulders slumping, her breath sighing out of her, like she's giving up the fight. "It started small. I liked your smile and that you got along with the other drivers. And then you started visiting my parents, and I would find excuses to go to their house when I was in town because you made me laugh and because I liked the way it felt to be near you. Every time I saw you, I liked you a little more. Until I was always doing everything I could to position myself in your path."

My breath rushes out of my lungs. It's like she has this whole history with me that I didn't know about. "I didn't see you. Not really."

"That's okay." She presses her hand into my thigh, and it's me suppressing a shiver now. I want her to move it higher. I want her to stop. I want her to never stop. Maybe it's pathetic.

She goes on, her voice a little more breathy now. "Do you see me now?"

I wrap my hand around the back of her neck, fist it into her hair like I could hold her still. I can't keep my mouth from hers any longer.

We're pulling at each other's clothes in seconds. I feel like I'll die without her touch.

I stand, ripping my shirt off over my head and reveling in the feel of her warm palms sliding up over my chest. She's already naked except her underwear, and the sight of her is intoxicating. She reaches for my belt, undoing the buckle, and watching her do it, the look on her face telling me how eager she is, drives me insane.

I stop her hands, and she looks up at me, confused, her hair wild around her face. I move her hands out of the way and pull my belt off, holding it in both hands. I lean forward and settle it across her thighs on the edge of the bed.

"I want to do something to you," I say.

I expect her to ask me what. I expect her to hesitate.

What I don't expect is for her eyes to go dark with heat and for her to say, "You can do whatever you want to me."

Fuck, this woman is everything.

"Get on your stomach on the bed."

She's quick to comply, scrambling up the bed and lying on her stomach, her face turned to the side. She tucks her hands up by her shoulders, and I know she thinks I'm going to spank her. What else would I do with a belt?

But that's not what I want. Although it's nice to know it's on the table. I settle onto the bed with my knees bracketing her legs. In my excitement, I forgot to take my pants off, and they're sagging low on my hips.

I reach for her wrists, pull both of her hands behind her and revel in the shocked little sound that escapes her. Using my belt, I clasp her hands together behind her back and secure them. By the time I've got it tight, she's panting a little.

"Do you like that?"

She doesn't say anything, but her eye meets mine over her shoulder. She nods.

I grab onto her hips, yank her up so that she's on her knees, with her face still pressed to the mattress. I stand and move around the side of the bed, take in the shape of her like this. I can see her watching me while I look at her. I know she wants to ask questions, maybe about whether or not I do this with every woman I have sex with.

I wouldn't want to tell her the truth. I don't know if it'll sound crazy outside of my brain. It's like wanting her this much has spun me out of control and now the only thing I know to do is to try and regain that control, tie her up so that I can think.

I push off the rest of my clothes and get back on the bed with her, my mouth immediately going to her hip, the outside of her thigh, the angle of her knee. And then I slip her under-wear down to her knees, leave them there so I don't have to move her. I want her to stay just like this.

"Do you have any idea how beautiful you are like this?" I ask, but before she can even think of responding, I put my mouth between her legs, and all that comes out of her is a long, tortured moan.

It's music to my ears.

I relish the way she wiggles, writhes, fists her hands behind her back while I eat her, sucking on her clit and then pressing my tongue inside her. Perfect. She's perfect.

Her breathing speeds up and I pull my mouth away, ignoring her sounds of protest. I know I should let her come, but I can't bear the thought of her coming without me inside to feel it happen.

"Are you still with me, *divina*?" I ask, lining myself up with her. The last time we did this, she said she was so nervous that she was having trouble concentrating on what we were doing. From the sounds she's making as I push into her, I don't think she's having that problem now.

"Yes," she whines as I settle my hips against her. I have to hold myself still for a moment, take a deep breath. She feels so good around me, squeezing me tight, and if I'm not careful, this is going to be over very quickly. "Mateo," she whispers. "Please."

I press my mouth to the slope of her spine. "Please, what?"

She keens, pressing her face into the sheets. My God, she's so sexy. I lick her spine and then bite. She gasps. "Please, fuck me, Mateo. Please. Please!"

I straighten, taking her hips in my hands. "Since you asked so nicely..."

I pull out and slam back into her. She groans, the sound muffled by the bed, and all I can do is smile. It feels so good to be with her like this. As I set a rhythm inside her, it's like everything else melts away.

Nothing else makes me feel the way she does.

Relief. That's what she is.

I hook my arm underneath her and find her clit with my fingers, slippery and warm. It's not long until she's moaning, crying out, and then finally, tightening around me, pushing me over the edge with her.

Arabella

"What's that?" He twists my hand until he can read what's on my screen. "An application?"

"It's nothing." I toss my phone on the nightstand, my body worn out after what we did earlier. I shouldn't have opened the stupid email, but I couldn't help it.

He presses in closer to me, settling his chin against my shoulder in a way that makes me smile. "Tell me."

I turn my head, my nose brushing against his. "It's just one of my professors from NYU. He's doing this documentary and he wants me to join his team."

"Documentary? Sounds interesting."

"Does it?"

He laughs. "No, not at all. Unless the documentary is about motorsport."

"It isn't."

"What is it about?"

"Everest."

His eyebrows shoot up. "Everest?"

"Yeah, I know it's extreme, but he assures me that I wouldn't actually have to climb Everest, just that I could go to base camp, which is apparently quite the climb on its own."

He's quiet for a second, and I can feel him floating away from me, the intimacy we've been sharing slowly dissipating. "So you're considering it?"

"Um, no, not really. It's just, you know, my contract with Albatross is only a year so I sort have to consider what comes next."

"That's not something you have to worry about." He props himself up on his elbow. "The team loves you. As long as you want a job here, you have it. But if there's some chance that you would want to do something else…"

"No." I sit up, too, holding the blanket to my chest. This conversation is already making me feel vulnerable enough without being openly naked on top of it. "Why would I leave? I have everyone's dream job. I get to travel the world, taking pictures of hot guys."

He growls, putting his arms around me and pulling me on top of him. "What other hot guys are you taking pictures of?" he asks, and I laugh.

"I'm not taking pictures of any hot guys besides you. You're the hottest."

His eyes scan over my face. "If you want to take the other job—"

"I don't. I want to be here with you."

"Well, I may not be here next season either. So maybe it doesn't matter."

"Don't say that."

"I'm serious."

I can tell by the look in his eye that he is. The thought makes my skin crawl. "Is that what the meeting was about today?"

"They're worried about the second half. The second-half curse, of course."

"Mateo, the second-half curse isn't real." I crawl off of him and set my head beside his on the pillow. I know that in the morning, before I leave for the airport, I'll bury my face in that pillow for one more scent of him.

"I know it's not real," he says, "but they have a point."

"Who does?"

"All of them."

"If you're consistently going down in the second half of

the season, isn't that indicative of a mistake on the team's part, not yours?"

He sits up, too, laces his fingers together in his lap. "No. Maybe. But I don't think the car is doing great in the first half of every season and then failing in the second half. This is my sixth season with Albatross." He shakes his head. "I don't think it's them. I think it's me."

"You're a legend."

"Maybe I'm just cracking under the pressure. Because maybe hearing that I'm under some alleged curse is easier than fighting and being close and then losing it."

I'm shocked to hear such a vulnerable truth come out of his mouth. "I think people would respect you more if you lost by a small margin than if you gave up in the second half."

He looks away from me. I'm focused on how strange it is for us to be having this conversation when he doesn't have any clothes on. His bare chest and shoulders and neck all just staring at me. I shouldn't be thinking about this right now.

"I want you to respect me." His golden eyes meet mine again.

His words break my heart. "You already have my respect," I tell him. "I've always respected you, even when you were out there beating my dad. Winning a championship isn't what makes you worthy of respect."

He nods, and I can see that the conversation is over, that he's lost inside his mind. We settle back into the pillows and turn the lights out. But just before I fall asleep, he says, "I respect you too," his voice so quiet in the dark. "And I would still respect you if you quit and took that other job."

I pretend not to hear him. Because I don't *want* to hear him. I don't want to hear him say he's fine with me leaving.

Lana

Hey, I'm sorry about what I said at the party. I totally put my foot in my mouth.

Ari, please. I didn't mean to hurt your feelings. I just worry about you, especially now that you're on that team.

Ari?

I understand. It's totally fair for you to still be mad. Just know that I'm here if you need me.

Love you, Ari.

Chapter Thirty-Eight
Round 11 - Stavelot, Belgium

Mateo Silva - 167 points
Lola Castle - 160 points
Archer Hayes - 140 points

Arabella

The ball bounces off the wall behind me. When I try to get behind it to hit it with my racket, I miss entirely, my arms swinging wide, spin, and fall on my ass.

"Oh, God, are you okay?" I hear Lola say as Mateo comes over and reaches down a hand to help me up. I have no idea if Lola and her boyfriend, Christian, are looking, but Mateo sets a hand on my waist, turning me slightly toward him, as if he could look through my athletic pants and see a bruise on my ass.

"You okay?" he asks, fingers flexing against my skin.

"I'm fine." I shove him away gently. "But I'm shit at this game." I rub my eyes as Lola approaches us, and say, more to her than him, "If it wasn't obvious, athletics is not my strong suit."

"But you take beautiful pictures," Mateo says, and Lola and Christian laugh.

It's the first time I've heard Christian laugh. He seems to be a kind of stoic guy. Devastatingly handsome, though. When we met in the parking lot, Lola explained to me that Christian is a former Marine, and that he works at a boxing gym in Baltimore that some of his Marine friends own.

Needless to say, he is very good at padel. He makes it look effortless.

"I think I'll sit out the next round," I say, handing my racket to Mateo, who takes it without question.

Lola hands her racket to her boyfriend.

"You don't have to do that," I say.

She waves me off. "Nah, it's okay. I could use a breather."

Together, we go through the glass door into the viewing area, where there are benches, looking in on the padel court. There are a few other people in there, who glance our way. It's hard to tell if they know who we all are, but it doesn't matter; they're kindly keeping their distance.

I reach for my camera, setting it in my lap and adjusting the settings.

"So no padel, huh?" Lola asks.

I laugh without looking up from my camera. "Yeah, I think maybe next time you guys wanna, I don't know, go tanning on the beach, sailing on a yacht, that's really more my speed."

She snorts and points her chin in the direction of my camera. "That looks fancy," she says. "I've seen those zoom lenses; they're basically telescopes. Do you have one of those?"

I laugh. "Yeah, I do. I don't have to use it very often, but obviously it helps during the races."

Once I've got the settings where I want them, I lift the camera to my eye. I can't hold back my smile when I catch

Mateo in the viewfinder. He's got a triangle of sweat on his shirt. The tips of his hair are all wet.

I didn't even break a sweat because I wasn't really trying. But Mateo can't help but be competitive, even when it doesn't matter. And it looks like Lola's boyfriend might be the same way. The two of them are going at each other hard.

"I think you're really good for him."

My smile falls, and I pull my camera away from my face and turn to Lola. She's wearing this expression that's not quite a smile, but almost.

"What do you mean?" I ask, nerves settling in my stomach.

Lola nods towards Mateo, drops her voice low so the other people in the room can't hear. "Mateo, he's just such a lone wolf. Sometimes I worry."

My eyes go back to him on the court. I know Mateo loves his family and that he has friends. Lola, and Arturo, and even Jayce. But she's right. He probably spends more time alone than he should.

"I can tell you really care about him."

I don't look away from him. What could it hurt, just to let someone see? What is Lola going to do? Tell Felix? She wouldn't.

"I do," I say. Simple. Just the truth. I finally look back at Lola.

Her expression hasn't changed, but I can see in her eyes the way she's calculating it. Trying to decipher. Her eyes slide over to the court, watching the two men through the glass. "I know what it's like to love someone who isn't used to letting themselves be loved."

Love. She uses the word so casually. I never said that I loved Mateo, but maybe I don't hide it very well. Jimena saw it, too. Is there any hope of ever being able to hide it?

She bites her lip. "It can be really hard trying to convince someone to open up to you, but he will."

I don't know how she knows all of this without me saying anything, but I just nod. "You won't tell anyone?" I ask, the words barely making it out of my mouth.

"Of course not." The two of us look over at the net again.

This time, Mateo is looking back, his eyes on me. She won't tell him how I feel, but maybe I should.

When we fall into silence, I say the first thing I can think of. "You're having such an incredible season. I know you hear this all the time, but I've always been such a huge fan of yours. I actually have one of your signed mini helmets in my apartment that Mateo swiped for me a few years back."

She laughs. "No way."

"Yeah. I was always cheering for you as much as I was cheering for Mateo."

"I think it's against team policy for you to say that. Careful or you'll get a fine."

"Oh, don't get me wrong, Mateo's going to crush you."

She laughs big, loud enough for the people on the other bench to look over at us.

"It's got to be really cool. First woman to ever win a world championship."

She shakes her head. "This season, I'm still trying to shake off the 'biggest injury in a decade' title."

I feel my heart sink at that. That would be a hard title to have. Even though Lola did have a huge crash last season and she ended up being taken out unconscious on a stretcher after her car went up in flames, the only reason it's the biggest injury of the last decade is because everyone else this decade who got seriously injured also died. It's a miracle that Lola made it out of that car. And a big reason she did, in fact, make it out was because of Mateo.

I watched that crash like everyone else, watched from my living room as Mateo started pulling Lola out of the car while the medics were on their way to her. My stomach was in knots, my chest tight from not breathing.

Like a slideshow, my mind immediately starts cataloguing Mateo's crashes, the little ones and then the very big ones, the ones he might not have survived under different circumstances. The images in my mind make me queasy. If I ever lost Mateo that way, I would crumble.

"Well, I'm glad you're here."

She sends me a soft smile. "Even if I beat Mateo?"

I snort. "Even if you beat Mateo. But you won't."

Chapter Thirty-Nine

Arabella

Out the front windows of the motorhome, I watch Mateo and Jerry walk down the main road, talking enthusiastically with hands and arms and eyebrows in that way that tells me they're discussing the race, strategy, tire degradation and pit stops. Especially that second pit stop, the one that was 9.6 seconds, plenty of time to knock Mateo almost completely out of the points. Mateo's racing suit dangles around his hips as he walks, and I feel ashamed for thinking he looks like something absolutely edible when he's having such a bad day.

As the guys walk in the door, I lift my camera and shoot. I'm supposed to give Mateo space on bad race weekends, and for the most part, that's not hard for me to do, but social media still wants as much of him as they can get, even when the race result is nothing to be proud of.

I remember those weeks when the notifications were few and far between. The weeks when the team didn't want to throw out post-race interviews and cute videos of Mateo because he was too busy licking his wounds or devising his next plan of attack.

"...what they're doing. I know it's not their fault. I know things go wrong, and there's nothing that can be done about that, but what happened to Plan B? What happened to the strategy?"

"Mateo, we're just–"

My camera clicks and both men stop walking and look over at me. I pull my camera from my eye and let it rest against my sternum.

"Sorry," I say quietly.

I expect them to move on, but when I look up, Mateo's eyes are still on me, his expression unreadable. Most of the crew is down in the garage, packing things up or watching the podium ceremony, but a few people are working on breaking down the motorhome already, wiping down tables and packing away the bar.

Mateo turns and says something low to Jerry, and Jerry nods. Most likely, the two have agreed to put the conversation on hold until the team meeting that I know will go late tonight.

When Jerry leaves, heading in the direction of the offices, I'm not really sure what to do, standing awkwardly in the middle of the motorhome with my camera hanging from my neck.

I left the garage as fast as I could earlier. As soon as Jayce and Mateo were off to do post-race interviews, I left, feeling numb in the pit of my stomach knowing that Mateo would take the results hard.

Earning a single point almost halfway through the season when you went into the weekend six points ahead of your competitor is tough stuff. The kind of stuff that Mateo lets crawl under his skin and live there.

Mateo glances around and then pulls out his phone. At

first, I think that's it. That he's upset enough about the race to just all-out ignore me. I start to back away, decide I'll head to a back office to work, but then my phone buzzes in my pocket as Mateo turns for the stairs.

Mateo
Wait thirty seconds and meet me in
my room.

I don't look up at him as he walks out of the room, pretending to do something else on my phone for at least a minute before I look both ways and head for Mateo's room, trying not to be nervous about the fact that his open door is right next to Jayce's, just down the stretch of hallway from Felix's.

I slip into Mateo's room and shut the door behind me, reaching to lock it just in case.

Mateo is halfway out of his driver suit.

"What are you–"

He cuts off my question with his mouth. His hands slide into my hair and he backs me further into the room, until I'm pressed against the wall in the bathroom. I've melted against him, going pliant in his arms.

Without taking his mouth from mine, he reaches over and turns on the shower. Just the sound of the water running has my blood pumping wildly. I always knew there were showers in the driver rooms, and I would imagine Mateo in here, water dripping down his bare skin.

"Get in," he says, ripping his fireproofs off over his head. I start to reach for the hem of my own shirt, but he pushes my hands out of the way and pulls my clothes off me. There's something especially erotic about letting him take off my clothes. Each piece of skin he bares to the warm air makes me feel more and more like I'm doing something bad, the kind of bad that makes me wet between my legs.

Mateo pushes me into the shower and climbs in beside me. He doesn't give me a moment to breathe. He covers my body with his, pressing me between him and the wall. His mouth finds my neck, and his hand immediately moves between my legs. His fingers stroke up and down my pussy, spreading the slickness all across my labia.

My mouth falls open, the pleasure already too much, and Mateo says against the skin of my neck, "That's it. That's what I need."

This is making him feel better. This is what's going to bring him back after that terrible race. Not strategy meetings. Not race replays. This. Being here with me, finding his pleasure with me.

As if he's reading my mind, his fingers dip and plunge into me, and his other hand clamps over my mouth before I can let out a sound that will surely be heard through the wall.

"I want to feel you on my fingers," he says, making my muscles tighten around him. "I need you to come for me." The heel of his hand grinds into my clit, and after just a few pumps, I'm shaking, my legs almost giving out underneath me.

As soon as I'm coherent, aware of the sound of the shower running and his heavy breath at my ear, I say, "Fuck me. Now."

He doesn't hesitate. Hoisting me up, he helps me wrap my legs around him and sink down onto his waiting cock. My eyes roll back in my head, my whole body weak for him. As he bucks into me, I bite down on my lip, desperately trying to be quiet as he fills me, but nothing has ever felt as good as he does right now, his fingers digging into my skin and his mouth open against mine.

"Mateo," I whisper, but he shakes his head, his eyes meeting mine as he fucks me.

I want to tell him I love this side of him. I want to tell him that I love every side of him, his sadness and his anger and his joy and his passion. I want all of it. Forever.

Instead, I tell him the only way I can. I take his face in my hands and kiss him while I let him use me, punishing me with all the anger and fear I know he feels right now.

He slams into me again and again, and all I can do is hold on. He presses his mouth right against my ear and whispers, "Touch yourself, *querida*. I need to feel you come around me." Like he's afraid I might not have heard him, he wraps a hand around my wrist and pushes it down between our bodies.

I do what he tells me to, letting him hold me up as I rub circles around my clit, knowing I need to get myself there again for him. I fist my other hand into his hair and say so quietly I'm worried he won't hear, "Use me."

He lets out the tiniest of grunts, and I feel him pulse and come inside me. The feeling pushes me over the edge, the way he pants against my collarbone sending me spiraling.

A knock sounds on the door. Mateo claps his hand over my mouth to keep me quiet, as if I haven't already stopped breathing altogether.

"Yeah?" he calls to whoever is outside the door, as casual as if I'm not currently pulsing around him. As if his cum isn't dripping out of me.

"Meeting," Arturo says back, voice uninterested.

"I'll be out in a minute."

We hear the subtle sound of Arturo's shoes moving back down the hallway, and Mateo removes his hand, allowing me to suck in air.

Mateo pulls out of me. "Did I hurt you?"

I shake my head, even though it's not entirely the truth. He did hurt me a bit, but I don't mind. "You need to go."

There's regret in his eyes, but he nods. "I'll go out first. No one will even think to be watching the door if they think I'm not in here. You can get yourself cleaned up and sneak out."

I nod. He cleans up quickly before changing into his team kit to go to his meeting. He stops at the door and turns to look at me. I've only just begun to put my clothes back on.

He hesitates. One second, then two.

"Fuck." He rushes across the small room, taking my face in his hands and kissing me deep, so deep I want to beg him to stay, even though I know he can't. He pulls back, golden eyes finding mine. "It kills me every time you're gone."

Before I can say anything, he turns and rushes out of the room, leaving me standing there, half-dressed among his scattered belongings.

Arabella

I step out of Mateo's room, glance both ways. His room is at the very top of the stairs, the second floor of the motorhome, tucked into the back hallway. It's almost impossible for someone to see accidentally. But my heart still pounds as I step out and shut the door. I've made it almost to the end of the hall when someone steps into my path. Brigit.

She's got a file folder in one hand and her phone in the other, and when she almost runs into me, she screeches to a stop. She must be on her way to one of the back offices.

"What are you doing up here?" she says, her eyes floating over my shoulder to the door behind me. Mateo's door.

"I, um... I was just..."

"Were you in Mateo's room?" She doesn't ask it in an accusatory way, more just curious. "I just passed him down in the hallway. Are you looking for him?" she asks.

"No, I, um… He wanted some tea."

"Tea?" she says.

"Yeah, I think he's planning on coming back. And he wanted some tea in his room."

She hesitates, brow furrowed. "That's not your job."

"No, I know, but Mateo's my friend. And he asked, so it's no big deal."

She nods, but her expression hasn't changed. She inches around me so we can switch places. Me by the stairs, her by Mateo's door. With the hand holding the phone, she reaches out and knocks a knuckle against Mateo's door, seemingly without realizing it.

With her eyes on the nameplate, she says, "He does espresso on race days." Her blue eyes shoot back to mine. "And your shirt's inside out." She doesn't say anything else, just turns and walks towards the offices.

I can hear my pulse in my ears. I pull my shirt away from my chest and look down. Sure enough, not only is it inside out, it's also backwards. Because I'm a moron. I close my jacket around my shirt and rush downstairs to find a bathroom.

Arabella

Later, after all is said and done and the motorhome is packed up, I find myself lingering around the garage, putting finishing touches on things, packing and then repacking my bag, waiting for Mateo to be done with his meeting. I've been in here for two hours, but I don't want to leave without talking to Mateo, not after what happened between us.

The sex may have been excellent, but I know it was only excellent because he was upset, and I just want to make sure he's okay.

The door of the office creaks open. I pull something out of my bag, trying to make sure I look extra busy, like I have reason to still be here, even though I don't.

People start filing out, and I glance up. None of them even notice me. Everyone on the team has their jobs, a well-oiled machine, and unless somebody's fucking up, they're mostly not paying attention to each other.

Mateo and Jayce step out last. They're talking, and Jayce pats Mateo on the shoulder as Mateo's eyes meet mine. Jayce looks over, and Mateo says something to him. Jayce nods and leaves. There are still others lingering around the room, packing up supplies and hardware. I shove what's in my hand back in my bag and zip it closed.

"Hey," Mateo says. Images flash in my mind of earlier, him hoisting me up against the wall, wrapping my legs around him, thrusting into me hard and rough.

I drop my voice as low as I can. "Are you coming by my room tonight?"

He taps his first two fingers on the table, sticks his other hand in his pocket. "Not tonight. I told Jayce that we'd drinks."

"Oh, okay."

His eyes shoot up. "We usually spend a lot of time together during the season, but I haven't been because you've been with me." He nods. "Yeah, so we're just going to do some catching up."

"You could come after."

"It'll be late," he says, "and I know you have an early flight, so don't worry about it. I'll see you next week."

"Two weeks," I say, the words heavy in my stomach. "It's two weeks before I see you again."

His eyes finally hold mine. "I know. Don't worry. We'll talk soon."

Arabella
How was your night with Jayce?

Mateo?

Chapter Forty
Round 12 - Zandvoort, Netherlands

Lola Castle - 185 points
Mateo Silva - 168 points
Archer Hayes - 152 points

Arabella

The second I walk into the motorhome, the first person I see is Mateo. He and Jayce, Felix, and Jerry, and a couple of other people sit at a long table against a window, probably talking race strategy for tomorrow, and I have to walk by that table to get over to the bar.

I wouldn't normally stop at the bar first thing, usually waiting until late morning after I've done some preliminary documentation before having a snack, but I can't resist walking by the table and catching Mateo's eye. He leans back in his seat, casual as ever, and cranes his neck toward me as I go past. As I do, I hear Jerry say, "Okay, so we go plan A, but plan B is going to be probably a little more reasonable."

I don't hear when Mateo excuses himself and comes over to the bar, until he's leaning his elbows on it. "You had a good two weeks?" he asks as we wait for someone to come over.

"Yeah, it was fine." We're not looking at each other, both of us staring straight ahead at all the fancy appliances, an espresso maker and a toaster that looks like it has Bluetooth.

"I missed you," he says, his voice quiet.

My breath huffs out of me, but other than that, I don't react. What I want to do is fall at his feet and beg him to love me.

But instead, I say, "I would think you were too busy to miss anyone."

At this, he turns toward me with his whole body, one elbow still on the bar. "I'm sorry for how I acted in Belgium. After the race and then ghosting you."

I shake my head. "Don't apologize for any of it." I try to tell him with my eyes that what he did to me in the shower was perfectly okay. The rest of it was tough, but I'm smart enough to know that sometimes Mateo will need space. I'm also smart enough to know that we haven't defined what's going on here in any real way, and I shouldn't have expectations.

We talked over the two weeks we were apart, but not nearly as much as I wish we would have. We haven't established a rhythm for when we're apart yet, and I don't think long-distance comes easily to him. It's different for me. I've had only the version of him on my phone for so long.

"What do you do when you're home?"

I raise an eyebrow at him. "What do you mean?"

"I mean that when you're not here, working, what are you doing? You know, when you're in Montreal."

I just blink at him for a moment. I've known Mateo for so long and have spent so many years grasping for any bit of information that I can get about him in interviews and articles, social media. I know all of his hobbies and his pastimes. I know his favorite vacation spots and which sports he likes the best, padel and skiing. But I sort of forgot it didn't go both ways. Even before I officially met Mateo, I was learning about him through the years of watching my father and him compete in the sport. And even though Mateo and I met when I was in college, we didn't spend much time around each other, not enough.

"I work," I tell him. "I spend a lot of time on social media trying to find trends and stuff. I spend a lot of time playing around with my software..."

"What else?" He's serious. He really wants to know.

"I like to go jogging."

His eyebrows go up. "Yeah?"

I nod. "Montreal is beautiful. You know this."

He nods.

"I like to go running in the mornings. Take in the atmosphere."

"You take pictures on your runs?"

I shrug. "The camera's pretty heavy, but sometimes I'll stop and take pictures on my phone."

His eyes scan over my face, drop to my mouth.

"The usual, Mateo?" Nick, the one who's usually behind the bar, startles both of us. We whip around to look at him. His eyes are on Mateo, smile big.

"Yes," Mateo says, and Nick turns to me.

"What can I get you, Arabella?"

"I think some orange juice."

He nods and turns his back to us, bending down to pull supplies out of a cooler.

"And when you're done jogging, what do you do?" Mateo picks back up the conversation like nothing happened.

I have to look away from him. I can't think with him looking at me like that, like he's trying to see straight through my bones. "I guess it sort of depends. I spend a lot of weekends with my best friend, Lana."

He nods. "She was at the party."

"Right." I don't mention that we haven't spoken since the party, that she said things that cut me deep. "She lives in Quebec City, so we sometimes meet halfway and have lunch and stuff on non-race weekends."

He nods. "Sports?"

"No, you're the athlete here, sir, not me. I like to read. I like to go to the farmer's market. I'm learning how to cook. I'm not very good at it."

Nick sets two cups in front of us. A tall glass of cold orange juice and a steaming mug of tea with a string hanging over the side. Mateo takes both of them, holding the tea close to his chest and offering me the orange juice. Holding his eye, I wrap my hand around his that's holding the glass. I shiver when he slowly slides his hand out from under mine, our skin brushing.

He winks and I roll my eyes as he heads back to his table. I set my orange juice back on the bar and lift my camera to my eye, snapping several photos of the meeting that's happening before heading back out.

Arabella

Papa
How's Mateo today? Optimistic?

I look down at my phone as I walk behind the buildings of the paddock, trying to avoid crowds so that I can get back to the motorhome.

My father's question is a complicated one. How is Mateo?

He certainly seems to be rather cheery, but I think it's clear that, with Mateo, you can never really tell what's going on in his head. He may seem cheery, but I know he's struggling under the weight of this weekend's expectations.

Arabella
In good spirits but definitely stressed.

I've just sent the message when an arm wraps around my middle. A squeak makes its way out of my throat just before someone spins me around and amber eyes meet mine.

And then Mateo's mouth is on mine. I can't even convince myself to fight him, even though we're out in the open enough that this is a terrible idea. Anyone could duck behind the buildings at any moment. But his tongue sweeps into my mouth, and his arms come around me, and after two weeks without him, it's paradise.

I'm surrounded by him, just like I like to be, all my senses taken over by the smell and taste and feel of him. We part, and he looks down at me.

"We absolutely cannot do this here," I whisper to him.

He nods. "Right." He takes my mouth again, kissing me in a slow, languid rhythm, like we have all the time in the world and absolutely nowhere to be. All of me trembles, and he has to hold me up, bracketing me between him and the wall while his fingers undo the buttons on my polo and dip inside to caress the curve of my breast.

Finally, he lets me up for air, taking my face in his hands. "I needed a little good luck."

"Are you insane?" I say, buttoning up quick and fanning my face. At least if someone does come around the corner, I can come up with some excuse for why I'm flushed. It's dreadfully hot outside.

His tongue glides over his bottom lip. "I haven't touched

you for two weeks. You looked a little stressed. Just thought I'd help out."

"Oh, am I the stressed one?" I say. "You're going to be on track in two hours."

He shrugs. "I'm used to the pressure."

I roll my eyes.

"Hey," he says when I start to step away from him. His hand comes up to grasp my elbow and turn me back toward him.

"If you're about to ask me for a blowjob..."

He chuckles. "No. Summer break. Have you thought about it at all?"

Have I thought about summer break? Have I thought about three straight weeks of not seeing Mateo? Have I thought about the fact that we're going to be separated when he's going into the second half of what is probably the most stressful season of his entire career? Have I thought about the fact that missing him is going to chew away at my bones? Yes, I've thought about it.

"Not really," I lie. "Just going to be relaxing at home. Why?"

He shrugs. "My big house in Barcelona is going to be very lonely."

Wait. Is he saying what I think he's saying?

"What do you mean?" I ask him.

He grins. "I mean, come spend summer with me. It'll be amazing." He pulls me to him, wrapping his arms around me. "We'll spend some time on the beach. We'll go cycling and play padel."

"We're not playing padel," I say.

He raises his eyebrows at me in question.

"I'd have to go home first to pack Spain-appropriate clothing. My flight is already booked."

"Is that a yes?" I know I shouldn't. I know my parents are

expecting me to come home. And that it might be a little suspicious if I suddenly just have the means to take a three week-long vacation.

But I can't say no to Mateo. How could I possibly say no to spending three weeks with him in his house in Spain? I can't. So I don't.

I say yes.

Mateo

See? I knew you were good luck.
Maybe I should kiss you before every
race if it means a win.

Arabella

No objections here. Heading to the
airport now. See you in ten hours.

Chapter Forty-One

Arabella

Laid out before me is a big plot of land with a beautiful Spanish home right in the middle of it at the end of a long, winding driveway that takes us to the front door.

Mateo helps me carry my bags inside. I'm frozen, looking around at everything. The place is immaculate. I know he probably has a cleaning lady that comes every day, but it's like a museum in here. Tile floors, tall ceilings. There's a foyer as soon as we go inside, with a place to leave our shoes. Mateo sets my bags down.

He takes me on a little tour, through an open doorway into a kitchen, and then around into a sitting room. It's all very impressive, but I didn't realize how exhausted I was until we got here.

"Why don't I get you something to drink?" he asks, motioning towards the couch, sitting in front of a fireplace that's turned on, even though it's warm outside.

I sink into his big sofa. It's so cozy, and I could just fall asleep right now, but at the same time, my body is so aware. I'm aware of the smells, the sharp scents of citrus and cinnamon that seem to float in the air, the fabric of the couch under my fingers. There's something about seeing someone's home, seeing the things they find relaxing and comfortable, the things they like and want to surround themselves with every day.

I've known Mateo for almost six years, but it's not the same as knowing him in this way, in his home and in his private life. I've gathered little things about him over the years, little pieces that I stash away, save, bury in the ground like a squirrel with a nut, things like the music he listens to at the gym, the food he cooks in his motorhome, the brand of tequila he likes best, all gathered from interviews and social media posts and overheard conversations.

But in an odd way, I know as much about him as everyone else in the world does. The things I know about him from being where I've been, where I'm positioned near him in the universe, are things like what he looks like when he thinks no one's looking and the kinds of jokes he tells at the dinner table, the way he talks about the other drivers when he's not on the track, things I'm sure people want to know, and that I only know by chance.

Outside the windows on either side of the fireplace, I can see the lights of Barcelona shining bright.

He's gone for quite a while, and when he returns, he hands me a steaming mug of coffee. I raise an eyebrow at him, and he smiles.

"It's decaf."

He sits beside me, arm draped over me so I can press my face into his shoulder. For a long moment, we just sit in silence, breathing. Enjoying. I can hear the steady beat of his heart under my ear.

I sip the coffee. It's dark, not sweet at all, and honestly, it feels so much like Mateo. I've never seen him eat anything sweet.

"I'm so happy you're here," he says. "The last few days, I've been counting down the minutes until you arrived."

I can't help the smile that creeps up my face. That's the most Mateo Silva thing he could have said. His calculating mind, put to good use. Just for me.

He leans forward and puts his mug down on the coffee table, the one that looks like it was cut directly from the bark of a tree. It's very trendy, and I imagine him hiring a designer to pick it out for him. My eyes fall to something I didn't see before. On the edge, there's a stack of books, a cactus, and in front of it all, a puzzle, half put together. Vincent van Gogh's *Starry Night*. I giggle and lean over to touch the pieces with the tips of my fingers.

"Wow, you really are an old man, aren't you?"

He throws his head back and laughs. It does something to my chest. I love seeing him laugh. "I am an old man," he says. "I've been exploring some new hobbies. Puzzles, video games, books. Testing out what I like."

I set my head back against the back of the couch, my eyes feeling heavy. "That sounds lovely," I say.

"I think I'd like a quiet life with you."

I barely process his faraway words. And then I fall asleep to the sound of his voice.

Arabella

I wake when the sun hits my eyes. There are no curtains on the massive windows overlooking Barcelona. I sit up, something falling to my lap. Sometime in the night, Mateo must have covered me with a blanket. It smells good, like fresh laundry. Hand-knit by someone, maybe his mom or Jimena. I glance at the puzzle on the table. I wonder if knitting is one of his many new hobbies.

I sit up and see the still full mug of decaf coffee I left on the table last night. It was rude of me not to finish it. But then, it was rude of me to fall asleep on the couch, too.

The house is quiet. I think Mateo must still be asleep, but when I toss the blanket off of me and walk into the kitchen, I see him there in his breakfast nook, doing something on his laptop. He looks up at me and smiles.

"There are more eggs," he says. "And coffee, caffeinated this time." His caramel-colored eyes are even brighter in the early morning sun.

"I'm sorry I fell asleep on the couch."

His thick eyebrows furrow. "I don't mind. You can sleep anywhere you like. It was a long day. Don't apologize."

I help myself to eggs and toast, my eyes flitting periodically over to Mateo at the table. He's zeroed in on his laptop, and while it doesn't bother me that he's distracted—it's what I would expect from someone at the top of their industry the way Mateo is—I know he needs time away from it all. He needs to unplug.

I set my plate and my coffee across from him and take a seat. "Hey, Mateo?"

"Hmm?"

I lean across the table. "You're not supposed to be working. It's summer break," I whisper.

His eyes flit over to me, and then a slow smile spreads across his face. He shuts his laptop. "You're right. I'm sorry."

"Don't apologize," I mimic back at him. "You need a break from it all."

He sighs. "I can never get my mind off of it entirely."

"I wouldn't expect you to be able to."

He leans back in his chair, spears a piece of melon with his fork. "Have you thought anymore about Everest?"

I almost choke on my eggs. "What do you mean, have I thought about Everest?"

He shrugs. "I didn't know if you missed the opportunity."

"I don't need the opportunity." I put down my fork and rest my arms on the table. "I have a job."

His expression never changes. He's just calculating. Gathering his research. Doing his mental math. "Are you certain you don't want to do it?"

"Why do you want me to take the job?" I ask him. All the joy I felt at waking up in his house has all gone up in a puff of smoke. "I don't understand what the big deal is."

"No big deal," he says. He gets up and comes to my side of the table. He pushes in close beside me. "I'm not trying to stress you out. And I'm not trying to get you to leave the team. I just want you to be happy. That's all I want."

"Then why do you want me to go? I'm happy with you."

He takes my face in his hands. "I don't want you to go. I just want you to make the decision that's right for you."

I brush the tips of my fingers across his soft lips. "I just want to be wherever you are."

He opens his mouth to say something, but then closes it again. Opens it, and closes it. Until finally, he says, "Let's go for a swim."

Arabella

Mateo dives into the pool beside me and I laugh. This is not exactly a diving kind of pool. Do people dive into infinity pools? He comes up and slicks his hair back, pushing the water out of his eyes and smiling so big at me that I swear his teeth sparkle like some kind of dentistry commercial.

"What do you think?" he asks.

"What do you mean, what do I think?" It's a pool. Sure, it's a very nice pool, but a pool nevertheless.

He wades over to me, takes my face in his wet hands, smearing water along my jaw. I haven't gone under yet. Just wanting to enjoy the moment a little bit more before I get my hair wet.

"I want you to be comfortable here," he says. "I want you to love it. I'm hoping you'll spend a lot of time here in the future."

As cheesy as it sounds, I'm pretty sure my heart skips a beat. "Really?"

"Of course," he says, letting me go and swimming backwards away from me. I love this side of him. Carefree, cheerful. "I wish you could be here all the time," he says. "God, I miss you every time we're not together."

I would tell him I could come between races, that I could spend breaks with him, but I know I couldn't really mean it. As much as I would also like to be with Mateo, I can't pay for an apartment in Canada that I don't use.

"I think about you every second I'm here alone," he says, swimming back to me. His face has gone serious. "I think about you when I eat meals, when I go for runs." He presses his mouth to my jaw and I sigh, melting against him. "I think about you when I'm in the shower. I think about you when I'm in bed at night."

"What do you do when you think about me in bed?"

"I think you know," he says, and I giggle. "And I can't wait to have you in my bed finally." He wraps his arms around me.

And then, without warning, he pulls me down under the

water. As soon as we're under, he lets me go and I swim back to the surface.

"You asshole!" I say, splashing him when he comes up to join me, laughing.

"You needed to get your hair wet," he says. And then he puts his hands into said hair and kisses me.

Chapter Forty-Two

Mateo

"You should be asleep."

I'm not particularly surprised when I hear her voice. I knew she would discover she was alone in bed eventually. She's wearing one of my Albatross t-shirts. It almost fits her, just barely grazing her thighs. I'm only a few inches taller than her, though I have much broader shoulders.

"I've never been very good at sleeping," I tell her, setting the wrench I'm holding down onto the floor of my garage and reaching for a rag so I can wipe the grease off my hands. I'll have it under my fingernails for the next few days, but it will be gone by the time we head to Austin, before she has to take pictures of me where I have to look clean and presentable.

"I remember," she says, walking into the garage. I want to tell her not to. She's barefoot. But I scan the ground in front of her, make sure there's nothing there she could step on. A stray screw. A puddle of transmission fluid. When I'm satisfied the floor looks clean, I sit back on my haunches and wait for her to come to me.

She stops beside me, the smooth shape of her legs right at eye level. I want to reach out and touch her, but I don't want to get her dirty. Not when she's so perfect.

I lift my eyes to her, stopping to admire the way her nipples have peaked under the fabric of the shirt. If she stands here too much longer looking like that, I'm going to get hard.

"You used to call my dad in the middle of the night," she says, bending down, setting her hand on the tire well of my 1965 Shelby Cobra. "Sometimes, when I was staying with my parents on break, I would put my ear to the door and listen to your conversations. You would talk about racing for hours."

"It sounds so boring when you say it like that," I tell her.

Her smile falls and she shakes her head. "You're anything but boring. I used to wish I could hear your voice, too. I wanted to soak up everything I could get of you. I was hungry for it."

It's strange to hear her talk about our history this way. Those years looked so different to her than they did to me.

But now, having her here in my arms like this, she feels like the whole universe, bottled up and set before me.

She reaches out to take my hand and I pull back.

"I'm not clean," I say. "You'll be covered in it."

She smiles. "Then let me be covered in it. Please, touch me." She sets my hand on her leg, guides it up her thigh, under the hem of the shirt, leaving black streaks along her skin. I fight back a growl at the image of it.

How many times have I come down here in the middle of the night when I couldn't sleep and spent hours working on my cars or scrolling social media or going over data from the last race?

Always alone. Always in the quiet of the night. Always feeling like some creature so different than everyone else I know.

I pull her to me, wrapping myself around her and taking

her mouth when she straddles me on the cold garage floor. She doesn't care that we're on the floor or that the air smells like motor oil or that it's the middle of the night.

"I'm so lucky to be here with you," she says against my mouth, and I just shake my head.

"I'm the lucky one." Can't she see? Can't she see the way she saves me? The way she comforts me? The way I don't deserve her?

All I can do is show her.

I shove my hands up under the shirt she's wearing, feeling her soft, warm skin. I take her breasts in my hands, run my thumbs across her nipples, and revel in the sound of her soft, sweet moan.

I press my mouth to her neck. "Fuck, I want to tie you up."

"Then take me upstairs."

This almost makes me laugh. With the way she's grinding her sweet, naked pussy against the front of my sweats, I wouldn't make it two steps before throwing her down and shoving myself into her.

"I can't wait that long."

I push the shirt up and take her nipple into my mouth, loving the feel of it pulling into a hard peak on my tongue. She starts to reach for the hem, like she's going to take the shirt off, but I stop her.

"Leave it on."

She only pauses for a second before she grabs onto my shoulders. She always seems to be able to read my mind, and we move as one as I shove my pants down just enough to let my cock spring free and she grabs onto my shoulders so she can push up onto her knees and take me inside her.

She sinks down on me, and we both moan. She's so hot and tight and absolutely perfect for me. I bury my hands in her hair and tilt her head back so I can suck marks into her chest, her neck, the underside of her jaw.

I take her face in my hands, relishing for a moment her blissed out face—eyes closed, mouth open, brow wrinkled, before I say, "Open your eyes."

She does, her brown eyes meeting mine, holding even as they go glossy with pleasure.

I think back to that first night in her hotel room, the way I could tell she was overwhelmed, that she was struggling to meet my eyes, that her mind was in a million different places.

I'm not letting her go anywhere tonight. I'm not letting her fall into her thoughts. I need her here with me. I'll always need her here.

Her eyes start to flicker away from mine. It's something I've noticed, the way she has trouble holding my gaze when we're being intimate like this, and it feels like fear, nerves, something that has no place here with us, not when we're like this.

"Look at me," I say, more forcefully this time, and her eyes shoot to me, her hips stuttering as she rides me.

"*Mateo*." My name is barely a whisper on her lips, like a plea. I want to suck it out of her mouth, the way she always speaks of me with this reverence I haven't earned.

Her hips rock against me as I press my forehead to hers, hold her to me with a tight grip in her hair.

"Don't look away," I tell her. "Not for a second, or we stop."

A wrinkle of displeasure appears between her eyebrows, like she wants to argue with me. So I reach down and grab onto her hips, holding them steady so I can fuck up into her.

Her mouth opens on a keening cry that makes me move faster.

"Do you understand how much I want you, Arabella? How much I need you?"

Like I knew she would, she makes the sounds again, a needy sound that makes me desperate for her. I want to listen to her make those sounds every second of every day. I want to record her and listen to it when she's not around, when she's back home in Canada and I'm here alone, dreaming of her.

Her eyes start to fall closed, and I shift, holding her up with a tight grip on her ass so I can slip my cock out of her.

She makes a choking noise, her eyes flying back open. "Mateo!" This time, when she says my name, it's a painful sound. "No. Please. Please."

"What did I tell you?"

"Okay," she breaths against my mouth. "Okay. I'll keep them open. Please don't stop. Please keep fucking me."

I lower her back down, letting her sink onto me before I pick up our rhythm again. This time, she carefully keeps her eyes trained on mine, and it's me that struggles to focus. In my peripheral vision, I can see her tits bouncing, and I desperately want to watch them.

But I want her eyes more. Want her focus.

Her breath starts to speed up, coming out of her in huffs as she bounces, and I know it won't be long. My balls are starting to tighten, and she's gotten so wet that her juices are starting to slick both our thighs.

"Oh!" she says, her fingers digging into my shoulders. "I can't... Oh, Mateo, I can't..." She's starting to come, and she's struggling to keep her eyes on mine as her legs start to shake.

"Don't close them," I tell her, as I feel myself inching toward the edge. "Let me see. Let me see every second."

She breaks then, her inner muscles squeezing me tight, her mouth hanging open as she takes my face in her hands. As soon as she goes limp in my arms, her mouth finds mine, kissing me as I groan and fill her up.

We keep kissing long after my orgasm has passed, long after I've gone soft inside her, tongues mingling even as her body begins to droop with exhaustion and our skin has gone cold.

I kiss her until I realize I'm holding her up, that she's fallen asleep with her mouth against mine. And even then, I plant one, two, three more warm kisses on her before hiking her high against my body and carefully getting to my feet.

I carry her out of the garage, leaving my work behind.

Mateo

At 3 AM, I'm still awake, staring into the darkness of my bedroom. My eyes have completely adjusted to the dark, and I turn and look at Arabella, lying beside me in my bed.

I feel like someone who accidentally found themselves on a roller coaster, clicking and clicking and clicking toward the top. And then, suddenly, you're at the apex and you're looking down, and you know that if you don't get off now that you're going to go careening into a place you have no control over.

I quietly get out of bed and move over to the desk where Arabella left her laptop. When I turn on the screen, I see that it needs a password. I type in Albatross because that's the password on my computer. It's a no-go.

I glance over at her. My God, she's so beautiful. The background on her laptop is a mountain range probably in some Scandinavian country.

I stare at the screen for a long moment, and then sigh, leaning forward to type my name into the password box. I don't know if it's self-serving or optimistic, but I'm not surprised when the computer unlocks. Something big and scary and suffocating smacks into my chest when it does.

What have I done? I knew when I got involved with Arabella that it was not a simple thing, that it was not a casual thing, that it was not something that could just be done and then forgotten.

But I don't know if I could have ever anticipated what we've experienced these last few weeks. Could never have anticipated the way we've become so attached, how much I feel like I can't live with her.

I open her emails and scroll through them, looking for the application or a letter from this professor of hers. I don't exactly know what I'm looking for, but most of her recent emails are Albatross schedules, so I just read anything that isn't from the team.

When I can't find the email, I think maybe her professor sent it to her cell number instead. Maybe he texted her a link. The only time I saw it was on her phone.

But then I open her trash can. And it's right there. *Everest_Doc_App_Cedillo.* She deleted it. She was never going to apply. And that knowledge makes my chest ache.

She wants to go. I know she does. And I know she'll never go as long as she has the chance to stay with me at Albatross. I know she'll never make the choice to leave me.

If I thought Formula 1 was really what she wanted, I wouldn't even be considering this. If this work was as exciting to her as it is to me or to Pedro, things would be different. But I've seen her these past months. She doesn't love the sport. She's here for me. I'm why she's throwing away this job that looks like it would be amazing for her.

I think about this last week together here in Barcelona, the way she always has the camera up to her eye. The way she'll smile at me around the lens. The way I'll catch her staring off into the distance, that little line between her eyebrows like she's trying to figure out a way to bottle up every beautiful thing in the universe and just stick it in her pocket.

She deserves to do that all the time. She deserves to do what makes her happy.

But she's never going to do it on her own. She's never going to leave as long as she has a place in Formula 1 and as long as she has me behind her, telling her how much I want her on the team. Every time I've told her how happy it makes me to have her here, I thought I was helping her feel more at home, more like she belongs.

But now I know I'm what's holding her back.

I follow the link in the email. I fill out the application and send it. And then I get back into bed and I settle my head on the pillow and watch her sleep. Because the season is three quarters of the way over. And I don't know how many more chances I'll get to do this.

Chapter Forty-Three

Arabella

In the end, it's almost ironic that it's the social media accounts that bring us down. The day it happens, a week and a half into my idyllic Barcelona vacation, I'm jogging through the hills of Spain at sunset.

Mateo is supposed to be with me, but he got a call at the last minute while I was putting on my shoes. Arturo with some question. So I went without him. No big deal. I've done it many times before.

I'm listening to Cassie Reese as I jog, the music turned up dangerously loud, when the melody is drowned out, notification after notification after notification.

The social media notifications find me first. They always do. They're instantaneous. But then I get the emails, Google hits with Mateo's name and mine wrapped together. Text messages from Lana, and the last one from Mateo.

Mateo

Where are you? Come home.

Mateo

It takes Arabella twenty minutes to get back to the house. By then, I've already run through a million different strategies in my mind.

People from the team have been calling and I've been ignoring them. The last thing I want is to start making plans before Arabella and I have spoken.

She throws open the door and slams it shut behind her, her chest heaving under her orange sports bra. If circumstances were different, I would have been dragging her to the ground and fucking her right there in front of the door.

The anger and stress I feel at the current situation is just making me want to do it even more. But we need to talk.

"What happened?" she asks, panting.

I can only imagine how far away she was when I texted, how fast she sprinted to get back.

"You didn't look?" I ask.

She throws her hands up. "The sun was shining on my screen. I didn't really want to slow down long enough to figure it out. I just wanted to get back here to you, so tell me what's going on."

I pull up the photos on my phone, the ones that are all over F1 social media, and hand it to her.

She spends a long time studying it. I can tell she's doing exactly what I did, trying to figure out how long ago the photo was taken, where it was taken, who could have taken it, who could have sold it.

A very clear picture of me in the hall outside her hotel

room. The door to her room is open, and she's smiling at me as she reaches for me, our hands linked, in full motion.

She runs a hand over her face, leans back against the door. "This is the hotel in Italy," she says.

I nod. I already figured out that much.

"It could be a lot worse," she says. "It's not exactly incriminating, is it?" She shakes her head. "This is not direct evidence of anything."

"Me showing up to your hotel room in the middle of the night?"

She shrugs. "We're friends. Everyone knows we're friends."

She's right, but I don't know that it really changes anything. People will start rumors. They'll start to analyze things they saw themselves. They'll start to question.

"We're toast, no matter what."

"Have you spoken to anyone?" she asks.

I shake my head. "I wanted to speak to you first."

At that, she sets my phone on the table by the door and comes over to me, taking my face in her hands. "It's okay. We'll figure it out."

"Of course we will." She's right. It could certainly be a lot worse. It's not like either one of us is married. It's not like we're competitors.

"It's okay. I mean..." Her eyes look back and forth between mine, run down my face and back up again, analyzing. "I'm, you know, okay with people knowing."

I can see the worry in her eyes. She's worried that I would prefer to hide the whole thing, when it's the exact opposite. "I'm not the problem here. I don't mind everyone knowing," I tell her. "But I think we both know someone who won't be happy."

Her hands tighten just a little bit on my jaw. Then they drop away from me. "I should call him before he sees everything. My parents barely pay attention to social media. It's really doubtful they would have already seen something."

"Your father watches F1 news. This is going to be all over F1 news."

"I know."

But then something begins to loosen inside me, begins to let go, like a wet knot finally coming free. "Maybe this is a good thing," I tell her. "Maybe it would be nice not to hide anymore."

As I watch, the worried lines along her face begin to shift and her mouth pulls into a wide smile. She leans in and kisses me.

I know we have a lot to handle. People to call, media to weather.

But for right this moment, she's still just mine. And no one can take her from me.

The world can wait until tomorrow.

Chapter Forty-Four

Arabella

I come awake with a gasp. I stare into the dark, not sure what it was that woke me, but when I clutch the blankets to my chest and look over, I realize Mateo is awake too, pushing himself up in bed, his eyes on me in the dark.

"What was that?" I ask him.

Before he can say anything, it comes again. Someone banging at the front door.

"Stay here," he says, getting out of bed and pulling on a pair of athletic shorts.

"Absolutely not," I say, snatching up the Albatross shirt I left beside the bed and throwing it on to follow him into the hallway. He doesn't argue with me as we both cautiously walk into the entryway.

The doorbell sounds, making me jump. Mateo presses himself to the door, putting his eye to the peephole. I'm waiting for him to tell me there's a masked serial killer on the other side, but instead, he looks at me with this expression can't I can't read, like he's waiting for something terrible to happen.

"What?" I ask.

He doesn't say anything, just reaches out, unlocks the door and opens it.

After that, everything happens so quickly, it's a blur. Whoever is on the other side of the door bursts into the house, ramming straight into Mateo.

I gasp, my brain working much faster than my body. Mateo knew who was there. He wouldn't have opened it the way he did if it was someone he didn't know, someone he thought would attack him. But now there's a man on top of him, his hands wrapped around Mateo's throat as he pushes him down into the stairs. And then it clicks. Like two pieces of a jigsaw puzzle fitting perfectly together.

My father.

"Pedro," Mateo chokes out. He clutches my father's wrists, his biceps bulging as he tries to push my father off of him.

"What the fuck is wrong with you?" my father growls, letting go of Mateo's throat to cock his arm back.

"Stop!" I shout, rushing towards them, but I don't make it before my father's fist connects with Mateo's face. "Papa, no!" I scream. I don't know what else to do other than to wrap myself around my father's arm, holding it back so he can't hit Mateo again. "Stop it! Let him go!"

My father is vibrating. He's like a dog with his teeth wrapped around an intruder. I've always known my father was strong, but trying to hold him back now, as Mateo struggles out from under him, is like trying to move a two-ton boulder.

"Stop it! Stop it!" I keep saying into his ear.

Mateo moves and my father and I land on the stairs together. When he realizes he's not going to get another hit in, my father tries to grab me, like he's going to drag me bodily from Mateo's house.

I shove his hands off and push away from the stairs. I go straight for Mateo, press my hand to his face to look at his swollen cheekbone while he gasps for air.

"You disgust me," my father says.

I turn to look at him, feeling his words like a punch in the throat, and I know they must hurt Mateo more than the actual punch did. I can see the hit blooming pink across his cheekbone.

My father's eyes are deadly focused on Mateo. "Ari," he says without looking at me. "Pack your bags. We're going home."

"Excuse me?"

This seems to break my father out of some kind of trance. His eyes finally find mine. "You're not staying here."

I take a step toward him, feeling murderous. I've never been this angry at my father before, but he's never spoken to me like this, not even when I was a child. "You don't get to tell me what to do," I say. "I'm an adult."

"Fine," he says, finally pushing up off the stairs, his hands still clenched into fists.

I realize he's in his lounge clothes, the sweatpants and t-shirt he wears when he's at home on a Sunday afternoon, watching sports and letting my mom cook for him. It's like he heard the news and immediately got on a plane, not even bothering to change.

"I trusted you," he says in Mateo's direction. "How could you?"

Mateo shakes his head. "You don't understand what's going on here, Pedro."

"Don't I?" he says, taking a step towards Mateo.

When he moves, I do too, standing between the two of them, blocking Mateo with my body.

My father doesn't seem to notice. He walks right up to me, until I'm staring directly at his throat. "Don't I know what's going on? I know exactly what's going on. I trusted you to look out for my daughter and you did this. She's half your age. She is a child."

Without even thinking, I shove my father back and he stumbles before smacking into the wall that leads to the kitchen. "I am *not* a child," I shout. "I'm twenty-five years old and I may be your daughter, but you don't get to make my decisions for me and you don't get to talk about me like I'm a teenager. And you *certainly* don't get to hit a man just because I'm involved with him."

"You don't know what you're doing, *cariño*," he says. "You're young. You don't know any better."

"Oh yeah?" I say. "And how old were you when you married Mom and started having babies, huh?"

"That's different," he says. "I wasn't having babies with a woman twenty years younger than me."

"It doesn't matter."

"And not only are the two of you doing something absolutely sickening, but you've lied about it as well, right to my face. How long has this been going on, hmm?"

I can feel Mateo trembling behind me, full of adrenaline and anger.

"I asked you to look out for her," my father growls, leaning around me like he's just remembered Mateo is still here.

"It's not what you think, Pedro," Mateo finally says. "It's all very new to both of us, okay? And this is why we didn't tell you. Would it have made it any better if we had gone to you a month ago and told you this was happening? Would you have taken it any better than you are right now?"

"I'm not going to let you do this to my daughter," my father says, his voice low, full of rage.

"You don't get to decide," I say. I reach back for Mateo's hand and he offers me his fingers, wrapping them around mine. "This has nothing to do with you," I tell my father. "For once in my life, I am doing something that has nothing to do with you."

His eyes squint at this, showing off the crow's feet on either side of his face. I'm caught for a moment by the look in his eyes, the eyes I know so well in the face that's so familiar. "You've ripped my heart from me," he says. This time, I can't tell if he's talking about Mateo or me or both of us. "I don't ever want to see either of your faces again."

"Papa," I say, feeling like I've had all the wind knocked out of me. I don't know what to say or what to do. He came in here and shattered everything. Even if I stop seeing Mateo right now, that doesn't suddenly fix everything. The relationship between Mateo and my father, between my father and me, is permanently annihilated. There's no going back now.

"I don't know either of you," he says. Then he's gone, wandering back down the stairs of Mateo's home to the car I can see through the open doorway, its back door flung open, parked at an angle in the U-shaped driveway.

A sob escapes my mouth. I don't realize I'm about to collapse until Mateo has wrapped his arms around me.

Arabella

There's nothing left to do when my father leaves except go back to bed, which feels preposterous because how do you go back to bed when your father just disowned you?

Mateo and I crawl back into his bed fully clothed, settle under the covers silently, lay beside each other, and stare up at the ceiling.

There's nothing left to say, nothing left to do, and after a moment, it all just comes crashing down on me, and I start to cry.

What a horrendous thing it is to love someone so much and to have the other people you love so much hate that love.

Mateo rolls over on his side to face me. He pulls me into his arms and I tuck my face into his neck and cry and cry and cry, until there's nothing left but me gasping for air.

"I'm sorry," he says. "I'm so, so sorry."

"I don't want you to be sorry," I tell him. "Don't be sorry for being with me."

He shakes his head. "I could never be sorry for that." He brushes the wet hair out of my face. "You can call him tomorrow. You can go see him."

This is the first time I've ever felt guilty for the way I feel about Mateo. I wasn't stupid enough to think that it would go over well once people found out. I know how it looks. I know how people think. I know how big the gap is in our ages. I know all of these things. I just don't care about those things. I just care about him. But my dad cares. Not just because of how it looks, but because we've taken a reality that he knew to be true and changed it, turned it on its head, confused him.

"I don't want to."

"Why not?"

I pull back to look him in the eye. Can he really not see? "Because he made me choose," I say, sitting up, looking down at him in the dark where I can just barely make out the features of his face. "He made me choose, and I choose you."

"Why?"

"Because I love you." I can't hold the words in anymore. I can't make them stay inside me. I can't hold any of the emotions back.

He pulls me back down to the mattress and presses his forehead to mine. "I don't deserve that kind of devotion."

His words make my stomach hurt. The fact that he

doesn't think he deserves my love makes me want to claw right into his chest and burrow there.

"Yes, you do," I tell him. "And you have it."

He doesn't address the fact that I just told him I love him, that I said it in the midst of this complete dumpster fire of a night. And he doesn't say it back.

Chapter Forty-Five

Mateo

I get started on damage control before the sun is up and Arabella is awake. I talk to Felix, and we decide that he'll address the media today and I'll address the media next week in Austin. Arabella won't address the media at all, if she can avoid it.

I scroll through social media comments, through text messages and emails. It's never ending.

Yesterday, it felt so far away. It felt like this thing that couldn't touch us because we were all the way in Spain.

But it doesn't feel like that today. Today, it feels like all of it is looming over us, like we're in a bubble and everyone else is standing just on the outside, ready to pop it.

All I can think about is Arabella crying in my arms last night. About the bruise I can feel pulsing on my cheek. How we somehow managed to utterly fuck this up. We tried not to hurt anyone. We did something the two of us thought was right and okay.

And yet, somehow, we're still here.

And I'm sick at the idea that Arabella would throw it all away for me. Her relationship with her parents, her reputation with the team, an opportunity to do something she's passionate about.

Because now people will think they know what's going on; they'll think they understand who she is. It's all about to get so much worse for her.

She said she loved me, and I don't know what to do with that. Because if I have never deserved anything in my life, this is the thing I have deserved the least. The love and commitment of a beautiful, kind woman like Arabella.

She comes downstairs later, and I wish I could say I'm surprised when she brings her bags down with her, but I'm not. I know she needs space. I could feel it last night.

"I have to get home," she says as she stands in the foyer. "I have to get prepped for Austin next week."

I don't argue with her. I know it would be no use. "I'll drive you to the airport."

She shakes her head. "I already called an Uber."

I walk over to her slowly. I can feel the wall she's put up around herself, and I'm not sure if I should keep my distance or if I should tear the thing down. All she's done is tear my walls down, but I don't know how to deal with hers. I'm not used to them. She's always opened herself up to me.

Because I don't know what else to do, I take her face in my hands and kiss her. I can taste her sadness on her lips. I want to tell her we'll get through this, that we'll figure it out. But maybe there is no way through.

"Text me when you get home. Please."

She nods, looks up at me with sad eyes. I wish I could take the sadness away from her, but I know I can't. I watch her walk out to her Uber, feeling like she's taking part of me with her.

Porkupike: I guess we should have all seen that one coming.

Cinnamonster33: Geez, this is really nepo baby to the extreme, isn't it?

podium_king: Another woman trying to sleep her way to the top.

r@cing_s1m: *@p0dium_king* where exactly would she be trying to sleep her way to?

quiiickshiftz: Mateo never saw a pretty girl he didn't want to dick down.

Chapter Forty-Six
Round 13 - Austin, USA

Lola Castle - 203 points
Mateo Silva - 193 points
Archer Hayes - 160 points

Arabella

This must be what it's like to be Mateo. When I walk into the paddock, all eyes are on me. People turn cameras in my direction, cell phones, follow me with their eyes.

I'm not supposed to be on this side of the lens.

I keep my head down and keep moving, focusing on getting to the motorhome and getting to work. It's been a week since I left Mateo to fly back to Canada, a week of late night phone calls and rushed text messages as we tried to weather the storm while he got back to work.

The media hasn't been kind. I've been called every name in the book: a slut, a nepo baby, a pot stirrer, a gold digger. They've said only the worst of me, and I've just had to take it. It's not like I can say anything to defend myself. Albatross has a carefully crafted media presence, and I was very quickly told to keep my mouth shut and let Mateo and the team handle everything.

People start to call out my name. I ignore them and keep walking. It isn't until someone grabs my arm, pushing in close, that I start to panic. I turn to whoever it is, ready to tell them off, to shove them off me if I have to. I don't get a chance because Arturo does it for me. "Hey, what the fuck?" he says, dislodging the stranger's hand and then stepping between us.

He puts his arm around my shoulders and his hand up like he's trying to shield me from paparazzi.

"Thanks," I say as we head towards the motorhome.

As soon as I step into the motorhome, it's like when you're at a party and you step outside and shut the door behind you and all of the noise just stops. Everyone turns to look at me. They stop what they're doing. They stop talking. The only ones still moving are the cooks, making omelets and avocado toast.

For the last six years, every minute I wasn't with Mateo during race season, I *wished* I was with him. I wanted to be in the paddock. I wanted to be at every race. I wanted to know how he was feeling every second of the day. I wanted it all the time.

And now, I just wish I could be anywhere else.

In my fantasies, it was never like this. When I would daydream about this, never thinking there was any universe in which it could actually happen, everyone was so happy. The media loved that Mateo was with Pedro Cedillo's daughter. Papa was excited because he loves Mateo. Mateo's parents would welcome me with open arms.

The version of me that fantasized about those things was an idiot.

On autopilot, I head for the back office I'm used to hiding in to get work done, and I'm surprised when Arturo follows me, waiting in the doorway, even as I take a seat.

"How is he?" I ask. If anyone will know it will be Arturo. He's the one that's glued to Mateo every minute he's in the paddock.

The corners of Arturo's mouth turn down. "He's worried about you."

"That's not what I wanted at all." I say it out loud even though I don't intend to.

"What did you think was going to happen?" Arturo says, keeping his voice low as he steps into the room, his eyes going to the people on the other side, all of them focused on their own work. "He told me what happened... with your dad."

"Is he mad?" My voice breaks, and I glance over at the engineers discussing something between themselves. They don't seem to notice I'm in emotional distress.

"No," Arturo says. "No, he's not mad at you. He's mad at himself. He just wants to know that you're okay."

I nod. It's not like I thought this was going to be easy. Especially not after what happened with my dad. But I guess I wasn't prepared to feel so alone throughout all of it.

Last week, as soon as the news hit, I had to go back to Canada and Mateo had to go to England to visit the factory, and even though we talked every day, we were on opposite sides of the planet.

"Felix wants to see you."

My eyes shoot back up to Arturo, towing over me. "He does?"

He nods. "I guess he and Mateo have discussed a lot, but they want you there to discuss as well. You can finish your work in the garage." Without giving me a moment to process, Arturo reaches for my bag and slings it onto his shoulder. I guess he's used to carrying Mateo's stuff around, but I'm certainly not his boss, and this is not in his job description.

I follow him back out of the motorhome, not missing the way everyone's eyes follow us as we move through the front lobby, where crew members and sponsors and spectators are taking pictures and getting food and just generally staying out of the Texas heat.

Outside, for the first time in my life, I have microphones shoved in my face. They seem to be coming from all directions.

"How long has this thing with Mateo been going on?"
"What does Pedro think about you and Mateo dating?"
"Did you take Mateo from Cassie Reese?"

The questions begin to swirl in my brain, and even though I know I shouldn't and can't answer their questions, I feel myself wanting to speak, wanting to defend myself, wanting to tell them all where to shove it. But my body seems to be torn between speaking and not speaking.

"Out of the way!"

I take a deep breath when I hear Mateo's voice, like a balm to a screaming burn.

He reaches for my hand and pulls me in the direction of the garage without looking back.

Mateo

"Is this going to be a problem?" Felix crosses his arms and leans back in his chair. I can already tell this meeting is going to be a waste of time, that this is just one more way for Felix to enforce his authority.

"Why would it be a problem?" I ask. In the seat beside me, Arabella is silent. I get the feeling she has no intention of speaking during this meeting. It's unfortunate, but she understands her role here, her role on the team. She's important to me, but she's not important to them.

Felix gestures vaguely toward the door. He doesn't have to

say it for me to know what he's talking about, what just happened outside. Arabella pulling attention, all those media people asking her questions, mobbing her. "I need your head in the game," Felix says to me. "I don't really care who you're sleeping with or dating or whatever it is you're doing, okay? What I care about is whether or not you're showing up and you're doing your job."

Arabella makes a noise in the back of her throat that has both of us looking at her.

"Do you have something to say, Miss Cedillo?"

Her eyes come up, shift from Felix to me. "I mean, are you serious?" she asks, catching me by surprise. I watch her carefully.

"Excuse me?" Felix asks. I can tell he's trying to be patient, but patience has never been his strong suit.

"All Mateo does is his job. All he's focused on is what's going on here at the track. He has his head so far in the game that he can barely sleep at night, and you're going to question him now because he has the audacity to be in a relationship?"

Felix sighs loudly. "Arabella, I understand that you grew up in this world and you think you know what's going on, but I don't think you do. The last thing we want right now is bad press. The media is already questioning Mateo's abilities, both on the track and off. If you were anybody else, this wouldn't be a problem. But you are not just somebody else, okay? You are the daughter of Pedro Cedillo. And so, everybody out there wants to know what the hell is going on. Don't even get me started on the fact that they're having a field day with the fact that you're twenty years younger than him."

"Seventeen," I correct him.

"Get a grip," he barks back. "We can't afford to handle this right now. We have five races left in the season." He points at Arabella without looking away from me, talking about her like she's not in the room. "If she becomes a distraction..."

"If she becomes a distraction, what?" I ask.

Felix sighs and lets his hand drop with a *thud* onto his desk. "There is exactly one expendable person in this room, Mateo."

I look over in time to see Arabella's face go pale. So that's it. If Felix deems Arabella a distraction, he'll fire her. I look at what I've caused. Arabella swallows, and I know she's trying not to cry. This job may not be her dream, but I know she wants to be here, even if I don't understand her motivations.

And now the fact that she's with me is threatening everything she's worked so hard for.

"Just..." Felix begins and then trails off. "Just keep your distance until the race." He addresses Arabella. "Find something else to shoot, okay? Spend some time with the guys in Jayce's garage. Walk down the paddock. Take a picture of the car park, if you have to. There are tons of celebrities here. Go take pictures of people that aren't Mateo. Put some distance between the two of you until the race is over and until all of this cools off. Got it?"

Arabella, her jaw clenched tight, nods.

"Yeah," I tell him. "We got it."

And without waiting for another word, Arabella shoots out of her seat and leaves the room, the door crashing shut behind her.

As soon as she's gone, Felix shakes his head. "You couldn't have picked someone a little less complicated?"

I'm floating in the middle of an ocean, and a wave in the distance is getting bigger and bigger, ready to crash down on me.

"I didn't pick her," I say, leveling him with a stare. "She picked me."

Mateo

"Mateo," the reporter says in the pre-race press conference, "it recently came out that you've been in a relationship with the daughter of Pedro Cedillo. How has this affected the team?"

I sigh. Here we go. I knew it was coming, but they gave me false hope by asking Lola and Archer questions before me. And they asked them good ones, about the state of the car so close to the end of the season and Lola's championship hopes.

But they're asking me about Arabella.

"It hasn't affected the team, not at all," I say confidently. "I have been seeing Arabella for quite a while without anyone knowing and it has had no effect on the team or the championship or anything that's going on at Albatross."

"How does Pedro feel about the two of you seeing each other?"

"I'm done with the questions about Arabella. Moving on."

The room is quiet for a second as the media regroups. They move the attention away from me for a moment, and then someone asks, "Mateo, where did you get the black eye?"

I almost forgot about the black eye. It makes me wish I had learned to put on light makeup, like Jimena's always suggesting I do, to cover up how much I've aged when I'm standing next to all the young guys. I thought it would have faded enough for the cameras, nothing more than a banana-colored monstrosity now, but clearly, I was wrong.

"We're five races away from the end of the season," I say into the microphone, "and there are ten points between Lola and me. At this point, anybody could take it. And everyone's too concerned about what's going on on my face, or who I'm seeing." I pause, pull the microphone away from my mouth. After I take a deep breath, I pull it back. "As drivers, we have to find a good balance between our personal lives and our professional lives. Mine just happen to intersect. I don't have a habit of getting involved with people I work with, but Arabella is different. We've been friends for a few years now, and I know that not everyone in this room, or everyone who's listening to this or asking questions, understands what's going on here, but it's not for them to understand. All you need to understand is that I'm going to go out there on Sunday, and I'm going to race Lola."

I turn to look at her. She sends me a gentle smile.

"And most likely, one of us is going to win. That's all you need to know."

Part of me wishes I had never opened my mouth, and another part of me wishes I could just tell everyone in this room right now that Arabella has become so important to me, that she's burrowed down deep under my skin, and that I don't know what to do about it, that I don't know how to do right by her, that I'm lost. Lost in her, lost in our predicament.

When they dismiss us, all I can do is sit there on that couch, watch everyone file out, and wish I could just disappear.

Mateo

I can feel the defeat in my blood when we pull around the last corner. There's nothing left, not in the car, not in me, not on the track. I cross the line behind Lola and slow as we go around again.

I did my best to keep my head in the game, I really did, but I made mistakes and Lola didn't, and that's why she went across the line first. There's no separating any of it anymore. Arabella and this fucking car, this race, it all takes up the exact same amount of space in my brain now. Everything is fighting for dominance, and on a normal day, that might have been fine. I've been managing it just fine for the last two months.

But it's different now because before, when I was ripped apart, when I was analyzed, when I was put under a microscope, it was just me, and it was fine if I was up at night worrying about it, and it was fine if Felix was chewing me out, and it was fine if I couldn't get any fucking peace.

But now that Arabella is involved, it's not fine anymore, and I can't get it out of my head. That look on her face when Felix threatened her job, the way she cried in my arms back at home, the way that being with me is slowly but surely draining her, taking everything away from her that she loves.

How am I supposed to focus on a fucking race when I've done that to her?

I stop in my designated spot, get out of the car, and wave to the crowd the way I'm supposed to. Luckily, they can't see my face. I weigh in, do my interview, and then Lola and I stand together while they interview Archer.

I can feel the cameras on me. I can feel everyone watching. Lola glances up at me under her eyelashes.

"Is she doing okay?" she asks, her mouth barely moving, because she knows there will be some video later, someone analyzing us, trying to read our lips. They've done it before; they'll do it again.

"We're fine," I tell her.

She tips her head to the side. "You have a really good thing," she says. "Don't let them take it from you."

I nudge her with my elbow. "Says the woman who's trying to take my championship away from me."

She smiles, rolls her eyes. "Someone's gotta stop you and your ego." Her eyes go over my shoulder. "Oh, shit."

I spin around, and my eyes go straight to the Albatross garage. Just outside of it, a cameraman has the huge camera up on his shoulder pointed right at her. She tries to duck around him, but he follows her, locked in on her in a sea of faces.

I see her stop and say something to him, the anger on her face evident, even though I can't hear what she's saying. Without thinking, I start toward her, but before I can take two steps, Lola has a hand wrapped around my arm.

"Let her handle it," she says in my ear. "She's got to learn how, and you're going to make a scene that you can't get out from under."

I know she's right, but every muscle in my body is telling me to go to her.

She shouts something at the cameraman and then ducks under him too fast for him to follow and rushes over to where the rest of the team has gathered. She disappears into the crowd.

Chapter Forty-Seven

Arabella

Mateo is swept away as soon as the podium ceremony is over, and I decide not to wait for him. I know he'll come find me as soon as he's done with his responsibilities. I gather my stuff and go back to the hotel to order room service and wait for him.

It's almost midnight when he finally comes. He doesn't even have to knock. I hear his shoes come down the hallway, swishing on the low carpet, and then feel him on the other side of the door. I open it and he slips in like a ghost. As soon as we're inside where they can't follow us, he pulls me into his arms, burying his face in my neck.

"I'm sorry," he says. "This whole weekend was awful."

"It's not your fault."

I feel him sigh against my collarbone. He's never going to believe me. He's always going to blame himself.

He pulls back, takes my waist in his hands. "I missed you," he says, and my pulse flutters hearing him say that. Even after everything, all the shit we went through, it still feels unbelievable that he's doing all this for me, that he would want me this much or at all, that he would miss me when I'm not around.

"I'm sorry you were worried," I say, thinking about what Arturo told me.

He shakes his head. "Don't be. You've got your own things to worry about."

"I just needed you so bad," I say. I didn't even know I was feeling this way until now, that I did need him this much. For the last week, while I was trying to sort through my life and also get ready to come back to work, I thought I was fine, that I needed space from him to get my head on straight. But I don't think that's what I needed at all. "I just don't know what to do. I ruined everything." I choke the words out.

The whole time I was in Montreal, I kept thinking all I had to do was drive across town and I could talk to my dad, try to make him see reason. But I knew I wouldn't be able to handle it if he slammed the door in my face, if he refused to open it at all.

"What?" he asks, his voice soft and incredulous. He takes my face in his hands, cradles it gently. "You haven't ruined anything. You've given me everything. Everything I didn't even know I wanted," he says. When I don't say anything, he continues. "You make me feel less lonely, less worried, less invisible, less scared, less disposable. You have made everything in my life bearable. This season... I can't do it without you. I can't handle life without you."

I choke on tears this time, but I can't stop them. I launch forward and kiss him. I'm surprised by how soft it is. How gentle. How easy and natural. Loving him has always been so simple.

Even now, everything else is a question mark, bow I feel about him is in bold, capital letters.

I feel steadier now. I grab onto his arms. "We just have to get through today and then tomorrow and then the day after that, one day at a time, okay? One race at a time. Then the season will be over, and then next year, no one will care. We'll be old news."

He nods, but none of the stress leaves his eyes. I can't really blame him. It's there for me too, swirling under my skin, the uncertainty of where this is going now.

I slip my hand behind his neck and pull his mouth to mine. I just need it to be like it was. I need it to just be us, before the entire world went to shit and brought us with it.

His hands cradle my jaw as he slips his tongue into my mouth, making me moan. But before I can really sink into it, he pulls back.

"Hey," he whispers, lips still brushing mine gently. "You had a rough day. We don't have to do this."

"I want to," I say against his mouth. *I need to.* I need to feel him, to be entwined with him, to just be his, not sharing him with anyone. "You don't want to?"

He groans, his hands tightening on me. "Of course I want to, *mi vida.* All I think about is having you in my bed."

"Then take me to bed, Mateo."

He hoists me up against him and turns, laying us both down in the sheets. Pushing me toward the headboard, Mateo gets to work on my clothes, pulling my shorts and underwear down my legs and pressing his hand between my legs.

I moan into his mouth, but then he's gone. I start to protest, but then I realize what he's doing. Picking up my discarded underwear, he tests the strength of them with both of his fists and comes back to me, shoving my hands up above my head.

I smile as he does it, watching the concentration on his face as he uses the underwear to secure my hands to a decorative swirl sticking up out of the solid wood headboard.

When he tightens the knot, I give an involuntary grunt.

"Too tight?" he asks, but I shake my head. It's uncomfortable, but I don't imagine we'll be at this very long, considering the solid length of Mateo's hard-on against me. I can certainly bear it if it means Mateo keeps looking at me the way he is now, like I'm made of diamonds.

He runs his hands from my shoulder to my breast, shoving my shirt up so he can graze his fingers over my nipple, making goosebumps pebble along my skin.

"Fuck, I want you," he says, and with my hands above my head, I watch him take off his clothes, my mouth watering at the sight of his hard cock. But he doesn't give me a chance to enjoy it. He's back on top of me quick, his mouth on mine.

"Please," I whisper into his mouth, and he smiles.

"You gonna beg me?"

"I will. If you don't give it to me right now, I will."

He gives a little chuckle, and then he starts to press into me. The relief I feel when he fills me up is intense. This is where I belong, right here beneath him, giving myself to him in every way he needs me to.

He thrusts inside me, and I sigh in pleasure, watching him lose himself and wishing I could put my hands on him, wishing I could pull him close and never let him go.

As he moves inside me, his hands curl around the backs of my knees to push my legs wider, and his mouth wraps around one of my nipples. I turn my head and realize there's a full-length mirror on the wall. And there we are, Mateo holding my legs up, his dark head bowed over me, his gorgeous hips thrusting into me.

"Holy shit," I breathe.

I watch Mateo relinquish my breast and raise his head. He follows the line of my sight, and then our eyes meet in the mirror. His mouth stretches in a devious grin.

"Are you watching us, baby?"

My reflection nods.

"So fucking hot," he says before putting his mouth on me

again, thrusting in hard as he bends to lick a wet stripe along my rib and then nip it with his teeth.

With my eyes still on the mirror, I whine, "Harder."

He gives my rib one more lick and then meets my eye. He pulls almost all the way out of me and then slams back in, making me moan, even though that's not what I meant.

I shake my head, sliding back and forth on the pillow. "No. Bite me harder. Mark me, please."

He turns my face away from the mirror so that I'm looking right into his eyes. "What?"

The desperation inside me is so big. "Please. I want everyone to see it. I want everyone to know I'm yours."

I see the calculation in his eyes. There's heat there, too. I know he wants it, but I think my words have made him nervous. I writhe under him so his cock moves in and out of me, even though his hips are still.

"Please," I beg him. "I want you to mark me so they all know I'm in your bed every chance we get, that you use me, that you take me, that I belong to you. Give me something to look at when you're not around."

His breath saws in and out of him, and then he bends, presses his open mouth to my neck, right under the curve of my jaw. I let out a long sigh of relief knowing this is going to happen. I didn't know how much I needed it until now.

He nips me gently at first, like he's testing the feel of my skin between his teeth. And when I gasp and dig my heels into his back, he bites down hard, sucks. And I moan loud, a cry I know will be heard through the wall. I don't care.

He bites me one more time, like he's making sure. And that's when I come undone, pulsing around him without him even rocking inside me. He groans loud in my ear, and I know he can feel it.

"Fuck," he says, his pitch higher than I've ever heard it,

and then he starts to thrust inside me hard, and I know he's coming too, can feel the spill of him after a few pumps.

I don't realize I'm crying until Mateo has released my hands. Until they've come up to frame his face and I realize we're both wet from where my tears have fallen.

He presses his forehead to mine. "Why are you doing this to me?" he breathes out. And I know what he's saying without him saying it. I know the way he feels for me has grown bigger than he ever intended. I know he feels what I feel.

"You did it to me first," I whisper.

He rolls off of me and pulls me up against him, tucking me into his side. I listen to his heartbeat as it slows over time. Once it's back to normal, a nice, steady rhythm, Mateo says, "I belong to you too, you know."

And even though he never says he loves me, I think, for now, it's enough.

GridG1n: *to the tune of Goodbye Yellow Brick Road* Goodbye second-half curse

DDDriftdynasty: *@GridG1n* Season's not over yet

GridG1n: *@DDDriftdynasty* Oh get a grip. Mateo's going to win.

DDDriftdynasty: *@GridG1n* Lola's still first in the championship and dominating! And Mateo is worrying about his dick.

Psychobasketballfish: Holy shit did you guys see that hickey on Arabella????

Chapter Forty-Eight
Round 14 - São Paulo, Brazil

Lola Castle - 228 points
Mateo Silva - 211 points
Archer Hayes - 175 points

Mateo

Pain lances through me as I hit the wall. Tail first, and then the rest of the car. I take a deep breath, and after a minute, the shooting pain in my spine subsides.

Fuck. That's all I can think, going over and over again in my head. *Fuck, fuck, fuck.*

Crashing in Q3 will put me starting the race tomorrow in tenth place. Fucking tenth place.

"Mateo, are you okay?" Jerry asks through the radio. I don't want to answer, but I know people are waiting, listening to hear from me, even as I stare at my crumpled wing, my tire that's upside down on top of the hood. I know Arabella is listening.

"I'm okay," I say, disconnecting my steering wheel and pushing my way out of the car. There's no use in dwelling on

346

it. I can't undo it now. But it's not as if the media has ever let anyone move on from anything.

She's the first person I see when I get back to the garage. She's kneeling on the pavement the way she likes to do. She says she likes the angle from there, that it gives me good light.

She's got her camera pointed at me and a part of me wants to tell her to put it away. She's really good at being able to interpret when I want the camera in my face and when I don't. When I can tolerate it and when I can't. But we're down to the wire now, and I'm sure she has her orders.

As I walk quickly toward her, I remember what she told me once: that there were days that went by when I wouldn't have my picture taken and I wouldn't be on social media and I'd disappear, and her only connection to me would be severed.

Radio silence, she called it.

Unbearable, she said.

So I let her take the pictures, whether it's for her or for someone else on the internet. Maybe it's for me ten years in the future, when I don't have a career and I'm looking back and remembering these moments.

As soon as I get to her, she straightens. She falls in line with me and Arturo. It's what she's entitled to now. A special place at my side, where before, she would have walked a few steps behind.

"It's just tenth place," she says. "You're still in the points if you don't lose any places and you know you'll pull ahead early."

I shake my head. "If the fucking Onyxes block out the front row, it'll be a beast to get ahead of them."

She cradles her camera in her palms the way she does when she's nervous, when she needs something to anchor her.

"You're Mateo Silva. You're faster."

I try to smile at her but I don't think I manage it. Instead, I grimace. A shot of pain goes up my back.

She skitters to a halt on the concrete just outside of the garage and takes my face in her hands. "Are you hurt?" she asks, her voice already laced with panic.

I shake my head, aware that we're being watched. "Just a little rattled, that's all."

She keeps her eyes on me, and I know she can see right through me. She won't settle for some surface answer, for lies. But I'm not going to give her anything more than that. Because I'm not going to have her worrying about me.

"I gotta get back to work," I say as we head into the garage.

She has to stay because Jayce is going into Q3, but I keep walking, straight out of the garage.

Mateo

"You're sure you're okay?" Arabella asks as she runs her fingertips down my spine. It feels good, but it doesn't cancel out the pain in my shoulder, the pain that spreads like a shockwave down my entire right side every time I move. But I'm not going to tell her that. The last thing I need is Arabella panicking when I get back in the car for the race tomorrow.

Instead, I take a deep breath, focus on the feel of her fingers, on the scent of her hair as she leans over me, and say, "I'm certain."

With my head turned away from her on the hotel bed, I can only hear her as she shifts, and then I feel her lips on my spine as she softly kisses her way down, stopping at my hip.

I groan and close my eyes. She has no idea how much she helps me, how much *this* helps me, just having her near and knowing she's not going to leave.

"You're so quiet," she whispers. "What are you thinking about?"

I would laugh if I didn't think it would just make matters worse. "The race tomorrow. They suspect bad weather."

I feel her settle on the bed behind me, and I twist to face her, let her reach out to run her fingers through my hair the way she does. "You love rain on race day."

I can't hold in a laugh this time. "Yes, normally. I'm good on a wet track. But there's a difference between a slick track and a monsoon."

She nods, hair shifting on the pillow. "You're going to do great."

Even though it hurts, even though it sends lightning strikes of pain through my side, I wrap my arm around her and pull her toward me. "I just need my good luck charm."

She giggles softly and wraps her leg over my hip. "And what's that?"

"You." I press my lips to hers, and kiss and kiss and kiss her until we both drift off to sleep.

Chapter Forty-Nine

Arabella

I'm in the garage with everyone else when I feel the ripple of panic shiver through like a tidal wave. I'm not wearing headphones, just watching the telecast like the rest of the world, but I see them react at the pit wall, the way Jerry and Felix turn to each other sharply. I see Jerry's mouth moving, see the concern start to slowly cross his face.

The mechanics all start to stand, and that's when I know something is really wrong. We've done our pit stops for the race. There isn't anything left for the mechanics to do unless something goes wrong. Something has gone wrong.

My eyes meet Brigit's, but I know I can't go to her if she has work incoming.

Without waiting, I rush over to the wall of headphones and try to stay out of the way of the commotion.

Jerry's voice immediately sounds in my ears. "Are you sure you're okay to continue? We don't want any injuries, Mateo."

"I'm fine, mate," Mateo says.

My gut clenches at the sound of his voice. He's not fine.

His words come out strangled. I glance up at the screen beside me, huge in the back of the garage.

Ten laps left. Even as I watch it, the number counts down. Nine now. I want someone to tell me what's going on. I can feel the panic starting to well in my chest.

"You have nine laps left, Mateo," Jerry says.

"I'm fine," Mateo barks. "I can't cut out now."

I shoot a look to Brigit again. The mechanics are all up, ready to move if Mateo has to call the race. But I know he won't. The rain took Lola out seven laps ago. Mateo can't throw away the opportunity to overtake her in the points.

All day, I've known something wasn't right. Mateo's been running slow. He's sitting in sixth place right now, a four-place improvement. The atmosphere in the garage was already tense. Conditions were already bad because of the storm. Everyone was already worried. Calculating points. Watching times. Poking their heads out into the pit lane to see who's retiring. And now this.

It's pouring down rain.

Yesterday, when Mateo crashed during qualifying, he told me he was okay. But he was walking funny. He went to his trainer and swore he was sorted for today, but I know Mateo almost as well as I know myself, and I knew there was something he wasn't telling me, something he was trying not to give oxygen.

When his voice cuts back in again, I hear the grunt before he speaks. "It's the bouncing," he says. "It's not normal."

The bouncing. So, it's the car too, not just the weather. None of the other drivers are complaining about bouncing. They're so close to the ground, being dragged down and pushed up over and over. Mateo is forty-two years old. His body is not handling this well.

Everyone's perched on the ends of their seats, gripping pant legs, fisting fingers.

I rip the headphones off, take a deep breath. I know I have to listen. I need to hear the reassuring sound of his voice. Every second of Mateo's silence is killing me, but so is listening to him suffer.

And then, on the big screens over our head, I see my own face. On instinct, my eyes drop, looking for the camera person outside the garage, panning in on my face. I know I shouldn't, that it'll only stoke the fire, but I turn my back to the camera, watch on the big screen on the back wall as the cameraman moves on.

A hand lands on my shoulder, and I turn to find Arturo.

"What's happening?" I ask him. He nods to a corner of the garage, and I follow him over.

He lowers his voice as he bends down to speak to me. "He wouldn't admit it, but he hurt his back yesterday," he says. "I heard him tell the PT. They did some alignment, massages, stuff like that, but he got back into the car too quick. It's not like he had a choice."

"Is he going to be okay?" I ask, dread settling in my stomach.

"Of course he is," he says, placing a hand on my shoulder and giving it a squeeze. "Of course he is, Arabella. Come on, we're talking about Mateo."

I know we're not talking about life or death here. I know he's not going to die of a bad back. But I'm afraid he's going to keep driving until he can't anymore, until his pain is irreversible.

"Mateo knows his body," Arturo goes on. "He knows how much he can handle and he's an athlete. His body bounces back easier than a normal person's because he takes care of it. The car's fucked. The track's rough. And he would have been fine with all of that if he hadn't hit the wall yesterday. He's just trying to heal and bounce back. He's going to be okay."

Arturo's called away and I'm left standing there.

Seven laps to go.

Then six.

Mateo finishes fifth. Even with his back hurting, even in so much pain he could barely talk, he still managed to get in front of Archer on the second to last lap.

Even when it's over, I have to just sit there and wait. I'm not allowed on the track. Only the mechanics are.

Arturo squeezes my arm as he goes by.

I stand in the garage, hands balled into fists as I try and see down into the pit lane to where the cars are parked. There are so many people and so much going on that I can't see anything. People pass by me. I'm careful not to make eye contact with any of them. No one got the whole story. All that was broadcast was Mateo complaining about the bumping. But it was enough for people to know he's in pain, enough for people to be questioning what's happening, enough for people to be looking to me.

I see his blue and silver suit and fight to keep myself from going to him. I do the only thing I can think to: take pictures. I take pictures because the internet is going to want to know what happened. There are people out there that care about Mateo. They deserve to know that Mateo is okay, if he even *is* okay. When he's finally on our side of the rope, I go to him and throw my arms around him.

He's got his helmet off, his suit unzipped. Even though I know he's hurting, all I can do is hold on to him, put my fingers in his sweaty hair and grip because I feel like he's going to float away.

"Are you okay?" I ask, my voice choked. I'm very aware that people are watching, that they'll take their own pictures and talk about us online, but I don't care.

"I'm okay," he says, pressing his hands to my back.

"Come on," I say. "I'll walk you to medical."

"No," he says. He steps back from me and takes both of

my hands in his, kisses both of them. "You've got to go to the media pen. Arturo will take me."

"I don't care about the media pen," I say, feeling anxious and desperate. I have no interest in taking pictures of Jayce at a time like this.

But he just lets go of my hands, walking backwards away from me. "Go do your job, Ari. I'll see you in a bit."

Arabella

As soon as Jayce is done in the media pen, I rush to the medical tent, finding Mateo sitting on the edge of a cot, talking to one of the F1 doctors.

When the doctor sees me, he pats Mateo on the shoulder and says, "I'll leave you to your PT. Stay limber for Mexico, yeah?" He nods to me and then heads to the other end of the tent, where it looks like Thane is being looked at. It wasn't an easy race for anyone.

I step up to Mateo, his head hanging between his shoulders. Mateo wouldn't show anyone he was in pain, even me, unless he couldn't help it.

As much as I want to put my arms around him, feel the warmth of him under my skin for my own peace of mind, I keep my hands to myself, scared to hurt him even more. "What did the doctor say?"

He sits up straight, pushing his shoulders back with a wince. "It was actually my shoulder. I must have jarred it harder than I thought during quali. But we've got two weeks before Mexico. It'll be fine by then."

I feel an ocean of dread tumble over me. "Right. Mexico."

His eyes meet mine, his brow furrowing. "What is it?"

I know I should probably just keep my mouth shut, but

after everything we've been through, I don't know if I can anymore. "I'm just...wondering how much longer you're going to be able to do this."

At my words, his brow furrows even deeper, and I notice for the first time the bags under his eyes. "What? Ari, it's a shoulder sprain. It's not like I broke my back."

I feel a lump form in my throat and look down at the floor to avoid his eyes, my gaze catching on his racing shoes, navy blue with the team logo on the side.

"I know that," I say, keeping my voice low. "But that was so stressful, Mateo. You were miserable out there."

He throws his hands up and I look up just in time to catch him wince again. "It's part of the sport. If everyone threw in the towel when they got injured, there would be no one left to drive."

"I'm not just—" I start to say, but when the doctors on the other side of the tent look our way, I lower my voice. "I'm not just talking about today. Don't forget I've been watching your career like everyone else. I know what you've been through. But you're not twenty-five anymore. How long before you *do* start breaking your bones?"

He stares at me for a long moment and then finally stands up off the cot gently, his race suit dangling around his hips. When we're standing eye-to-eye, he says, "I thought you supported what I'm doing here."

"I *do* support it. There is literally no one who supports you more than I do. But you can't go on like this forever. When will it be enough?"

"When I have another championship," he says through gritted teeth.

"Will it? Will it be enough then? You're doing all of this to win this championship so you can stay on the team, not so you can leave it."

He clenches his jaw and doesn't respond. He knows I'm

right. He's not going to leave if he wins the championship. It's just going to stoke the fire.

After a long moment, he swipes his cap off the cot where he left it. "What do you care anyway, Arabella?"

I jerk back, feeling like he just hit me. "Excuse me?"

He runs his hand through his sweaty hair before putting his hat back on. He sighs loudly. "Why are you doing this, Arabella? Can't you see that I make you miserable?"

"What are you talking about? I'm not miserable."

He shakes his head. For months I've been working my way past his defenses, and in a single day, it's like he rebuilt the whole wall. And then those amber eyes meet mine, steady. "You gave up your career, your family, your life, for what?"

My mouth drops open. "Gave up? I didn't *give up* anything. I got the one thing I wanted most." I step up to him, take his face in my hands and make him look at me. "You just don't get it, do you? Even after all this, you still don't get it."

"Get what?"

"You are everything to me. And I *choose* you, every time, over everything else."

His eyes fly back and forth between mine. "You shouldn't." He wraps his hands around my wrists and pulls my hands away, stepping away from me. I watch him turn his back toward me, watch the slight tremble of his shoulders. Is he in that much pain? "I thought you understood me. I thought you understood what I was trying to accomplish."

"I do understand. I really do. But I think that *you* are more important than this sport."

He spins around and I see, out of the corner of my eye, everyone in the tent turning to look at us. There's no hiding anymore what's happening here. "I am nothing without this sport," he says, voice loud and angry.

"That's not true." My voice is loud now, too.

He throws his hands up. "Then, what am I? If I take it all

away, the driving, the championships, everything I've built over the last twenty years, what's left?"

"The man I love."

The words ring out like a bell between us. When I said them before, it wasn't in the light of day like this. He can't just ignore them anymore. And he doesn't. He looks me right in the eye, sweat and rainwater dripping from the tips of his hair, his chest heaving like he just got out of the car.

"You're not just a sport to me. You're not just a world champion. And I can't watch you do this to yourself anymore."

"Then you should go."

"Fine, I'll go. We'll just talk about this later." I don't want to leave him here, not when he's in pain, but he clearly has a lot going on in his mind right now and we're not getting anywhere.

"I don't think we should talk about it at all. I think this has to be over, Arabella."

The reaction of my body is violent. I've been flayed open before him. "What are you talking about?" My voice comes out a whisper.

Mateo crosses his arms and looks up at me. "You asked me why Elena left. You want to know why I don't have anyone? Here it is. Because this is what I choose and that's never going to change."

I feel picked apart. Shattered into pieces. Melting. Drowning.

My body takes over like I've been programmed for this.

"If that's what you want." The words feel far away, like someone's speaking them outside of myself.

"It's what I want." He lifts his chin, stands a little taller. So I give him what he wants. I nod and leave the tent without looking back.

No new messages

Chapter Fifty

Arabella

When I was a sophomore in high school, I had to get dental work done. The dentist stuck me with a million needles, and it felt like my gums, my teeth, my entire skull was full of Novocain.

I couldn't feel anything for hours and hours. Even the next day, things just weren't quite right. Food didn't taste the way that it should have. All the flavors, the wrong shade. And the touch of anything in my mouth, even my own tongue, felt strange and unfamiliar.

That's how I feel leaving Brazil and going back to Montreal. Numb. And like things are never going to feel quite right again for the rest of my life.

When I get home to my quiet apartment, I don't know what to do with myself.

I can't go see my parents because they don't want to see me, and all of my friends are in New York, far away from me and this idiotic choice I made to move back to Montreal after college. Everyone except Lana, who I haven't spoken to since the party.

I can't sit here in this apartment. I can't sit still. I can't stop moving. I can't face emptiness and silence. If I let my brain process what happened in Brazil, I'll break, like someone taking a hammer to ceramic. I'll crack and I'll shatter and I'll never be able to put myself back together again.

So, I go to a bar. I go to the loudest bar I can think of. I go to a bar, and I order a drink. And then I order another drink and another.

Until my body goes from metaphorical numbness to literal numbness. Until the room starts to lose its sharpness. Everything becomes a bit of a blur. And that's nice. Dizziness takes over the pain. Nausea takes over the heartbreak.

I can't feel my heart stopping if the whole world is spinning like a top.

"You doing okay there?" I hear a voice ask, though I'm not entirely positive where it's coming from.

I'm staring straight ahead at the dance floor, watching people move, wrap their arms around each other, wrap their legs around each other, push pelvises against pelvises, throw heads back, taste a little bit of skin.

"Hey," the voice says again.

I blink a few times to clear my head, but it only kind of halfway clears anything. The world still looks like late night traffic with an astigmatism.

I turn my head and look into an unfamiliar face. A guy who looks like he's seven feet tall, his legs not knowing where to go as he sits beside me on the yellow vinyl couch, his light brown hair sticking up like he spent a long time in front of the mirror to perfectly gel it that way.

"Do I know you?" I ask.

He laughs. "Hello to you, too," he says.

"I'm not feeling particularly generous tonight," I snap, tripping over the words that can't quite find their way on my tongue. I didn't come here to socialize. I came here to stop the bleeding.

"I recognize you." he says. "I'm a big fan of Formula 1. You're Pedro Cedillo's daughter, right?"

I set my jaw on my fist and look over at him. I'm suddenly aware of how tired I am. I sag, feeling the heavy sigh through my whole body as it comes out of me. "Please, tell me how well you know me, stranger. Tell me how amazing my life is because I'm the daughter of Pedro Cedillo. And please tell me how lucky I am to work for Formula 1. And please..." I choke on the words as they come out. I think I'm going to puke, but I force them out anyway. "And please tell me what a whore I am for having the bad judgment to fall in love with Mateo Silva."

His eyebrows shoot up. "I definitely wouldn't call you a whore."

"Sure," I say. "Sure, sure, sure. I totally believe you. You might not say it, but you'd be thinking it." I look out over the dance floor again, watching lights swirl in different colors.

"I'm not sure I understand what makes someone a whore just for sleeping with a person they're dating."

I narrow my eyes at him. I don't really know what he's saying, and I don't really care. "*Was* dating."

"Oh. Sorry. I hadn't heard."

"Do you need something?" I ask.

I'm surprised when he smiles. "No, I just wanted to come say hi to you. Make sure you're okay."

"I am not okay," I say. And I'm surprised when it comes out on a laugh. Because at this point, I don't know whether to laugh or cry. I don't know whether to go dance or rip my fucking ribs open. I don't know anymore.

"You're in love with him, huh?"

All I can I do is stare at him. "Who are you?" I ask.

"My name's Josh."

"Josh," I say, setting my head back against the couch until I realize that doing so somehow makes the world spin even faster. I sit back up, swallow down bile. "Listen, Josh," I say. "I've been in love with Mateo Silva since the day we met. You want to hear the really fucking sad part?"

"Sure," he says, leaning in a little bit closer.

"The sad part is I took that stupid job at Albatross just to be near him. I don't want to work in Formula 1. Do you have any idea what it's like to go to work every day, work your fucking ass off, and have everybody there think you only got the job because of who your father is? It's hell. And it's especially more hellish when you're a woman. And it is the seventh circle of hell when you are a woman who is sleeping with the boss. But the boss happens to be a man you've loved for your whole life and who you've known longer than any of those assholes. They don't even know him. But I do. I know him. He let me in past that wall and then he just took it all away because I had the audacity to fucking care about whether or not he kills himself for a fucking sport."

Josh isn't laughing anymore. He's just staring at me, his mouth turned down in the corners. "You're right. That sounds awful. Listen, you seem really out of it. Why don't I call you an Uber?"

I scoff. "I'm not going to sleep with you just because you call me an Uber," I say, my head feeling too heavy. I let it fall into my open palm.

"I really don't want to sleep with you," he says.

"Fuck," I shout. And even in my haze, I see several people turn in our direction. "That certainly is one way to kick someone when they're down, you know, telling them that you don't even want to fuck them."

He heaves out a little grunt of a noise. "I'm not saying you're not attractive and that I'm not attracted to you. I am. You're very beautiful. But I have no interest in sleeping with a woman who's as drunk as you are and who's probably going to cry the whole time over her ex-boyfriend."

The word comes out of his mouth so easily. *Ex-boyfriend.* Is that what Mateo is? He was never really mine, was he?

"Your car's on the way," Josh says.

I don't know how long we've been sitting in silence, but he helps me up off the couch and walks me to the front of the club.

"Hey, thanks for not being a total piece of shit," I say when he opens the door and ushers me out onto the curb. "I didn't deserve this kind of kindness from a complete stranger today."

He reaches out and uses his finger to swipe at one of my tears before it drips from my chin. "Sure, you did," he says. "Everyone deserves kindness. And hey, you know, maybe if he knew all of that stuff... Maybe if you said to him what you said to me, it would change things."

I sniffle. "Nothing's ever gonna change, Josh, but thank you." I get into the Uber and slam the door behind me.

Arabella

I stumble out of the Uber and almost eat it on the curb, managing to catch myself on the door before I knock my teeth out.

"Are you okay, ma'am?" the driver asks.

"Yep, I'm good. I'm good," I say, holding up a hand so he won't be tempted to get out of the car and help me. I don't need help. I just need to get inside and pray that when I lay down, the world stops spinning.

I stumble up my steps and, after three tries, manage to get my key into the first door. There's two, the outer door and the one in the vestibule. And then, of course, I have to somehow make it all the way up to my apartment.

By the time I get to the elevator, I sort of feel like I'm going to fall asleep. Yes, the world is spinning, and yes, I'm pretty sure I'm going to vomit, but I'm also just so tired.

The kind of exhaustion that goes all the way down to the marrow of my bones.

I still have six awful weeks before this job is over and done. What do I do if Felix offers me another contract after everything that's happened? I can't possibly stay, can I?

I gag in the back of my throat, not sure if it's the alcohol or the idea of leaving Mateo behind forever.

When the elevator doors open, I push myself up off the wall and stumble into the hallway. It's a long walk to my door, but at least it's a straight one. As I get closer to my door, I see there's someone sitting in front of it, crumpled on the ground next to a duffle bag.

"Lana?"

Her head comes up and I realize she was asleep, half folded against the wall beside my door.

"Hey," she says, and then I vomit on the hallway carpet.

Arabella

The sound of my cell phone ringing wakes me up.

It takes me a moment to orient myself. That's what happens when you spend half your time in hotel rooms. Every time you wake up, you have to calculate whether you're at home, or in Italy, or Mexico, or Abu Dhabi.

"Hello?" I don't bother to look at the name before I answer because there are very few people who would call me this early in the morning. But even as I'm trying to clear the sleep from my brain, I think: my parents aren't speaking to me, so it's definitely not them; Mateo and I are also no longer on personal speaking terms; and Lana is on the bed beside me. Who else is left?

"Arabella? Hey, it's Mark. Sorry it's probably a bit early there."

"Professor Whitaker," I say, sitting up. I scrub the sleep out of my eyes and look over at Lana who stirs, squeezed into my full-size bed.

"Listen, I apologize it's taken me so long to get back to you about your application."

"My application?" I say, pushing my hair out of my eyes.

"Your application for the Everest doc. I would normally have contacted you right after I saw it come in, and I was really excited, but we've been interviewing people, trying to get things set up, meeting with a million different sponsors, and now we possibly have a network involved? Anyway, I just didn't get an opportunity. So I wanted to talk to you today and let you know how pumped I am that you've decided to join the team."

For a moment, I just blink. I'm so very confused. Obviously, Professor Whitaker sent me the application a while ago, but I didn't fill the thing out. I ended up deleting it weeks ago.

"Anyway, it's fine if you can't really talk now, but there's a lot of prep to go over so I want to schedule some meetings with the team. We're going to try and coordinate it so that we can do as few of these meetings as needed to get information out. I'm going to send some times that me and some of the head folks are available and if you could just look over them and let me know when you would be available too, that would be great."

I feel like he just recited the Greek alphabet to me and asked me to repeat it back to him.

"Okay." I'm not really sure what else to say.

I don't want to tell him that I definitely did not send an application...because maybe this is the best thing for me. Maybe I should take this job. Even if I somehow applied for it in my sleep.

I reach for my laptop sitting on my nightstand.

"You're not going to regret this. It's going to be amazing."

"I bet. Thank you, Professor Whitaker."

As soon as I end the call, I open up my laptop. Beside me on the bed, Lana says, "What's going on?"

"I have no idea," I say. Little bits and pieces of last night are starting to come back to me, but I have to push them aside because I have to focus on what I'm doing. I open up my email. I scroll through all the emails I've sent and received over the last few weeks.

I feel Lana shift beside me, looking over my shoulder as I scroll through the emails. I go back one week, then two, then three, then four, and there it is.

The original email had a link in it to a form, and when that form was filled out, a copy of it was sent to my email, and it's all there. My education, experience, all my vital information, even a short paragraph about why I think I would be a good fit for the job.

But as I read through it, I know for certain I didn't write it. Not that I ever thought I did, but I would have never said these things about myself. That I'm hard working, that I'm focused and dedicated. Not because I don't think they're true, but because I don't think I would have been able to gather the courage to use such words to describe myself.

"You applied," Lana said. I haven't been able to look over at her, but any anger I've felt over the last few weeks has fully disappeared. It's hard to be angry at your best friend when you've been shattered by the person you love. I only have so much room in me for hurt.

"I didn't," I say.

She sits up straighter and I look over to see her scanning the application. "I don't understand," she says. "Are you, like, sleepwalking?"

"I don't sleepwalk."

My eyes slide back to the date. And everything clicks.

Summer break, while we were in Spain.

"Holy shit," I say, my voice breaking.

"What is it?" she asks, taking my laptop from me, like there's some clue that she'll be able to decipher.

"Mateo," I say, feeling the sob rise up in my throat.

"Mateo sent the application? Why would he do that?"

The words barely make it out of my mouth. "Because he wants me off the team."

Then I start to cry.

⚑

Arabella

"Look, you don't know that," Lana says as she puts a cup of hot tea in front of me on the coffee table. "You could talk to him about it, ask him why he did it."

I pick up the cup and take a long sip. "Talking to Mateo is not something that's particularly easy these days."

She sighs and sits next to me on the couch. "Yeah, all those videos that have been circulating on social media after everything came out haven't been great and then Thane mentioned the two of you got in a pretty huge fight in the medical tent."

"Thane?"

She grimaces and shrugs. "He follows me on Instagram. He DM'd me. He was worried and said Mateo refused to talk about it."

I take in a shaky breath. I can't just cry all the time, but everything that's happened over the last few weeks has just built up and built up, and I haven't been letting it out because I think letting it out felt like admitting that it was all real. I keep holding my breath, waiting for Mateo to realize we belong together, and instead, he did the exact opposite. He did what he could to get rid of me.

And he did it in Spain. Things were so good in Spain before my dad got there. At least, I thought they were.

"What happened?" Lana asks.

"We broke up," I say. "In Brazil, last week."

She pulls her knees up to her chest and puts her arms around them. "Can you maybe tell me the whole story? I feel like I missed everything, and by the time I knew what was going on, it was already over."

So I do tell her everything, from the moment I got my letter from Albatross to last night, getting drunk at the bar because the thought of sitting at home made me sick.

She scrubs her hands over her face. "I'm sorry for what I said at the party."

I'm already shaking my head. "It's fine."

"It's not fine," she insists. "I guess I just thought that you kind of had a silly crush on this person who didn't really care that you existed. I didn't know you were, like, *really* in love with him. And I was scared you were throwing your life away on him."

I nod. I knew she was trying to protect me, and now, after everything, maybe she was right. "At the party, things were still kind of tentative. You know, nothing had really happened by that point, but it wasn't very long after."

"You're sure that he did this application thing to get rid of you? Whatever reason he had, he's made it pretty clear he wants you to follow your passion. Maybe he was just trying to give you a nudge in the right direction."

"This is not a nudge in the right direction," I say, pointing at my laptop, still open and staring at me from the coffee table. "This is taking control of someone's life."

"Well, you said yourself that he likes to be in control." She makes a face, probably because when I made that comment, I was talking about the sex.

"I just don't know what to do now."

She makes a pitying face. "You can't keep accepting crumbs. You deserve more than that."

I know she's right, but the words still feel like something sharp in my chest. "But I love him so much."

She reaches over to take my hand. "You have to go cold turkey after this season. No more F1. No more Mateo. Go to Everest. Get away from it all."

"I feel like you just shot me."

"I know."

I know I'll do what she tells me, that I'll take the Everest job. I just don't know if going to Everest will make any difference. I love him too much to stop.

Dear Team,

Included below is a list of MUST-HAVES for base camp. I've also sent your stipend via PayPal so you can purchase things at your leisure over the next several months. Please let me know if you have any questions. This list is not all-inclusive and we'll update you as we get more information. – Mark W.

Moisture-wicking base layers
Insulation layers (fleece or down jackets)
Outer layers (waterproof and windproof)
Trekking pants and shorts
Hats and gloves (with liners)
Socks (wool or synthetic trekking socks)
Hiking boots with good ankle support
Camp shoes
Backpack (50-70L capacity)
Trekking poles
Sleeping bag (4-season with a liner)
Headlamp
Extra batteries
Sunscreen
Lip balm
Water bottles/Hydration reservoir

Personal First-Aid Kit (we'll also provide extra for the team)
Daypack
Pack cover

Chapter Fifty-One
Round 15 - Mexico City, Mexico

Lola Castle - 228 points
Mateo Silva - 221 points
Archer Hayes - 200 points

Arabella

I feel like a spy holding on to a secret. All weekend, while the world celebrates Mateo and the fact that he seems to have overcome the second-half curse, I'm waiting to get him alone so I can confront him about the Everest application.

How could he do this?

How long has he wanted me gone?

I get my chance after the qualifying race on Saturday. The motorhome is quiet, most of the team having taken off to get a good night sleep before the race tomorrow, and everyone else who's staying to work on the car still down in the garage.

I stand inside, packing up, and watch Mateo walk down the paddock, heading right toward the motorhome. I feel like it's eight months ago all over again. My heart is pounding as he approaches.

When he steps into the empty motorhome, his eyes find me immediately. He stops in his tracks, wide eyes on me like he can't begin to imagine what I'm doing here. And then, without a word, he turns and heads straight for his room.

I clench my hands into fists and look around, making sure there's no one watching before I follow him. I know I'm breaking the rules and could get in so much trouble if Mateo took it upon himself to make my life difficult, but I don't care. I walk right up the stairs to the second-floor hallway and slide open Mateo's door.

He spins around to face me, and when I realize he's got his shirt off already, I regret not waiting for a better time. One thing no one tells you about break-ups is that the attraction to your ex doesn't just magically die, no matter how bad they hurt you, and the sight of Mateo's chest, of that tattoo over his heart, makes all my skin heat up.

Fuck.

"Arabella?"

I shut the door behind me. "Did you send in that application for the documentary?"

He doesn't answer me. He sighs and bends over to grab a fresh shirt from his bench. I wait patiently as he pulls it on over his head, but as soon as he does, I start in again.

"I know it was you. You're the only person who knew besides Lana, and she didn't have access to the application. Why would you do that?"

His hands fall to his sides, and he meets my eye, but he still doesn't say anything.

It's infuriating, and the next time I speak, the words come out through clenched teeth. "You ended it, and now you're sending me away, is that it?"

The surprise on his face shocks me. He finally speaks. "That has nothing to do with it."

"Then why?"

"Because this isn't what you want."

I take a step toward him, every muscle in my body poised to attack. "You don't get to decide what I want."

"I've been watching you all season. You don't love Formula 1. You want something else. So you should go after it. Don't just be here because you think it's what makes sense. I've tried to tell you this before. It shouldn't come as a surprise that I want more for you."

I want to scream, but I know I have to stay quiet so no one in the motorhome knows we're fighting right now, that we've broken up entirely. "And I've tried to tell *you* that I'm here for a reason. If I didn't want to be here, I wouldn't *be here*. I took this job because I *wanted to*."

I don't realize my eyes are on his feet until I'm watching them shuffle closer to me. I look up and almost gasp at how close he is.

"I know your reasons for being here. I know why you wanted the job. And you deserve better."

"Stop it," I say. "You don't get to make my decisions for me."

"You weren't going to make it yourself, even though you know it's the right one. Did you take the job?"

"I hate you." I hate that my voice breaks when I say it. I hate it because he knows it's a lie just as well as I do. But I *want* to hate him. I want to be able to make the decision to walk away from him as easily as he made it for me,

"I know." He tips my face back, and I whimper when his mouth lands on mine.

It's been two miserable weeks without tasting him, and when his lips slip over mine, his tongue delving into my mouth, I forget about everything else. I grab fistfuls of his hair and open my mouth to let him in as far as he can get, desperate for the warmth of him.

Then you should go.

His words from Brazil slice through my mind, and I jerk away from him. I can see the sadness in his eyes, the way it mirrors what's inside me.

"Stay away from me, Mateo. If you have a problem with me being on the team, maybe *you* should leave." I turn away from him and slide the door open, not surprised to find Arturo on the other side. The look on his face tells me heard some, if not all, of our conversation.

I step into the hall but like some kind of compulsion, I turn back to Mateo. "Good luck in the race tomorrow." I rush down the hallway, barely holding myself together.

I'm sorry for kissing you
I'm sorry for kissing yo
I'm sorry for ki
I'm sorry for sending the application withou
I'm sorry for sending the application w
I'm sorry for sen
I'm sorry for hurting you
I'm sorry for hurti
I'm sorry for

Mateo
I'm sorry for everything

Chapter Fifty-Two
Round 16 - Abu Dhabi, United Arab Emirates

Lola Castle - 253 points
Mateo Silva - 239 points
Archer Hayes - 215 points

Mateo

"Shit," I shout as I lose yet another match to Lola. I toss my racket down and bend over, grabbing my knees.

Across the court, Lola laughs. "You're really off your game today," she says,

"Yeah," I sigh. "You can say that again." I walk to the sidelines to grab my water bottle, and Lola comes to join me as I drink.

We both sit down on the court and press our backs to the wall, looking out to the parking lot. There are several people out there with phones, a few more with some pretty expensive looking cameras.

"Do you think they got enough?" she asks quietly, her mouth barely moving.

"Probably. Maybe this will get some of them to shut up about how much we hate each other."

She rolls her eyes. "So ridiculous, pitting friends against each other. It's a sport, not war."

The padel game in an open court was Lola's idea, and it was a good one. The media has been trying to paint us as some kind of enemies, two people who hate each other because we're both so close to winning a championship, and maybe if we were other people, we *would* hate each other. After all, back in the day, Pedro and I hated each other, and then went on to hate each other for a decade after that. It was mostly on his side, but I didn't try to change his mind.

Pedro is very good at holding a grudge.

Lola and I have always been friends. She's pleasant, the kind of person who likes everyone. And after the accident last season, she became the person on the grid I'm closest to.

This championship isn't going to change that.

"What about the Arabella situation?" she asks, lifting her own water bottle to her lips. "How did you figure out how to get the media off your back about all of that?"

I haven't, and that's why we haven't told anyone that we've broken up. Because as awful as the media was when we were together, I'm afraid it will just get worse if they find out we ended it. Maybe they'll say I was using her. Maybe they'll say she was using me. Either way, they won't be able to understand what happened between us. Felix asked us to keep it quiet when we told him, the first good idea he's had since this whole thing started. He wanted to keep the media focused on the championship, and I don't blame him.

Two more races and it's all over.

I take a deep breath, and I'm shocked when I start to cry. It comes out of nowhere. One minute, I'm fine, and the next minute, I'm fighting for breath.

"Hey," Lola says, putting her arm around me. "Hey, what's going on?"

I gasp for air, trying to calm myself. "I broke her heart, but I had to do it."

"What did you have to do?"

I cover my face as much as possible. I can only hope the cameras have moved on to something more interesting by now. "I had to let Arabella go."

She's quiet for a long time, and I don't know what I expect, but she eventually just lets out a quiet, "Why?"

I throw my hands up. "Because she was throwing everything away for me, and I couldn't let her do it."

She opens her mouth, sucks in a breath like she's going to say something, and then closes it again. "What is she throwing away?" she finally asks.

I tell her about Pedro, about Everest. I tell her things I'm not sure Arabella would want me to tell her, but I tell her anyway. I trust Lola.

When I'm done, she presses her back to the wall and nods. "Okay, yeah, I get it. I want to tell you that you did the wrong thing, but I'm not sure you did. It's just that...people make sacrifices for love, just one of many things we do. She wanted to be here with you, and you kind of took that choice out of her hands."

"Because she was making the wrong choice."

"It doesn't matter. She was making the choice she wanted to make." She bites her lip and turns her face toward me. In the early morning sun, I'm not surprised by how pretty she is, golden hair, green eyes, soft skin. "What makes you think you're not worth it?"

"What?"

Her face twists and hardens a bit, more like the Lola I'm used to seeing in the paddock. "I mean, yeah, she gave up a cool job. And yes, her dad hates you. So what? You guys could have figured it out."

"He hated me for a decade for winning that championship. You don't think he's not going to hate me just as long for dating his daughter?"

"Who cares? Arabella is an adult. She can make her own choices. What makes you think you're not being just as bad as him? She's a grown woman. Pedro wanted to control her, and now you do, too."

"I don't want to control her."

"But you *are*, whether you want to or not." She hoists herself to her feet and reaches down a hand to help me up. "She deserves the opportunity to make the choice she wants," she says when we're eye-to-eye again. "That woman is obsessed with you. If you want her, let her choose to want you back."

Mateo

I've been through a lot of breakups. I've broken up with women. They've broken up with me. It's always difficult, and I always get over it.

Not once have I gotten a good result in a race and felt nothing because my entire being was so consumed by a breakup.

But today, as Jerry screams in my ear, ecstatic about the fact that I just won another GP, effectively closing the gap between Lola and me, I don't make a sound, even though I know the media will zero in on my radio, hoping for a celebration. A celebration I can't give them.

"Good work, team," I say when I finally find some moisture in my mouth. "Thank you for all your hard work this weekend."

I still put on the show. I wave to the crowd when I get out of the car. I accept Lola's handshake and try to make myself smile, even though I know she won't mind if I don't. I stand in front of everyone, take the microphone. I smile and I talk about how happy I am, how incredible it is to be this close to the championship. I hold my head high.

And I can't feel any of it.

It should matter.

I should care.

But I don't.

On the podium, I spray Lola with champagne, laugh as she returns the favor. Feel like I'm crumbling, falling into little pieces in front of millions of people, and when I stand up there and look down one more time, searching the crowd for Arabella's face, I don't see it. Because she isn't there.

Arabella

I watch the post-race coverage from my hotel room. I'm not obligated to stay for the podium since good photos ops from that angle are few and far between, so I don't go. But as soon as I'm alone, I watch it on my phone, hunched over in my bed.

Part of me feels like I might cry, but another part of me just feels like there are no tears left. There's nothing left inside me except this bizarre happiness. Mateo is going to win the championship. He's actually going to win it. I can feel it all the way down to my bones. He's going to win.

And as someone who has spent the last six years cheering for him (longer than that, even if I could never tell my father that), believing in him, and wanting nothing more than to see him win a championship, this is going to be the best year of my life, and the worst.

The best year of my life, the year I got to kiss Mateo, fall in love completely with him, mean something to him.

And the worst year of my life, the year I lost him.

The commentators agree with me. They talk about how they feel that Mateo's race has become immaculate, that he's not making little mistakes like he used to, that the improvements on the car are flawless.

The recipe for a perfect season.

PitCrewHero: I can't believe this is really happening. Mateo Silva back from the dead.

F1Rush7: Mateo finally winning another championship was not on my bingo card

F1time: Why is everyone so surprised? Mateo is the GOAT. I wouldn't be surprised if he won next year too.

Larrylaps: Lola is still first place! Let's not pretend Mateo has already won it. Chill.

Chapter Fifty-Three
Round 17 - Suzuka, Japan

Lola Castle - 271 points
Mateo Silva - 264 points
Archer Hayes - 230 points

Arabella

"All right, everybody, I'd like you to welcome our newest addition to the team, Arabella Cedillo. She's going to be our photographer on the trip, so you might not see her face as much as you see her camera lens."

A kind laugh goes through everyone on the video call, and I give the camera a small wave. I've sequestered myself in a back room of the motorhome, hoping the meeting will be quick before I have to be out on the paddock. The sun isn't even all the way up. Luckily for me, timelines worked out that I could just get up a little earlier to join the meeting; for most of the team, it's firmly afternoon.

"Arabella, you and Sammy will be doing the most," Mark says, referring to the cameraman in the top corner of my screen. "We're going to have one more camera person. They're just going to have a handheld cam, and we'll have a boom operator, but neither of those roles have been filled as of yet. We've got some stuff in the works there."

Mark taps away at something on his keyboard. "Arabella and Sammy, I'd really like you to familiarize yourself with the weather reports, so you'll know when the light is going to be best, that sort of stuff. We'll plan schedules around what you two think is going to work. I know I don't need to tell you this. You're both highly trained professionals."

At this, he gives a little laugh, and someone else on the call says in a mock yell, "Yeah, go Albatross!"

Maybe it's the fact that this is the last place I was expecting to encounter Mateo Silva fans, but the comment sends a rush of cold through me.

"Sorry," a middle-aged woman with sunburned skin says. The box at the bottom of her screen tells me her name. It's Rachel. She gives a nervous laugh. "I'm a big Formula 1 fan. It's so exciting that you're going to be on this trip with us."

"Yes," Mark says, "we'll have a lot of downtime, and Arabella will get to entertain everyone with her stories of her Formula 1 days." Another titter goes through the group.

I think Mark intends to change the subject, but then Rachel breaks in again. "It must be so exciting that your boyfriend is about to win a championship. He's definitely going to beat Lola Castle, no?"

I feel frozen. Even when I'm discussing a trip to Everest, I can't escape him. What makes me think I'll be able to escape him when I'm on Everest itself?

"I definitely think he's going to win, but I might be a bit biased," I say with a smile.

Even now, weeks later, the only people who know that Mateo and I have broken up are the doctors who were in the tent that day, the Albatross crew, Thane, and Lana. I'm sure Mateo will break the news after the championship. But he hasn't said anything, and neither have I, because the last thing I want is to take any kind of attention away from this huge moment in his career.

The meeting moves on, but I'm stuck. It doesn't matter how far I run, and it doesn't matter if I change my career or change my identity. I couldn't escape being the daughter of Pedro Cedillo when I joined Formula 1, and now, I'll never be able to escape this.

I'm always going to belong to Mateo Silva.

"Would you still want me if I wasn't a Formula 1 driver?"

I look up from my laptop. I didn't even realize the sun had begun to rise in earnest, low in the sky, leaving us in a mostly dark room, the light blue shade of the walls making me feel like we've dropped to the bottom of the ocean.

Mateo stands in the door, his hands in his pockets. I can't read his face in the shadow of the room. I can only make out the shape of his body, a little slumped, his head hung low. I can feel his eyes on me though, like they're beams of light straight from the sun.

I shut my laptop, my meeting long over, and stand. I should move, but I feel petrified to my spot by his question. I can't take anymore. I'll bow under the weight of everything I feel and everything that's happened between us. And with his question, I snap, like a dam breaking open, letting loose its contents.

"My admiration of you came from your determination to win your first three championships. I respected the way you were always proving everyone wrong. Your confidence and your strength kept me going every time I came up against anything in life I didn't think I could handle." I lift my chin, meeting his eye. He's inching toward me, one slow step at a time around the table I've been sitting at.

"I've loved you since I was nineteen. I fell in love with you the first time we met. Do you remember it? The summer after my freshman year of college."

He nods, eyes soft.

"It wasn't because of your money, and it wasn't because you were a good driver, and it wasn't because you were famous. It was because of all the times you made me laugh and all the times you looked *at* me instead of *through* me and the way you stared off into the distance like you were trying to understand life, even when you were the most famous man in Spain."

My words are choking me, and I don't realize I'm crying until the hot tears drip from the edge of my jaw and land on my collarbone. "There's nothing that could make me stop wanting you. Believe me, I've tried."

With a loud exhale, he rushes toward me, closing the distance between us and taking my face in his hands. But before he can kiss me, I turn my face, a whimper of pure agony making it past my lips.

"Arabella..." he breathes.

I shake my head, my face still turned away from him. "You ripped my heart to shreds, Mateo. I will love you until the day I die, but that doesn't mean I'll let you use me up and shove me aside."

"That's not what I want to do. That's not it at all. I–" He drops his hands and takes a step back. I can make out his face now, the cut of his jaw and the droop of his eyes, the sharp point of his nose. "I thought if I pushed you away, you would figure out that you deserve so much more."

My gaze meets his sharply, my mouth opening and closing in bafflement. "Deserve more? More than what? More than *you*?"

He throws his hands up. "More than giving up an extraordinary life just to follow me around."

It's like he's reached his hand into my stomach. Why does

he keep dredging this up? Why can't he let me go? "But I *wanted*—"

"I know. And I knew that as long as I was here, and as long as we were together, you'd never have the life you wanted."

The lump forms in my throat again, and I swear to myself that I will not cry in front of Mateo. "All I wanted was *you*." The words come out a whisper.

He shakes his head, and I realize he's put some real distance between us now; he's backing away. "You want more. And I want you to have more."

I can't keep arguing with him like this. I can't keep begging him to want me as much as I want him. "I can't do this, Mateo. Maybe we should just...stick a pin in this conversation until the season is over."

He nods. "Okay." He sighs. "I—" Whatever he was going to say, it seems caught in his throat. He takes another big step back from me and then leaves me there in the shadows of the rising sun.

Arabella

The extended contract offer shows up in my inbox two hours after Mateo wins the Japanese Grand Prix. It's from Julie, not Felix, which I appreciate because I don't think there's any world in which I could have a conversation with Felix right now. Not after everything he's said and done to me and Mateo.

I read over it, as much as I can understand at least. It's a two-year extension. Two years, probably exactly what they'll offer Mateo once he wins the championship.

It even comes with a raise, though I'm not sure if that was

Julie's idea or if it's because Felix knows he's been an ass to me these last few weeks.

Either way, it's a good amount of money. Plenty to take care of the apartment and my bills. It lays out the possible restructuring of the team after this year and next, which I can't even think about right now, not when that conversation I just had with Mateo, a conversation I can't even begin to understand, is still so raw.

If this had hit my inbox a month ago, there would have been no question. But everything's different now. And even though everything is different, and even though I already officially have another job, all I can do is stare at the email.

Because I wish my life was different. I want to be accepting this job offer and be following Mateo around the world for another two years. I want to go back in time and undo whatever unraveled.

Even after what happened with my dad, we were fine. We were totally fine. And then we just weren't.

I think about that night in the hotel room, about the thing Mateo said without saying it. I don't know what went wrong. All I know is there's no way I could accept this job offer and spend the next two years of my life close to someone I love desperately but can't have.

I open up a reply and type out a short message.

Julie, please give me the week to think about it.

It's an exciting time for Mateo Silva fans

Sixteen years after his last World Driver's Championship win, Mateo Silva is perfectly poised to win another, his fourth, and the whole world is watching. Yesterday, Mateo won the Japanese Grand Prix, bringing him to an exact tie with fellow world champion, Lola Castle. The Singapore Grand Prix is going to be one to watch...

Chapter Fifty-Four

Mateo

When I pull up in front of the familiar house in Montreal, I realize my hands are shaking. It's ridiculous to be this nervous. I get into a verifiable death trap every single weekend, but this is going to be the thing that does me in. I take a deep breath and get out of the car, the one I rented because I didn't want some Uber driver witnessing me getting my ass kicked, if it comes to that.

I knock on the door and hear Pedro's footsteps as they make their way down the long front hallway. It doesn't bode well that all I can think about is the last time I was here. I don't think Pedro would appreciate knowing I made out with his daughter in his backyard.

He's smiling when he opens the door, which tells me one of two things has to be true. Either he was expecting somebody else and I'm intruding, or this is just how he answers the door because he's a nice guy and genuinely looks forward to having people show up on his doorstep. The complete opposite of how I would respond if someone showed up uninvited.

Of course, his smile falls as soon as he sees me, and he immediately tries to slam the door. But, seeing as how I came prepared, as soon as the door starts to close, I stick my foot in the gap, and then I grab the door with both hands, holding it still.

"Pedro, I know you don't want to talk to me."

"Get the fuck off of my property," he growls.

"Don't you think it's worth having a conversation for the sake of your daughter?"

He clearly doesn't appreciate me saying that. He opens the door wide and then slams it hard on my foot. I wince. I'm in trainers, so I don't have a lot of protection.

"Don't talk about my daughter," he says.

"That's exactly what I came to talk about," I bark back. "Look, I get it. You hate me, that's fine. But you don't hate Arabella, and that's why you have to let me say what I need to say. Okay? Please. I understand that you would never do it for me, but I need you to do it for her. Just ten minutes."

He takes a deep breath, chest moving up and down once. And then he lets go of the door. "You have five minutes," he says. "And you'll say what you need to say right here. You're not coming inside my house."

I put my hands up. "Fair enough."

"Pedro?" Melanie calls from inside the house. "Who is it?" She peers over his shoulder, and I see the surprise on her face. Through all of this, she's been quiet, which I've found to be a bit surprising. As far as I know, she hasn't tried to contact Arabella. Melanie has never been the type to let Pedro take over and do whatever he wants, which tells me she's most likely just as angry as he is. But either at me or Arabella, I'm not sure.

"Mateo," she says when she gets to the door. "What are you doing here?"

"Melanie, it's nice to see you."

She sighs, her shoulders falling. "I'll make us some lemonade," she says. "We'll talk on the back porch."

That's where we find ourselves a few minutes later, the three of us sitting at the glass table beside their pool.

"I think the most important thing for you to understand," I tell Pedro once he's got his angry eyes on me, "is that I love Arabella."

I hear Melanie's little intake of breath. She really wasn't expecting me to say that. Maybe that's the problem. They thought somehow that this was a fling. It's anything but, and maybe they just needed to hear me say it. Maybe *I* just needed to hear me say it.

"So, what?" Pedro says immediately. "You think can come here and tell me that and I'll give you my blessing?"

"No. That's not what I think at all."

"Then what are you doing here?"

I wipe my sweaty palms on my shorts. "I'm here because I'm going to give up everything for her, and I don't think I can do that until I know she's not losing her family for me."

I expect him to argue, but instead, he just frowns at me skeptically. "What do you mean you're going to give up everything for her?"

I shrug. "I've only ever wanted one thing in my life, you know that. But it's not what I want anymore. She is. So I'm going to give it up. But I broke her heart."

His expression changes back to anger at that.

"What did you do?" I'm surprised when the question comes from Melanie.

I turn to her. "I told her we couldn't be together, and at the time, I meant it, but I don't mean it anymore. I'm dying without her. I thought it made sense for us to go our separate ways, and now I know that the only thing that makes sense is for us to be together."

Her face softens, and I start to think that maybe I've got an ally in her after all.

"I want to give her everything," I tell Pedro. "But that everything includes you, both of you. I can't give her the life she deserves otherwise."

They're quiet for a long time, and I honestly feel like I've said everything I need to, but I can tell they're still waiting for more.

"If you need to hate me for the rest of our lives, Pedro, I understand. Honestly, I'm used to it. You've always hated me, even when you didn't." I feel it all rise up in my throat again, this emotion that I can't seem to tamp down on a normal day anymore. "But she loves you so much. She can't live without you. She can live without me. Of that, I'm certain. She's doing it right now. And she'll keep doing it. But she can't live without you, her family." I say this last bit to Melanie. "And I'm ready to try and get her back, but... I won't do it unless I know that you will be her family when we're on the other side of it."

Melanie bursts out of her seat, her hands covering her mouth. She's crying. "Of course, we're always her family," she says. "Of course we are. This is just a... a road bump."

Pedro doesn't look so convinced. He hasn't moved. Hasn't looked away from me. "Of course," he says.

"You told her you never wanted to see her again," I remind Pedro.

He nods. "I know."

"She didn't do anything wrong, Pedro. You know she didn't do anything wrong. I understand how this looks. I'm not stupid enough to not have thought it through. To not have seen the problems that we could face before we made the decision to be together. I understand. I'm much older than her. I'm technically in a position of authority over her professionally. Not to mention *our* history, of course. And I understand."

Pedro watches me, eyes narrowed.

"But we're adults. And... I can't help what happened. I can't help that, for some reason, she wants me. It's something I never knew to ask for or hope for. And now that I have it, *had* it, I just can't let her go. It doesn't matter what it takes. If you say no today, I'll just come back tomorrow. I'll keep doing this. For the rest of our lives, if I have to. Because I know there's not going to be anyone else for me, and I'd rather spend the rest of my life completely alone than with anyone that isn't Arabella.

Melanie sniffles. And finally, after the longest silence I've ever felt in my entire life, Pedro says, "Tell me what you plan to do."

Chapter Fifty-Five
Round 18 - Marina Bay, Singapore

Lola Castle - 289 points
Mateo Silva - 289 points
Archer Hayes - 248 points

Arabella

I was seven when Mateo won his first world championship. In a lot of ways, it's my first memory, the first one that really mattered, watching on the sidelines with my mother as Mateo and my father went wheel-to-wheel.

My father came in fifth in the race where Mateo took the championship. My father was always an excellent driver, a world champion himself, but not the driver Mateo was.

I have memories of Formula 1 races the way other people have memories of picnics and Christmas trees and roller coasters. It was how my family spent the weekend, whether my father was driving or not. Private jets, motorhomes, hot asphalt.

Formula 1 was just always something that happened in the background while I was living my life, a reality I had as a child that apparently other children didn't have. And Mateo's name was a curse word in our house until six years ago.

Maybe it will be again, forevermore.

Whatever the opposite of numb is, that's what I am on race day in Singapore, waiting in the garage for the boys to arrive. Mateo has been avoiding my camera lens all weekend, and now it's race day, he and Lola are tied, and my brain is a pit of chaos.

Because when all is said and done, I'm still Mateo Silva's biggest fan. And I'm still so in love with him. Trying to change it at this point would be like trying to change my own DNA.

Singapore is a great track for Mateo. He's notoriously good at it, always getting a good result.

"We'll see." That's all he said in the interviews when people were trying to get him to break, to admit he's nervous as hell being tied with Lola going into the last race of the season. It's going to be one of them, no matter what.

And I want him to win so bad my stomach hurts with it. Every single muscle in my body is tense to the point of trembling. Because of course I want him to win. And if he wants to keep going after this season, I want that for him too. All I've ever wanted was the very best for Mateo. All I've ever wanted was for him to get exactly what he wants in life. Whatever that looks like.

I try to distract myself by taking pictures. I get pictures of the lights under the navy blue sky. I get pictures of the pit lane stretched out in front of the garage. Pictures of the other teams as engineers and team bosses set up at the pit wall.

Two garages down, my eyes catch on Lola's down at the Onyx garage, talking to her race engineer. When she spots me, she sends me a sad smile.

I heard someone say once that the drivers can never really be friends, something I know isn't true. Because these people here, they're the only people who understand each other.

Nobody can be in their shoes. I think about the way Mateo and my father couldn't be friends when they were driving together, how they found their way back to each other. Until I ruined it.

If Lola wins today, it won't break my heart. I won't feel any kind of anger or resentment towards her. Because she deserves it just as much as Mateo does, and I don't think he could ever hate her for it either.

I smile back at Lola and wave because I want her to know I support her and that she should fight her hardest, no matter what.

No emotions, just drive.

I give her a thumbs up and she laughs and winks at me before disappearing into her garage.

I go back inside, and I wait. And I wait and I wait. The car is ready and needs to be moved out onto the track. People are beginning to murmur quietly. It's far past the time for both of the drivers to be down on the main straight.

When Jayce comes through, his face is red and splotchy. I start to lift my camera but lower it when I see his face. He pushes past several people in the garage, and as he walks by me, he glares.

I watch him go, something stirring in my stomach at the look on his face. I glance at my phone again. Time is ticking by and I can hear engines revving down on the track. The formation lap is going to start any minute. The car should be long gone. What's happening? Where is Mateo? I know he knows what he's doing better than anyone else on the grid. He doesn't need me to sit here and think I know better than he does.

But I'm worried. Everything is wrong. The crowds are beginning to part on the track, mechanics pulling away to go back to their garages, media getting out of the way.

There's still no sign of Mateo.

I catch sight of Arturo coming down the stairs and rush toward him, even as all eyes in the garage go to him.

"Where's Mateo?" I hiss.

His jaw grinds. He doesn't look at me at first. He just crosses his arms and looks ahead. I can feel everyone in the garage watching us. I follow Arturo's eyes to Felix and Jerry at the pit wall. They're yelling at each other, arms flying everywhere.

"What the hell is happening? What's going on?" I ask Arturo again. I'm not asking for answers anymore. I'm demanding them. Arturo's eyes finally drop to mine.

"He won't come out of his room."

"What?" My chest pulls tight, like a rubber band ready to snap. "What are you talking about? It's time. He was supposed to be down forever ago. This is very bad."

"Yeah, I know it's bad," he snaps, glancing at his watch.

They're very strict with their schedules in Formula 1. I reach for Arturo's wrist, look at his watch.

He has three minutes. He's not going to make it. It takes three minutes just to get down to the garage.

Oh my God. This isn't real.

I un-sling my camera from my neck and shove it at Arturo before racing up the stairs. I don't know what the hell is going on, but I'm going to get Mateo.

I sprint across the paddock and burst in to the Albatross motorhome, completely empty, only the clanging of dishes in the kitchen where the cooks are washing up.

I rush straight up the stairs to Mateo's room and bang on the door. "Mateo!" I shout.

The door opens immediately, and there he stands. I'm shocked by how quiet it is here. The way that the sounds of engines and commentators and crowds are so far away. They have to know by now that Mateo's car is missing. They have to know by now that he's not going to make it to the start of the race.

"What are you doing?" I shout. "You have to get your ass to the garage."

He looks far too calm when it feels like my heart is going to burst in my chest at the stress of what's happening and where we've found ourselves. This cannot happen. He cannot miss this race.

I grab onto his arm, starting to tug him out of his room. But even as I do it, it processes in my brain that he's not even wearing his suit. This can't be happening.

He chuckles. "Arabella, stop."

"No!" I say. "What the hell do you think you're doing?"

"I'm not doing it. I'm not racing."

His words almost make me gag. "Yes, you are!"

"I'm not." He wraps his big hand around my wrist, pulls me away gently. "I don't want to go out there. I don't care about the championship."

"Yes, you do. Felix—"

"Felix already knows."

I don't even realize I'm crying until he reaches out to wipe the tears off my cheeks.

He can't do this. One more race. If he just wins one more race... That's it. That's the championship.

"You can't do this," I say. "You've worked too hard."

He steps up to me so close the tips of his shoes touch mine. Not his racing shoes. Just his regular trainers.

"I don't care about the championship," he says again. "I don't want it. I just want you."

I don't have time to even figure out what he means by that. I just start talking, saying anything. "You can have me," I say. "You can have me if you go out there. You can still have me." I don't even know if that's true. I just feel like I need to say anything to make this go away. To undo it. To rewind time and make him go down there where he's supposed to be.

"No," he says. "I can't have you and Formula 1. If I go out there and I win the championship and my contract is extended, I won't ever be able to walk away. If I go out there and I lose and I leave with you tonight, you'll always wonder if it was because I really wanted to or because they forced me out."

I'm sobbing hard now, tears dripping onto my neck. Because I know he's right.

"You'll regret it," I choke out, feeling my body sag in defeat. "You'll always look back at today and you'll regret the choice you made." The thought makes me sick.

A soft smile spreads on his face. "I'm not going to regret choosing you over Formula 1. I already regret what I've done to us, and this is the only way to fix what I destroyed."

"Please," I beg one last time. "Please, don't do this."

But it's too late. I know it's too late. I can hear the crowds screaming in the stands. The motors all taking off at once.

The lights have gone out.

It's over.

I pull his hands away from my face, my whole body trembling. "Why?"

"Because I love you," he says, forcing another sob out of me. "Because I love you more than a championship. I love you more than driving. I love you more than Formula 1. I love you more than all of it. I'm ready to let it go. I'm ready to go where you go. You told me I deserve devotion. Let me show you that you deserve it, too."

I am a kaleidoscope of thoughts and emotions. Just a shivering pile of goo standing in front of him.

He's saying everything I've always wanted him to say, but I never wanted him to say it like this. I never wanted him to do this. I never wanted him to not finish the season or to come so close to the championship that his fingers are grazing the trophy just to throw it all away.

"I have to go," I say, because I can't think of anything else to say. I can't process what's happening. I can't tell him I'm so in love with him that I want to claw my heart from my own body.

"Of course," he says, wearing a sad smile. "You have a job to do." He gives me just the slightest push toward the exit.

"Come with me. At least, come watch."

He just shakes his head.

It hurts, but I turn and leave him standing there.

Mateo

I stand in the middle of the paddock. Close my eyes and tip my head back. Listen to the sound of engines down on the track. The crowd is going wild. From where I stand, I can see all the billboards displaying the remaining laps.

It's almost over.

Lola is going to win. And rightfully so.

I know a part of her will always wonder if she only won because I backed out. And I did take that into consideration when I made my choice, but I had to do what was right for me and Arabella. And it isn't as if I was her only competition on that track. I was just the only person close enough in points to have a chance at taking the championship.

I watch as the screen arching over the finish line flashes. Lola's face appears, WORLD CHAMPION bursting bright and colorful behind her. Fireworks pop overhead. I smile. I remember the day I won my first championship so well, every single second of it. The taste of the champagne is practically fresh on my tongue.

I know Arabella thinks I'll regret this. I'm not going to say I never will. That wouldn't be true. I probably will regret someday never seeing if I could do it again.

But I won't regret choosing her. I won't regret leaving with her tonight. Walking away from Albatross. Paying the fines, facing the penalties, apologizing to the team I know I've hurt, putting in the work to completely disconnect myself from it all.

I close my eyes again, listen to the commotion, the music, the fans, the fireworks, the cut of engines as everyone else crosses the finish line.

This time, when I open my eyes again, she's there. A silhouette of her outside of the Albatross garage. She has her camera around her neck, her arms down at her sides. She's just watching me.

It's like an old school Wild West shootout, her on one side, me on the other. So far away that I can't even really make out her face, but I know the shape of her, the color of her hair, the curve of her hips. I've memorized her, whether it was intentional or not.

I start walking.

I didn't know how I would feel when it was all over. I think a part of me thought I would feel relieved. And another part of me thought I might feel the ache you get in the back of your head when something is incomplete and unsatisfying.

But I don't feel that way. I just feel whole, happy.

I'm not sure when the photographers arrived. People have started to file out of the garages, flooding into the paddock for post-race events and press.

I've got my eyes on her as I get closer and closer. By the time I get to her, by the time I take her face in my hands, I can feel the crowds beginning to press in, but they don't matter. She's all that matters.

I kiss her. I kiss her because it's been too long since I've had oxygen, and that's exactly what she is. She's oxygen. She's everything.

She kisses me back, hooking her hand around the back of my neck, her tongue finding mine. I know this moment isn't just ours. It'll be on every website and every social media outlet in minutes. But for now, I just want to enjoy the taste of her because we'll never be able to make it back to this exact moment.

She breaks away from me, pressing her forehead to mine, gasping for air. Her eyes shoot to the side, where a camera is pointed at us. I duck into her line of sight so she has to focus on me and only me.

"Why did you do that? I can't believe you did that," she says. "I didn't want you to quit for me."

"I'm not. I'm quitting for you *and* for me. I'm quitting for *us*. Because I love you. Every time I've ever been in love or some version of love, it's always come on so quickly, like a fire burning hot and then fizzling out. I always thought that maybe I finally found someone that I loved as much as I loved driving. I know how that makes me sound, but it's the truth. But I fell in love with you slowly, so slowly, like an ocean wave creeping up and pulling me under. I don't love you as much as I love driving; I love you far more."

She shakes her head, her mouth pulling wide until she's my favorite, beautiful version of herself, the version I didn't know until a few months ago. A version who loves me even though I don't deserve it. A version who's loved me without me noticing. A version who came all this way just to be with me. Changed her life just to be with me. How can that even be possible? How could I ever earn her?

"What now?" she asks, her voice quiet under the din of reporters pressing microphones into our faces, shouting my name, asking questions even though I haven't given them any reason to think I'll be answering them.

They want to know why I did it. They want to know, just like her, what's next. It'll take a long time for everyone in this sport to process what happened here today, including me, including Arabella.

We'll handle all of that. We'll deal with it later.

"Everest?"

She grins. "Everest."

Arabella

I have to sit outside the garage for a very long time as Mateo meets with the team and the FIA officials. Brigit sits beside me for a little while, holding my hand, excitedly replaying moments from the race.

Lola comes by, and I hug her tight and congratulate her. She cries into my shoulder, clearly overwhelmed and exhausted. Her boyfriend pats me on the shoulder and carts her away. I'm sure they're going to party at the clubs, to celebrate with the whole city.

And then it's just me. I sit outside the office in the Marina Bay building and eat a bag of pretzels left over from catering. I listen to the voices on the other side of the door.

There will be a lot of consequences for the choice Mateo made. There will murmuring and rumors and anger. And I hope Mateo can handle that. That he's okay with it. That he'll forgive me and himself for it.

The door of the back room opens so swiftly it slams into the wall and Mateo comes marching out. I half expect him to be angry or sad, but he just smiles at me. And it's a real smile, not a fake one.

He comes to me and takes my hand, pulling me up out of my chair. "Room service?" he asks, so casual, like he didn't just tank his entire career for me. He pulls me out of the building, our hands clasped. "I want to throw you down on a bed and not let you back up until it's time to leave for base camp."

I giggle, turning into the bashful teenage girl he always reduces me to. "Sounds good to me."

We head out to the paddock, walk through the quiet streets as crews work to pack up their motorhomes.

"What did they say?" I ask him once we're out of earshot of the garage. People still watch us as we go by. I know they're curious, especially since Mateo has refused to speak to the media.

He makes an unconcerned face. "It's fine. Don't worry about it. There's legal stuff, lots of money, but in the end, what can they do? I'm an individual, and they don't own me."

"Not anymore," I say and smile over at me.

He winks. "You do, though." I giggle. "Did you see it?" he asks as we walk. He doesn't have to elaborate. I know that a part of him will wonder forever if he could have beat Lola when she was at her best and most competitive.

"Yes."

"Was it amazing?" His voice isn't sad so much as curious and full of wonder, as if he's never experienced someone winning a championship before.

"Yeah," I say, "it really was. She was so good. She almost didn't win."

"What?" he says, thick eyebrows furrowing as we step through the turnstiles out of the paddock.

"Yeah, Thane caught up to her at the last minute. Not that it would have mattered. It's not like anyone could have beat her for the championship. Her win was solid the second you didn't walk out on the track, but he gave her a run for her money anyway. Archer probably could have, too, but I'm sure the team told him to hang back."

"Of course they did," he says, chin up, eyes focused

forward as we walk back to the hotel. "Archer would never ruin Lola's race."

"I don't know. I think Archer's gunning for her spot."

"No way. He'll never catch her."

"How long do you think Lola is going to stay on?" I ask. I love this, talking Formula 1 with Mateo. I may not know the sport the way he does, and I may not love it the way he does, but I grew up in it. And I know it as well as I know myself.

"She's still young. She's got a solid decade ahead of her, unless she decides to cut out earlier than she has to. And as a three-time world champion, she'll always have a seat on offer."

I feel so good, so solid with his hand in mine. I can't believe this man is mine. This man that I have wanted and craved and loved my whole life sacrificed everything for me. You don't do that if you're going to walk away. You don't do that if it's just for a little while. It's the kind of thing you do when it's forever.

Mateo stops talking. I look up at him, trying to figure out what caught his attention. And then I stumble over the pavement. Mateo holds me up, but I still find it hard to walk when I see the figure waiting outside my hotel.

I would know the figure of my father anywhere, that bright red polo he wears with his khaki shorts, his hair always far too long.

"Papa?" I ask when we're close enough for him to hear me.

He turns, his eyes immediately dropping to where our hands are clasped.

"What are you doing here?"

His eyes move to Mateo then. "I didn't want to miss it. I knew it was going to be a race that would go down in history."

I look over at Mateo, back at my father, standing on the wet streets of Singapore like he didn't tell me a month ago that he never wanted to see my face again.

"Wait. You knew...?" He knew that Mateo was going to sit out of the race. But...how would he have known that?

He nods. "Yes. I knew. Mateo came to talk to me about it before he did anything."

All of the air rushes out of my lungs. I don't even have the brain power to try and sort through that right now. All I can think about is the fact that my father is standing in front of me.

"So...you were there?"

"No," he says. "I watched on the TV at the bar." He jerks his head in the direction of the hotel.

"You came all the way to Singapore to watch the race from the bar of a hotel?"

He runs a hand down his face, looks down at his feet. When he looks back up, his steady gaze focuses on me. "I couldn't get myself to go to the race, to face you in the midst of it all."

"Why?" I ask, even though I know that was the right decision. I don't know if I could have dealt with my father's presence on top of everything that happened at the race today.

"I was ashamed of myself."

Mateo's fingers tighten around mine, and I know he's feeling everything I'm feeling right now. Anger and sadness and confusion.

"I should have known better," Papa says, his voice sounding like gravel. "I should have known that if the two of you were going to take such a risk, being together with all the circumstances against you, that it was serious, that it meant something." He pauses, takes a deep breath. "I was just... surprised."

I know I should be nice in this moment. That I should be receptive to him, especially when he's asking for forgiveness, if that's what he's doing. But the anger takes over anyway. "Surprised? Surprise doesn't get you on a plane all the way to Spain. Surprised doesn't get Mateo a black eye."

"I know," he says, interrupting me. "And I'm sorry for all of that. I was just worried, and I didn't trust either of you when I should have."

"Yes," I say, "you should have."

"I don't know if I really believed Mateo would go through with it, sacrifice everything he's ever wanted and worked for." His chin wobbles and I'm surprised. It's a rare thing to see my father cry. But I suppose if anything was going to make him do it, it was going to be the idea of a championship within reach, only for it to be snatched away. "I can't believe you did that for my daughter," he says.

I want to say something, but I can't. The words don't come. They sit in my throat, getting harder and harder to swallow by the second.

"I love her," Mateo says.

My father doesn't seem surprised by this. He just nods, like he always knew it. I desperately want to know what they said to each other between the last time we were all together and now.

"I'm sorry to both of you." He turns, like he's just going to walk away, like everything that needed to be said has been said. I reach out and grab onto his elbow.

He looks over his shoulder at me and I gesture towards the hotel. "Come and have a drink with us?"

He sighs, clearly relieved. Mateo claps him on the back, hooks an arm around both of our shoulders, and guides us inside.

Epilogue
1 Year Later

Arabella

"Do you regret it?" the podcaster asks.

"Regret what?" Mateo asks, his voice coming through my car speaker, as if he doesn't know exactly what the podcaster is asking. I don't normally listen to Formula 1 podcasts, mostly because I find it's a lot more peaceful now to be separated from it as much as possible.

I catch races here and there with my dad, and I've been to a couple with Mateo in the last year. When we were up at base camp on Everest, Mateo was the hot ticket. Nobody could get enough of him.

Now that we're back, though, I've honestly weaned myself from everything, but Mateo did this podcast just before we left for the documentary. *Away We Go*, it's called, and I'm not going to miss a single moment of any kind of press Mateo does.

"Do you regret walking away from a championship?"
Mateo hesitates.

"*Turn right onto McCord Drive*," my GPS app says, cutting off the podcast for a second.

"I don't know that I did walk away from a championship," Mateo says, very diplomatic. "Nothing was ever guaranteed."

"Okay," the podcaster says, staying patient, even though he's clearly frustrated that Mateo is dodging his question. "Do you regret dropping out of the race?"

Mateo gives a little hum in the back of his throat. I've heard him make that sound more times than I can count. "No. No, I don't regret it. I didn't regret it then, and I don't regret it now. I walked away because there was something more important."

"Arabella Cedillo," the podcaster says, without missing a beat. I grip my steering wheel harder. "Everyone speculates that you walked away because she asked you to."

"She didn't ask me to do anything," Mateo says.

The podcaster sighs. "I just can't quite figure out why it was necessary to leave before the race and not after. You could have won one more championship and then retired a happy man."

Mateo gives a humorless laugh. "Luckily, I don't need you to understand. I don't need anyone to understand but me and the people who it concerns. Either way, I *did* retire a happy man."

The podcaster gives a rueful laugh. "I get it."

Mateo goes on. "I'm not sure why the fans feel like they have to know everything. You know, on the other side of a screen or on the sidelines, the track, they only get part of the story, and they think they know the whole thing, but they don't. And they don't need to. It's over now."

"So we won't be seeing you back?"

Mateo snorts. "Even if I wanted to come back, nobody would have me now. But you'll see me at the races. I'll always be around."

"Well, we appreciate you coming out today, Mateo," the podcaster says. I think his name is Bruce or something. "And we'd love to have you back anytime. If you ever want to tell the whole story, you let us know."

Mateo chuckles. "I'll keep that in mind."

Conveniently, the podcast ends as I pull into the driveway. Mateo is already there, talking to the realtor, his hands in his pockets and a kind smile on his face, as always. When he hears my car, he turns, his smile changing from polite to something much brighter.

They immediately start to walk toward the car. I can hear their voices through the windows as they get closer.

I roll down the window and Mateo leans his head in, giving me a long kiss before pulling back and draping his arms over the window frame. "I think this is the one," he says, eyes shooting to the big white house. "You're going to love it."

I turn off my car. "Yeah?" I get out and join him in the driveway. "Are you sure?" I ask him.

He shrugs. "If you want to keep looking—"

"I don't mean about the house." I turn to him and lower my voice so the realtor can't hear. "I just mean, you know, are you sure about Montreal?"

He takes my shoulders, squints at me. "You know I'm sure," he says. "We had a deal. I retire and you make all the decisions from here on out."

I laugh. "I don't remember making that deal."

"I made it for you. So now it's on you. Where we live, where we go; it's whatever you want."

"Maybe I want to move to Valencia to be closer to Jimena and baby Diego."

He throws his hands up. "So we get another house in Spain."

"We can't afford that," I tell him. "You're not a Formula 1 driver anymore, remember? No Formula 1 salary."

He smacks me on the hip, gives me the smallest shove in the direction of the house. "That was the other deal I made though, Miss Cedillo."

"What deal?" I ask him over my shoulder.

"To give you everything you could ever want. And I'll do anything to make it happen."

Read Lola's Book

Read about Lola's dramatic season (mentioned several times in *Dangerous Strategy*) in her own book, *Give Your Heart Away*!

Want More Mateo and Arabella?

Visit my Patreon page to read bonus scenes!

Grab Your Free Ebook!

Grab a copy of *Love Is an Open Door*!

She can't seem to slam the door on the guy she hates.

Brooke has had enough. After dumping her cheating boyfriend, dropping out of her graduate program, and being forced to move out of the city she grew up in, the last thing she needs is a jerk of a neighbor who slips not-so-passive aggressive notes under her door at all hours.

But what is she supposed to do when the guy who yells at her for singing in the shower turns out to be the same gorgeous man she saw jogging shirtless? The same man who seems to be watering her balcony plants? The same man who breaks down her door when he thinks she's in trouble...?

She isn't so sure she can trust the guy next door, but she knows she can't ignore him, either.

Acknowledgments

I have so many people to thank!

I've written a lot of books, but this book was by far the most technically difficult to pull off, and I wouldn't have been able to get through it without a lot of people sharing their experiences and knowledge.

First of all, thank you to all the Formula 1 teams and their social media managers. Their behind the scenes content and garage information sessions were invaluable, especially the McLaren, Aston Martin, and Red Bull teams. The *F1: Chequered Flag* podcast was incredible for learning the ins and outs of the cars and what's going on at the factories. And a special thank you to Kym Illman for such excellent YouTube content on F1 photographers.

A huge thank you to the drivers. The Formula 1 drivers know what happiness they bring the fans, but I'm not sure they'll ever understand the impact they truly have on all of us. I hope this book illustrates just a fraction of how important the drivers are to the fans and how invested we are in their successes.

Thank you to my F1 community, especially the girls at *the off season race club* and *Worldwide F1 Girlies*. I just love you all. You make every race weekend even more enjoyable, and I love getting to fangirl (and argue) with all of you on the daily.

My husband, Jeremy. No one else has to put up with as much of my blabbing as you do. Thank you for nodding patiently as I talk about drivers you don't know and races you don't care about. Thank you for sleeping next to me on the couch while I watch the late-night races and for not batting an eye when I say we have to make tapas or scones for a special race or hang a Spanish flag from our wall. A true ride or die.

And lastly, in our current world, I want to say thank you to everyone who's standing up against hate. The romance community is one that often fights hard against sexism, racism, homophobia, transphobia, and everything in between. Keep fighting.

About the Author

B. Randall wrote her first novel at fourteen and hasn't stopped since. She's published over a dozen novels, both young adult and adult romance. She's also a freelance editor, working primarily with indie romance and horror authors. When she's not writing, she's listening to podcasts, drinking way too much Dr. Pepper, and watching Formula 1. She lives in Dallas with her husband.

Also by B. Randall

The Berserkr Gym Series

Come In With The Rain

Make It To Me

Take My Love

Find Me Here

Let Me Fall

Give Your Heart Away

One Last Auction

The Vegas Duet

A Man After Midnight

Late Night Talking

Braving the Waves

Love Is an Open Door

Love in Slow Motion

Anywhere But Here, Anyone But You

Serving Tegan

Writing as Winter Randall

My Best Friend's Mate

The Vamp and I

Five Nights With The Fire Monster

King of the Fire Monsters

Snowed In With The Mountain Monster

Touched by the Shadow Creature

Minotaur Sugar Daddies

My Gargoyle Protector

www.ingramcontent.com/pod-product-compliance
Lightning Source LLC
Chambersburg PA
CBHW061043310726
48969CB00004B/1060